Machine World

by
B. V. Larson

ISBN-13: 978-1507755433
ISBN-10: 1507755430
BISAC: Fiction / Science Fiction / Military

Earth's Legion Structure, circa 2125

Earth's fighting forces are divided into two major strata. Most of the ships and troops are under the command of Hegemony, a planetary force focused on home world defense. The balance of the military is organized into independent legions.

The legions are hired out to fight off-world in other Frontier 921 star systems. The troops in these legions represent virtually all Earth's forces with combat experience.

The highest ranking officers are all members of Hegemony. The rank of tribune (equivalent to a brigadier general in the past) is the highest honor obtainable by a member of any independent legion.

The ranks are as follows:

Consul: Equivalent to a five-star general in Earth's multi-national past. The rank of consul is a temporary one, only created in times of all-out war with neighboring powers. Multiple consuls are possible, if Earth should find itself in wars on multiple fronts.

Praetor: A four-star general. This is a rare rank, but not a singular one. All consuls are drawn from this pool of top officers.

Equestrian: A three-star general. This rank is the highest rank that may actually take to the field in war and is charged with handling an entire front in wartime. An Equestrian might lead the defensive efforts of an entire world or multiple worlds.

Imperator: A two-star general. Imperators are often utilized to coordinate the efforts of multiple legions involved in a single conflict.

Tribune: A one-star or "brigadier" general. All legions are led by a tribune, and they have an unusual degree of autonomy within their mission parameters. A legion is made up of ten to fifteen cohorts. Half the cohorts are light troops with poor gear, and half heavily armed and armored. Some legions have specialized cohorts attached that are designated as auxiliary.

Primus: The equivalent of a colonel. A primus leads a cohort, which is made up of ten regular Units, about twelve hundred soldiers strong.

Centurion: A centurion is a battlefield commander leading approximately a hundred and twenty troops. The equivalent of a captain, centurions lead their unit into battle personally. They are the highest-ranked front line troops.

Adjunct: Adjuncts operate as lieutenants supporting their centurion. There are normally three adjuncts in every unit.

Veteran: The highest rank attainable by enlisted personnel. Those warriors honored with the rank of veteran are equivalent to the master sergeants of the past. There are several veterans in each unit, and it is their job to support the officers.

Specialist: Specialists are lower-level non-commissioned officers. They're valued for their training more than their command skills. They have a wide variety of specialties, but the most common three are bio specialists, weaponeers and techs.

Regular: A regular troop is an experienced individual who has been proven in battle. They're more likely to be issued expensive armor and weapons, placing them in a cohort of heavy infantry rather than a light infantry formation. This rank is equivalent to that of a private first class.

Recruit: The starting place for all new soldiers. These are the least experienced people in the legion, and consequently they're always placed in light infantry cohorts with the cheapest weaponry. Good alien-made equipment is expensive, and normally it's only issued to people with proven skills.

Recruits are often referred to as "splats" due to their tendency to experience frequent, violent death.

"A coward dies many times before meeting his actual death."
– Julius Caesar, 48 BC

-1-

Earth had gone through several dramatic changes during my years as an adult. First, we'd been thrown into an economic tail-spin when Cancri-9, better known as Steel World, had canceled our most lucrative legion contracts. Years later, we'd been given a boost in budget coming from the Empire's coffers to handle local defense. Times were good back then.

Things had shifted yet again this year. After reestablishing contact with the cephalopod race at Tech World—and somehow ending up in a state of undeclared war with them—Earth was tightening up her collective belt all over again.

It wasn't that we didn't have money. The Mogwa, a race of Galactics that were struggling with their peers for dominance among the Core Systems, essentially owned our backwater province. Either as part of their strategy or because we were just a small line-item in a vast budget, they were still sending us funding in the form of hard Galactic currency.

What *had* changed was Hegemony Government's state of mind. Our worldwide politicians and bureaucrats were rationing everything, spending every spare credit on our military effort. I understood the goal, but it was annoying.

4

Gone were the days when a trooper could buy himself an alien-made contrivance for the fun of it. All the best imported stuff went straight to the legions. They'd stopped paying us in Galactic Credits too, opting instead to issue Hegemony Credits to soldiers. What's more, the established rate of exchange was ruinous. In the past, about a thousand Hegemony Credits had been deemed worth a single Galactic Credit—but they were now giving us less than half that after the accounting was all said and done.

"Crooked government stooges!" Carlos complained bitterly over a beer in legion Varus' Chapter House in Atlanta. "At least we've finally got a cheap pub in our Chapter House."

I nodded and sipped a sour beer. They had it on tap, and they sold it cheap. That was about all I could say that was positive about this bitter, foamy, piss-water. I suspected the reason they'd opened a bar at one end of Atlanta's row of legion Chapter Houses was a sneaky one. The bar was a trick, an inexpensive way to buy off troops like Carlos and me. Sure, we'd lost half our income in some kind of shady, computerized money-shuffle, but at least we could get drunk for less to drown our sorrows.

Making a face, I gulped my mug dry and slammed it down. The bartender behind the counter winced, looking at us in concern.

"You two aren't about to make trouble, are you?" she asked.

"What?" demanded Carlos. "Do Varus troops have that bad of a rep?"

"You're getting there. We had a serious fight last night. They had to call in the MPs. There were two deaths, and one of the revives has been placed on hold pending an inquiry."

I shook my head, snorting. "Let me guess, they're holding up the Varus guy's revive, right? What was his name?"

The bartender shrugged and frowned, thinking for a moment. "A big guy. Sargon was his name, I think."

"Hot damn!" I said. "I wish I'd been here to watch his back. Poor Sargon."

Carlos nudged me. "Why don't you go charm the Imperator? I bet she'd squeeze out a revive for him if you handled her right."

Carlos was talking about Imperator Turov, who'd had a questionable relationship with me last year. I gave him a sour glance and waved for a fresh beer. The bartender poured it, but I could tell she was wary about feeding us any more alcohol.

"That business with the Imperator is all over with, Carlos," I said. "She doesn't care if I live or die now."

I lifted a fresh mug toward my face, but the beer never reached my lips. A hand interposed itself, touching my wrist to block the path of my beverage. The hand was fairly strong, but pale-skinned and thin-boned.

Getting between a drinking man and his brew was rarely a good idea, but it was especially ill-advised in the case of a Legion Varus trooper. We just didn't take that kind of crap from anyone.

Without even thinking about it, I rotated toward the intruder. My other hand was already balled up into a fist, and it levered back almost on its own, ready to deliver a hammer-blow. Behind the bar, the bartender had already hit the floor. She was probably summoning the cops on her tapper—but I didn't much care.

The only thing that stopped me from slamming my fist into the face I saw standing over me was recognition.

"Winslade?"

I could tell right off he knew he'd miscalculated by grabbing my wrist. His hand leapt off mine and he backed up a step.

"McGill," he said, trying to pretend I hadn't scared him. "You know striking an officer is a flogging offense, yes?"

"Yeah," I said slowly, as if gauging my options. Finally, I lowered my fist and purposefully turned back to my beer. I took a drink, made a bitter face, and waited for him to explain himself.

Winslade was Turov's lapdog. He was a suck-up and worse. He'd abandoned Legion Varus for Hegemony at the same time Turov had. That was a shameful thing in the eyes of any off-world combat legionnaire. We knew that men who

6

couldn't handle real fighting often sought cush jobs in office buildings on safe, reliable dirt.

"You're drunk, aren't you?" Winslade demanded. "That's great. What else should I have expected?"

"This is a bar, sir," Carlos pointed out. "And we're off-duty."

Winslade nodded. "You *were* off-duty. You're back on as of now, McGill."

He finally had my complete attention. "What's up, Adjunct?"

He was a prissy officer, as they went, and I could tell he didn't like my lack of deference. I could see his annoyance in the way his lips twitched and his eyes narrowed—but I just didn't care about that right now.

"I'm here to transport you up to Hegemony Central. In Northeast Sector."

"I know where it is," I said, frowning.

The worldwide seat of Hegemony Government had been established on a chunk of land that had long ago been known as Connecticut. I'd never thought much about why the powers-that-be had chosen that small plot of the planet to elevate to the status of a new capital, but I supposed it was the same reason they'd built Washington D. C. in the first place: it was close to where the important people lived.

"Why the hell are you taking McGill to the capital?" Carlos demanded, immediately jealous. "What about me? If he did anything cool, it was only due to my private counseling."

This statement seemed to amuse Winslade. He'd gotten over his rush of fear concerning my fist, and he was back to his usual slick, self-confident attitude.

"What if I'm taking him up there to be properly permed?" Winslade asked.

"Well then," Carlos said, "in that case I'm not responsible. In fact, McGill has been acting strange lately. Like he's hiding something. Maybe you should go out to his shack in the swamp and mess with him tonight. He loves that."

Winslade nodded at Carlos dismissively and gestured to me with his fingers as if he was beckoning to a dog. "Follow me, McGill."

7

"You're a hog," I pointed out rudely. "An officer, but still a hog. I need orders from my own legion."

Winslade's face remained confident and bemused. "Have you checked your tapper lately, Specialist?"

Frowning, I looked down at my arm. The mail light was blinking red. A priority message was waiting for me in my inbox. I didn't even have to read it. I knew Winslade had me.

"All right," I said, accepting that I was beaten. Winslade was the kind of guy who waited until he had all the cards before making a move. There was no point in arguing with him now. It would just give him the thrill of backing me down.

I slapped a twenty credit piece on the bar and stood up. "See you, Carlos. Let's go, Winslade."

I followed the officer to the door.

"He's paying for mine, too," I heard Carlos tell the barkeep.

I shook my head. I'd meant to leave the girl a big tip. It was the least I could do after scaring her half to death.

Exiting into the parking lot, I followed Winslade to a sleek black contraption parked out on the periphery of the puff-crete pavement.

"Is that an air car?" I asked, surprised.

"Yes. Personal use. Don't tell me you've never been in one before?"

"I rode in one that I liberated from a Galactic once," I said, giving him a grin.

His face froze in a mask that told me I'd given him more information than he wanted to hear. He opened the canopy, and I climbed over the wing and slid onto the plush saurian-hide seats. He climbed in the other side.

"Don't talk like that," he said seriously. "About Galactics, I mean. Not even if you're joking around."

"You think they're bugging the alien-made cars now?"

"Maybe," he said, licking his lips and powering up the air car.

The strange vehicle vibrated for about ten seconds then launched into the sky with alarming power. We rose up into the clouds and leveled off. The only sounds were the thrumming of

8

the engine and the muted rush of air flowing over the dual canopies.

"What do you want from me, anyway?" I asked.

"Xlur wants you. He's waiting for us up at Central."

This statement, at long last, cut through my state of intoxication. Up until then, I'd been just another hard-drinking trooper in a foul mood. Now I knew things were serious.

Xlur was one of the Mogwa. He was, for all intents and purposes, a pharaoh on Earth. A god-king who wielded the ultimate authority of the Galactics within the boundaries of Frontier 921.

I'd met Chief Inspector Xlur previously under unfortunate circumstances. I sincerely hoped that he didn't recognize me this time around.

-2-

Whenever Winslade crawled out from under his rock, I knew Imperator Turov must have ordered him to do it. Sure enough, when we got to Central we landed on top of Hegemony headquarters and were transported via a smart-elevator to her office.

She started off by making a speech, which I quickly tuned out. I found myself staring at her rear while she strutted back and forth over her new, plush carpet.

We were near the top of what had to be one of the biggest buildings I'd ever seen in my life. Hegemony headquarters made the old Pentagon building look like a joke. It was shaped like a ziggurat and contained a thousand stories of stacked puff-crete, reaching as high as a mountaintop. Outside Turov's slanted, floor-to-ceiling office window, I could see clouds scudding along far below us, obscuring the surrounding city streets.

My eyes roved from the fantastic external view to Turov's butt and back again. Once in a while she caught me looking, but she didn't complain. I honestly thought she might be enjoying my distraction. Sometimes she did stuff like that, wearing uniforms with smart-cloth cinched up a few notches beyond tight and marching around to show herself off. Since her last revive, she'd been restored to an unreasonable point of youth and beauty in her life. She looked like she was about twenty years old even though she was twice that in actual age.

"James," she said, interrupting my reverie. "Wake up. You must pretend you're an officer when you meet Xlur."

"You want me to impersonate an officer?" I asked. "Why's that?"

"Because I don't want to explain why a noncom was involved in an Interstellar diplomatic disaster."

"Why does Xlur want to see me at all, sir?"

The Imperator made an irritated gesture. "I don't know. It was the Nairbs that made the initial request. First, they demanded a roster of the people involved—we thought maybe they were drawing up charges. Now, I'm not so sure. Xlur has taken up the matter personally, but instead of lodging formal accusations, he's demanded this interview. The four of us talked to the cephalopods in person, so we must all be present when Xlur calls upon us."

"Well, I've got a solution to this business of rank, sir. All you have to do is make me an officer. Primus sounds nice, but I'd settle for adjunct if I had to—"

"Shut up. You haven't even been confirmed as a veteran yet. I find this kind of blatant rank-climbing personally disgusting, McGill."

I released an involuntary snort and looked at her in surprise. "I was just making a joke, sir."

"Well, it's not funny. Just don't volunteer any information and we'll get through this."

I was annoyed, but I managed to shut up. Hearing how disgusting rank-climbers were was ironic, especially coming from Turov. She'd clawed and scratched her way to Imperator using every dirty trick in the book—in fact, I thought she'd invented a few new ones along the way. But pointing that out wasn't going to improve her mood, so I dropped the matter.

Xlur arrived to speak to us shortly after that, and everyone's mood changed. At first, Imperator Turov did all the talking—or rather I should say, schmoozing. She was a natural, I had to give her that. For all the harsh treatment she could dish out on the head of a subordinate, she was nothing but love and biscuits when it came to talking to real brass.

Chief Inspector Xlur was the final authority in Frontier 921. Thousands of star systems were under his direct management. He was a Mogwa, and his kind owned our local patch of stars.

Physically, the Mogwa were spidery aliens with a central body mass that looked like a black widow's thorax. Xlur had six limbs that operated as arms or legs interchangeably. Each of these limbs terminated with hands that could be used like feet or to manipulate objects.

For all his power and position, I didn't think Xlur liked his job much. He complained about it constantly.

"These worlds of yours are called the Dark Worlds by the Mogwa," his translator box rasped. "They are dreary and unpleasant. I find this fringe of cold, lonely planets depressing. In the Core, the countless nearby suns never allow one to fall into gloom. What you might term 'night' is to us a brilliant display of color from a dozen nearby stars, more beautiful even than our blazing days."

I noticed that Adjunct Leeson was giving me the stink-eye, as if he expected me to blurt out something. I avoided his stare. It was true that I wanted to suggest to Xlur that he should pack right up and head back to his shiny home planet, but I managed to hold my tongue and stand at attention. After all, I wasn't born yesterday, and the cheap Chapter House alcohol had pretty much drained from my system by now.

"Worse, there's nothing in the way of culture out here," Xlur continued, "nothing like the splendor of the Core Systems."

"We must apologize abjectly for our lack of amenities, Chief Inspector," Turov said.

She was good. She even sounded like she meant it.

Besides Turov and Leeson, Graves was present. The four of us had all spoken to the squids the last time we'd made contact with them on Tech World—just hours before the violent "diplomatic incident" in question.

"So," Xlur said when he'd finished disparaging our backwater planet, "you told this renegade individual named Glide that he should leave Galactic space. When he refused, you took no action. But when he attacked the megahab at Tau Ceti, you destroyed his ship. Am I correct in these essentials?"

"A masterfully condensed description of the event-sequence, your excellency," Turov said.

"I see. You realize that this places the Empire in a dangerous position? If the cephalopods decide to strike, our defensive forces are out of position."

We all looked uncomfortable.

"We were hoping, sir," Turov began, choosing her words with care, "that the fleet might soon be returning home again. It has been more than two years since—"

"No," Xlur said firmly. "The Battle Fleet will not return anytime soon. Eventually, of course, Mogwa ships will silver the skies of every cephalopod planet to cast down righteous revenge upon these barbaric invaders. But for now, you must find a way to manage on your own. Your task is to stop any incursions these creatures might attempt. As Enforcers, it is your duty to police this frontier province."

Turov licked her lips. "Hegemony is aware of this requirement?"

"Naturally."

"And we've been provided with an expanded budget in order to meet your—?"

"Imperator Turov," Xlur interrupted sternly. "You step beyond your station. I've already discussed such matters with your superiors, and I have no intention of discussing them with you."

"I apologize profusely, Inspector. My curiosity got the better of me. I will not ask more on this—"

"See that you don't. I'm finished with my line of questions. My person shall now be escorted to the air car on the roof."

"At once, Inspector!"

It was odd, watching Turov bow and scrape before a foreign dignitary. We knew that she'd always been like that, the sort that treated a superior like a god all the while crapping on her subordinates. But it was different to see her do it with an alien.

Still, I had to admit, she'd handled this interview well. Xlur seemed satisfied with her answers, and I'd never been asked a direct question. That suited everyone just fine.

When we reached the roof, Xlur complained bitterly that his air car wasn't waiting there to whisk him away into space.

That's when I did what I'd been cautioned not to do: I opened my mouth.

"Well sir, we don't have an infinite number of air cars to go around on Earth," I said. "Sometimes, we all have to wait our turn."

Xlur shuffled his bulk around and arranged his optical organs to study me.

"What is this creature, and why is it addressing me?" he demanded.

"That's Adjunct McGill, Inspector," Turov said quickly. "He's one of our lowest-level officers. He's present because you requested that all the personnel who were in contact with the cephalopods be available for questioning."

"Do I infer from your statements that this being had some direct contact with the barbarians?"

"Well, yes..."

Xlur lifted a wavering limb in my direction. "Being— McGill," he said. "What did you say to the barbarians?"

I squirmed. Everyone did. My mother always told me the best policy was honesty, but I'd never believed her. Still, I didn't see any harm in answering forthrightly on this occasion.

"All I did was answer their questions, sir."

Xlur shuffled a pace closer. "Then you confirm that you spoke to them directly? I wasn't told this. I thought the being called Turov did all the talking, while the rest of you were mere witnesses. Turov, tell me, who is lying here? Must I request video feed and transcripts? I'd hoped to avoid that level of effort."

"Uh," she said, looking very uncomfortable. "Sir, you must excuse me. I didn't think it was significant, but McGill here did answer at least one question from the cephalopods directly."

"One question? What was it?"

"They asked—" she began.

"No!" boomed Xlur. He made a slashing motion toward her with one of his limbs. "I want *this one* to talk. The McGill-creature. Speak!"

14

"Uh…well sir, it went like this," I said. "The squids—that's what we call them here, sir—the squids asked me about the bombing of their colony world. They wanted to know exactly how it happened."

"And what did you tell them?"

"The truth, sir. I saw the bombing with my own eyes. The Nairbs did it with nine hell-burners. Every organic structure on that planet was broken down to component molecules within an hour of the bombing. It was a glorious demonstration of Imperial power."

While I'd been speaking, the air car had come down and landed behind Xlur. He ignored it and stayed focused on me. All around me, the other officers were looking at one another with increasing alarm.

"I want you to be very precise, McGill-creature. You told the enemy that the Nairbs erased their colony?"

I was unsure what the fuss was all about, but I pressed on as best I could. The other officers had white faces and gritted teeth. They didn't seem to have much faith in me.

"Uh…yes sir," I said. "That's how the bombing went, after all."

"Disaster," Xlur said. "You've done incalculable damage."

"How so, sir?"

"Silence." He turned his baleful orbs on each of us in turn. "Are you all dedicated to your Empire?"

"Of course we are," Turov said. The others murmured in agreement. Only I didn't join in.

"Draw your sidearms!" Xlur ordered.

My heart rate accelerated. I'd seen this sort of thing before. I purely expected this nasty alien to order my fellow officers to gun me down. They reached for their holsters and did as he ordered, and I did the same. If they were going to fire-squad me, at least I'd go down with a gun in my hand.

"You will all now self-execute!" Xlur commanded the group.

We all blinked in surprise. Faces tight, the officers looked at one another in confusion and disbelief.

"May we ask *why*, Chief Inspector?" Turov asked. All the blood had drained from her face, just as it had from the faces of the others.

"Because you have involved the Empire in a war we do not need! Our diplomatic corps has been working hard to convince the cephalopods that humans were directly responsible for this disaster. Only when this creature spoke did I realize you gave them damning testimony disproving our premise. You informed them that representatives of the Empire chose to destroy their colony. They'll never be satisfied with the destruction of your pathetic species now. They'll continue the war, grinding farther into our territory at a time when we can least afford the distraction."

Things suddenly clicked on in my brain as he said this. First off, I'd always wondered what had happened to the last "Enforcers" the Galactics had appointed to the post. By all accounts, they'd disappeared. Could it be that the true role of an "Enforcer" species along the Frontier was equivalent to that of "scapegoat"?

"But Your Excellency," I said, not fully understanding his reasoning. "Why do you want us to self-execute? Aren't you better off leaving us to defend our world as best we can and maybe damage the squids further?"

"A few humans will make no difference to the outcome. The enemy kingdom consists of three hundred worlds."

"If we make no difference, why should we be executed?"

"It's the principle of the thing," Xlur said, drawing himself up taller and ruffling his limbs. "You brought this inconvenience down upon my person, and I will feel better if you're expunged. Now, get on with it!"

"Chief Inspector Xlur," Turov said formally. "I request that a grievance be filed—"

"There will be no grievances!" he roared at her. "That is for justice dispensed by Nairbs and other underlings. A Galactic Citizen, especially an Inspector such as myself, is not bound by bureaucratic nonsense. I demand that you all self-execute. If you do not, I will order this planet erased immediately!"

Shaken, we gripped our weapons with tight fingers and eyed one another.

16

Graves moved first. Without a change in his expression, he put the muzzle of his gun under his chin.

"I lived for Earth, and I die for her."

He shot himself and pitched forward on his face.

Adjunct Leeson went next. He looked at me, shaking his head. He spoke through clenched teeth. "Fuck you, McGill!"

Then he shot himself and fell on top of Graves.

I looked down at the two of them, breathing hard. Xlur made a burbling sound. I wasn't sure if he was laughing or farting, but either way, I didn't like it.

"This pleases me," Xlur said. "Finish the process."

Turov released a hissing breath. I looked at her.

"Why do you always make these things happen, McGill?" she asked.

"It's a gift, I guess."

"Well?" she demanded. "Do something to fix it!"

I lifted my pistol. After all, as far as I was concerned, I'd just been given an order by a high-ranking officer.

Without hesitation and with a steady hand, I shot Xlur right between the orbs. He flopped and died, making more of those farting sounds and bleeding blue ichor on the rooftop.

Xlur didn't look any better in death than he had in life. In fact, I thought he looked a little worse. He definitely smelled bad—like rotten fruit.

"Are you insane, McGill?" Turov screeched at me.

"You told me to do something."

"You can't fix things by shooting a Galactic! He'll remember all of this when they revive him upon his ship! You've gotten us all permed at the very least, if not our entire planet!"

"Don't worry," I told her, "I've got a plan. Hand me the Galactic key, will you?"

She hesitated, and I was honestly surprised by that. Could she be so greedy and paranoid? Even when faced with the destruction of the entire human race, she didn't want to trust me with her most prized possession—not even for a minute.

"Hurry, we don't have much time!" I said, holding out my hand and making a grabbing motion.

She slapped the key into my palm with a snarl. It was a seashell-shaped device that had powers that were belied by its mundane appearance. Essentially, it operated like a skeleton key, allowing the user to break security systems. Only Galactics were supposed to have them, and as far as I knew, Imperator Turov was the only human who possessed one of these highly illegal devices.

Quickly, I located Xlur's tapper. It was embedded in the cooling rubbery flesh of one of his appendages. I touched it with the key, which bypassed any passcodes he might have set and opened the settings menu.

Fortunately, I was able to read the symbols his system displayed. Galactic technology was designed to be used by a wide range of beings on thousands of worlds. Interfaces had to be usable by almost anyone and therefore followed universal standards.

Working fast, I performed the tricks that Natasha had showed me a year or so back and erased the most recent copy of Xlur's mental-backup.

The Mogwa's tapper operated pretty much the same way ours did. Every few minutes it recorded changes to the neural network in the host's brain and uploaded them to the nearest relay station. This often worked even after death as the tappers didn't stop operating right away unless they were destroyed. That's why we could remember our death experiences right up to and including the gory details at the finish.

But the upload didn't work instantaneously. It was a transmission of periodic snapshots. It took time to send the data, and the tappers had to share bandwidth with other traffic. With any luck...

"I think I did it," I said after fooling with the interface for about a minute. "His latest mind-snap was in the upload queue already, but I just erased it. Hurry up, help me."

I grabbed one of Xlur's limbs in each hand and pulled.

"Help you do *what?*"

"We've got to get Xlur's body into the air car."

Grimacing, she helped me carry the flopping alien corpse to the air car and shoved it into the passenger seat. The driver looked more than stunned.

"I can't deliver *this*, sir!" she told the Imperator, horrified. "They'll perm me for sure when I get up to the ship—"

Turov fired two shots. The first blasted a large hole in the driver's arm, destroying her tapper. Before she could even scream, the second shot blew the driver's brains all over the upholstery.

"What the hell...?" I demanded.

"The driver has to be in the pilot's seat for this to be believable. Don't look at me that way—I'll have her revived and debriefed later."

This woman was ruthless. I shook my head. I didn't like including an innocent bystander, but I knew Turov was right.

Part of me was impressed that she'd managed to grasp the essence of my plan and improvise improvements so quickly. Most people just stood around gawking when I pulled stunts like this.

We loaded up the bodies, and I made sure the air car was in full manual mode. I nudged the stick forward just a bit, and it drifted to the edge, nosed over, and dropped down the side of the building like a sled.

We stood there side by side, watching it spin and blossom into flames a few hundred meters downslope.

"Too bad about the pilot," I said.

"Are you kidding me? That's all you have to say? You almost got our world erased *again!*"

"Didn't you hear what Xlur said?" I asked. "We're screwed anyway. The Galactics are out there talking to the squids, telling them that we're the troublemakers. We pulled the same blame-game on them back on Tech World. Remember?"

I could see by the look on Turov's face she did remember. We'd been together when she'd told the squids that we were an independent and neutral entity. That we weren't part of the Empire proper, but rather mercenaries who worked for them on a for-hire basis. The purpose of that lie had been to deflect the squids into attacking the Empire rather than Earth. Apparently, the Mogwa had come up with the same idea.

Both the Mogwa and Earth had tried to put the blame on the other side. I had a feeling the squids weren't really going to care. When they came for us, they weren't going to be choosy. They were going to kill everyone who got in their way.

Turov holstered her sidearm and put her gloved hands on her hips. "What are we going to do now?"

"We'll report this as an accident. With luck, Xlur will be annoyed but too busy to seek petty revenge. The bigger question is what the squids will do next."

"That's not what I meant," she said, rubbing her temples. "What are we going to tell Hegemony? They have to know about this. They have to know that Earth is being abandoned by the Empire. Three hundred star systems—isn't that what he said?"

"You're talking about the size of the squid kingdom? Yeah, I think that's right."

"I just don't believe this," she said, shaking her head.

Walking away from the wreckage and the fallen bodies of Graves and Leeson, I headed for the elevator. Turov followed. We were both a little dazed.

Emergency flying vehicles were converging on our location. I thought it might be a good idea if we weren't around to have to answer any embarrassing questions when they got here. The emergency people didn't need any details as far as I was concerned. They'd queue up the revives and, unless a hold was put on any one individual, all the victims of this "accident" would be returned to life soon enough.

When we were in the elevator car riding downward, Turov put out her hand toward me and gave me an expectant look.

I glanced around quickly. I didn't see any cameras. I shrugged and took her hand in mine. I figured maybe she needed a little comforting. Possibly, this was an opportunity to spark up the brief love affair we'd enjoyed back on Tech World.

She shook my hand off of hers with a violent motion.

"No, you idiot!" she hissed. "Give me back the key!"

"Oh, that," I said, and fished it out of my pocket. I handed it over to her with some reluctance.

The Galactic key was quite possibly one of the most powerful devices on Earth—maybe *the* most powerful device. Giving it up wasn't an easy thing for anyone to do. I'd put it in my pocket, and it had felt like it belonged there. Now that it was gone, I missed it.

Turov turned the key over twice in her hands then put it away. I wondered if she was checking to make sure it was the same one. Like I said, she was as paranoid as the day was long.

"Do you think this ruse will work, McGill?" she asked when she was satisfied with the key.

21

"You mean about crashing the air car? I sure hope so."

She shook her head. "I can't believe what just happened. I can't believe you took such a chance."

"The way I see it, I didn't have much choice. I didn't want to go down saluting an alien and blasting my own brains out."

"I don't mean that part. I mean you took the chance that I had the key on me. What if I'd left it in my office or something?"

I chuckled, shaking my head. "I know you pretty well by now, sir. You wouldn't do that. What good would it be locked in a safe somewhere? If you ever need that thing, it has to be on your person to be useful. I knew you had it in your pocket. It's just in your nature."

She didn't say anything after that which spoke volumes to me. I knew I'd guessed right.

-4-

I spent that night in a hotel in Central City. The city consisted of a ring of modern buildings which surrounded Hegemony's ziggurat. Looking out through an immense window at the streets and towering structures, I couldn't help but stare at the monstrous headquarters building in the middle of it. The hotel was over a hundred stories tall, but was utterly dwarfed by the primary structure.

Staring quietly, I tried to come to terms with the events of the day. I'd just murdered the highest ranking being in this part of the Galaxy on that distant roof. It didn't seem real to me now.

The hotel was nice, but the prices were incredible. I didn't have any Galactic credits anymore, and Hegemony credits spent like water in this town. Still, I decided I might as well treat myself since I was stuck here anyway. Turov had ordered me to stay local in case any of the brass from Central demanded a briefing. I knew what she really wanted was a witness to back up her story when it came down to it.

Along about midnight, I fell asleep. Drunk on fifteen flavors of alcohol, I passed out and began snoring in front of the wall-screen. I'd treated myself to the minibar, despite the fact I knew better. Credits were leaking out of me like air out of a half-credit balloon.

The door chimed, but I didn't get up. I sort of blearily opened my eyes then shut them again. The door chimed several more times and a knocking sound began.

With a groan, I heaved myself to my feet. I reached for my pistol and took it with me to the door.

Honestly, when I opened it, I thought I might find a pack of goons there out in the hallway waiting for me. I could hardly have blamed anyone who'd sent them. After today's impromptu murder of a Galactic official, right here on Earth, I had no right to expect anything other than arrest or outright assassination.

I opened the door anyway, and I was pleasantly surprised. Instead of goons, Imperator Turov stared up at me. She was still wearing her uniform. I wondered if she slept in it.

"Imperator, sir?" I asked. "Do you know what time it is?"

"You've been drinking again?" she asked, walking past me. She looked around the hotel room as if she expected to find someone. "Are you alone, Specialist?"

"Yes sir—at least I was."

"We have to get our stories straight, McGill," she said, sitting on my couch and brushing away a clattering pile of tiny plastic vials. They were mostly empty, so I didn't mind.

"Uh…" I said, closing the door and sitting beside her. "Is there going to be an inquiry or something?"

"What do you think?"

I nodded. "Who's asking about what happened?"

"Everyone is. The press, the Hegemony Consul himself—everyone. No Galactic has ever died on Earth before. Did you know that?"

"No, but I could have figured—"

"This is a *big* deal, McGill. Pull yourself together."

"I'll try, sir," I said, opening a can of pop and wondering if her visit was purely business. Right now, it kind of looked like it was, but a man's mind always wandered after midnight.

"Even Graves is baffled about the details," she continued worriedly. "Fortunately, I don't think he's foolish enough to tell anyone if he suspects what actually happened. He'll keep quiet, but I still wished we'd had the forethought to erase his mind and Adjunct Leeson's."

"Hmm…I don't think there was time. We had to create that accident and move on before the emergency people got there."

"You're probably right."

24

"Have you contacted Graves and Leeson yet?"

"No, I was not able to do so. They got revives, but they were picked up by Hegemony goons."

"Hmm," I said thoughtfully. "I'll tell you who your weak point is: Leeson. He's a good man, but he doesn't have the kind of elastic mind that these situations require."

Turov shook her head and chuckled. "Elastic mind, huh? Is that what you call it? Yours must be like a giant rubber band in your skull."

"I'll choose to take that as a complement, sir. Would you like a drink?"

I could tell she was tempted. She'd smiled at me while talking about my rubber-filled skull. A smile and a drink after midnight—well, that's the sort of thing that gets a lady into all sorts of trouble after a stressful day at work.

"No James," she said with a hint of regret. "I'll pass."

From the appraising look in her eyes, I figured she knew what I was really asking. I sighed but didn't press the matter.

We talked after that, laying out the details of our plan to bamboozle anyone who asked exactly how the disaster had gone down. Maybe it would work, or maybe it wouldn't. It was hard to say.

By two a.m., Turov was gone. Unfortunately, I found it hard to go back to sleep after her visit, and I stayed up until just before dawn.

* * *

The next morning my tapper woke me up. I'd put it into silent mode, but a summons from Legion Varus broke through such settings.

The tapper didn't just chime, it vibrated. No one liked that feeling; the nerves in your arm jiggled and tingled irritatingly. It was like having someone buzz your funny-bone with a jolt of electricity.

Gasping awake, I fought to make my eyes focus on my tapper.

"Varus summons," I read out loud. "All able-bodied personnel are ordered to transport themselves to the Mustering Hall immediately."

I headed for the showers with a groan, massaging my temples. I seriously doubted if I qualified as "able-bodied" right now. After washing up and eating, however, I found I felt a lot better. Checking out of the hotel without even daring to look at the total at the bottom of the bill, I took the cheapest public tram I could find to Newark, where the North America Sector's Mustering Hall stood tall.

The trip reminded me of my initial visit to this place years ago. Back then I'd been a kid, as green as long grass. A lot had changed since those days. Physically, I was no more than a year older—but my mind was a different thing entirely.

I contacted a few of my friends with my tapper, but no one seemed to know what was going on any more than I did. Probably, they knew even less than I did.

Walking up to the smart-door on the Mustering Hall, I applied my palm to the pad beside it. The door buzzed but didn't open.

There was a long line behind me. They groaned and shuffled as I tried the door repeatedly, each time achieving the same results. Everyone had to log in through that door, and they didn't want to wait around for me to get through.

"Come on, splat!" shouted a regular trooper a few spots behind me in line.

I turned on him, glowering. It was then he must have noted the specialist's stripes on my sleeve and the Wolfshead of Varus on my shoulder.

He was a regular from Solstice. I could tell his legion by the rising sun patch on his shoulder. Solstice was a well-known outfit—but they didn't have the same kind of rep that my legion did.

"Uh, sorry Specialist," he said. "Proceed, by all means."

I pushed my palm against that door at least ten more times. Each time it buzzed, turned red, and made me wait a few seconds before I could try again. Behind me, the crowd had begun to filter away in disgust. I didn't care. They could go around to another entrance on the far side of the building if they wanted. It was a bit of a walk, but—

The door opened suddenly. This baffled me, as I'd just tried again and gotten another red hand symbol.

The mystery was immediately solved when I realized two Veterans had opened the door from the inside. They were Hegemony, and they were all out of smiles today.

"Specialist James McGill?" the closest man asked.

"That's me, Hog."

His face darkened a shade or two. Calling a Hegemony man a "Hog" was an insult that had preceded countless bar-fights.

"From Legion Varus?" he asked.

I slapped my Wolfshead patch and looked at him like he was an idiot.

Roughly, the two men reached for me.

Now, at this point, I feel I have to explain myself. I've not had an easy life in the legions. Far from it. When faced by others from diverse outfits, I'd never been treated well. In fact, the last time Hegemony had sent MPs to my house down in southern Georgia District, I'd sent them home for a revive. All three of them.

On top of this history of bad blood, I had a hangover today, and I was steaming mad at that damned door.

I broke the first man's arm. That was something of a surprise to me as well as to him. I did it on reflex. He reached, and I grabbed his wrist and pulled him forward, off-balance. I brought my knee up and his extended arm down. The two parts met around where his elbow was—bending it backward until it snapped. This action took about a half-second.

Shocked by this turn of events, the second man backed up and reached for his sidearm. I put my hand on my own in response. Neither of us drew, we just stared at one another for maybe two long seconds.

The first guy was on his knees, hissing like a snake. He was too concerned about his dangling arm to do much else.

"McGill?" asked the second man. "Why the hell did you do that?"

"You don't just grab a man from Varus. And you don't draw on him either, not unless you want to run yourself through the guts of a revival machine for fun. Now, Hog, why don't you tell me what this is all about?"

The hog swallowed hard. "We've got orders to bring you up to the Equestrian's office. That's why the door stopped you until we could get here."

The Equestrian. I let that roll around in my head for a second. The rank of Equestrian was one notch higher than Imperator, which was Turov's rank. True brass. I'd never even laid eyes on an Equestrian. Outwardly, I didn't let any of these thoughts show, but it was a struggle not to look impressed.

"Am I under arrest?" I asked.

"No—not officially."

"Can I see your orders?"

With a look of concern for his arm, the man showed me his tapper. I nodded.

"Seems like you've got the right of it," I said. "Lead the way."

"That's it? You're happy now? Why didn't you just submit to us when we asked the first time?"

"Because you didn't *ask*, that's why. You tried to grab me."

He grumbled but led the way. I followed him into the Hall and up an escalator. Behind me, the hog with the broken arm staggered in the rear.

"I'm going to have you up on charges, McGill," the injured man said.

"Uh-huh. You didn't identify yourself or your purpose. I'm a member of an independent legion, and you tried to grab hold of me without cause. That's assault, Hog. Look it up."

He shut his mouth but kept following. I wondered if he might burn a hole in my spine. If he did so, I would respect him for it—but I didn't think he had the balls. Hegemony troops rarely did. The sort of man that opted for the softer duty of guarding Earth wasn't the kind to break the rules right here in the Mustering Hall.

We reached the Equestrian's office without further incident. I was surprised to find a familiar face there, that of Tribune Drusus, overall commander of Legion Varus.

"Ah, there you are—damn it, McGill," Drusus said, catching sight of the hog with the broken arm.

I couldn't recall ever having heard Drusus curse before in my presence. He was a naturally calm man despite his high rank.

"Sorry sir," I said, clearing my throat. "There was a misunderstanding."

Drusus shook his head. "Thanks for finding my Specialist," he said to the hogs. "Why don't you gentlemen go get yourselves fixed up?"

They looked at the Equestrian, who nodded. Then they disappeared, grumbling.

The Equestrian watched me for several seconds as he steepled his fingers. He didn't look like he had a sense of humor.

"I'm Equestrian Nagata," he said with a slight Japanese accent. "You may have heard of me."

I hadn't, but I smiled and nodded. "It's an honor to meet you, sir."

Nagata grunted. "You are a violent man, McGill, from a legion of famously violent soldiers. Would you agree with that assessment?"

"Uh…" I said uncertainly. I glanced at Drusus for a hint, but he was wearing a poker face. I went with my gut. "Yes sir, I would have to agree. We wouldn't be much good otherwise. We're fighting men, after all. That's why people hire us."

Nagata nodded. "Well said. All right then. I'm going to give you and your renegades a chance to show us what you can do. But first, I need some truthful answers out of you."

"Okay, sir."

"Did you kill Chief Inspector Xlur?"

Again, I glanced at Drusus. He looked a little paler to me now, but that might have been my imagination. He gave me no help.

"Yes sir," I said. "I did."

Nagata nodded slowly. "Could you explain your reasoning for taking this drastic action—a move that might well result in the extinction of our species? I assume it wasn't because he didn't show you respect when he asked you to escort him to the roof?"

"No sir, that wasn't it at all. Galactics never show any human any respect."

"Hmmm…yes. I don't suppose they do. Could you elaborate?"

"Well sir, it went like this…"

I quickly explained the events that had transpired on the roof of Hegemony headquarters. I didn't edit or embellish— except for the part about using the Galactic key. Instead, I told him I'd been trained in technical matters and explained how a recent revive could be deleted by a man with quick fingers on a tapper. That was mostly the truth.

What helped was Turov's visit the night before. She'd anticipated this moment and had given me a script. About ninety-five percent of it was the truth. Really, I didn't think there was much point in trying to lie about it. Hegemony brass was full of weak, cowardly men. But they weren't stupid.

While I spoke, I glanced now and then at Drusus. He looked like a man who was listening to his own eulogy.

"So sir," I finished up, "we didn't have much choice. Xlur had just ordered us all permed, and in addition, he was talking about erasing Earth. I took action because I had to."

"Such drastic action—taken without planning or forethought? Done alone?"

He'd touched upon something I hadn't made a big deal out of: Imperator Turov's part in the matter.

"Not entirely, sir," I said, as if I'd left a detail out accidentally. "Turov helped me."

"Ah, I see! Did she not, in fact, *order* you to do this?" Nagata demanded, leaning forward and looking hungry all of a sudden.

Like a bolt of lightning, the situation was suddenly plain to me. They were after Turov, not a lowly specialist. Sure, they could perm me with a wave of the hand over their tappers if they wanted to. But a bigger head might be called for. A person who I'd be willing to wager wasn't all that popular among her peers. Maybe, for all I knew, Turov was already bucking for Nagata's job. I knew Turov would never be satisfied until she

30

reached the rank of Consul itself. After that, who knew what might be next?

"She did ask me to take action," I said carefully. "But I have to admit that I could have taken that in many different ways. Another man might have self-executed right then and there. After all, that's what Graves and Leeson had just done. Instead, I moved down the only path I could think of that might save all of us."

Nagata shook his head, staring into space. "Such hubris. Such risk-taking. It is inconceivable that an individual like you was placed in that kind of position. You held the lives of billions in your hands."

"And he didn't hesitate," Tribune Drusus said, suddenly reentering the conversation. "He took bold action which turned out to be the correct choice."

Nagata kept shaking his head. "Insanity. I should by all rights move to disband your outfit, Drusus. People at Central have been saying so for years."

"Use us instead," Drusus said. "Why destroy your toughest unit in the face of an interstellar war?"

"Oh, I don't know…maybe because you helped *start* this war?" Nagata shouted the last part of his sentence at us.

"Again," Drusus said calmly, "I ask that you use us, Equestrian. Place us where we'll be most useful."

Nagata glared at Drusus, but then he began to nod slowly after a few seconds. His sudden anger appeared to dissipate.

"Very well. I know *exactly* where to deploy your legion of outcasts, Drusus. You'll serve us yet—even if your murderous specialist here doesn't feel like it."

-5-

I bedded down that night on cold puff-crete in the sub-basement under the tram station. This part of the Mustering Hall was dank and dimly lit. Most people didn't even know it existed. Overhead, the trams rumbled and squealed all night long.

Various people from my unit as well as many others filtered in and found a spot to camp nearby, but they barely looked at me.

Carlos didn't show up as I'd expected him to do—maybe because he hadn't bothered to look for me. Others wandered by, and I recognized some of them, but they didn't stop to talk to me either.

The word must be out. Specialist James McGill was to be avoided at all costs. I was bad news, and somehow, everyone knew it.

I was in a bit of a blue mood myself. Camping out in the cavernous sub-basement was quite a come-down from the pricy hotel where I'd spent my previous night. There wasn't any beer to be had and precious little food. Once we'd reported in down here we weren't allowed to go back up into the Mustering Hall proper where we could at least buy a burger. We were informed that we were shipping out at dawn, and that we'd best shut the hell up and stay put in the meantime.

When a familiar face did finally find me, it was late. Most troopers were snoring, and I'd joined them.

A kick in the ribs alerted me that I wasn't alone. I rolled to my feet and stared at my assailant.

"Is that a snarl I see on your face, McGill?" Veteran Harris asked. He looked amused, and his fists were on his hips. His eyes were tight and serious despite his light tone. He wasn't happy with me—he rarely was.

Veteran Harris was a big black guy who was as mean as cat dirt. He was an experienced soldier and the most senior noncom in my unit, but he'd never quite gotten used to my style.

"Oh, it's you Vet," I said. "Come to tuck me in?"

"That's right. Me and my friends want to talk things over with you."

I glanced over my shoulder. Sure enough, three more veterans stood behind me with their arms crossed. They wore Varus patches, all of them. This made my heart sink a little. I couldn't pull any crap on them about not being under their command. All of these men were from my outfit, and they had every right to give me an order.

"What's this about, Vet?" I asked nonchalantly, even though I figured I already knew.

Veteran Harris and I had never quite seen eye-to-eye. In fact, he'd killed me a few times, and I'd returned the favor in my own way. When we were both in the path of a real enemy, we'd always fought back-to-back—but if we were on our own time, well, we just didn't get along.

"We want you to refuse your advancement to candidacy," Harris said, coming right out with it.

"Why would I do that, Vet?"

"Because we don't think you're ready yet for that kind of responsibility."

"With all due respect, I disagree," I said.

One of the men behind me jabbed me in the left kidney at that moment. It was a sharp blow, not full-force, but it was enough to hurt pretty bad—and it kind of pissed me off.

I grunted but didn't fall to my knees. I didn't even turn around.

"You want do this right now?" I asked Harris.

Harris' face clouded in momentary confusion. "Do what?"

"The test. The trial. Whatever hokum you've come up with to determine if a man is ready to be a veteran or not." As I said this, I stood at attention and clasped my hands behind my back. "Maybe beating on a man from behind is part of your hazing routine," I said.

I reached into my back pocket and retrieved a combat knife. I didn't draw it out into the open. The sub-basement wasn't pitch dark, but it was pretty near it. The only light was shining into my face from a few scattered lanterns. As long as I kept the knife behind my back, I was pretty sure the guys standing behind me wouldn't see it.

"I don't think you're getting the message, McGill," Harris said.

I kept my hands behind my back and angled the blade of my knife toward the men behind me. I smiled at Veteran Harris.

"I don't think I am," I said. "But I'm ready, and I'll take your best shot with my hands behind my back. How's that?"

Harris got into my face. "Are you threatening me, Specialist? I think you're threatening me."

"No Vet. I just don't get it. Why don't you ladies explain it to me?"

This last I tossed over my shoulder toward the men behind me. A fist was driven at my back again in immediate response, targeting my right kidney this time. It came in harder—which was bad for the guy throwing the punch.

I'd gambled dangerously this time. That punch could have come at another spot, for instance, but I had calculated that it wouldn't. This guy seemed fascinated with kidney-punches. He could have gone at the left kidney again—but I'd guessed he'd go after the right since his first shot to the left had failed to knock me down.

An odd, screeching sound came to my ears after I took that second punch in the back.

"What the hell is wrong with you, Johnson?" Harris demanded.

"My fingers—two of them are off!"

Harris snapped his eyes to mine. He nodded appreciatively. I was still standing and there was blood all over the knife behind me. Fortunately, it was another man's blood.

"We're not Hogs," Harris said dangerously. "We're your superiors."

"I know that, Vet," I said. "That's why you're still on your feet."

Harris threw up his arms in disgust. "All right, fine! You want to go for it, don't you? I don't know why I bothered to try to explain things to you. I'm some kind of kind-hearted fool. I tried to come here and give you a friendly warning. I tried to do the right thing for a man I've fought shoulder-to-shoulder with. What you don't understand is that this isn't about you being a good fighter, McGill. We all know you can fight. We just don't think you're ready to lead men into battle. As Varus veterans, it's our responsibility to make that call. Do you understand what I'm saying?"

"I hear you loud and clear, Vet," I said.

Veteran Harris sighed and stalked away into the night. "Pick up your damned fingers, Johnson," I heard him say, "and quit that whining!"

After they left me, I settled back down using my ruck as a pillow on that hard, cold floor. I closed my eyes, crossed my arms, and pretended to fall asleep again.

But I didn't sleep. I couldn't stop thinking about this trial and what it might entail. I got the feeling it wasn't going to involve a multiple-choice test and a good-natured round of arm-wrestling.

Still, I was more determined than ever to get through it. Call it a character flaw, but when people told me I wasn't good enough for something...well, I tended to get stubborn about it. I just *had* to prove them wrong.

-6-

We were rousted out of our sleeping bags before the sun rose the next day. Hustling aboard early-morning trams, we were sent rattling down the tracks to the spaceport.

There, waiting for us under the pink skies of dawn, we found a long line of lifters. I shuffled aboard the closest one and less than an hour later flew up into space.

None of these events were new to me. I'd been deployed on alien planets several times before and on each occasion I'd been shipped off into space to travel to the target world. This time, however, I had no idea where we were going or who we were supposed to fight...but come to think of it, that part wasn't all that unusual, either.

The only surprising element of the new campaign was the sight of two more ships following *Minotaur* in space. In the past, the legion had always flown out aboard a single dreadnaught-class ship, a starship capable of warp drive. One ship, one legion—that was how it had always been. This time instead of one dreadnaught there were three.

We found our bunks, and before we could stretch out on them *Minotaur* entered a warp bubble. We were quickly propelled right out of the Solar System.

At the first morning roll call the next day, I raised my hand to ask Centurion Graves about the other ships.

"Sir?" I asked when he reluctantly called on me.

"What is it, McGill?"

"Why are there two other ships following *Minotaur*, sir? Are we heading out with three legions this time?"

"Close," he said. "There are two full legions on this trip, Varus and Solstice. In addition, we have a third ship with extra equipment and an auxiliary cohort for each legion."

I frowned at this answer. I recalled the Solstice regular who'd yelled at me at the smart-door yesterday. It made sense that Solstice was going with us, as they'd been visible all over the Mustering Hall, too. But auxiliaries? Where had they come from?

Although I'd never gone through the process before, I knew that joining up with other legions and auxiliary cohorts was SOP for special missions. A full cohort of techs, for example, was useful when handling engineering projects or drone-based units. Bio cohorts were known to exist as well, on hand in case we were tasked with giving aid to an alien world with a rampaging pandemic. Our people were especially sought after under such circumstances as humans couldn't catch a disease that had evolved to kill an alien form of life. Such missions were considered cakewalks, however, and I doubted Varus would be treated to any such easy task. From what Equestrian Nagata had indicated, this was going to be a rough campaign.

"Then can I ask—" I began, but Graves cut me off.

"No. Shut up, McGill." He looked away from me and ran his eyes over the assembled unit. "Now that we're up and flying, I can tell you our destination. We're going to Gamma Pavonis, a white F-Class star a little larger than our own Sol."

We looked from one to another, confused. I couldn't recall ever having heard of such a star before.

"That's right," Graves said, taking in our baffled looks, "we're heading off the charts this time. This star is over thirty lights out from Earth in a new direction. To the best of our knowledge, we've never been there before. Let's join the Imperator's briefing channel."

Imperator Turov's face flashed up on the wall behind him. The entire wall was made up of photosensitive organic LEDs, and they made her image glow with life. This was the first time I'd see Galina Turov's new, younger self magnified. She really was a sight for sore eyes.

For about a minute, she fooled with her tapper. Finally, she looked up.

"Commanders," she said, "please signal the last few units that it's time to connect to my channel."

She looked down again, waiting.

During this warm-up time, Natasha had been eyeing me rather than Turov. Natasha had been placed near me as we were both specialists and accordingly had been assigned to a front row spot.

I stared up at Imperator Turov expressionlessly. Sure, I wanted to smile about those lips which she'd glossed up. Each lip had to be thicker than a man's arm on that huge screen, but I didn't dare show interest. Natasha and I had an on-again, off-again thing going, and I knew that if she caught me grinning at Turov I'd be in the "off-again" stage indefinitely.

"Do you think she's doing this on purpose?" Natasha asked me.

"Doing what?"

Looking disgusted she nodded toward the screen. "Making us watch her. She has a captive audience of about twenty five thousand right now, and she's not even making a speech."

"Oh, that," I said. "I don't know. I'm kind of hungry. I could really use some breakfast about now."

This was not total bullshit, but it was pretty close. I *was* hungry, but I could probably watch Turov's little pre-game show for another ten minutes before I got bored with it.

Finally, the Imperator got on with the briefing.

"Good morning troops. I will attempt to answer all your questions at once with this briefing. We're moving out today, not as a hired mercenary band, but rather as an organized force representing Earth. Our contracts have been paid by Hegemony, using Galactic credits. I've been chosen to lead this campaign personally by my superiors because of my intimate knowledge of our true enemy."

Frowning, I absorbed her words. Our *true* enemy? She could only mean the squids.

"Renegade forces abound along the fringe of the Empire. Frontier 921, being at the edge of explored galactic space, naturally borders dangerous barbarians. One such untamed tribe calls itself the Kingdom of the Cephalopods."

I glanced at Natasha. She was frowning, too. We were both worried. I'd been holding out a thin hope we'd been assigned one of those easy escort-missions I'd heard so much about since I was a kid. Instead, this looked like we were marching to war—real war. At least Natasha seemed to have gotten over the idea that Turov was flirting with everyone.

"The target world's atmosphere is somewhat similar to that of Earth. It's made up primarily of nitrogen, about seventy-five percent, with an oxygen content just under ten percent. That's where the similarities end, however. The world's surface is made up of an icy frost of methane and bubbling petroleum byproducts. There are lakes and even small seas of liquid methane—but very little water."

"Sounds like a real garden," I said quietly.

"Sounds like an ice-ball," Natasha said. "It must be if there's liquid methane."

"Sounds like you two need to learn when to shut the hell up," Harris said from behind us.

We both straightened up and stared at the giant Turov on the forward wall.

"The surface temperature varies between minus one-fifty and minus two hundred degrees C," she continued.

I winced. An ice-ball indeed.

"Interestingly," the giant face went on, "science tells us there might be some kind of life on this world producing the oxygen in the atmosphere. If so, this life must be quite alien and subsist by using methane as a primary energy source. The cloud layer is so thick that photosynthesis, as we understand it, is probably impossible."

The world she was painting in my mind was an unpleasant one: Frozen, with deadly substances everywhere. The air might be breathable if we filtered it and warmed it up by a few hundred degrees, but that was about it.

"The reason we're interested in this planet is strategic," Turov continued. "Galactic Intel tells us that the cephalopods are probing this world and maybe building an advance base there as it's close to Empire space. Their strategic goals are easy to discern. The world is mineral rich. Metals and radioactives are plentiful."

That made more sense to me. If the target world could be used to build ships and weapons right on the border, both sides would want the planet.

Turov continued her lecture. "If there is an indigenous population, it's probably primitive and negligible. We will arrive with three ships and two legions. Any cephalopod forces will be eliminated if they refuse to vacate the system."

This caused me a pang. Sure, the Nairbs had blown up one of their worlds when they'd attacked our ship, *Corvus*. And later, I'd personally had a hand in destroying their ship when they attacked a megahab full of Tau civilians on Tech World.

But this was different. We'd be invading, striking first. As far as the squids were concerned, I was pretty sure they figured this planet was theirs for the taking. Interfering with that using Earth's legions—well, I hoped the hog brass knew what they were doing.

"On to the last item of today's agenda," Turov continued. "Legion Solstice, Legion Varus, I would like to introduce you to two new cohorts. They're both cavalry units from Zeta Herculis."

That got our attention. I hadn't known what to expect, but two cohorts of specialized troops from Zeta Herculis? That had to be damned near the bottom of the probability chart for me.

Zeta Herculis, better known as Dust World, was Earth's one and only colony. We'd been allowed to keep it on a technicality. Normally, civilizations in the Empire were permitted to inhabit only a single star system. But since we'd colonized this lonely, dry planet back before the Empire had discovered us, we'd been "grandfathered in."

"These two auxiliary cohorts *do* include some colonial troops," Turov said. "They'll be attached to your existing legions. Cross-training will take place on the third ship, *Cyclops*, as there's plenty of open space available on her decks."

"I bet there is," I said quietly.

Natasha's eyes snapped toward me, and I shut up immediately. Romance-wise, this might be yet another bad turn. I'd taken an interest in one of the colonists on Dust World, years back. Her name was Della, and I'd probably never had a stranger relationship in my lifetime. Including Natasha and Turov, that made this a potential three-girl situation, and I'm simply not equipped to handle that kind of pressure.

"I will now list off the units I want transferred to *Cyclops* for immediate cross-training."

Turov began to read off various unit designations from one cohort or another. Units from both Varus and Solstice were specified. There were quite a few of them.

I finally noticed Natasha was staring at me.

"What?" I asked her.

"I know what you're thinking."

"You do?"

"Yes. Don't play that dumb-guy thing with me. You're thinking about Della."

"Who?"

She made a disgusted sound.

"Oh yeah, Della," I said as if just recalling the name. "That crazy colonist chick. Do you know she killed me twice back on Dust World?"

"Then why do you still want to see her?"

I shook my head, baffled. "Where's this coming from?" I demanded. "She's probably not even on that ship—I mean, what are the odds?"

"Pretty good. She was one of their top fighters."

Candidly, I had to agree with her, but there was no percentage in admitting that. I laughed quietly instead.

"Natasha, get real! That girl is fifty lights away—and anyway, why do you care so much? Do you want to start going out with me again?"

"Certainly not."

I tried not to smile, but I failed. I knew she wanted to go out. Why the hell else would she care so much about the ghost of Della, someone who probably wasn't even—

"Legion Varus, 3rd Cohort, 3rd Unit," Turov announced.

It could have been my imagination, but I thought maybe the Imperator had given the camera a little flickering smile as she listed my unit designation.

"I don't believe it," Natasha said. "That bitch."

"What's wrong?" I asked. "She said we'll train with auxiliary cavalry, right? That sounds pretty cool."

"Not if it was her idea. Not if she picked us off the list for this special assignment. Didn't you see her smirk at the camera? We're doomed."

I shook my head. Natasha could be overly dramatic sometimes.

-7-

The flotilla dropped out of warp near an orange-looking K-class star system encircled by lifeless worlds. Before we went back into warp, my unit was transferred off *Minotaur* and onto *Cyclops*. The ships were all armed Imperial transports, so they looked pretty much the same. *Cyclops* had the same bulbous hull and a full broadside of sixteen big guns for armament.

The main hold of *Cyclops* was occupied by a stack of modules in the same manner as the other two ships. The number of modules was smaller, however, and they'd been pushed together to form a single mass about three modules high. On top of these modules was a wide, flat area about a kilometer square.

My unit was brought in first before any other unit had transferred. Marching into the hold in a column four abreast, we exited the lifter's ramps and were ordered to climb up to the top of that stack of modules. We hustled, not wanting colonials to see us looking weak.

We jogged up a set of steps made of steel tubing to the top. I noticed one thing along the way: the gravity was turned on full-force. Usually while traveling in space, the transport ships maintained a centrifugal force of half-gravity. That level was both heavy enough to keep us fit and light enough to make it easier to get around with heavy equipment. But today my body weighed over a hundred kilos, and my kit must have been twice that much. Fortunately, my exoskeletal armor helped out with the load.

43

Once we stepped out on top of the modules, we were wowed by an unusual sight. Arrayed on this large, flat surface were long lines of fighting machines. I recognized them immediately.

"Hey," Carlos said, coming up to me with a broad grin. "I know those machines! Turov drove one of these babies when she snapped off your head back on Tech World."

"That's right. But as I recall, she killed you first with one snip."

"Whatever."

"These look bigger," I said, marveling and stepping toward them, "and improved."

They were bigger. As we walked closer, we could see they were at least three meters tall. I bet when they stood up and were fully operational they'd be even taller. When Turov had driven a suit like this, it had been little more than a heavy-built exoskeleton wrapped around her body. These machines were more leggy. I figured right off that the pilot's legs probably only went down to about the knee-joint while his hands terminated where the elbows were.

"They look like mean ostriches," Carlos said.

"No," I replied. "I'd say they're more like a small T-rex. Ostriches don't have tails that whip around or big foreclaws."

"Good point. I bet getting yourself murdered by Turov while she was driving one of these suits turned you on, didn't it McGill? You're sick."

"I'm not the one who can't stop talking about it."

"Come on, let's pick out our machine and start riding!"

Carlos trotted toward the line of hulking metal vehicles. I walked after him watching them warily. They all seemed unoccupied, but one could never be too—

Up and down the line, about every twentieth machine perked up when Carlos was about a hundred meters away. Carlos' rapid approach faltered then stopped altogether. He glanced back at me with a worried expression.

Veteran Harris moved in front of the group. He was smiling, and right away I knew he was in on the surprise.

"They're quite something, aren't they?" he asked with his throat mike cranked up to top volume. "Fantastic fighting machines—we call them dragons."

I walked to Carlos and slapped him. "See? I told you they weren't ostriches."

He waved me away.

"I'm sorry to say," Harris continued, "that these fine dragons are about to be totally wasted on a unit of sorry shit-sacks like you. I told them not to do it, but the brass never listens to me."

"Uh..." I said in concern. "Some of those suits are occupied, Vet. Who's in there?"

"Your trainers. Zeta Herculis people. Think of them as advisors."

"They built these things?"

One of the machines started walking then. It stalked forward on its hind legs like a predatory bird. It flexed foreclaws that terminated in sharp grippers, and the tail moved on its own to balance the machine when it leaned and stepped. Twin, stubby cannons were built into the barrel-like chest. Inside the dim-lit faceplate, I could make out the vaguest outline of a human face. We felt like little kids facing a Halloween monster. Reflexively, our line of troops fell back a few steps.

"We're here to train you in the proper use and maintenance of these systems," the pilot's voice boomed. The amplified voice was kind of creepy coming out of the robotic fighting vehicle. It was as if some kind of mechanical nightmare was talking to us.

None of the Varus people approached any closer.

Harris grinned. "Stand down, Scout," he said then turned back to us. "Now, this is how we're going to do things today. We're going to have a little sparring contest. A full unit of Varus regulars up against—"

Already, troops around me were shifting into a fighting stance. We were no strangers to surprise drills—Varus loved them. Unfortunately, they were often deadly to the troops getting surprised.

45

A number of men around me unlimbered their rifles and dropped to the deck. Up and down the line of dragons, nine more had started moving. This was pure Legion Varus: training on the fly.

I took a half-second to glance over my shoulder. Just as I'd thought, our officers were nowhere to be seen. Adjunct Leeson and Graves were no doubt sipping a cold one and watching this contest on a vid screen in the officer's mess by now.

As a weaponeer, I knew I was critical to any chance my side had to take out these machines. By my estimation, my belcher was one of the few systems heavy enough to punch through the enemy armor.

Accordingly, I threw myself flat and shot the nearest one in the leg. This seemed to take everyone by surprise. Harris was still talking, describing his contest, but I was done listening. It was me or the dragons, that's all I knew.

The target machine took the hit, and for a second I thought it was going to stay up, but it didn't. The leg buckled and the machine went down on one knee, servos whining.

Harris charged at me, shouting.

"HOLD!" he roared. "No guns! Neither side is supposed to damage—"

The machine's rider seemed to take exception to my breaking of the rules. Smoothly, two cannons protruded from the chest cavity and barked.

Harris was in a bad place at a bad time, right between me and the dragon I'd just crippled. He was hit in the back and blasted off his feet. He went into a tumble that finished up about five meters to my left. His eyes were as dead as boiled eggs, and his back was a smoking ruin.

All up and down the Varus line, my fellows opened up, rattling fire at the line of active machines. The machines rocked back with the shock, then returned fire with their cannons. The weapons seemed to have short range but explosive power. If I had to guess, I'd say they were firing rocket-powered grenades of some kind.

"HOLD YOUR FIRE!" boomed a command in our headsets. It took me a second to recognize the voice of Centurion Graves.

46

Somehow, Graves managed to cut through the confusion. A few more shots were popped off by both sides, but we lowered our weapons and stared at one another distrustfully. Three of the dragons were damaged, and at least twenty troopers were dead.

"No guns, no shields, no force-blades!" Centurion Graves' voice ordered in my headset. "Both sides are to use only melee weapons. This is to be a hand-to-hand contest. GO!"

Reluctantly, I dropped my belcher. The temptation to launch one more salvo was strong in me, but I managed to resist it.

"What are we going to do, McGill?" Carlos shouted from nearby, breathing hard.

"We're going to have to get in close and take them apart by hand."

"Shit!" he said, and I had to agree with the sentiment. "Those grippers—there's no way. This is a setup. We're supposed to get slaughtered."

All up and down the line, the Varus troops were forming up in knots. They had a grim look on their faces. The enemy line formed up as well, transforming into a wedge-shaped group of seven functioning dragons.

With all my heart, I wanted to extend my force-blades and do battle—but I didn't. Instead, I advanced and a knot of troops formed around me.

Veteran Harris was down as was Sargon. That left me as the senior noncom in my platoon. This was my chance, I decided, to show I could lead men if I had to.

"All right," I said. "Form up, spread out. We're going to have to—"

That was as far as I got. The enemy wedge charged. There weren't that many of them, but they were ferocious. They came on with those powerful legs churning. If I had to guess, I would say they could run twice as fast as a man.

The wedge plowed right into a knot of troops to my left. They went down like bowling pins. Screams and roars sounded from both sides. Men struggled in their exo-skeleton suits, but they couldn't compete in either strength or weight. The troops had out knives, but although they gouged the armor of the

47

machines and even cracked a few faceplates the squad was soon just a struggling mass under the crushing weight of the machines.

It was already clear to me what the enemy was going to do. They'd charge each group of us as we formed up and break us, destroying us in detail. The leader was already rotating a predatory head, the dragon's tail lashing with a whining noise as it fought to maintain balance, standing on the backs of fallen troopers.

"Break apart!" I ordered. "Squad, spread out. Their commander is looking for a target, and we don't want that to be us."

They did as I asked, separating and dispersing with rapid side-steps in every direction.

"Good thinking, McGill," Carlos said. "Let these mechanical monsters wreck everyone else first. With any luck—"

"Shut up, I'm trying to think," I ordered, and for once in his life he did what he was told.

"Natasha?" I asked. "Can you do anything?"

"Like what?" she demanded, breathing hard.

"I don't know. Maybe you could remotely hack the dragons or something."

"Tried it. No go, McGill."

"Okay. Plan B."

"They're charging again!" Carlos shouted.

The cavalry had chosen another group of victims by now, and they charged in tight formation. This squad of troops had retreated to the edge of the battlefield and stood with their backs to a hundred meter drop. The results were almost as bad as the first time, with one exception. The troops managed to push one of the dragons over the side.

That gave me an idea.

"Squad, follow me! Attack! Redirect all suit-power to your legs!"

Without explaining, I ran across the field toward the struggling knot of men and dragons. The Varus troops were losing—badly. But they weren't all dead yet. Using only grippers, the machines had to pretty much amputate limbs methodically to win.

We crossed the intervening distance quickly. In powered suits, we could run almost as fast as the machines could when we sent the full power of our exoskeletons to our legs.

"What the hell are we doing, McGill?" Carlos shouted.

"Hit them. Like a football tackle. Knock them over the edge. It's the only way."

"McGill's right!" Kivi shouted, somewhere behind me. "Let's push them over the side!"

The best part of the next minute as I later looked back on it all had to be when the enemy turned to see us coming. They had to be thinking "what the hell" but before they could react, we were on them.

My boots were clanging on the metal roof of the modules with perfect, powered rhythm. My face was a death's-head snarl of rage. Lowering my shoulder, I crashed into the nearest dragon.

The shock was tremendous. The vehicle was so massive it was as if I'd just rammed myself into the bumper of my parents' family tram back home. The machine rocked but didn't go down. The driver must have set himself for the impact.

But then Carlos came in beside me and added his weight. Finally, the machine began to move. It was sliding, I realized, sliding on the bloody mess they'd made of the last squad who now formed heaps of helpless dead on the ground.

We struggled, grappling their legs and heaving. One machine went over the side, taking a howling trooper with it. They crashed to the bottom of the hold, and I dearly hoped the rider had died for his sins.

Still, the contest was uneven. There were only five dragons left against ten infantry. While we'd shoved and grunted and forced them back, they hadn't been idle. Those grippers reached out snapping and snipping. Heads and arms were lying everywhere.

Ten of us—we couldn't do it. I decided as the dragon Carlos and I were working on got a gripper on my left elbow that I'd do my damnedest and die well. My arm didn't come off right away as my weaponeer's armor was heavier than that of the average trooper. If I could kill just one more of them—

Wham! I felt a slamming weight against my back. My despair had been premature. More men had arrived. Legion Varus troops, seeing our plan and seeing it was working, had charged from all around the battlefield.

More and more of them joined in, adding their weight to ours.

I couldn't see—I could barely hear. So much blood had splattered my cracked faceplate, and everyone was roaring in my ears so loudly I didn't even realize I was near the edge until I went over.

There was a sick feeling at the final second. It was a moment without parallel when I realized I was falling through the air and crashing down to certain death.

The dragon I'd been struggling with all this time was under me, and I was riding it down. It felt like I was falling all the way to Hell itself.

I don't remember hitting the bottom. I think I was knocked out at least for a few seconds.

I came awake groaning. I flipped up my faceplate painfully, and I could see again.

A tangled mass of death lay all around me. One of the machines and three or four troopers squirmed, but most were still.

On impulse, I reached up and opened the faceplate of the nearest machine—of the one I'd ridden over the side.

To my shock, I recognized the face inside.

"Della?" I asked in a coughing whisper.

She didn't answer me because she was as dead as a stone. I stared into her face. It was strange meeting up with her again—it was even stranger to know I'd just killed her.

A cheer swelled louder and louder above me. I flopped and rolled onto my back, looking up. A line of Varus troops stood along the edge, shaking their fists and whooping.

"Look at McGill!" Carlos shouted. "He's still alive!"

More cheers went up. Grinning through bloody teeth, I forced one gauntlet to wave at them before I passed out.

Bio people are lazy. They don't like to fix the bodies of the badly injured. They preferred to recycle broken flesh and start new. Theirs was a throw-away culture, and I was therefore surprised when I woke up in the infirmary in my old, badly damaged body.

"Seven broken bones, not counting ribs," Bio Specialist Anne Grant read from her tapper while standing next to me.

I had to turn my head pretty far to see her as my right eye had swollen shut.

"Contusions, punctures and a collapsed lung," she went on. "We even had to remove your spleen. Do you know how long it's been since I've bothered to do that, James?"

"No, but I'm pretty sure you're going to tell me," I said with stinging, cracked lips.

"Eight years, I would guess. That's how long ago I signed up with this crazy outfit. We just don't do organ removal. Not from a living person, that is."

"Sounds like it would be boring, just running the revival machine all day."

She gave me a reproachful look. "And you, you're hurting aren't you? Is this better than a fresh revive?"

I didn't know why she was giving me a hard time, but I was getting tired of it. After all, I was the one in agony. She'd only suffered inconvenience. Then again, maybe I was just feeling sorry for myself.

"Actually," I said, "I'm feeling pretty good. I figured I might go for a jog around the top of those modules later today. I've got a few kinks in my legs I need to work out."

She shook her head and huffed. "Those aren't kinks, they're staples. I nu-skinned the hell out of them, but they'll still sting for a week. They're sunk in all the way to the bone."

Groaning, I levered myself into a half-sitting position. Her small hands pushed on my chest.

"Lie back down, please. You'll pass out if you get out of bed now. Graves wants to talk to you. I think that's why you're still alive."

I let her push me back down. In truth, it felt a lot better that way. I was a mess. As a person who's been killed and injured countless times, I could tell this was a bad one.

Graves showed up about ten minutes later. His face blocked out the medical lights that were glaring into my eyes, and he examined me with all the tenderness of a rancher poking at his prize bull.

"McGill? Are you lucid yet?"

"Right as rain, sir."

"Good. I wanted to talk to you. With all the revives going on today I knew it would be a while if I let you stack up in the queue with the rest. I hope you don't mind."

"Mind that you stopped me from being recycled? No sir, I don't mind."

He slapped my thigh, and I winced. He didn't seem to notice.

"That's the spirit! I want to thank you, McGill. That was a fine bit of improvising you did out there on the field today. We didn't expect that play. Sure, Winslade and the rest of his auxiliary people are screaming about the damage you did to their machines—but do you know what I said to that?"

"Uh...what sir?"

"That they could go screw themselves, that's what. It was Winslade's idea to prove how powerful his machines were by abusing all the new troops who arrived to train on them. I'm sure he didn't expect much in the way of damage, but that's just too damned bad."

I was fuzzy, but I was pretty sure he'd mentioned a name that I didn't think should be mentioned when talking about combat units.

"Sir?" I asked. "Did you say Winslade? As in, Adjunct Winslade?"

"The one and only. Turov's sidekick has finally cashed in his marker. He's a primus now—hadn't you heard?"

A primus was in charge of a cohort in a regular legion or in some cases an independent auxiliary cohort. Commanding an auxiliary cohort gave a primus more prestige and responsibility than a regular commander who was permanently the subordinate of a legion's tribune. Usually, such special cohort assignments went to people who'd held the rank of primus for several years and who had done well in that capacity. Winslade was none of these things.

"I'm not surprised he managed to swing a command rank," I said, "but isn't this a stretch? A primus is two jumps above an Adjunct. Last I'd heard, he still didn't have much in the way of combat experience to begin with."

"I know," Graves said, "I know. I've been with this legion for decades, and they've always promoted one snot-nose or another over me. That's the way of things sometimes. When forming up a new auxiliary cohort, you would think they'd look for officers from the existing fighting forces, but no."

"They took and promoted a Hog right over you? It's just not right."

"Well, let's forget about that," Graves said. "Let's talk about your tactics. What inspired you to try to shove the dragons over the side?"

I explained how I'd seen a group along the edge which had managed to throw one down. I then quickly ordered my followers to charge into the melee before the dragons could finish butchering the first group.

"Excellent," Graves said. "That's what I'm talking about, right there: Leadership on the field, improvisation—and victory. I don't regret a thing."

I frowned. "What would you have to regret, sir?"

"Your upcoming trials have been challenged. The 3rd Unit veterans came to me, and they told me I had to pull your

53

advancement to candidacy. Did you know they were against it?"

"I had a feeling, sir."

"Well, I won't lie—this might go badly for you, but I think you might be able to pull it off somehow. See you on the other side, McGill."

He stood up and gave me a grim nod. Then he left the infirmary. I looked after him and tried not to worry.

* * *

The trip out to Gamma Pavonis was a long run. I had plenty of time to heal up and join in the training exercises with the rest of my unit.

Driving the dragons around turned out to be fun. I'd seen Turov do it back on Tech World, but at that time I hadn't known who had built these machines. Apparently, the colonists from Dust World had produced the prototypes when seeking a system they could sell to other planets. They'd settled down as nanite vendors in the end but not before producing some pretty interesting designs to share with the human-only market.

What got me most was the inventiveness of the colonists on Dust World. They'd been a splinter group cut off from Earth for nearly a century. They hadn't known they shouldn't be making new tech devices freely, that it was against Galactic Law. What impressed me the most, however, was how many cool things they'd invented with such a small group. During the same interval, Earth had pretty much stagnated technologically. Due to its very nature, the Empire progressed very slowly.

I recalled from my new-history courses back in school that the twentieth and twenty-first centuries had been a time of explosive growth in human knowledge. We'd invented all kinds of things that were taken for granted today. Humanity had been quite innovative back in the days before the Galactic bureaucrats came and put a damper on all our creativity. In order to legally make a product in the Empire, you had to first make sure that no other civilization held the patent. The colonists from Zeta Herculis hadn't known about these restrictions and had plowed along inventing whatever they damn well pleased. I had to admire their spunk.

The dragons were one such invention. As they were already producing nanites as a trade good to cement their position in the Empire, they'd decided to use the battle vehicles as a trade good with Earth itself. It was just as illegal for a single planet to have multiple interstellar trade goods as it was to have none or to trade something that someone else did. But, apparently, no other planets produced suits like these and so humans were in the clear to build and sell them among themselves.

Over the next month or so, I'd come to understand how the new auxiliary cohort fit in with the rest of Legion Varus. My Legion had gone into space this time with a lot of extra recruits. These troops now served to swell the ranks of all ten of Varus' existing cohorts. In the meantime, veteran troops were moved into the new auxiliary cohort. My unit, being one of the ones trained in the use of heavy armor, was a natural choice to learn how to fight in dragons as they were essentially larger, heavier, self-powered battle armor systems.

Centurion Graves became a unit commander under Winslade. It seemed unfair, even downright mean, to put him in that position, but Turov had never been one to worry about justice when she made a decision.

And so I learned how to drive the strange dragons. Probably the most difficult part was learning how to operate the hand controls manipulating the grippers at the same time I was directing the twin chest cannons.

The chest cannons operated in two modes. You could use them on full-auto, which essentially meant the suit's computer system chose its target and fired the cannons wherever it wanted to, or you could manually control both the arms and the cannons with your own hands. This was accomplished by squeezing metal triggers with your palms and three smaller fingers, while at the same time using your thumb and forefinger to make pinching motions to control the grippers. In reality, most troopers chose the middle ground of letting the computer aim the cannons while they chose the moment to fire by either verbally commanding it or by using their fingers.

It was all pretty much as difficult as it sounded. I remarked about it to Carlos while we were undergoing our final trials.

"Tell me about it," Carlos said. "I feel like I should have a bugle hanging out of my ass. I'm a one-man band, here."

Throughout the days of training I was naturally in close proximity with Della. We were both riding dragons, of course, but I could still see her face. I had to wonder what she was thinking.

I knew without asking what Natasha was thinking. She didn't leave me any mystery about it. Every time I looked at Della or watched her climb in and out of her dragon, Natasha seemed to notice. I didn't know how I was supposed to avoid noticing Della all that time, so I didn't bother to try. After all, we took showers together, dressed together, and sparred together all day long.

Since Natasha seemed to care so much, I decided to make a play for her at dinner the night before we finished our training.

"Natasha," I said, "hey…how about you and I—"

"Forget it," she snapped.

"What? You haven't heard what I was going to say."

"James, I've heard it all. We all have. All of the women in this unit."

"Sheesh. I was just going to—"

"I know. I suggest you go ask Della instead."

"Wait," I said, "Della doesn't even look at me. Haven't you noticed that?"

"Of course I have. That's why I'm angry. She's still very aware of you. Go talk to her. She wants you to."

I shrugged. "Fine. Just fine. I'll do that."

I found Della in the colonist module which was in the lowest tier of the stack aboard *Cyclops*.

"Hi Della," I said, "I thought I'd come down here and—"

Della put a finger to her lips. She walked toward me, smiling. When she came close I checked her hands for weapons, and I became alarmed. She had one hand behind her back.

Like I said, Della and I had a strange relationship. We'd made love and fought to the death about the same number of times. It could go either way with this woman.

56

When she got close, I backed up a little. Laughing, she lifted both her hands, palms out. They were empty.

I smiled sheepishly. "Just checking," I said.

"I know," she said. "But I've changed, James."

"Listen," I said hesitantly, "I wanted to apologize for pushing you off the stack of modules and killing you the other day. I didn't know it was you inside that metal monster at the time. You understand that, right?"

"Yes. You shouldn't feel any remorse. After all, I *did* know it was you, and I still tried to clip your arms off. It was all part of the exercise."

"No hard feelings then?"

"None at all."

I smiled. "Good. We can be friends again. Say, how about—?"

That was as far as I got. She cut off my words by jumping on me. That's the only way I can describe it. One second I was unsure how I stood, even fearing for my life, and the next we were in a lip-lock.

We found a place off by ourselves on the Green Deck, which was pretty easy to do on *Cyclops* since the ship had only about twenty percent of the usual number of troops aboard.

Green Deck was like a public park, a place traditionally built aboard all large ships to simulate an outdoor environment. It was always popular with couples seeking a get-away during off-hours. During the day it was used for combat training.

Overgrown with trees and riddled with sheltered nooks behind rocks and bushes, there was always a spot you could find that was secluded and at least semi-private. Artificial birds sang and brooks babbled, giving people the exact level of cover-noise they needed.

We made love, and the sex was as good as it had always been with Della. She was possibly the most uninhibited girl I'd ever been with. I chalked that up to her upbringing on an alien world.

"That was great," I said afterward. "You aren't still trying to get pregnant are you?"

"No, of course not," she said. "I wouldn't do that now, it would be inappropriate."

I sighed in relief. Last time we'd been together, Della had been interested in procreating with me. Apparently, that was all over with.

Putting my arms behind my head, I stretched out on the grass and stared up at the simulated starry sky.

"Aren't you interested?" she asked.

"Interested in what?"

"Don't you at least want to know the name I chose?"

I frowned in confusion. "What are you talking about, girl?"

"Our child, of course."

Words failed me. "You mean…?"

"Of course. We succeeded the last time. Her name is Etta."

I stared at her. Both of my eyes must've been as big around as a Georgia peach. She laughed at me, laughed right in my face.

I jumped up like I'd been stung. "What are you doing out here in space?" I demanded. "Where's our kid? You didn't bring her aboard, did you?"

"No, I wouldn't do that. She's far too young. She'll make an excellent Scout someday, but she's not ready yet."

"No… I didn't mean that. Who's taking care of her? That's what I want to know."

"Her grandfather, among others. You remember the Principal Investigator?"

I made a sour face. "How could I forget?"

"Don't worry," Della said, "Etta will be fine. With your genes and mine, she's as immutable as a stone in the desert. Everything will make way for her. Nothing will break her."

"But…listen, where I come from, parents care for their own children directly. If I'd had a kid back on Earth, I wouldn't have joined the legions and come flying out here to the stars. I would have stayed home and raised it."

She cocked her head to one side and looked at me quizzically. "Are you upset?"

"A little, yeah," I admitted.

"You didn't enjoy the sex?"

I snorted. "Of course I did."

She shook her head and combed leaves out of her hair with her fingers. "You people from Earth, you're so sensitive. You worry about everything. How can life be worth living if you worry all the time?"

If there's one thing I'd never been called before, it was a worrier. But this was different. Della had gone and gotten herself pregnant—with my help of course—and now I'd been placed in an unaccustomed role of responsibility. It was a shock.

Heaving a sigh, I sat down beside Della, and I looked her straight in the eye.

"We should get married," I said.

She frowned. She plucked at the grass around her knees and twisted the blades around her fingers. "I would've liked that," she said, "a year or so back...but I can't now."

"Why not?"

She smiled at me. Her expression was almost shy.

"Because, James...I'm already married."

-9-

Della's twin revelations came as quite a shock to me. Not only was I a father, the parent of a kid I'd never seen and possibly never *would* see, but she'd gone and gotten married in the meantime.

Even stranger was her apparent attitude toward fidelity. I mean, she was a married woman and yet she'd slept with me without even telling me about it. I just couldn't get over that. Culturally, we were about as far apart as two people could get.

Needless to say, I was confused. I went back to my bunk that night and thought about it, unable to sleep for nearly *ten* minutes. That's not normal for me.

When I finally did fall asleep I dreamt weird things. I dreamt about squids, and deserts, and beautiful nutty women.

Around about three in the morning, my sleep was interrupted. Straps looped over my chest, legs, and throat. My eyes snapped open, and I moved to get out of bed, but I was pinned down to it. The room was dark and my roommates were gone. Figures stood all around me.

As an experienced fighting man from Legion Varus, I pride myself on being prepared for violent action at all times. This was just one more of those times.

My right hand slid out of the grasp of the man who was trying to pin it down. I managed this trick with the aid of the combat knife my parents had given me some time back. Knives in my time were sharper than they had been in the past. Using advanced metallurgical techniques and molecular alignments, a knife could be made to cut through flesh and bone as easily as paper. One could even puncture steel plate if driven with sufficient force.

But of course before that could happen, the owner of the knife had to be a man paranoid enough to sleep with such a weapon in his grasp. I happened to be just such a man. Fingers, straps, blankets—they all parted before the glittering white line of my knife's edge.

One of my assailants started howling, he also released his grip on my forearm. My blade flashed up to the man holding a strap around my neck. This guy was quicker however, and he managed to get his two hands around my wrist before I could drive the point of my blade into his face.

"Dammit McGill!" Harris hissed. "Stop struggling. This is the beginning of your trial!"

"Sorry Vet," I said.

Someone snapped on the lights. I looked around at the men that surrounded me. They were the same veterans who had accosted me back on Earth.

My knife made a sweeping motion, and they hastily withdrew their hands. I slashed my bonds and sat up on my bunk.

"You boys really should let a man know when you're going to pull a stunt like this," I said. "Somebody might get hurt."

Harris put his big face into mine. "You're coming with us, candidate."

"Sure thing, Vet. Lead the way."

They retreated from my bunk while I got to my feet, stretched, and pulled on my clothes.

As none of them were wearing armor, I didn't bother to put on mine, either. They led me to Green Deck, and we followed the stream that wound through the middle of the forested section. The stream terminated and spilled into a tiny artificial canyon, forming a waterfall. We walked down a path to the bottom of the canyon.

Overhead, I could see stars sliding gently by through the simulated glass dome. I could tell that the stars had shifted since the last time I'd looked at them with Della some hours ago. The pinpoints of white light moved with almost imperceptible slowness, like the hands of a clock.

We reached the end of the path and stood at the sandy bottom of the canyon. I spotted a group of several other candidates. Their heads were in sacks, and they lay on their bellies with their wrists tied to their ankles. Each of them was trussed up like a Christmas turkey.

"Oh, I get it," I said. "I was supposed to be tied up, wasn't I?"

One of the veterans stepped up to me angrily. I recognized him in the starlight. He was none other than Veteran Johnson of 1st Platoon.

"You're mocking us aren't you?" he demanded.

"Why no, Vet," I said. "Whatever gave you that idea?" I knew I shouldn't do it, but I gave him a little grin.

"Settle down, Johnson," said Harris. "You'll get your chance."

Johnson never even looked at Harris. He kept eyeing me instead. "You know what would make me happy, McGill?"

I glanced down at his hands. Sure enough, one of his two gloves looked half-empty. I realized then that he'd drawn the short straw a second time while dealing with me.

"Let me guess," I said, "a couple of extra fingers?"

He threw a punch at me, which I ducked. He caught a little bit of my left ear, but it was no big deal.

Harris was between us instantly. He pushed us apart and shoved his face into each of ours.

"We're doing this one by the book," he said. "You hear me?"

"Loud and clear, Vet," I said. My eyes never left Johnson's. We stared each other down for about two more seconds before backing off.

"McGill?" Harris asked in a sarcastic tone. "Would you mind going over there and standing with the rest of the candidates?"

I did as he asked. Moments later, the veterans slashed their captives free. I looked from one face to the next in the starlight. Two of them I recognized. One was none other than Weaponeer Sargon. The other was a short stocky woman built like a fireplug. She was from 1st Platoon, but I couldn't remember her name.

"Here's the deal," Harris said. "All of you have been advanced to candidacy, but only one of you will be given the promotion. As the existing veterans of third unit, it's our job to watch and judge this contest. Your boundaries are the walls of this canyon. Do not exit the boundaries. To do so will result in immediate disqualification."

As he spoke, I began to frown. It was dawning on me that this was some kind of arena-combat scenario. The other candidates were already eyeing each other and separating. I took this time to examine my surroundings more closely.

We stood on a beach that was only about ten meters wide. The canyon was circular and about hundred meters across. The walls were quite forbidding. They were sheer and vertical. The only easy path out of the canyon was the foot trail we'd come down on, which wound its way up along the walls and under a waterfall at the far end.

I'd gone swimming down here a number of times in the small, cool, deep lake that formed the center of the canyon.

"Oh," Harris said, "one more thing. McGill? Would you be so kind as to give me your weapon?"

"You mean my knife?"

"Exactly."

I drew it out, flipped the blade so that I held the tip and flicked it at him. He flinched, but didn't jump out of the way. The blade stuck in the sand between his boots.

Smiling grimly, Harris picked up my knife. "The last man—or woman—who's left alive in this canyon tonight is a veteran. That's it, no more rules. *Go!*"

The fireplug-woman moved first. She caught Sargon by one foot and pulled backwards. He went down on his face, growling. A thin, rat-faced man joined her. Together, they dragged Sargon out into the water.

I thought about intervening, but I didn't have time to see how that struggle ended. Something hit me, blindsiding me, knocking me back into the water.

A dark figure loomed over me outlined by the stars. He had a big rock in both hands, and a snarl on his face. I fought to get my hands in between that rock and my skull. He still managed to deliver a glancing blow, and I could feel the blood leaking out of my scalp.

The veterans were cheering. They called out encouragement, catcalls, and slammed their hands together in applause when someone landed a hard blow.

The guy with the rock kept coming after me. Feeling a little dazed, I decided to disengage. I swam away with long strokes toward the center of the lake.

The guy with the rock didn't follow. Instead, he ran off toward the foliage along the shoreline.

The fireplug-woman with her rat-faced companion managed to drown Sargon. There was nothing I could do, and it made me angry.

They'd teamed up, plain as day. That seemed unfair. I could only wonder if they'd known ahead of time how this trial was going to go. I hadn't seen them talk or negotiate anything in the canyon. I could only surmise that they'd been in cahoots from the start.

"Well played, well played," Harris said, talking to the fireplug and her sidekick. "I feel compelled to reward success."

So saying, he produced my combat knife and tossed it at the feet of the woman.

Both she and her partner lunged for the knife. I treaded water, watching.

"What's this?" Harris chuckled. "Treachery? So soon?"

The stout woman had landed on the knife first with rat-face on her back a fraction of a second later. Four hands clamped onto the hilt of one knife. They rolled, grunting, but in the end, the rat found his throat slashed and the woman stood over him panting.

More applause, appreciative shouts.

"Come on McGill!" Johnson shouted at me. "Quit hiding out there in the lake!"

I turned and swam for the waterfall.

"Well now," Harris said, "that's just plain cowardice, McGill."

Harris drew his sidearm, an old gunpowder weapon, and shook all the cartridges out of the gun except for one. He threw

64

the weapon at the guy who'd hit me with the rock. "Here, catch!"

Any of my teachers from Atlanta's primary education system could have told you years back that I'd never been the most attentive student. But even I, when faced with overwhelming evidence, can figure out where the cards lay.

These veterans had no intention of letting me win this contest. In fact, it looked to me like they were going to cheat if they had to. No matter what, I was destined to lose. They'd probably set up the fireplug and her rat-buddy to nail Sargon right off, so I wouldn't have anyone to team with.

Seeing that there was a gun in play, the fireplug lady ran off around the lake to the far side. Grinning, the dark complected squatty-looking man with Harris' gun circled the other way. I could tell he wasn't interested in taking his single shot at long range. He wanted to get in close and make sure of a kill. Both of them headed toward the waterfall on opposites sides of the lake.

I came up under the waterfall breathing hard. I could see two figures approaching through the mist, one from either direction. This gave me an idea. If they could cheat, why couldn't I?

I dove, swimming deep into the cold water. I took long sweeping strokes. I was well below the surface. Each pumping motion of my arms and legs took me back toward the shoreline where this had all started.

When I surfaced, gasping, it was just in time to hear a shot crack the air. The veterans whooped. They were standing knee-deep in the lake around me.

I stood up in the water. Johnson was the man nearest to me. His luck was consistent.

"What the hell—?" he shouted. "McGill? All you do is run from every fight. You have to be the biggest chicken—"

That was as far as he got. I stepped up to him, pulled his sidearm out of his holster and aimed over his shoulder. I shot Veteran Gonzales, who had just turned in our direction to see what the fuss was about. My surprised target went down on his face with a loud splash. The back of his skull was gone.

Johnson began struggling with me, but as he was missing a finger or two he couldn't stop my hand from bringing his gun around and placing the muzzle against his chest.

Boom!

I don't think Johnson could believe his bad luck right to the end. He stared up at me as he was dying, even after the lake water covered his face.

Harris slammed into me a moment later. The pistol flew out of my grasp. We traded blows for two long seconds. I knew the game might be up. I was getting tired, and my head injury from the guy with the rock was throbbing. Hell, I'd have been lucky to beat Harris one-on-one when I was fresh.

Harris snatched the fallen gun out of the water. He aimed it at me, his sides heaving with exertion.

"God *dammit!*" Harris roared. "How is it, McGill, that the every time—?"

Harris made a choking sound. I saw the squatty little guy who'd smashed me with rock minutes ago. He'd snuck up behind Harris and rammed my knife home. He must've taken it from the woman candidate after having shot her.

Not to be taken out so easily, Harris turned, ripped the knife out of his own back, and ran down his attacker with it. I followed at a safe distance to watch what transpired with morbid curiosity.

Harris cut the man to ribbons with my knife. All the while, he bled profusely and released a steady stream of profanity.

Harris turned to face me at last. His sides were heaving, and his body was slick with sweat and blood.

"Whatever possessed you to attack your superiors yet again, McGill?" he asked me in a hoarse voice. "You have to know you're disqualified now."

"Well Vet," I said, "I guess I just didn't understand this contest from the beginning."

Harris began laughing. It was a hitching, gasping, gargling sound. He shook his head and sighed. "You're a real piece of work, you know that boy?"

"Yeah, I guess I do."

Harris slumped forward. He looked surprised, like he was going to vomit or something. Then he slipped onto his face in the water. A few last bubbling, bloody snorts came out of him—then he died. It was blood loss that had done the trick, if I had to guess.

Uncertain as to where this left matters, I retrieved my knife, wiped it clean, and walked up the path.

When I got to the top I was met by four officers. Centurion Graves, Adjunct Leeson, Adjunct Toro, and Adjunct Mesa were all standing up there together. I realized they must have watched the trial from the edge of the cliff surrounding the canyon.

Swaying a bit, I saluted the group.

"Specialist McGill reporting, sirs."

"Don't you mean Veteran McGill?" asked Adjunct Leeson.

"That's ridiculous," Adjunct Toro snapped, her face was red and her teeth were clenched in anger. "McGill didn't follow instructions."

"Hell," Leeson said, "he never does that."

"Well, I vote that he be disqualified," Toro said. She'd never liked me much, so I wasn't surprised.

Graves turned toward the last adjunct. "What do you think, Mesa?"

Mesa looked me over like he smelled bad meat. "I don't think I want this man as a veteran in our unit," he said.

My heart sank, but I stood there, resolute. If they were going to kick me back to specialist, I wasn't going to cry and whine about it. Sure, the game had been rigged. There'd been no way I could win outright with the vets distributing weapons to the other contestants. But complaints weren't going to convince anyone to change their verdict.

Graves shook his head thoughtfully. "I'm afraid I'm going to have to overrule the majority of my adjuncts in this instance," he said. "For me, the deciding factor came to light when the last candidate attacked Harris. It was apparent through that action that he believed the fight to the death announced by Harris included the veterans themselves."

"Not so," Adjunct Toro piped up again, "all that proves is that McGill's bizarre actions confused everyone."

Graves shrugged. "You've got a valid complaint. But the fact is, and you can check the vid recordings to back this up,

Harris *did* say the last man to walk out of that canyon alive would be a veteran. He did not specify that the veterans themselves were not participants. I don't think any of you can argue that McGill isn't the last man standing."

The two who voted against me grumbled but didn't say anything else.

"McGill?" Graves asked, turning to me. "What have you got to say for yourself?"

"Well sir," I said, "you described the situation pretty well. Harris inserted himself into the contest when he began to distribute weapons at random to the candidates. At least, that's how I saw it."

Graves nodded. "Very well. As far as I'm concerned, you're our newest man with the honorable rank of veteran. Congratulations."

He reached out a gloved hand, and I shook it.

Just like that, I'd achieved a new rank. I knew there would be no love lost between Harris, myself, and the rest of the noncoms, but I didn't much care. They'd never been too sweet on me to begin with.

-10-

I found my new rank to be a little bit daunting. Sure, I was far from a rookie, but I knew there were soldiers with more experience than I had in this unit. They looked at me with a strange mixture of jealousy, curiosity and maybe, just maybe, a hint of respect.

It was that last item on the list that worried me. I had to *earn* that respect in order to keep it. I had to prove myself worthy of it. Yes, I'd pulled a fast one during a simulated battle with the dragons from Dust World, but that was a far cry from leading a squad throughout a campaign on an unknown planet.

One of the nice things about my new position was the command structure the auxiliary cohort had embraced. Rather than being made up of infantry with units led by centurions with the strength of one hundred twenty men each, Winslade's cohort was more limited in size. We were considered to be cavalry. Each squad was led by a veteran, like me. The squads were broken up into two maniples of five troops each, just like the Roman cavalry of ancient times. One of the maniples was led by a specialist, making him second in command, while the other was led by the veteran directly. That meant each squad was made up of an even dozen riders and their dragons. The specialists placed in charge of a maniple were mostly weaponeers, but there were also a number of bios and techs in the mix.

Because all of us were outfitted with large, walking, fighting machines, we didn't have as much need for our

69

traditional infantry-oriented roles. I was a little sorrowful I wasn't going to be carrying a belcher into battle this time, but I got over it quickly the more I worked with the dragons. They were quite obviously superior weapons systems.

Harris took the other squad in our platoon, and Leeson commanded above him. Although I was effectively just one more trooper piloting a dragon, the difference this time was I'd been placed in charge of eleven other guys riding along behind me.

A little over a third of the infantry who tried out qualified on the dragons, and I was proud to note that almost everyone in 3rd Unit had survived the winnowing process. That was due in large part to our success with the initiation trials on the rooftop battlefield. Most units had been slaughtered. In fact, my group was given the grim task of annihilating the last units to come over from *Minotaur* to kick off their training. I wasn't proud of it, and the butchery was intense, but I had to admit afterward that it was a valuable lesson to both sides. No trooper could fail to appreciate the power of a dragon after being killed by one. The pilots working the controls were undeniably impressed as well.

The troops that performed badly during the training exercises were sent back to *Minotaur* to fill out other ranks as needed. Once we were down to the best of the best, the training commenced in earnest. During a period of about three weeks, we trained hard every day. In all that time Veteran Harris never spoke to me. In fact, he did his damnedest not to even look at me.

I understood. After all, I'd made a fool out of him and the other veterans in my unit. That wouldn't sit well with anyone.

Della and I had had lunch together a few times over the weeks following our first encounter, but I'd made sure things didn't go any further than that. If she was married, I was determined to respect her vows—even if she didn't.

During my fourth week aboard *Cyclops*, the brass announced that the target star system directly ahead of our three ships was now easy to see with the naked eye. This wasn't exactly true, as we were in a warp bubble and vision was interpolated, but it was still an exciting change.

Going up to the observation deck the night before we arrived at Gamma Pavonis, I sat quietly with many others and watched the white star grow fractionally larger every hour. Kivi joined me that night as I maintained my vigil.

"James?" she asked. "Are you up here by yourself?"

I made a vague, waving gesture toward the numerous couples that surrounded us. The observation deck on any warship tended to attract people who wanted romance, if not privacy. They lined the walls up against the curving hull because the couches arrayed there were darker than those in the center. That left me with a big central couch.

"I'm hardly by myself," I said, smiling.

Kivi smiled back. "You know what I mean."

"Yeah, you're right. I don't seem to be as popular with the ladies this time out."

Kivi cocked her head and looked at me curiously. "That's not what I hear."

I shrugged. I turned to examine the white star again. Was it a pixel or two larger now? Maybe.

"Depression?" Kivi asked. "Can this be for real?"

Chuckling quietly, I shook my head. "I'd hardly call it that. Can't a man question his place in the universe without people thinking there's something wrong with him?"

"No, they can't. At least, not in your case. Other people can be self-possessed and introspective—but not James McGill. I have to admit I'm curious as to the cause of your unprecedented mood. Let me guess, it has something to do with Natasha and Della. Am I right?"

"Maybe."

Kivi climbed onto my couch without asking. She scooted across it until she bumped her hip into mine.

"Oh yes," she said, "the view from here is much better. Now, tell an old girlfriend what this is all about."

"What if I don't want to?"

"Then I'll have to guess."

I shrugged. "Go for it."

"Okay. Let's see... Natasha always has believed deep down that you're her private property. And Della...well, that girl is just plain crazy. I can see plenty of ways that a man might get caught between those two and yet shut out by both."

I liked Kivi, and I liked how she felt all warm and vital laying there next to me. But her words were starting to make me feel a little uncomfortable. I squirmed a bit. I couldn't help it.

"What's wrong?" she demanded. "The McGill I know would've grabbed me by now. Oh my God…"

Frowning, I turned to look at her. Her eyes were wide and they searched mine intently.

"It's *true*, isn't it?" she asked.

"What's true?"

"I'd heard rumors. Someone told me Della is pregnant. It's got to be something like that. The James McGill I've always known would of moved on by now to find another girl if it was anything less."

I shook my head and smiled ruefully. "Wrong," I said. "She's not pregnant. She already had the baby."

Kivi's mouth fell open comically wide. She punched me then, right in the gut. I grunted and grabbed her small fist before she could do it again.

"What kind of an asshole are you, James?" she demanded in a harsh whisper. Her mood had shifted as quickly as an autumn wind—but that was Kivi for you.

"Why are people always asking me that?" I wondered aloud.

She scooted away from me about a foot and crossed her arms over her ample breasts.

"So," she said, "let me guess how this happened. Back on Dust World you met Della, screwed her, and left her there. Now, she's out here in space trying to make a living training our legions to use these dragons while your kid is back on Dust World growing up alone."

"You make it sound like I did this as part of some kind of evil plan. Well, I didn't. She was the one who wanted to get pregnant. She chased me on Dust World for that express purpose. Now I find out I've got a kid, and I don't quite know what to do about it."

Kivi was quiet for maybe ten seconds. To be honest with you, it was kind of nice.

"It was *her* idea?" she asked suddenly. "The getting pregnant part, I mean?"

"Yeah, sure. Think about it. Those colonists were living separated from Earth with a limited gene pool. To their way of thinking procreating with new humans was almost a duty."

Kivi nodded thoughtfully. She scooted back toward me and threw one leg over mine. I jumped a bit reflexively not quite knowing where she was going with this.

But then she kissed me, and I figured it out. The winds had shifted back the other way.

We made out on the observation deck as I hadn't done for years. Kivi, as I've said before, is not a shy girl. Even though we were in semi-darkness, I didn't quite feel comfortable with some of the things she did while climbing over me on that couch. But it'd been a while since I'd made love to a woman, so I let her open our tops and kiss me passionately.

At one point, I heard some giggling off to my left. I put a gentle hand on Kivi's cheek and lifted her face away from my neck.

"How about we go someplace else?"

"Screw them," she said hotly. "It's nothing they haven't seen before."

"Yeah well, we're giving them a live show, here."

She made a frustrated sound and hopped up off the couch. She tugged on my hand until I followed her. There were more whispers and giggles from the dark around us as we left the observation deck.

I figured she would want to go to Green Deck, but we didn't make it that far. When Kivi gets hot, she gets *really* hot.

We made love in an ammo storage compartment. The metal containers were unevenly surfaced cold planes against bare skin, but Kivi didn't seem to care. After a while, neither did I.

-11-

When we arrived at Gamma Pavonis, we came down directly from above the local plane of the ecliptic. In other words, instead of moving from one planet to the next, getting closer and closer to the central star, we dove straight down toward the target world's northern pole.

It was no secret we were coming. Three Imperial capital ships, dreadnaughts all, can't hide on approach. Once we turned off the Alcubierre drive and transformed from glowing blue-white spheres of light into what looked like a trio of comets with hundred-kilometer long plumes of exhaust, any alien watching the scene would have to be blind not to know what was coming next.

The good news was that they couldn't have detected us until we came out of our warp bubbles. As I understood it from the techs, we were technically visible as a bubble of light while the drive was active, but since that effect was moving faster than the speed of light in relative terms, there was no time for the light thus produced to reach the eyes of anyone watching. We were, effectively, out-running our own shadows.

But once we turned off the big drives—well, that was it. There isn't much in space to occlude the view of a sensor, and any kind of traditional engine produces heat, light and other energy readings that were very visible. I wasn't sure what kind of sensors the squids might have, but I was pretty sure they knew we were coming in hot.

About the squids—I had no doubt that they were at least watching this system. If both the Empire and their Kingdom were interested, they had to have a survey team out here at the very least. I said as much to Natasha, who gave me a look then sighed and answered civilly.

"You're right," she said. "You've got to be right, if you think about it. They will have seeded this system with sensors and listening posts. We only hope that they didn't—"

That was as far as she got. An alarm went off. It wasn't a ship-wide klaxon, but it was a flashing yellow-orange bar on her tapper. She looked at it then glanced at me in alarm.

"I've got to go," she said.

"What's wrong?"

"They're summoning all the techs to battle stations."

She looked scared, and I didn't blame her.

"What's going on?" I asked her. "Should we be preparing for action?"

"I don't know. Follow your tapper and the arrows on the deck. You know the drill."

She turned to go, but I put a hand on her shoulder. I gave her a hug—no kiss, no rude squeezes, just a friendly hug. After stiffening up for a second, she relaxed, hugged me back and wished me luck. She left smiling.

I watched her race off down the passage toward the weapons deck. There were arrows now, just like she'd said. Green ones meant tech-only. Those lit up first and stayed lit, glowing on the deck plates.

As I walked farther down the passages and ramps, the red arrows lit up. Red indicated combat arms, which meant me. I watched, but the other colors stayed dark. Blue was for bios, in case of a medical emergency. Golden arrows meant *everyone* should follow them, and they were usually reserved for abandoning the ship.

The way shipboard actions worked on an Imperial vessel was, well—odd. The Skrull who crewed the ships weren't allowed to fire the weapons systems. In Frontier 921, only humans were licensed—literally—to fight in star systems beyond their own. Because of this, a tech like Natasha was invaluable. She had the skills required to run the ship's sensors and operate the broadsides in a battle.

Natasha herself was not part of my dragon-riding squad. She'd failed to impress the brass while operating a combat machine. She just didn't have the killer instinct, or at least not enough of it to satisfy Graves and the rest. But she was a good tech, so they'd decided keep her aboard *Cyclops* to operate the guns if we needed them.

Watching Natasha vanish around a corner, I decided not to wait around for the brass to deploy us. I knew the battle decisions were being made right here aboard *Cyclops*. Of the three ships, this one had the smallest complement of troops as it only housed the cavalry. For that reason Turov had brought her command staff here and had taken over Gold Deck, making it her operations center for the entire task force.

Knowing my fate was being decided by staffers up on Gold Deck didn't make me happy. Sometimes, it seemed like the officers treated us like hamsters in cages. They ignored us until it was time to give us orders, then provided arrows and instructions a moron could follow. They only noticed failure after that—or that we weren't moving fast enough.

I trotted after the red arrows to my squadron's prep room. We didn't have a formal service deck, not yet, but we had our own section of the module with bunks all around and a row of tough polymer crates that enclosed our dragons.

"All right, listen up!" I shouted, slamming my hands together.

It was gratifying to see troops hop off their bunks and gather around. Even Carlos hustled, and when I had everyone's attention I went into my routine.

"We're going to prep up like this is a hot action. We haven't gotten the official call yet, so don't wet your pants, but who knows? It could come at any time."

"Is this a boarding action, Vet?" demand Carlos excitedly.

I smiled. "We can only hope. I would like nothing better than to meet up with a pack of squids while riding these sweet machines."

The others echoed my sentiments. We'd been training for more than a month, and we were itching to try out our new equipment on an honest-to-God enemy.

We dressed in thin smart-suits not unlike those I'd worn as a light trooper. They were vacuum-tight in a pinch, but really, it was like wearing a garbage bag. If our dragons failed us, we'd probably die fast.

Opening up the crates, we coaxed out our machines and climbed over them, checking gauges and—

Wham! A tremendous sound rang through the ship. I knew that sound. There was only one thing that could have caused it.

"Broadsides have fired!" I shouted. "Be on your toes, we must be in fleet action!"

"This is bullshit," Carlos said, picking himself up and trying to get his machine into a squatting stance for mounting. "They should tell us what's going on!"

"If we need to know something, we'll be told," I said firmly with a conviction that I didn't feel. I knew from long association with the legions that the brass was perfectly capable of forgetting about ground troops in the belly of a transport. In fact, if they figured it would be easier to let us all die and be revived later, they might well engineer our deaths for the sheer convenience of it.

But I was a veteran now. I wasn't supposed to whine or complain. I was supposed to reassure those who did. It felt a little odd, but I thought I could get used to it.

Finally, someone felt the urge to tell us what the hell was going on outside our ship's hull. A voice and a face appeared on one wall. It was none other than Primus Winslade.

"Troops," he said, looking a little flustered. "*Cyclops, Minotaur* and *Pegasus* are in action. We've met up with unexpected resistance. There appears to be some kind of fortification on the smallest of the target world's three moons. The moment we exited warp and showed ourselves, this moon fired missiles at us. They're currently inbound. Everyone is to prep their equipment and march to the lifters. I want my cohort off this ship and in transit *now*!"

Winslade sounded nervous. He didn't say how many missiles or what kind of warheads they had. He probably didn't know.

Carlos slapped my shoulder. "Hey, do you realize what's going to happen if those missiles get through our defenses and blow up one of these ships? That's it. Permed! A whole legion. Or maybe it will be our lucky turn to get cleaned out. After all this training, too. I want—"

"Shut up, Ortiz!" I boomed. I realized I should have said those words about a full minute back, but I was a little slow sometimes. I wasn't used to being the veteran. "Get your rig walking—with you inside of it!"

Everyone went back to prepping their machines. About ninety seconds later, I rolled up the big bay exit door, and we went clanking down the passageway toward the lifters.

Red arrows lit up the floor. That was us—combat arms. I hoped they'd load up the rest of our support people, too. We needed everyone on this drop.

I didn't even bother to look back to see if the rest of the dragons were following me. If they weren't stomping after me with their tails lashing, well, they could die in the module with the bio people.

Wham!

The broadsides had fired another salvo. I was nearly thrown off my artificial feet. Servos whined, and I drew a three-clawed gash on the closest metal wall. But I stayed up and marching. My team was behind me, and I could see there were no stragglers. My HUD showed they were all there—a row of wicked marching machines right behind me.

Among all the squads to reach the lifters, we were third. I felt proud. Veteran Harris was there ahead of me, however. He gave my team a glance but didn't nod or wave. He looked like he smelled something foul.

Leeson waved me closer. He was inside one of the dragons as well. His claw-arm looked strange as he made a human-like gesture. I hurried and clanked up to him.

"Good job, McGill," he said. "You're right on time. We'll be the first lifter to abandon this ship if Toro's platoon gets down here."

Graves came clanking in next. I thought he looked uncomfortable in his dragon. He didn't ride it, it rode him.

"This damned thing fell on its nose when the broadsides fired the second time," he complained. "Where the hell is Toro?"

Leeson threw up his grippers. "She's late."

The broadsides boomed a third time, and about one second later, Toro and her team arrived. She was leading all of them with her two veterans right behind her. I recognized Johnson and Gonzales. I wondered how glad they were to lay eyes on me.

"About time, Toro," Graves said. "Get your machines secured. We're dropping."

"Sir?" Leeson said. "The pilot wants to know if we can fly. The missiles, sir—"

"Tell him to decouple in twenty seconds. Positions, everyone!"

We dropped our visors all around, and we backed our machines into the hanging clamps that were supposed to secure us during flight. Moments later the floor became the wall, and then it became the ceiling.

About half of Toro's group wasn't ready. Their machines went sliding and crashing across the deck, slamming in a pile-up against the hull a hundred meters down. Some managed to grab onto things with their grippers, and a crewman was crushed.

"Toro, dammit," Graves fumed. "Get your people under control!"

"We must be in trouble out there," Leeson said, grunting and hanging on to his clamps with his grippers. "What's the word from Winslade?"

"There isn't any," Graves answered.

I noticed Leeson hadn't moved an inch during the inversion. He was using his grippers to hang on, like they were arms. He instinctively hadn't trusted his clamps. I thought that was a pretty good idea, and privately ordered my squad to do the same. Pretty soon, every machine in sight was hanging on for dear life.

The lifter righted itself after about a minute. We pulled hard Gs during a slewing turn, then there came that undeniable feeling of falling at high speed. My stomach was in my mouth, and my heart was pounding in my ears.

Could *Cyclops* have been hit? What about Natasha and the rest? I didn't know anything except that I was about to land on an alien world I hadn't even had the time to lay eyes on yet.

"Hey, McGill," Carlos said. "I'm sorry, I mean *Vet*. Look at this stream—I'll pipe it to your tapper."

He sent me a streaming feed. Lord only knew how he'd gotten access to it. The image was grainy, and it skipped and fuzzed out now and then, but the scene was unmistakable.

Three ships hung over a gray-white, mist-clad world. Distantly, a moon of dark rock floated. It was covered in puffing explosions. Were those our strikes or more missiles firing up from the moon base? It was hard to tell, but I figured it was our own broadside shells slamming home. I'd seen them strike before, and their power was daunting. Whatever missile base was firing on us was sure to be toast with three of these ships hammering at it.

The one worrying thing, however, was displayed as the view shifted. I realized then that the vid was from someone aboard our lifter. Probably a tech who'd released a buzzer and had it fly to a porthole. Buzzers were insect-sized drones that were often used for scouting or even spying by legion techs.

One of the three capital ships was on fire. It was *Pegasus*, Solstice Legion's transport. Normally, fire wasn't possible in space, but with the released oxygen escaping with other gasses, she was a briefly lit torch. She'd been hit—hit bad. My heart sank to see that.

Out of the bottom of *Pegasus*, tiny capsules were firing like bullets. Hundreds of them shot out as if the ship was bombarding the planet below.

I knew those capsules didn't contain explosives. They were carrying troops. Each one was a drop pod firing down through the atmosphere into the murky clouds of this new world.

My heart went out to the Solstice legionnaires. What a way to enter a war! There was no way they'd reached their optimal

80

drop altitude. The legion commanders had to be panicking to order a general drop from such a height, trying to save their—

That's the point I'd reached in my thoughts when *Pegasus* exploded. I closed my eyes and said a silent prayer for the thousands that still had to be aboard her.

-12-

I've been to war in three star systems over the years, with Gamma Pavonis being my fourth deployment. That doesn't make me some kind of grizzled old-timer, but it does mean I've been around the bush a few times.

I could tell already, this campaign felt *different*.

In the past, there'd always been a certain degree of restraint. There'd always been orderly rules applied, to some degree, to each battle I'd witnessed. Hiring out as mercenaries to various planets with internal problems, one never knew when things might get hairy, but there were certain things you could trust would or would not happen.

One such rule was the sanctity of Empire ships. No one, I mean *no one*, fired on Imperial warships. To do so not only meant your own destruction but very likely would result in the destruction of your entire species.

I found myself commiserating with some of those old-time European generals. This must have been how it had felt for them when they met enemy troops who didn't line up in colorful costumes and fire their guns all at once. There was no sense of honor or reticence in these aliens. They meant to kill us all. They didn't care about our contracts, our revival machines or the consequences of their actions. They meant to kick our collective asses anyway they could.

To me, the fact the enemy had destroyed *Pegasus* indicated that we were engaged with the squids. These guys might not have spines, but they had balls. They didn't care two hoots about Imperial might or the threat of eventual annihilation. This was war of a different caliber entirely. All-out war. A total war.

Taking a deep breath, I cut Carlos' feed to my tapper when we hit the upper atmosphere. I couldn't see anything but white clouds after that, anyway. We hit a patch of turbulence right off, and it kept getting worse as we went down. Whatever this atmosphere was made of, it was thick. The vapor never broke from the mesosphere on down to the troposphere. We were bouncing and thumping every kilometer of the way to the surface, and more than a few of my troops puked.

"Shut those visors the second you're done throwing up," I ordered. "You never know when we'll take a hit and lose pressure."

"Permission to get out of my dragon, sir," Carlos asked. He'd toppled over onto his nose, and was having trouble getting up. Servos whined and his claws gouged the metal of the ship's floor.

"Permission denied," I said, clanking over to him. I threw out my grippers and caught hold of his tail, which was whipping around, trying to get him back into balance. I hauled him up onto his hind legs and clanked away.

"Hold onto something—anything," I told them. "I'll try to get a weather report from the techs."

As a veteran, I was now permitted to log into command chat and listen in. It would have been considered bad manners by my officers if I'd said anything, so I kept quiet. On the inside of my helmet, the names of the speakers lit up in green when they spoke. That was helpful because a lot of the transmissions were sketchy.

Winslade's ID flashed up first. "What's your status, Graves? Give me a count of effectives."

"We're at full capacity, sir," Graves responded. "4th Unit is on the same lifter with us, and I think they're as ready and able as we are."

"No casualties?"

"No sir. My unit was on the first lifter out of the ship. We didn't take any flak."

Winslade chuckled unpleasantly. "That figures. Your team is made up of the fastest rats in this part of the galaxy."

I wanted to jump in and yell at Winslade, but I held my tongue. We'd followed our orders, that's all. If we moved fast, it was because we'd been prepared, not because we were chickens.

"What are your orders, Primus?" asked Graves.

"Looks like you'll be on the first lifter down. Spread out and secure the LZ for the rest. Report back any resistance or hazards encountered. Winslade out."

That was it, then. We were going to be the point formation on this invasion. I relayed this to my team, and they produced a general chorus of groans.

"Okay people, hustle up. Let's be ready to scramble when we touch down. The second that ramp drops, I want to see nothing but metal tails and dust as you rush out there to surround the lifter."

We didn't have long to wait. The general rule when making any kind of assault from space was to get the flying part over with as quickly as possible. Every second we were in the air increased the odds the lifter would take a hit and wipe out whole units of troops at once.

The pilot seemed to be exquisitely aware of this reality. He maneuvered the lifter like it was a dive-bomber, taking us down to the deck in a screaming swoop then pulling up at the last second.

A message came from the pilot. "We're about to hit the surface. Crouch your machines and wait it out."

This was a maneuver I'd practiced but never executed under live conditions. To keep upright, our machines could crouch like nesting birds if we wanted them to. We all folded the legs up—just in time.

The bottom of the ship shuddered and my teeth rattled. We landed hard, the shocks on our landing struts groaning and bucking.

A few of us nosed over and smashed down, and we busied ourselves with pulling one another back up into a standing position. The dragons were top-heavy and not as natural to maneuver in as our own bodies, despite our training.

84

"Gather up whatever you can carry," I ordered. "We don't know what we'll find out there, and we might need just about everything."

I saw troops packing on saddlebags of extra ammo and the like. Then a gray-white line appeared in the hull, and everyone's turret-like head section rotated in that direction.

"1st Platoon, move out!" Graves ordered.

We raced along the aisles and down the broad ramp. It felt good to get out of the lifter. After having watched *Pegasus* explode, I'd been itching to get out into the open where ground forces could care for themselves.

"Swing right, McGill," Leeson ordered. "Harris, you take your team with his. Get clear, at least two hundred meters, then grab cover and park your machines."

We did as he ordered. Leeson himself was the last man of our platoon to exit the ship. He followed us to an outcropping of shiny rock. I couldn't tell if the rock was laced with metal or ice. Maybe it was a little of both.

The world itself was a strange one. I'd never been on anything like this place. It was foggy, with swirling gray-white mist everywhere. The place was bone-chillingly cold. I could tell that right off, even though my suit was pretty warm with the engine under my butt heating it up.

The surface of the planet had a light dusting of what looked like oily snow which I knew was probably frozen methane. There were rocks and spurs of mineral deposits everywhere. They were stark, and there was no sign of vegetation of any kind.

"What a garden spot," Carlos complained. "Let me guess, this is high summer, right?"

"Shut up, Ortiz," I said.

"But Vet, where are we going to sleep? Inside our suits?"

"We've got tents. We've got insulated gear. We'll be fine."

"Who wants to start a pool on whose waste-chute is going to freeze up first?"

I clanked over to him and put a fresh dent in his chassis. I understood as I did it that Harris would have done the same thing, for the same reason. He shut up after that, but he buzzed my helmet privately.

"What?" I demanded.

"Are you going to be a dick the whole campaign just because you got rank?"

"Carlos, you made a good point, in fact, you made plenty of them. But I need my people to be alertly watching for trouble, not pissing and moaning about the conditions."

"Well, at least you admit I'm right. That's better than Harris ever did."

"Right. Just try to support me by playing it straight, okay?"

There was a pause, but he finally answered. "Will do, Vet. Clearly, life is going to be pretty bleak on this snowball. We've got to make the best of it."

I was impressed by his attitude. Maybe asking him nicely and expressing a request in terms of helping the legion out worked better than just beating on him. I wasn't sure if Harris could have done the same, but that was history. Carlos was my problem now.

For about an hour, we patrolled around the lifter and certified that the region was unoccupied. We only found one odd thing during our search.

"Command?" I asked, holding up a mystery item with my grippers. "What do you make of this? Can you read my cameras?"

"Have you got your lights on, McGill?" Leeson asked.

"Yes. Here, let me defog my camera lenses."

Doing as I proposed was a delicate operation. I couldn't use a gripper for fear of cracking my external lens. Instead, I popped open my suit at the arm, letting it fall down and swing in the wind. My right hand and forearm were thus exposed, but inside a sealed vac suit.

I could feel the cold right off. It cut through the thin smart cloth without hesitation. Knowing I didn't have long, I reached out with my barely protected gloved hand and rubbed at the lens. Then I closed the arm and lifted the object in question up to the camera again.

"You see it now, sir?"

The object was rectangular. It had a corroded case and two metallic knobs protruding from either end of it.

"Yes…I'm passing on the vid to the techs. Looks like some kind of burnt-out battery."

"That's what I was thinking. That's acid leaking from it. To further support the theory, there's a very weak current flowing from the two metal poles."

"Can't be from us," Leeson said, "it's not our design, and it looks too old. That's a mystery all right, McGill. If it does belong to the squids, it means they must have been here for years. Wouldn't you say it looks like it's been lying out here for a long time?"

"Definitely, sir."

The connection broke, and I directed my recon team to pick over the area where we'd found the discarded battery. We found two more like it, also in disrepair. I logged the information and relayed it to command.

"Machines," Carlos said, looking over the third one. "This has to be a discarded battery from a big machine."

I thought about that. "But what kind of machine would be wandering around out here? And if it has batteries, how is it recharging them?"

"No clue," Carlos said. "Can we go back to camp now?"

We were recalled about an hour later. We headed back to where the Units had made camp under the lifter. We had polymer sheets draped down from the bottom of the landing ship to the rocky surface. Inside, the troopers who hadn't been sent out on patrol had been busy building a bivouac. We were grateful for their efforts. Even with hot engines, the extremities of our machines got cold, especially our metal-encased feet.

There was a large area, maybe two hundred meters in diameter, which was enclosed, heated and pressurized. The outer chambers were like airlocks. There, we garaged our dragons. The center of the region was almost homey. Condensation dripped from the belly of the lifter some ten meters over our heads.

"It stinks," Carlos complained.

I didn't argue because he was right. Melted methane—well, that's pretty much what a fart is.

We were cautioned against creating any open flame for any reason. Troops grumbled, but they didn't argue. No one wanted to burn their hair off playing with a lighter out here. The combination of warm oxygen from the lifter being pumped in so we could breathe easily, and the melting methane was a lethal mixture if combustion were to be introduced.

"Is this safe, sir?" I asked Leeson when I caught up with him to make my report. "The atmosphere in here, I mean?"

"How the hell do I know?" he asked. "That's up to the bio people and the techs to work out. If I die though, I hope they revive me without a nose."

I nodded in agreement. Adjunct Leeson was nothing if not a pragmatic man.

After some warm food, clean clothes, and a few hours of rest, I was awakened and summoned to an officers' meeting.

For a few seconds, I felt my heart race. I'd been summoned to the officers' tent plenty of times in the past. It had almost always been for the express purpose of chewing me out.

But not this time. From now on, I was expected to attend command meetings. Veterans were often invited to such affairs. We weren't expected to participate materially in the discussion of strategy, but we had to know what the plan was so we could help execute it.

Graves was there with three other centurions. Another lifter had landed about a kilometer off, and we'd joined forces. Graves was the senior officer so he seemed to be in charge.

On a makeshift command table in the middle of the group was a flat glowing diagram of the local region. There was a large silver patch directly north of us, representing a methane lake. To the east and west were badlands full of gullies and ridges. To the south, however, it looked like a wide-open plain.

"We're only about a hundred kilometers away from the next grouping of lifters." Graves said, zooming out the map so we could see the bigger picture.

I was immediately envious of the other group. There were six more lifters there, all clustered up in a valley. *Cyclops* only had ten lifters, so most of our troops had to be there. I scanned the map for the rest of the auxiliary cohort, but I didn't see it.

"Legion Varus is planning to land here, at the main camp, tomorrow morning," Graves told is. "Since the ships took out the moon base, we've seen no other resistance. The infantry have naturally chosen to reinforce Winslade at his largest concentration, making that our beachhead."

Frowning, I almost raised my hand. I managed to stop myself in the nick of time, and I was proud of that. To my relief, an adjunct beat me to the punch and asked the question I had rattling around in my head.

"Sir? Why don't we just get back aboard the lifter and fly there?"

"That's exactly what we're going to do—when our current mission is finished, that is."

The adjunct looked confused, and I joined him. Graves continued with a sigh. "We've been ordered to mount a rescue effort first. Remember Legion Solstice? The survivors abandoned *Pegasus*. They're scattered to the north of us, just past this big lake."

"How many, sir?" asked the adjunct.

"About two thousand of them."

The adjunct whistled. I grimaced and gnawed at my lower lip. *Thousands?* That was a lot of troops, and they were probably spread out over a large area. All of us were wondering if it might not be better to let them and their equipment go, and churn fresh troops out of the revival machines.

"These men are the last of Legion Solstice," Graves said, reading our expressions. "They're still alive, so we can't just write them off and revive them. Accordingly, we're going out there to render assistance. They've reported encountering some kind of mechanized resistance at their location. They're avoiding further radio transmissions, claiming it attracts danger of some sort."

"Danger? What kind of danger?" blurted Adjunct Mesa.

Graves gave the adjunct a stare. He swallowed and apologized.

"We don't know," Graves answered finally. "They've suffered casualties. They're spread out and unable to form a nice cozy camp like this. I asked if we could bring the lifters over to pick them up, but the request was denied. Command doesn't want to risk losing more of our assault vehicles."

"Command" meant Winslade, I thought to myself. I couldn't help but notice he didn't mind risking his cavalry, just the lifters he needed to get back off this rock. That was typical for any officer, but the ruthless ones were worse than others. They valued expensive equipment more than human flesh.

"This is where we get into the game, troops," Graves said, standing up and raising his voice. "We'll ride to the rescue in the morning. And by the way, this is a fast-rotating planet, so night is only about nine hours long. Get to bed as soon as you can."

We broke up and headed to our bedrolls which were alien-made products especially designed for humanoids suffering in cold climates.

"You know what the quartermaster told me?" Carlos asked as we bedded down. I didn't answer, but he kept going as if I had. "These sleeping bags are made from alien spider-silk. They can keep you warm down to negative two hundred degrees C, and they weigh less than a kilo. Perfect for troops on icy little shit-holes like this one."

"Thanks for the infomercial, Carlos, now let's get some sleep."

He finally shut up, and I was left to ponder Graves' words. What had he said? Something about Solstice having encountered some kind of mechanized resistance? I had to wonder what that was all about—but I didn't wonder for long. I was snoring within three minutes after sliding into my toasty-warm spider-silk bag.

The bag was nice, and it had me jealous of all those bugs who'd died in cocoons like this one. I'd never known what I'd been missing.

-13-

In the morning, we saddled up our dragons. We had some tough choices to make regarding load-outs.

These walking death-dealers were much more advanced than the one that Turov had used to such great effect aboard *Minotaur* back on Tech World, and they came with optional equipment. Even the armament had a variety of configurations. You could pack on extra generators, which gave the machine a shorter recharge time and more hours of running around, or you could take along extra ammo for the chest-guns instead. Another option was to adopt a more defensive arrangement, which meant about an inch of electromagnetic shielding that covered the hull, protecting the system from small arms and the like. Yet another choice involved a longer range gun system that rode on the spine of the vehicle and fired right over your shoulder.

"How should we do this, Adjunct?" I asked Leeson. "What kind of equipment does the brass want us to carry?"

"Well, we don't really know what we'll encounter," he said thoughtfully, "so I think we should go with a mix. I'll have Harris carry heavier generators with his squad, along with longer-range weapons and shielding. In contrast, your group will run light. No extra armament but extra cells instead, for endurance and plenty of speed."

I frowned but nodded. It was his call. Personally, I didn't think we should take the longer range weaponry at all. So far on this planet, I hadn't been able to see farther than a hundred meters past my nose. There was too much swirling mist. If we did run into a fight, it was going to be like having a battle in a blizzard. I didn't much like the idea of moving faster and rushing around blindly either, but Leeson was in charge.

We loaded up, and I rode out on point. Graves had organized his three platoons with two of them split light-heavy like mine, but 3rd platoon was all heavy. That amounted to four squads of slower machines in the center, and two faster squads flanking. The other units were farther off to either side of us. They were going to take separate, parallel paths.

On our screens inside the cockpit, it was pretty easy to keep track of where everyone was. I knew that if those screens and sensors ever failed, however, we'd be lost very quickly. Our GPS systems weren't working due to the strange atmospherics and the heavily metallic composition of the planet. We had compasses and scratchy radio, neither of which was one hundred percent reliable—and that was it.

The journey up north to the methane lake took hours, and it was a strange experience. Our light dragons could run at about fifty kilometers an hour, double that for short bursts. They could spring over obstacles, climb steep hills and even ford streams. But when traveling at high speeds, we were running blind. The mist and precipitation caked up on our visors and external camera pickups. Even under the best of conditions, we couldn't see far into the soupy air.

We reached the lake and turned east. After about an hour of running along the lakeshore, we ran into our first serious obstacle. I pulled up short and called it in.

"Leeson? This is 1st Squad. We've hit a big river, sir."

"How big?"

"I don't know—I can't see the far side."

He cursed for a few seconds then relayed my unwelcome news up the chain of command. When he finally got back to me, he had new orders.

"We'll be up to you pretty soon. 2nd Platoon just reported in from further south—same thing. We want you to scout the river for depth, McGill. Don't let that methane get up past your legs to the core of your chassis."

"Uh…right sir."

I wheeled my dragon to face the others who had gathered up and were letting their cells recharge off their fusion generators while they waited for new orders.

"We're going to find out just how deep this river is," I announced.

"Oh really?" asked Carlos. "Let me guess—it's my turn to die already, is it?"

"It would be, but I need your dragon," I told him. "Anyone feel like going for a swim?"

Dragons roamed along the shoreline, looking at the silvery surface of rippling methane. No one said anything. This must be why Harris had never asked for volunteers, I realized.

"Gorman, Roark—you're on," I ordered.

They groaned and cursed but wandered down to the edge of the flowing liquid. They both put in that first metal foot like they could feel the cold.

I goaded my machine up behind them. "Spread out!" I boomed. "I don't want you both going into the same hole. Kivi, Carlos, attach a tow cable to each of these brave souls."

With a steel cable taut on each machine, we watched them step out into the moving liquid.

"Ever seen a methane-drinking shark before?" Carlos called out to Gorman, who he had on his tether. "I hear they like shiny objects."

"Shut up, Ortiz," I heard myself saying. I had to admit, each day I spent as a veteran made me feel more sympathy for Harris. Could it be that this job shaped the man as much as the other way around?

I didn't get any more time for introspection, unfortunately. Roark ran into trouble about ten meters out. His dragon went down on one leg, even though the river hadn't looked to be that deep. One minute he'd been in about a meter of water, and the next he was floundering.

"What's got you, Roark?" I demanded.

"Not sure, Vet. One foot must have stepped into a deep hole."

"Shark! Shark!" shouted Carlos unhelpfully.

"Kivi, haul on that cable," I said. "Take the slack out of it."

She did as I asked, backing her mount up the bank. She pulled, but Roark's dragon wasn't budging.

Inside my dragon, I clenched my teeth. This wasn't the sort of problem I could afford to kick up the chain of command. I should be able to handle it myself.

Gorman had retreated out of the river and joined the group looking out toward Roark with concern. Instead of ordering Gorman back into harm's way, I marched out into the river after Roark myself.

"Careful Vet," Gorman said, eyeing my rescue attempt. "I got a feeling there might be more holes out here."

I moved warily. It wasn't an easy thing to do. The machine didn't have sensors in the bottom of its feet. I had to feel my way like a man driving a car over uneven ground, hoping he didn't get stuck.

As a precaution, I had my tow-line hooked up to my troops on the shoreline.

When at last I made it to Roark, I managed to use my arm segments to latch onto him. Bending my legs into a crouch then standing erect, I hauled him straight up.

There was resistance, that much I was sure of. Whatever he'd found, it wasn't just a simple hole. Something was trying to keep him down.

When we were both mobile again, I noticed that Roark still had trouble. His dragon tottered to the shore. I accompanied him in case he went down again, figuring his leg actuator might have gone bad.

"What is *that* thing?" Kivi asked.

I stopped and rotated my chassis to get a good look.

Kivi was right. There was something attached to Roark's machine. It was like a cylinder wrapped around the lower leg section, and there was a glowing amber light on top of it, too.

"What the…could that be a mine?" Kivi asked.

"Back up! He's gonna blow!" Carlos shouted.

The group scattered like hens. I stood there with Roark, who was trying to escape his fate. He had his grippers on the top of the cylinder, pushing down.

I reached out, seeing a group of wires on top. They were crude, thick wires. I snipped them with my grippers, and the amber light died. Using my dragon's powerful arms, I ripped the thing loose and dropped it on the rocks with a clang.

"Well," I said, "if that was a mine, it was a pretty piss-poor one."

The squad wandered back to us, looking paranoid. I decided it was time to report in.

"Adjunct Leeson, sir? The river is a problem. There seem to be devices in it, buried in the water. I don't know their function or who put them there, but they seem to be traps. They might disable anyone who tries to cross."

"Roger that, McGill. We've had other reports of a similar nature. Like that battery you found yesterday. Lots of discarded hardware. Command is suspecting that this planet was once inhabited, or maybe still is, by a technologically savvy species."

Who could it be? I thought of the squids right off, but it just didn't seem to be their style. This whole planet wouldn't have been appealing to them for colonization, just for resources. Who else might be living down here on this cold, mist-covered rock?

We were ordered to abandon our attempts to ford the river. It was too deep, too treacherous and too wide. Instead, we angled south off course and ran along the shoreline. Behind us, the main mass of troops arrived. I left the artifact we'd found on the beach for them to examine.

About a half-hour's run southward, we ran into something new. There was a cluster of low metal domes near the river. Don't get me wrong, the domes didn't have the fresh-forged look of our ships and machines. Instead, they were dirty and corroded. Everything about the place looked unfinished and crude. The domes were close to the methane, arranged in a semi-circle. We didn't march right into the middle of them as we were wary by now.

"What the hell is this?" Carlos asked. "Some kind of fishing village?"

When he said that, it struck me that he was right. That was *exactly* what it looked like. A fishing village.

"Carlos, check that hut up there on the hill."

" Shit…" he said then trotted his machine to the structure I'd indicated. There was a door of sorts, consisting of two heavy metal plates piled over one another. He levered it open, and it clanged and clattered to the ground.

"I didn't say to tear it up!" I shouted after him. "If natives live here, you'll scare the living—"

That was as far as I got. A figure sprang up out of the door of the shack and scuttled away. Now, when I say *figure*, you have to understand I'm not talking about a humanoid. I'm talking about something that looked like a centipede built out of rusty garbage cans with churning metal struts for legs.

"Holy crap!" Carlos shouted. "Did you see that guy? Did you *see* that?"

"Yeah, we sure did."

Carlos took off after the thing. It wasn't small, but it was a lot smaller than he was. Lengthwise, it was probably two meters long and a half-meter or so wide. Carlos caught up to it and launched himself up into the air, coming down on its back. He forced it down into the dirt, where it squirmed and kicked.

"Why's he killing it?" Kivi demanded.

"Carlos, she's right. Don't harm it. That thing must be part of the native population."

Carlos came back to us, holding the thing in his grippers. It squirmed and twisted but couldn't get away. It didn't make any sound other than desperate scrabbling noises.

"If this is a native, this is one weird place," Carlos said. "This—listen people—this is a *machine*."

We examined it, and we quickly realized he was right. The creature was all metal with cameras for eyes and jointed struts for legs. It looked like it had been assembled out of spare parts. There had to be some level of AI inside the brain-pan, however, as it was clearly pitiful and distressed.

"We should take this back to Natasha," Carlos suggested. "She'd get a kick out of dissecting it."

"I think we should let it go," Kivi said.

Something in her voice made me turn to look at her. She was staring back behind us. I turned around and followed her gaze.

There, looming out of the mist beyond the shacks, was a massive figure. It came up out of the methane river and moved like a rolling mass of interconnected plates. Shaped like a slug, it undulated to and fro as if uncertain. It seemed to be studying us.

"Carlos, put the caterpillar-thing down," I ordered. "Gently."

"Aw, I wanna keep him."

"Do as I order, or I'll fire on you!"

"Sheesh, all right. What's the—oh..."

He'd finally caught sight of the thing we were all staring at. He put the small machine down on the ground, and it scuttled off toward the bigger one.

-14-

We quickly retreated uphill, away from the village along the river. The mountain of metal plates shifted around the domes and followed us, matching our pace. As a measured response, we moved slowly and gently away from the village—or nursery, or whatever the hell it was.

"You think that's mama, Kivi?" I asked, whispering for some reason.

"I bet it is. If that little one is hurt, I suggest we offer up Carlos as a sacrifice."

"Hardly seems like a fair trade," I said. "We don't want to piss off the locals further by giving them our most irritating trooper."

"I didn't know!" Carlos complained. "How the hell was I supposed to know this world is inhabited by freaking machines? That's weird, man. Really weird. Who built them in the first place? How do they reproduce? What do they—?"

"Could you shut up for nine seconds, Ortiz?" I demanded. "I'm trying to report this in. Don't run, anyone. If it's like an animal, it's best to move slowly and confidently. Backward."

As we backed away from the village, the big machine eventually stopped following us and returned home. The bulk of it vanished into the white mists, and we were very happy to see the last of it.

"Uh…Adjunct Leeson? I've got an unexpected contact to report."

98

I gave him the story, and he kicked me up to Graves before I finished the third sentence.

"Have you got video?" Graves asked.

"Relaying and transmitting the file now, sir."

Fortunately, Kivi had had the presence of mind to flip on her suit recorders when we first met up with the village. The Centurion reviewed the file and let out a long breath.

"We've been suspecting something like this. A dozen reports have hinted around, but you're the first to encounter an actual organized habitation. Good scouting, McGill."

"Thanks. What *are* they, sir?"

"Native life, after a fashion. We've theorized about this, and the Galactics have hinted that some of the inhabitants of the Core Systems resemble these beings. They're electromechanical creatures. Robots, essentially."

"Some of the Galactics are robots?"

"That's what we understand," Graves said. "It's a miracle, when you think about it, that the various species from the Core Worlds were able to cooperate long enough to build an empire at all."

"I'm out in the field, sir. What should I do?"

"Be friendly with the locals. Get used to them. Maybe they'll get used to you. Machine life, McGill. Just think about them as flesh and blood. Wait a second—you didn't damage any of them, did you?"

"Not intentionally, sir."

"What does that mean?"

I explained about Carlos running one down and catching it, and Graves seemed tense.

"You have to keep a tight rein on your people, McGill," he said sternly. "We aren't marauders. Natives are key to any attempt we make to defeat the squids on this planet. We can't afford bad blood between us now."

I assured him I wouldn't harm any machines that didn't attack us directly.

"Good, good," he said. "We're working on this. Every tech we have on the surface is stretching their brains around it. Did you catch any transmissions?"

"Any what, sir?"

"Listen, machine life doesn't talk with a voice box. They send radio waves at one another. Did you record anything of that nature?"

"Uh...no, sir. We'll give it a shot if you want us to."

"All right. I'm going to send a tech out there to your position to help with the investigation. Go back into the vicinity of the village and watch the aliens. Don't get too close, however. From the sounds of it, you encountered a mother machine and her brood. You can't threaten her young, do you understand?"

"Loud and clear, Centurion."

He closed the channel, and I relayed his instructions to my nervous squad.

"Go back there?" Carlos demanded. "Are you nuts? Did you see the size of that thing? It was made out of metal, through and through. We couldn't stop it with these grenade launchers. It's as big as a building!"

"That's why we're going in slowly and staying well back. If it comes at us aggressively, we'll run. The mother-machine—whatever it was—it didn't seem very fast."

"Maybe that's because she hadn't charged us yet."

Despite Carlos' grumbling, we backtracked and came up over a rise to where we could see the village again. The moment our dragons showed their noses, the inhabitants clammed up. We had time to see a few of the small ones rushing to their little huts and slamming them closed. I figured they were probably already bleating for mama.

"Any signals on your scanners?"

"I've got something down in the kilocycle range," Kivi said.

We tuned in and saw a spray of jagged waveforms. The machines were communicating, but I couldn't make heads or tails of it, and neither could our dragons' computers.

"Let's back off," I said, and we retreated again. Once we were out of sight, I dismounted from my machine and walked up to the ridge again.

Specialist Sargon was heading up one of my two maniples. I put him in charge of the mounted troops with orders to rush to my rescue if I ran into trouble. I took Kivi with me as she was doing pretty well today in the absence of a real tech. I knew she'd been studying hard for that rank and saw this as her way to get a specialist's patch. There was no harm in giving her some field experience.

I felt exposed out on the surface outside of my dragon. We got down low and crawled when we reached the top of the hill. On our bellies in the cold mud, hearing our respirators hiss in our helmets, we crept up on the village and looked down at it curiously.

The village was alive again. Everybody had come out of their little clamshell huts to play. A half-dozen machines frolicked about, crawling over the landscape with what seemed like random, energetic patterns.

"Are you getting this?" I asked Kivi.

When I spoke, the machines halted and lifted up, looking around. Kivi put her helmet close to mine, and I heard her muffled voice.

"Don't use radio. They can hear it."

"Roger that. Voice only."

After lifting up the front part of their bodies and briefly cranking their forms this way and that, the machines went back to whatever they were doing.

They seemed to be excited. They had something inside one of the huts. Something large and metallic. They hauled it out together, working like a swarm of ants.

"You know," I said, "I bet those clamps buried in holes in the river were some kind of trap. They didn't blow up, so they aren't mines. Maybe these machines trap other machines."

"Everyone has to eat, I guess," Kivi agreed. "They must be running on methane for fuel, and they need metal to rebuild themselves and to grow larger. I've read about some forms of machine life in my studies. I think that the big one might smelt metal and have a construction system inside to build smaller units. It's all very strange, but not unprecedented."

"Right," I said thoughtfully, "they get energy from methane, and raw materials from the ground. This is a highly metallic planet with high quality ore outcroppings everywhere. I hadn't thought about it before, but this world is a paradise for a machine race."

"It might be more sophisticated than that," Kivi said. "These could be predatory machines that consume the less sophisticated types that graze on ore directly."

I nodded. "A food-chain. The techs will love this place."

The thing they were hauling up out of the ground was finally in the open. The little caterpillar guys swarmed all over it. We watched in growing concern.

"That metal they're chewing on—that's fresh and straight," I said. "I think it's manufactured."

"Yes. Don't you recognize it, James?" Kivi asked.

"Uh...can you give me a hint?"

"That's a dragon leg. You see the claw-like foot? It's been torn loose."

Staring at it, I knew right off she was correct. "You'll make a fine tech someday, Kivi. Let's get back to the others and report this."

We retreated from the hilltop, backing down the way we'd come. We had time to stand up on our hind legs—but that was about it.

There were machines behind us. They'd moved between us and our dragon-driving squad mates.

Seeing just one of these critters at a time from the inside of a dragon cockpit, they hadn't looked all that threatening. But standing out here in the open, wearing nothing but smart-cloth skivvies, I felt seriously exposed. The machines had all manner of pincers and scoops around their front sections which seemed to operate like an intake or mouth. They stared at us with their whining little cameras while their mouth-pincers worked the air hungrily.

"I see them, Vet," Sargon said in my earpiece. "We're ready to charge in and take them out. Just give the word."

"No, no," I said over my helmet radio. "Just sit tight. Graves didn't want us to hurt them."

"That's crazy. They're just machines."

"You have your orders, Specialist," I told Sargon. "If I die, you can take command and do whatever you want."

This radio conversation seemed to make the machines nervous. I was sure they could hear it but probably didn't understand it. Maybe it sounded like shouting or like a foreign language to them.

I put my hands up and stepped toward the group. There were seven machine creatures all lined up. Two of them were humped up, resting their foreclaws nervously on the backs of the others.

"They look like a nervous pack of animals," Kivi said, using her voice rather than her radio.

"Yeah?" I said. "Well, I'm feeling a little nervous, too."

I walked slowly toward them and squatted. This caused a response. The machines rushed closer.

Automatically, I stood up again. "Whoa, whoa!" I told the excited little robots.

When I stood up, they stopped approaching and went back to squirming on top of one another again.

"I'm getting the feeling these guys are young," Kivi said. "Young and not too bright. They're responding to your physical posture. Some animals are like that. If you stand up, they think you're bigger. If you get down and small, they figure you're food."

"Good observation," I said. "I'll make a point of standing tall. Can you fetch me a stick or something?"

There weren't any sticks, of course, as there were no plants on this planet—at least not ones we'd found yet. She came up and gave me something that looked like a length of steel tubing, about a meter long.

"There's trash like this all around their village," Kivi said. "For all we know, it's a bone to them."

"Yeah...I hope they don't take offense."

Using my metal stick, I drew a circle in the frosty mud at my feet. Then I backed away from it.

The largest of the creatures scuttled forward to examine the circle with his cameras. After about thirty seconds, he used a stubby leg to draw another circle inside the one I'd drawn. His was better than mine, more uniform.

"And that's what we call communication!" I said.

The machines looked at us expectantly. They rustled and churned their feet. Cameras craned to look at the circle, then at me.

"I think they want you to draw something else."

"Yeah, just like a pack of bored kids."

I proceeded to draw all kinds of geometric shapes. Each time, the robots imitated me. At last, my helmet buzzed.

"McGill, what are you doing out there?" Leeson asked me. "You were supposed to report in and return to base half an hour ago."

"Sorry Adjunct," I said. "I've made contact with the aliens, and they can't seem to get enough of me."

"That's just grand. Figure out a way to pat them on the head and leave. It's getting dark soon, and I want every dragon inspected and recharged for morning."

As I'd hesitated for a long time, the lead machine took the initiative. He—I'd started thinking of him as a "he" without being sure why—drew something new. Instead of a simple geometric shape, he drew a circle on top of an oval, with four longer ovals dangling from the central one.

"Ah," Kivi said. "You see that? He's drawn a picture of you, James!"

I examined the drawing and laughed. "So he has. You're a better artist than I am, robot!"

-15-

We got back to camp after dark. Returning late turned out to be a bad move. Trotting our dragons over the icy crust of this planet was hazardous in the foggy light of day. In darkness, it was downright dangerous. Two of us broke through the crust of frozen methane and had to be dragged out with tow cables. The group was weary and irritable by the time we reached camp.

When we did finally get back to our unit, I immediately regretted the fact the expedition had left the relative comfort of the lifter behind. Our new encampment wasn't much to look at without the sheltering roof of the lifter's belly above our heads. Our tents were soft, not much more than smart cloth bubbles. They never stopped whipping and flapping in the winds. The mist got inside, no matter how hard we worked to make the tents airtight.

"I didn't know a planet could smell this bad," Carlos complained. "Fart World, that's what we should call it."

"No," I said. "They've already got a name, haven't you heard? They're calling it Machine World."

"Well, I guess that will work. It's full of wacky machines. Did you ever figure out who the lucky trooper was who got eaten by your little friends?"

"No one got eaten. Just the dragon did. It was part of Harris' squad. One of the dragons broke down and they left it. When they came back for it hours later, it was gone."

"Scavengers. Jackals. That's what those little bastards are. You were crazy to go right up to them and start a drawing contest. What would you have done if they'd torn off your helmet for a snack and burned your face with acid?"

"I'm pretty sure I'd have died," I admitted. "But we've made contact. Maybe it will do some good in time. If people who've got more training with this than I do can continue the work, maybe we'll be able to communicate with these machines someday."

"I've got a better idea," said Carlos. "I've been talking it over with Kivi because I need a tech in order to try it out."

I frowned and stared at him. Carlos often got ideas, but they were rarely good ones.

"What are you up to?" I asked. "And why Kivi? She's not a real tech—at least, not yet."

"Hold on!" Carlos said loudly, lifting his hands up in front of his face. "Don't take a swing at me! I know you and Kivi are doing the nasty again, but that's no reason to—"

I almost hit him. I controlled myself with difficulty. "Listen, quit screwing around and tell me your plan. That's an order."

"Okay, okay. Here it is: we'll build a little box, see, just like the one you built with Claver back on Tech World."

"A box? What kind of box?"

"A com box, retard—oh, sorry. I mean *Vet*."

When dealing with Carlos, a man had to have a thick skin. There just wasn't any other way to get through a conversation.

"Keep talking," I said through gritted teeth.

Carlos seemed honestly surprised I hadn't hit him yet. I was a little surprised, too. But I wanted to hear what kind of cockamamie plan he'd hatched.

"Okay, here's the deal," he said. "These are machines, right? They have to communicate with codes and protocols of some kind. That means we might be able to hack them, to take them over. Wouldn't that be cool? What if you could just give this army of robots a command and have them all obey you?"

"What kind of orders?"

"You know. Stuff like 'kill that squid' or 'rip off Kivi's suit.'"

106

I nodded thoughtfully. It wasn't as insane as it sounded. But I knew it wouldn't be easy to do, and it might not even be possible. These machines were wild. They weren't slaves like our drones from Earth. They weren't built to take orders and obey them without question.

"So, why Kivi?" I asked. "You never said."

"Isn't it obvious? First off, none of the real techs would listen to me. But she did, and she needs rank as badly as I do. If we did something cool like this, we could be specialists within hours."

I'd often told him to go do something useful to prove himself, and I had to admit that this sounded like he was at least trying. It also sounded like Kivi would be doing all the work.

"As long as it doesn't interfere with your regular duties, I've got no objection." I wondered if I'd live to regret my words.

"Cool! Thanks James." He left to work on his little scheme.

I went to the dragon corral and cared for my mount personally. I'd taught my troops to perform minor repairs on their dragons rather than depend totally on the techs. Out here on a wild planet, your kit wasn't someone else's job, it was your life.

In the corral, I met up with Della for the first time since she'd dropped the baby-bomb on me up on *Cyclops*. We'd been placed in different platoons, and I'd been too busy coming up to speed on being a veteran in a brand new cavalry cohort to talk much with her. The truth was, I reflected, I'd been avoiding this moment.

"Hi Della," I said cheerily.

She gave me a thin smile and a nod. I'm not the best at reading feminine responses, but to me she looked a little put out.

"Hey," I said, walking up to her and wiping my fingers with a dirty rag. "I hope you didn't take things the wrong way up there on *Cyclops*. I've been so busy learning how to command a squadron of these dragons, I didn't have much time—"

"It's okay, James," she said. "Like I said, I've moved on."

"Yeah, sure. The marriage thing. Who'd you marry, anyway? I hope it wasn't that dickhead named Stott."

She smiled at me then, and it was the real thing this time. "No, not him. It's a man you don't know. A good man."

"Great, great," I said, turning away to go. I'd left things in an unclear state up on the ship, and I'd wanted her to know I wasn't mad at her or anything. I felt a little relieved I'd accomplished my mission. It was disturbing that some other guy I'd never met was taking care of my kid—but the whole thing was mind-boggling to me anyway.

"James," she said before I'd gone one step. "Don't you want to know more about your child?"

"Uh...I am curious. But I kind of figured that with you being married and all, I should bow out of the picture, if you know what I mean."

That was the wrong thing to say. Her face hardened. She was unhappy all over again. *Damn.*

I knew I was out of my element on this one. Sure, I could write a book on how a man should talk to a girl who'd caught him hanging around with a rival woman, or how to explain to a lover why you might have forgotten to send her text for a couple of days—but this? I was without clue.

Whatever my feelings, I could tell by the look in her eye that the ball was in my court. I took a random stab at serving it back.

"Why don't you tell me about her?" I asked brightly. "About Etta, I mean."

That broke the dam. I was treated to about an hour's worth of pictures and video and even a lock of the girl's hair to wrap around my fingers. I smiled at that last part.

"Blonde hair," I mused. "Real gold-colored, like mine used to be when I was young. Flaxen, my grandma used to call it."

"Do you feel better now?" Della asked, her eyes searching mine. She was trying to look cool—hell, Della was the ultimate cool-as-a-cucumber woman. But I knew she was gauging my responses carefully.

"Yeah!" I said, giving her a big grin. "Can I keep some of the hair?"

"Yes, certainly. I'll transfer the pictures and recordings to your tapper, too."

"Great."

We touched tappers, and it was all over in a second. I had a full dump of my daughter's pictures and videos on my arm—permanently. Right at the moment I wasn't sure if that was going to be a good thing for my mental health or not, but I could tell it made Della happy.

"Hey, when did you get a tapper?" I asked her.

"After you left Happy Valley, we absorbed as much of your technology as we could. We duplicated most of the simple things like your tappers."

I didn't consider tappers to be simple tech, but I nodded. They were complex machines embedded in the flesh of every full-grown human from Earth. They were powered by our bodies and symbiotic with our flesh. The screens even grew hairs sometimes, and you had to pluck them out.

"You guys are wizards," I said. "I've never been so impressed with a group of humans in my life. Stuck out there on Dust World with squids hunting you every so often—I never could figure out how you managed to build up a technological society under those conditions. Maybe we did send our best and brightest out into space a century back."

She was beaming now. I was proud of myself as well. I'd turned a cold-shoulder situation into a happy family reunion. That was quite an accomplishment for a rube like me.

"Well," she said, "we had help."

"You mean from the Galactics? Did they contact you after we left?"

"No, they didn't. They barely pay any attention to our part of space. From what I understand, that's a good thing."

"Yeah…" I thought about the Galactic I'd shot the other day. It was a very good thing the Empire was looking the other direction on that one. All my bullshit might get me past a Mogwa, but I'd never have managed to pull a fast one like that on the Nairbs or the Empire's Battle Fleet commanders. "If not the Empire, who helped you?"

She gave me an odd, almost shy look. "I'm not supposed to talk about that, James."

Frowning, I shrugged. "Okay...but who told you not to talk? You can trust me, you know. I'm in more trouble with the Empire than you could ever hope to be in your lifetime."

This cracked her up. I couldn't recall ever having seen her laugh much before, and it was a nice change today.

"I believe you," she said. "So I will speak of a mutual friend. But no one else must know."

"Uh...okay."

"Natasha taught me. She taught all of us. She took tappers from the dead—bodies you didn't recycle before you left—and she rebuilt new ones for us. She's quite talented, you know."

"She sure is," I said, looking as confused as I felt. "But when did she have time to do all that?"

Della stared at me for a second. "You don't know?"

"Know what?"

She winced, put her hand on my arm, and shook her pretty head. "Forget what I said. Erase it from your mind. It doesn't matter."

She walked away then, and I stared after her in bafflement. It took a full twenty seconds for the light bulb to go off in my dim brain. Sometimes, I'm pretty slow on the uptake. When I did get it, the bulb was like a flash of lightning in my skull.

"Oh shit," I whispered, eyes wide.

I ran after Della. She ducked me, walking into the tent with her squaddies. I chased after her and threw open the flaps. This pissed off everyone inside as it let the stinky air from the outer mechanical bay into the living quarters.

"Hey, close that!"

I did. Then I moved to loom over Della.

"We've got to talk," I said.

She was looking away from me, changing her clothes. She'd been in her grease-monkey suit, a coverall with nanofiber surfactants that shed any liquid that came in contact with it. She stripped this off and dropped her clothes in a heap on the floor, never even looking at me while she pulled a normal combat suit out of a locker.

Dropping one's drawers in a tent full of people wasn't all that unusual in Legion Varus. We had to live pretty close, especially on a planet with an atmosphere that wasn't quite human-flavored. Still, Della always had been even less shy than your typical trooper, due to her upbringing on a harsh colony world.

For just a second, I was distracted. Della's bare butt was as fine as the first day I'd laid eyes on it back on Dust World in an underground hot spring. Possibly, it looked a shade better than it had back then, as the cavern we had made love in had been pretty dark.

A big hand laid itself on my forearm, interrupting my staring session. I knew that hand and that firm grip—I'd know them anywhere. I turned to look at the face glowering at me. It was none other than Veteran Harris.

"Look, McGill," he said. "The lady has made it pretty clear she doesn't want to talk to you. I think you should show a little tact, and move the fuck on."

It was an awkward moment. I looked around and realized the whole squad was watching me. I outranked them all except for Harris, but that didn't make this situation any more acceptable. From their point of view, I was harassing a female soldier who was trying to get away from me.

"I'm sorry Vet," I said. "But Della and I need to talk for a moment. Do you mind?"

Harris shook his head. "You don't give up, do you? Quit chasing tail in my squad! Get on back to your own squad if you want to pull that shit!"

"What? No—hold on, Harris. That's not how it is. Della and I have a history. She had my baby, back on Dust World."

Harris did everything but cross his eyes at that statement. I could tell he didn't know what to make of it.

"Are you shitting me, boy? You're a real piece of work, you know that?"

"Yes sir. Everyone tells me so."

Shaking his head, Harris turned away. The rest of his squad melted as well. He ushered them out of the flapping, imperfect airlock. When they were all gone, he poked his head back in for one last statement.

"If she screams or something, I'm putting you down. You hear me?"

"Loud and clear."

He left then, and Della turned to face me. She had her arms crossed and her clothes on. I was vaguely disappointed, but at least she couldn't get away.

"You shouldn't press this," she said. "For the sake of our mutual friend."

"Natasha?" I asked.

"Yes."

"You know her—really know her. Don't you?"

She looked troubled. "I should never have said anything."

"I already know. From your reaction, I figured it out. Natasha told me, back on Dust World, that she might be a copy. I know about that—I won't tell anyone."

Della searched my face. "It's a violation. Hegemony Law, Galactic Law—nothing a person can do is much worse. There can only be one person with the same DNA sequence running around at one time. Natasha made that very clear to us."

I wasn't sure about it being the worst violation a person could perform, having committed a number of acts I would consider to be significantly worse, but I smiled reassuringly.

"I won't tell. Your secret is good with me."

"All right then."

We eyed one another for a few seconds.

"So," I said in a whisper, "She got off the doomed ship *Corvus* somehow and survived? I can hardly believe she made it across all that empty space to Dust World. Was she injured?"

"Yes. Radiation burns. Exhaustion. Only three of the techs returned to Dust World about a month after you left. The other two died within weeks, but Natasha hung on."

"How did they do it?"

"I don't understand it all," Della said. "I know they managed to rig up some kind of life-pod and used a slingshot effect around our star to reach planetary orbit. They finally made reentry a month after *Corvus* crashed into the star. Natasha was thin and sick, but we nursed her back to health."

Thinking it over, I could believe it. If anyone could figure out a solution to an impossible physics problem, it was Natasha. "I should have known she'd make it. I told her—the copied version of her, that is—that there was no way it could happen. I didn't want her to worry about it."

"We owe her so much, James. She taught us the tech that we didn't grasp. We had tech samples from the Empire and the Cephalopods. There were piles of forgotten debris all over the valley. She put it all together for us."

I nodded thoughtfully. Natasha was, flat out, the best tech I'd ever met. It made total sense to me that she'd be up to such a herculean task.

"She taught you, and you came up with trade goods. Nanites, dragons. Trade and viability. I'm sure you do owe her a lot."

"Your legion abandoned us. They left us to die, really. You're right, we owe her so much. She knew she could never go home to Earth again, so she did her best to make Dust World livable."

"One new colonist," I mused. "Just the kind you needed to get your world going. Did she hide when the ships finally came from Earth to trade?"

"She didn't have to. By then, she'd blended in with the rest of us. No one would ever have guessed who she really was."

Della's explanation was followed by an awkward silence, and I was the one who broke it.

"Okay," I said, forcing a tight smile. "Now I know everything. I'll be going now."

She stopped me with a hand. "There's one more thing. James, she never stops talking about you. She's in love with you. I can't figure that out, myself."

I chuckled. "Love, hate...they're just two sides of the same coin with James McGill."

-16-

Before dawn, I woke up with a hand pawing at me. I slapped it, but it kept coming back. Opening my eyes, I saw Carlos grinning down into my face.

Now, I don't know about you, but a hairy, round-cheeked male face was about the last thing I liked to see in the morning.

"What the hell do you want?" I demanded. "What time is it?"

"It's explaining-time for you, you big freak."

Growling, I came up off my bunk and landed on my feet. Carlos had pushed our friendship too far. I'd advanced in rank, and he hadn't, but he still thought he could treat me like that first day we met at the Mustering Hall in Newark.

"Whoa, fella," he said, pointing toward the tent flaps.

They parted to reveal Leeson. "About time you got off your ass, McGill. Mind you, I think we should just blast this thing and not even bother having you try to talk to it, but that's not my call to make."

"What?" I asked.

"Haven't you heard? That alien-looking mechanical bug-thing you made love to out on the ice is outside, trying to communicate. Now, get out there and figure out what it wants, pronto."

"Uh...yes, sir."

I scrambled into a vac suit and marched out through multiple fabric airlocks. The pumps wheezed and complained because I hadn't waited around long enough to let them seal up properly and scrub the air that got into our innermost quarters. Gas monitors beeped and farted neutralizing agents to counter the contamination.

Outside, it was dawn—or what passed for dawn on this frozen rock. In practice that meant the mist wasn't moving around as much as usual, and the diffused light was deep gray rather than the white of day or the black of night.

Hanging wisps of vapor swirled around one of the smaller machines, which whirred and clacked. In the still, windless air the gyrations of the machine appeared to be more pronounced. Its flailing limbs churned, digging at a patch of exposed dirt.

I peered at the alien machine. The thing *did* resemble the one I'd tried to make contact with the day before, but it was hard to be certain. They really did all look alike.

The camera-eyes noticed me, and they shivered a little. The machine stopped whatever it was doing and looked me over.

Finally, it broke off excitedly and ran toward me, gesturing with mouthparts. Running around like a dog, it tried to lead me to the spot where it had been working. I followed it to the flat area where it had been screwing around in the dirt. Squinting, I looked at what it had done.

"Pictures," I said. "Sketches. You came back for more communication, didn't you?"

The robot quivered and did a little spin around its latest work, but interposed itself between me and the other drawings. I figured it wanted me to see this image first.

It was a picture of a man, sort of, only the man looked like an oval with angled sticks for arms and legs. The man was inside a tent like the one I'd just exited. The tent was a bag-like affair encircling it.

"Okay," I said. "Me in a tent. Or at least, close enough. What else have you got?"

It backed away and showed me the next thing. This showed a series of blobs surrounding the man in the tent. I didn't get that one.

"Hmm. A bunch of somethings around the tent. Okay…"

The machine backed up further, showing me the last image. I frowned. I saw the man in the tent was lying flat, and the tent was deflated. It looked like a limp bag on the ground. The circles that had been encircling it were now piled on, drawn on top of the man, the tent—everything.

"Is this some kind of threat?" I asked. "Or a warning?"

Staring cameras regarded me. The artificial feet tapped at random intervals, making clacking sounds on the stones. It had no idea what I was saying. I heaved a sigh, got out my sidearm and used it to scratch in the dirt beside the images the machine had treated me to.

I drew two figures. One was the man-figure, similar in nature to the version the machine had drawn. The other was a machine, one that resembled the little guy I was trying to talk to. I had each extend a stick-like limb toward one another.

"So this is what passes for flirtation on Machine World, huh McGill?" Leeson asked. He'd been watching me with mild interest. "Why don't you draw two machines screwing? That will get you there faster."

He guffawed with laughter.

"I'm trying to make it look like they're shaking hands, not having relations, sir," I told Leeson. I offered him my sidearm. "Maybe you could do better?"

"Don't put that gun in my hand! I'd as soon shoot this mechanical bug as look at it."

While I talked to Leeson, the machine examined my image then moved to a fresh spot and began to work again. It left behind an image that was similar to mine, but the man-figure was all wrong. I had too many limbs, and they looked all curly.

Sighing, I tried but couldn't come up with a translation for the machine's work. Maybe it was too early in the morning. Leeson had no answers either. He finally got bored and left.

While I continued to examine the latest image the machine had drawn for me, a familiar specialist approached.

"Hey," I said in surprise. "What's up, Natasha? I thought you were still aboard *Minotaur*."

"We're all in the process of coming down now," she said. "Turov has been deploying most of the troops at the beachhead Winslade established south of here, but I was sent here."

I could have asked "what beachhead?" or made other rude remarks about Winslade, but I didn't. I was too happy to see

116

Natasha. I ushered her to the machine and showed her the drawings. She eyed them with great interest.

"Okay," she said. "I'm pretty sure that's you in the tent in the first image, or at least a generic human."

"Right."

"Then the man in the tent is surrounded, and finally destroyed. But what are those blobs that are performing the destruction?"

"I think they're the big machines. They look a little like conical piles of dirt. That's what the bigger ones look like."

She frowned at me. "So this guy is trying to tell us we're going to be under attack soon?"

"Maybe," I admitted.

"And you drew this last one? The one with the human making out with the machine?"

"We're shaking hands, dammit."

"Okay, okay. Then your friend drew something else—oh."

"What?" I asked. "I didn't get that one."

"Don't you see, James? That's a machine shaking hands with a cephalopod."

The moment she said it, I could see the sketch her way. It was as clear as day, now that I thought about it.

"He's telling me the machines aren't our friends," I said. "They're allied with the squids."

"Yes," she said. "We must report this to Graves."

I looked around a few minutes later and noticed the machine I'd been struggling to communicate with had wandered off. Reflecting on the entire episode, I wasn't sure if the alien had come here to warn us, to inform us—or just to gloat.

* * *

The next day went badly. We were out scouting the local region at dawn, in preparation for proceeding with our mission. There was no way we could have known what we were in for.

The first hint came when my helmet began to scratch with radio signals. I realized I'd left a channel open—a low-

117

frequency channel in the kilocycle range. I contacted Kivi first, who messed with her settings and confirmed it. I had her move off a few hundred meters from me to get a second directional reading.

The signals pointed out to the lake north of us. I contacted Graves without hesitation.

"Sir, we have machine readings—lots of them. They seem to be moving nearby. Triangulating with my team, I figure they're north, moving up onto the lakeshore."

"Machines?" he asked. "Like the ones in that village you found the other day?"

"Yes, exactly."

"I've reviewed the vids. The machines seemed pretty harmless. Even that big one shuffled off after you left the vicinity of the village. Just don't antagonize them."

"Right sir, but if I might add—there seems to be a lot of them, and they're coming toward your position from the north."

"Okay, okay. Go up there and scout them for me. Give me a count and a definite heading."

My heart sank. I'd been hoping I'd be recalled. But that wasn't Graves' style. Whether risking his own life or the lives of his troopers, he'd always been a pretty generous contributor to the reaper.

"Okay, saddle-up," I ordered. "We're going north to check out that contact."

We moved toward the lakeshore warily, trotting at about half-speed. The mists precluded a full-speed approach since we might have run into the targets blind.

As it turned out, it hardly made any difference. We were less than a kilometer from the mass of them when we realized what we were trotting our long-legged dragons into.

"Machines, Vet! Hundreds of them!" It was Carlos who sounded the alarm. Normally, I would have been suspicious of a line like that coming from him—but the tone in his voice indicated he was serious.

"Check them out. Have they detected you?"

"They're big ones, Vet! Like the mama-machine we saw back at the village. They're coming my way. I think they can hear our radios."

"Right. Wheel your mounts and ride!" I ordered my squad.

All around me, dragons turned and ran back the way we'd come. It wasn't our job to fight these machines. We were supposed to locate them and gather intel, that was it.

"Carlos, can you give me a count?"

"I don't know—I see at least four on my tail. Jeez, these things are big! They're fast, too. I—one of them is gaining on me. It just won't give up."

I reported in to Graves then noticed Carlos' blinking light. He was trying to contact me.

"Carlos, what's happening?"

"One of them caught me," he said, breathing hard. "It just plowed me over and knocked my mount down, but I'm still breathing. It hasn't breached the capsule yet. Permission to fire, Vet!"

I was surprised he'd bothered to ask. I wouldn't have. "Permission granted! Defend yourself! We're coming back."

"Is that a good idea?" Kivi asked. "We're not supposed to antagonize the locals. You were drawing pictures in the dirt with them yesterday."

"Yeah, yeah," I said. "That was before they attacked one of us. I told Graves I'd leave them alone unless they attacked first."

"Vet's right," Sargon said. "We've got clear rules of engagement. The locals have broken them. Maybe they'll respect us more if we show them we aren't helpless."

We plunged through the white mists and topped a small rise in the land. A machine loomed into view on the far side. It had to be the one that was trying to eat Carlos.

This machine was *big*. It was hard to judge, but I'd be willing to bet it was even bigger than the first mama machine we'd met up with. The configuration was familiar. A mountain of interlocking plates covering a body that looked like a giant metal slug.

Flashes of light erupted from under the machine as we approached. I figured that was probably Carlos trying to give it indigestion. I looked around but didn't see any other machines. If I had to guess, I figured they'd moved off while the lucky one that had caught Carlos tried to have a meal.

"Spread out. When I give the order, fire your grenades high," I said. "We don't want to blast our own man."

The squad went into action. Without being told, Sargon led his group around to the machine's flank.

The machine seemed to take notice of us, shivering and twisting this way and that as if nervous. But it didn't want to leave its kill. I could tell we were going to have to give it some encouragement.

"Fire at will!"

Everyone began raining grenades down on the machine. They popped and flashed but didn't penetrate. A few of its scales fell off but not enough. I knew what the problem was. Our weaponry was built to take out infantry not heavily armored targets.

"Carlos?" I called. "Can you still hear me?"

He didn't answer, and that's when I noticed his squad ID was red. His name, on the list of names in my cockpit, was listed as a dead link. I didn't know if he'd succumbed, or his radio had gone out. The effect was pretty much the same either way. We had to get past this thing's armor before it ate him entirely.

"I'm going in close!" I shouted. "Hold the grenade fire until I punch a hole in those outer plates."

I galloped forward, running my dragon at full speed. At the last second, the shivering alien machine lifted its lower edge. I realized that's how it must engulf things. It looked like I was about to run right under its skirt and spend some quality time with Carlos' corpse.

"Look out, McGill!" shouted Kivi.

Without taking the time to answer her, I engaged my dragon's exoskeletal legs with full power, stiffening the metal springs in the feet. I bounded high when I reached the machine, sailing right over the uplifted lip of it and landing with a sprawling clatter on top.

The footing was uneven at best. I didn't have more than a second or two before I knew it would reshape itself and send me crashing back down to the ground. After that, I knew it would swallow me.

Stabbing at the controls, I let my grippers fold back. Twin, high-powered force blades sprang from my dragon's arms.

Up close, the machine was more complex and bizarre than I'd realized previously. It had cameras—lots of them. Like a spider with eyes clustered between its legs, the cameras were nestled all over the place between the plates. There must have been a hundred machine-eyes watching me as I tore a hole in its armor.

Three times, I slashed. I didn't get a fourth try. Plates flew off, clattering and clanging to the ground. A good-sized hole had opened up, but I didn't know if it would be enough.

That was as far as I got before I was unceremoniously dumped on the dirt. A great flap of the outer rim rose up, the whole machine shivered forward—then everything went dark.

I was underneath it, being crushed down. The underside of the machine reminded me of a roly-poly from my grandma's backyard. There were hundreds of gray metallic feet and churning legs. They clacked and sparked on my dragon's armor. The experience left me with a panicky feeling. I knew this was how Carlos had died.

As my eyes adjusted to the gloom, I could see tools hanging down from the insides of the machine. Tools mounted on arms that moved independently. I could tell already that when these steel pipes, spikes and blades got through my dragon's hull to the soft meaty center, it wasn't going to be a happy moment for old James McGill.

"Squad!" I shouted on the com channel. "Can you hear me? I'm inside the machine, underneath it. If I use my launchers, I'll blast myself apart."

"Hang on, Vet," Sargon said. "We're mounting a general attack."

"Go for the hole that I cut in the thing's hull," I said. "Try firing grenades in there."

"We might blast you if we do that, Vet."

Thinking about it for less than a second, I made a hard decision. I was going to have to get lucky to live this time. The luck might as well come right now.

121

"I know," I told Sargon. "But I'll be toast anyway in less than a minute. Go for it."

I waited, cringing, while the machine tried to eat me. Hardened steel can take quite a beating, but right now I was wishing I'd opted for shielding and heavy weaponry rather than faster legs on my dragon's load-out.

A white flash boomed, overloading my optic nerves for a second. I was glad my ears were well-covered because the noise was deafening under the enclosed surface of the machine's outer hull.

I guessed one of my squad had gotten a grenade inside the machine. More explosions soon followed. It sounded like a rain of boulders on top of a metal roof.

Finally, the machine gave up on eating me. It peeled itself off my dragon and shuffled away. A dozen primitive legs thumped and clattered over me, and I was out in the open again.

Kivi's dragon helped mine to get up, but it wasn't any use. My mount couldn't walk.

"I've got a bad leg actuator," I said, going through a quick diagnostics check. "The left one won't take any weight."

"Get out of the cockpit," she said. "The rest of the squad is chasing the machine, but it might turn on them at any moment."

"What about Carlos?"

"He's dead. I checked."

"What the hell am I going to do on foot?" I asked.

"Climb on my back. Watch for the heat fins, they get really hot when I run."

I knew all about that. The heat generated by a dragon in combat was excessive, and they had fins rising up out of the back to help relieve it.

Ejecting myself from my mount, I climbed up onto Kivi's dragon and perched there like a man riding an over-grown ostrich.

"Sargon!" I called over the squad channel. "Come back, we're getting out of here."

My squad didn't need any more encouragement. They returned a few minutes later, and we all ran together. We didn't stop until we were far from the machines.

I reported in, and Leeson was pissed.

"You left *two* good dragons in the field for some machines to chew on? What do you expect to ride around on tomorrow, Veteran?"

"I know we have a few extras back at the lifter, sir."

"That's negatory, McGill!" he shouted. "Your flesh is nothing. That dragon is worth ten of you! Halt and wait. I'm coming to your position with Harris and another platoon. We're getting your machine back—Carlos' too."

I didn't think I could argue him out of it, so I didn't even try. I figured it was pointless, and I also kind of wanted some company in my neck of the woods.

About two minutes later, the whole unit showed up. We advanced at a run toward the last position where we'd made contact with the machines.

When we got there, we found the dragons—but we found something else, too. A few hundred meters away were at least a dozen of the large machines. The machines were piled up in a mound. At first, it looked like one massive mountain of trembling metal.

"McGill," Graves said, "you didn't describe these machines accurately. That mass looks to be a hundred meters high."

"No sir," I said. "I don't think that's one machine, that's about a dozen of them all piled up."

"What the hell are they doing?"

"Well sir, I'd be guessing, but I'd say they're eating the one we damaged earlier."

"Nasty," Graves said thoughtfully. "They're cannibalizing the weak. They look like beetles gnawing on a bone."

"We don't want to be here when they finish their meal, sir. They have quite an appetite."

"Roger that," Graves said. "Get three dragons on each of our broken-down vehicles. Drag them behind you on tow cables. We're bugging out of here right now."

We beat a hasty retreat, and I'd never been happier to run away in my life.

-17-

We were putting together an after-action report about an hour later when an unexpected guest showed up and burst in on our unit meeting.

Graves, Kivi, Leeson and I were all talking over the battle in our command tent when Primus Winslade himself swept in and sat at the end of the table. He sniffed the air as if it smelled bad—which it did.

"Primus," Graves said. "I'm so glad you could join us on the front lines."

Winslade wrinkled his nose. "There's a special scent in the air, Graves," he said. "It's the smell of failure. I'd know it anywhere. Why is your advanced scouting team bogged down out here? You've had a full day to cross a river, and yet here you sit in your encampment."

"The river is trapped, sir," Graves said. "We've encountered underwater systems specifically built to cripple machines. They're all over the local waterways. They're crude but effective. As far as we can tell, the machines feed on each other, and we've been trying to—"

"Let's stop the nonsense," Winslade interrupted. "I mean the part about 'trying' to do things. I need action, Graves. I was told you were a man who could provide it. That's why I put you in charge of this advance force. The Solstice troops we're trying to rescue might all be dead by now due to your indolence."

Graves rarely became openly angry, but I could tell Winslade was pushing his buttons like a pro.

"Is that right?" Graves asked. "Well sir, can you enlighten me on how things are going with the rest of the cohort? Are the majority of your units still sitting in your camp under the lifter?"

Winslade gave him an unpleasant smile. "No. Not any longer. We're all here—just outside, in fact."

Graves looked surprised. "When did your orders change?"

Winslade threw his hand into the air and twisted his mouth.

"Imperator Turov arrived at the site several hours ago. The location had been deemed relatively safe, so *Minotaur* disgorged all of Legion Varus at my base camp."

Graves nodded. "So, let me see if I understand the situation…as soon as the imperator landed she realized your cohort was sitting around, and she kicked you out to the front?"

Winslade was displeased. He gave Graves a hard stare for a moment before speaking. "Tactless, as always. I see now why you've been stuck with the rank of Centurion for half a century."

Graves' face was stone. "What are your orders, sir?"

"Turov has ordered all of us—the entire auxiliary cohort—to cross the river *today*. We're to advance to the last known position of the missing troops. I intend to follow that order immediately. Everyone, pack up and move out!"

That was it. There wasn't much of a plan, or any argument for that matter. Turov's orders were often like that, and I wasn't surprised Winslade operated in the same fashion. We stood up as a group and headed to the dragons.

Before we saddled up and rode out, I was issued a fresh dragon by the cohort quartermaster. Spare machines had been brought in with a lot of other critical supplies on the backs of our drones. The drones, or "pigs" as we called them, were like fast-marching mechanical oxen. They didn't move as quickly as the dragons, but they never got tired and each could carry several tons of weight over any kind of terrain.

As we gathered our equipment, I pressed Graves to let me choose a better load-out. I wanted heavy weaponry.

125

"Agreed," he said. "Speed might help when escaping those machines, but you can't win a fight by running from everything."

Grateful, I ordered my troopers to mount heavy guns on their dragons. We went without shielding as this new enemy didn't seem to be keen on shooting projectiles at us. Within an hour I found myself sitting in a dragon with a single cannon mounted on the spine, heavy generators and extra cells. This setup wasn't as fast, but it was lot more dangerous, and it could operate for an extended period of time.

When we finally reached the river, I don't think any of us were looking forward to the crossing. Behind us was a long train of drones and dragons. The group slowly lined up along the shore. Most of the cavalry wore heavy kits now. Spinal-cannons were everywhere. The quartermaster had complained he was out of back-up units if we got any of these weapons damaged.

"Leeson, McGill," Graves called to us.

"Right here, sir," Leeson reported.

"In his infinite wisdom," Graves began, "Winslade has seen fit to have our unit be the first to ford this river."

I nodded to myself in my cockpit. Graves *had* kind of flipped off the new primus when the man had crashed our little meeting. I could have told Graves how that was going to turn out. Winslade had been a vindictive little cuss when he was powerless. Now that he wore the insignia of a primus—well, it was time for payback.

"I volunteer, sir," I said.

"Excellent, but you'll need backup. Harris, I know you're listening. I need an experienced man behind McGill."

"On my way, sir."

About ninety seconds later I found myself marching into the silvery liquid.

"You just had to do it, didn't you McGill?" Harris complained in my headset. "Itching to die on yet another new planet? That's you in a nutshell."

"That's me, Vet."

"All right, enough bitching," Leeson said. "McGill, spread out your squad and cross at a walk. Harris, follow with your machines right behind them. Your job is to pull McGill's squad mates out of traps. Try to walk due west, everyone. If any of the dragons gets across without a problem, we'll mark the path and everyone will follow. Go!"

We had our orders. I was the first man into the river. I didn't feel fear, not really. If the river didn't get too deep—

"Vet!" shouted Gorman. "I'm down! Dammit."

We hadn't gone twenty steps. The other side was still an unknown. For all I knew, we had five kilometers to go.

"All halt," I ordered. "Can one of your men get Gorman out, Harris?"

"We're on it."

There was a brief delay before they had Gorman up and operating again. We'd learned by this time to cut off the trap and discard it. We kept going.

There was a trap encountered at intervals of about every ten steps. I could tell this was going to be a long day.

Watching my HUD, I began to frown. I was noticing a pattern. "Leeson, sir?"

"What is it, McGill?"

I was mildly surprised to realize he was in the river with us. He was in the rear, to be sure, but he was only ten meters behind my dragon.

"Sir, did you notice the last four traps? They started with Gorman, then Kivi, then—"

"Get to the damned point, McGill! Winslade is already crawling up my butt on officer's chat."

"Roger that. Sorry sir, but I think this might help."

"Keep talking and keep walking. You've got thirty seconds."

"There's a pattern, sir. The dragons that have hit a trap so far are finding them in a diagonal pattern. The first man hit was Gorman, the next one hit the man next to him, then—"

"I get it," Leeson said suddenly. "I see it on my HUD. By damn, you're not as dumb as a bag of hammers after all!"

"Thank you, sir."

Leeson barked out orders, telling people to regroup and move at a forty-five degree angle to cross the river. We marched like that for a full minute without running into anything.

"We can predict this," Leeson said excitedly, "and we'll get through it. But you have to tell me McGill, what kind of trapper fills an entire riverbed with traps using a perfectly even pattern?"

"A robot trapper, sir? They're nothing if not methodical."

"Another thing makes sense to me now," Leeson said in an uncharacteristically thoughtful tone. "This riverbed is dead-level. Right here, where the river has a natural shallow area, someone lowered it. They flattened this region of the riverbed out to make it more attractive to anyone trying to cross."

"Good thinking, sir," I said, and I meant it. "I think you're onto something there. All part of an efficient system of capture and—"

That was as far as I got before something strange happened. A surge of liquid methane came downriver and rolled into us. It didn't submerge our dragons, but it did rush over our knees in a wave that was at least a meter higher than normal.

"What the hell—?" Leeson squawked. "Where did that wave come from? What—?"

He got his answer in a physical form before I could say anything. A vast machine rolled up out of the mist. It came down the river behind the wave it had created.

I knew right off we were trapped. We could run back to the shore behind us, but if we continued on a diagonal course, we'd have to rush right into the machine that was bearing down on us.

"You asked who made the minefield, sir," I said. "I think there's your answer."

"Put a hole in it!" Leeson shouted. "Unlimber those spine-cannons. I want a volley on my mark. Target the center of mass. One, two...*Mark!*"

We all fired. There was a roar and a brilliant barrage of streaking lights. Smoke trails hung in the air behind our projectiles for a frozen moment before the impacts began to rain down.

The looming machine must have thought it had caught dinner and was going to feast on our metal carcasses. But it got the surprise of its life—which promptly ended.

The shells hammered through the plating and crashed into the guts of the machine, where they exploded.

The machine shivered and deflated like a vast balloon that had been punctured. The platoon shouted and roared in the victory. I had to admit, I felt a surge of relief as well.

But, I had to ask myself, what would be the repercussions of these clashes with the natives? Could we really expect them to be tolerant of invaders?

A part of me, too, wondered if this machine was the mama machine for the playful tikes I'd met and tried to communicate with at the nearby village. Would they go hungry now, without a parent to fend for them?

It was all very confusing, and I wasn't sure how I should feel about it.

-18-

After the incident in the middle of the river, we had no more trouble with the crossing. We'd figured out the pattern of traps and defeated the trapper. There were no further dangers to overcome.

An hour later, the full cohort assembled on the far side of the river. It had only been about a kilometer wide in the end, but it had seemed endless. When you can't see the far side of something, and danger is stalking you, time dilates, and a march becomes a slog.

When we set off again, Winslade was lashing at our backsides and making cohort-wide rants.

"That took *far* too long," he said into my earpiece. "It will be dark in only four hours. I know every legionnaire will want to quit by then—but it's not going to happen. We'll press on until we reach point-charley on your maps."

I looked it up. I knew I shouldn't have, but I felt the urge. When I found the next waypoint on our journey to the last known contact with the lost troops, I grimaced. There was no way we'd make it until midnight local time, even if we didn't run into another major obstacle.

Part of me understood why the officers were frustrated. We were supposed to be the cavalry, but we couldn't *move* like cavalry. We were in unknown territory swamped in mist, rough ground and danger. If they'd ordered us to charge into the unknown blindly, sure, we could probably make the run within the span of a few hours. But the officers had another, contradictory requirement: that we not lose their precious dragons.

"Quick gains on any battlefield often require risk," I said, quoting a military strategy book I'd read to prepare for my new status as a veteran.

"What's that crap?" Harris demanded. I'd forgotten he was still listening in on my squad chat. "You keep a lid on that, McGill. Someone might hear you."

"Someone already has," Graves said.

I flinched. I told myself I had to get used to the idea that I wasn't one more grunt mumbling to myself on proximity chat anymore. As a veteran, I had access to a lot of new levels of communication, and I'd just done the equivalent of a "reply-all" to the entire unit.

"For the record, I agree with McGill," Graves said. "We should just get this over with and quit walking like frightened infantry in expensive machines. With a vanguard of fast-moving troops, we can risk a unit and follow with a large column afterward. If the first group hits a major obstacle—well, we can decide how to handle it situationally. That way you risk losing a single unit, but the entire force moves at triple the pace. Risk equals gain, as McGill said."

My private chat line was blinking. It was Harris. I had no doubt he was calling to give me a reaming. He hadn't talked to me this much since I'd had my chat with Della in his squad's tent. Harris' distance had been just fine with me. Now, as I eyed the contact light, I wondered if I should open the channel or not. I decided to ignore it.

Another call came in from Graves. I took that one.

"McGill," Graves said, "I've come to a decision. I'm kicking your suggestion up to Winslade. Hold on."

A long, groaning sound came out of my mouth. I finally opened the private talk-line with Harris, who was still waiting.

"I don't believe it!" he said. "See? You see that? Are you even *listening* to Graves?"

"Yes, he just contacted me."

"That's what you get—but we *all* have to suffer! You see how this turns out, McGill? If you live again someday after this disaster is over and done, try to learn to keep your big mouth

131

shut, okay? That is, if you aren't permed along with the rest of us!"

He cut the channel before I could reply. It was just as well. I was all out of snappy comebacks anyway. I had a feeling he might be right.

The next few minutes were uncomfortable. Finally, the new orders came down.

"Good news, 3rd Unit," Graves announced.

What got me was that the centurion sounded honest-to-God happy.

"We're moving out, top speed," he continued. "My unit has been awarded the honor of forging the way. Leeson, take point."

That was it. Harris' worst fears had been realized.

"You heard the man!" I shouted. "Saddle-up, this will be a full-speed run. We're going to get this over with before darkness falls. With any luck, we'll be sipping auto-heated stew in a tent within four hours!"

We began to run. For the first hour, things went relatively smoothly. The land was flat and empty. There were boulders now and then, but no one wrecked their dragon.

But then our luck changed. We ran into a broken region of badlands. There were gullies, pits and wind-carved rocks everywhere. By this time, everyone in the cohort had a channel tuned to the low-frequency bands the machines used for communication. Our computers filtered out all but the strongest, close-range contacts. If the big machines came near, we would be warned by their radioed whale-songs.

There weren't any problems until we reached the midpoint of the badlands. In a particularly deep gully, we met up with a series of warbling contacts—a lot of them.

"Centurion Graves, we've got company dead ahead," I reported in.

"Roger that, I can see the readouts. Advance your platoon, Leeson. Give me an accurate count on the wildlife. Then I'll phone this in to Winslade to see what he wants to do. Remember to use only low-powered radio to talk, and hold your ground until told to do otherwise. Don't bring an avalanche of enemy machines back home to the main column."

Leeson ordered Harris to swing right and me to swing left. I had to wonder if Graves still hated me, or if his habit of picking Leeson, Harris and I to do his most hazardous missions was some kind of compliment. I figured it was probably a mixture of both, and possibly it had just become reflexive for him. Whatever the case, I found myself at the very front of the line yet again as we trotted our dragons between looming boulders, bubbling streams of methane and metallic-looking rocks with sharp edges.

We finally broke through to a region close enough and wide enough to see what we were facing.

I was confused at first. The machines were all in one tight area.

"Looks like that mound of machines we found eating their wounded brother back on the lakeshore," I said.

"Sure does," Sargon said, coming close.

We were peering down into a churning pit of machines. There were about twenty of them, and they were roaming around and appeared to be feeding. I knew the look by this time. The machines would kind of hunker down and shiver a little when they found something good to eat.

"Hey," Sargon said. "Look over there…is that what I think it is?"

I followed his dragon's outstretched gripper. Peering in the gloomy light, I nodded at last. "Yeah, I think so. That's a dead trooper."

We'd found the Solstice infantry—or what was left of them. Looking back down into the open pit area, I began to figure out what I was seeing.

"We're looking at the remains of the proud Legion Solstice," I said grimly. "They must have made a last stand here in the badlands. Trapped in this little box canyon, they fought and lost. These machines are feeding on the armored suits of their dead."

"Makes me sick," Sargon said. "Permission to destroy these scavengers, Vet?"

"Permission denied—for now. It's not my call."

Sargon looked at me. I could see his face lit up inside his faceplate by his instrumentation. He was enraged, and I didn't blame him.

"Come on, McGill," he said. "Since when did you play anything by the book? Let's charge down there and smoke those machines. If we move fast, it will be over before anyone knows what's going on. If the whole cohort shows up in the middle of the action, they'll back us up without a question."

"You could be right," I said, "but I'm playing this one straight. Sorry Sargon. I have the feeling we'll get the chance to blast plenty of machines apart before this campaign is over if it makes you feel any better."

Sargon shook his head and glowered back down the slope at the gorging machines. "If you're bucking for adjunct already, forget it. They don't often move an enlisted man up into the officers' ranks."

I knew he was emotional, and I didn't blame him. It looked like we'd found a wiped legion. I couldn't recall the last time Earth had lost one of the reputable legions like Solstice. Sure, we could revive them all if we got their data. That wasn't the point. It was a defeat, a humiliation.

"Two thousand years ago, in Roman times," I said, "the worst defeat ever suffered was in the forests of Germany. They lost three full legions on that doomed campaign. I feel now as if I can fathom some of the dismay the Romans must have felt at that loss."

Sargon's mood shifted. "Ha! Good one, McGill! Vicious, but funny."

"Huh?"

"You know they named our legion Varus after the commander of those three legions Rome lost in Germany, right?"

"Yeah."

"Well, the name was a joke, because we were meant to die over and over again," he said bitterly. "But now here we are, looking down at the remains of the Golden Legion. Solstice died here, not us. The joke is on *them* this time! Sorry bastards. Maybe their name will mean 'loser' someday, too."

134

Sargon wheeled around and left. I followed him. I made my report, and various officers came up to survey the mess.

All the while, I was thinking about Sargon's bitter words. I knew we'd been named after Publius Quinctilius Varus, the unluckiest leader in the history of the Roman Empire, and I'd heard that we'd been given the name as some kind of a joke.

But I didn't find it funny. It made me want to drag the hog generals out of their offices back home on Earth and put them into light-troop uniforms out here on the front line. We'd see who was laughing then.

Some of Sargon's dark mood was sinking into my mind.

-19-

Quietly, on a private channel, I asked Natasha to send out a certain radio signal that we'd isolated and recorded earlier. She'd theorized that it was sort of a dinner bell, a call from one machine to all those in the area that rich metals were available at a given location.

It turned out that Natasha's theories were correct.

I don't think Leeson, Graves or Winslade himself ever quite figured out how our first major battle with the native machine life started. Oh sure, the officers might have had their private suspicions. But they couldn't be sure.

Natasha, always faithful in these situations and equally accountable for the aftermath in any case, kept her pretty mouth shut.

There were about thirty of the big machines in the mountains around us when we transmitted the signal. We'd only spotted about half that number, but the rest came running when we sounded the dinner bell.

"James!" Natasha called on our private channel as the machines rushed up rough mountainous walls, quivering and clattering for a grip on the terrain. "I'm getting a response to my message!"

"You sure are," I said. "The machines are rolling in from all over."

"No, I don't mean that. Someone must be alive down there, underneath all the wreckage. They heard our signal and blipped back something in return."

"Really? Excellent. You need to have a little more faith in me, girl."

"I sent the damned message, didn't I? If we live, you owe me a drink."

"Done."

That was all the time we had for chit-chat. What was lucky for us was the lack of coordination in the machine attack. They acted more like a swarm of starving sharks than an army. Rather than timing the assault so they all reached us at once, they came in successive waves.

"On my target!" I roared, hearing Harris echoing the same command. I lit up the nearest machine with a laser marker built into my dragon. "Right flank, center of mass. FIRE!"

We took the first seven or eight down without mishap. But then they were rolling over the ridges above us and falling on us. Some had circled around, hitting our flanks. Other combat units had formed on hillocks farther to the rear, but they didn't have the same clear field of fire that I did. A few maniples were overrun and ground down by the sheer weight of the enemy machines.

Out of Graves' unit, six dragons were down and being consumed. A dozen more were in too close to safely use their big guns. Force-blades were extended, and the grim work of dismantling the enemy piece by piece began.

What saved us in the end, I think, was the greed of the enemy machines. Rather than pressing the attack, those in the rear fell upon their mortally wounded comrades. The smoking wrecks of machines we'd blasted were sent sliding back down into the valley where they flipped over and exposed their damaged guts. This was simply too tempting to the last waves of machines. They pounced upon the fallen and feasted.

After five minutes, it was all over. The enemy machines had all been destroyed, had fallen back, or were busy cannibalizing their own.

Graves approached me, and we gazed down upon a scene of destruction.

"We won that one," he said.

"Yes, sir."

"I didn't even see you fire the first shot to kick things off. How'd you manage it?"

"Manage what, Centurion?" I asked.

Graves shook his head disgustedly.

"By the way, sir," I said. "We detected a new message coming from under this pile of broken metal. We have confirmed it was transmitted by Legion Solstice survivors. They're down there, Centurion. Permission to attempt a rescue?"

"Since when did you ask my permission to do anything, McGill?"

"There's always a first time, sir."

Graves looked over the scene. "The remaining machines are broken or busy. Funny how they're ignoring us again."

"They're driven by hunger more than anything else. It's my theory that the smaller ones might actually be more intelligent. They don't have as much mass to keep fed so they can devote more processing time to higher pursuits."

"I hate theories," Graves said, "especially those hatched by noncoms." He eyed my squad. "You've only lost one squad member, right? Harris lost four. You know what that means, McGill?"

"That I'm going down there to check for survivors personally, sir?"

"Exactly."

"Can I take Natasha with me? We might need a good tech."

"All right. But don't get her killed this time."

As Natasha hadn't qualified to pilot a dragon, she was riding on the back of a drone. We rode our mounts down the steep, rocky slopes to the bottom and quickly reached the coordinates Natasha provided. At first, I didn't see anything special about this spot. Then we found an entrance shrouded by a polymer shell.

I rapped on the shell. There was no response.

Natasha ran her drone close to my mount. She was trying to look everywhere at once. There were still at least ten of the big machines moving around, eating the guts out of their friends.

"Just blow a hole in it," she said. "They might be too weak to respond."

"If I do that, I might kill some of them. This atmosphere is mildly toxic, and this might be their only pressurized refuge."

"Well, do something fast. Our refined metal is the most delicious thing in this region. To the machines, we're like walking chocolate bars."

Chuckling, I balled my fist and tapped an unmistakable pattern on the dome. *TAP-tap-tap-tap-tap-TAP-TAP.*

"What's that?" Natasha asked. "Morse?"

"Nah. It's what my grandpa used to call 'shave and a haircut, two bits.'"

I repeated the sequence several times, and at last the polymer dome rolled open. Inside were worried looking troopers with guns lifted toward our faces. The woman in the lead was the centurion of a light unit. She had a breastplate and rifle, but no full armor. Fortunately, her vac suit appeared to be in good condition, if a little dirty.

"Legion Varus," I said.

The centurion waved us into her den. "Come on in, Varus," she said. "Move fast."

We rushed inside, and when the last dragon tail was tucked underground, the small dome rolled shut again.

"Don't use radio," the centurion urged me.

"Don't worry. We already tried that."

"I'm surprised you survived."

We demonstrated our spinal cannons. She looked them over appreciatively. "We don't have much in the way of heavy weaponry. A few specialists with belchers that still operate, that's it. Snap rifles don't even get their attention."

I nodded, thinking it over. Light troops would be hard pressed to damage this enemy. The machines were just too big and too tough.

"My apologies for taking so long to get here, sir," I told the Centurion.

She looked at me for a second. "We didn't honestly think anyone would come. I'm Centurion Belter."

"Veteran McGill." I introduced my specialists, Natasha and Sargon. We checked on the status of the surviving group. It was pretty good, all things considered. They had supplies and weapons. The injured had already died out, which made things simpler.

"Do you have a confirmation list?" Natasha asked.

Grim-faced, Centurion Belter touched her tapper to Natasha's. "That's it. We've lost a lot more however, I'm sure of it."

"How many people do you have hiding down here?" I asked.

"There are a few other groups like this one. Altogether, I would say there's more than a full cohort. Fortunately, the caverns are huge. We think smaller machines burrowed these tunnels years back."

I whistled. Somewhere between eighty and ninety percent casualties. Solstice hadn't been wiped, but it had been a damned close thing.

"We've been trying to tunnel our way out," Belter explained. "That's been the survival plan all along. The trouble is the ground is full of metals and hard to dig through. We managed to connect tunnels with some the other survivors in these caverns, but that's all we could do."

I thought about the surrounding cliffs of metallic ore. There wasn't much chance the legionnaires could dig through the walls of the valley to safety. It was too far, and the earth was too dense.

"We killed most of the machines," I said. "I suggest you get your people together and follow us out. Our dragons can kill these machines with focused fire."

She shook her head. "It's too late for that tonight," she said. "Nightfall is coming soon. That's when most of them show up."

Staring at her for a few seconds, I blinked, then narrowed my eyes. "Are you saying the thirty-odd machines we encountered isn't all of them?"

Centurion Belter laughed. "Thirty machines? No, that's like low-tide around here. Tonight, there will be three hundred. Maybe more after the word gets out that there are freshly dead machine carcasses to feed on. You see, we've managed to make small breakout attacks before, but it's always caused more machines to show up."

"Uh…maybe we should get out of here right now."

She checked her tapper. "Too late for that. In fact, you'd better warn the rest of your unit to come down here to hide. They'll be all around us in these spikes, crawling in to feed at this spot. It's like a watering hole for them—high grade ore walls and all. That's why we've been trapped here, not daring to leave."

Without jawing anymore about it, I retreated to the surface. Sure enough, I could see fresh machines coming in over the lips of the valley walls. Racing my dragon up to where Graves waited, I informed him personally.

"We've got to tell Winslade about this, sir," I said.

"What the hell have you gotten us into now, McGill?"

"I didn't make these crazy machines, Centurion."

"No, but you helped ring the dinner bell! Yes, I heard about that, never mind from who." He sighed and tried to think. "All right," he said after a moment. "I'm sending a courier now. Stand by."

In the end, Winslade arrived to see the enemy massing all around us. There were twenty machines roaming the valley, gorging themselves on refined metals. I could tell from the look in his eye that he was worried. He was a hog, not a true fighting man. Death wasn't a normal part of existence to his desk-flying kind.

"How many did Centurion Belter say were coming?" he asked me.

"Hundreds, sir."

"We can't rescue the Solstice troopers," he said decisively. "We don't have time, and we can't outrun these machines if we're babysitting troops."

"Your orders, Primus?" Graves asked.

"Get ready to pull out," Winslade replied.

We did as he ordered—but we didn't make it. The machines had been gathering slowly and steadily, but as darkness fell over the badlands, they came on in a surge. They were all around us in the gullies and slithering over the hills, moving in from every direction toward our location. They were coming home to sleep, or feed, or mate, or whatever. It didn't really matter. We were surrounded.

141

In the end, we had to race down into the valley and stash ourselves in the caverns. The machines gave chase, but after we blasted a few and closed the polymer domes, they gave up. To them, plastic was a strange, possibly nasty-tasting material. They avoided it, and we were left in peace.

Except that we were trapped underground, along with the survivors of Legion Solstice.

Winslade chanced a powerful transmission up into space the next morning when most of the machines had retreated. We'd hooked up a transceiver just outside of a tunnel mouth and blasted a high-powered compressed message up into space. The message reported our situation to Turov, who had left the surface and returned to her ships.

On the planet, a fair-sized group of officers and noncoms had gathered in one of the central chambers. Overhead, the roof of the place glittered with nodules of ore and embedded crystals. We hadn't really gathered for any formal purpose. Leaders tended to clump up together to plan and talk. We hadn't known what else to do. For the most part, we were waiting on the word from above.

Winslade was out of his depth, I think. He hadn't put forward any comprehensible plans of his own other than to guard the entrances and wait out the night.

Winslade and Turov conversed privately. He was the only one who could hear what she said. When Winslade closed the com channel, his face was even whiter than usual.

"They're going to use the broadsides," he told us with a flickering smile. "They're going to smash these machines all at once!"

I knew right off why he was sweating. A murmur swept the room. Overhead, the ceiling sent spills of dust down into our faces. The machines, stirred up by his transmission, were rioting, tearing at the ground. I hoped they couldn't get through, or at least that they would get bored and give up before they managed to dig deeply enough. There were, by reported count, more than a hundred of them hanging around tonight. More arrived every hour.

"The big guns?" asked Graves. "Fusion-powered shells landing right here, on top of us?"

"That's exactly what I mean," Winslade said.

"Primus?" I said, speaking up in the stunned silence that followed Winslade's announcement.

"What is it, McGill?" Winslade asked with a resigned voice. He was tapping at his tablet.

"Sir, such a move might well kill everyone in this room."

Winslade's eyeballs slid sideways from his tablet to look at me. "That is supposition, Veteran. This is an officer's meeting, and I would appreciate it if—"

"Sir?" I asked, interrupting him again. I was going for broke, but hell, I figured we were all about to die anyway. "Can you and I have a private word, sir? I might be able to help."

Winslade eyed me quietly. I stared back.

He had to know what I was thinking. I had a special connection with Turov. He knew that—everyone did.

"Dismissed!" he said, waving us away.

I hung around as the officers filtered out. Graves passed me and gave me a flat frown. He shook his head slightly, discouragingly. In return, I gave him a smile and a bright nod. Sighing, he left.

Winslade's eyeballs slid to me again when the last man had vacated the chamber. "I meant you too, Veteran," he said.

"Sorry Primus, I misunderstood. But can I say one thing?"

"If you must."

"Those broadsides—have you seen them fire on a planet before, sir?" I asked. "I was in *Minotaur's* tactical fire control center when we bombarded Tech World, and do you know what? If those shells come arcing down into this general vicinity, we're all paste."

"You may be correct, but that's not our decision to make."

"Oh sure," I said, "the fleet people might get around to reviving all of us eventually. But what do you think will

144

happen to your auxiliary cohort if all the dragons are destroyed? Do you think the hog brass will give you a budget to buy a hundred new ones? Might it not be easier—and much cheaper—to disband your command and call it a bad idea?"

Winslade grimly watched me as I mouthed these damning words. He'd never been a man with a pleasant expression, but if looks could kill, I'd have been struck dead.

"Don't you think I know that, McGill?" he hissed. "Is this private discussion just an excuse for you to gloat before we're all blown to atoms?"

"No sir, I'm trying to solve our mutual problem."

"Which is?"

"Turov, of course. Are you aware I have a special relationship with her? I might be able to put in a good word."

He chewed his lower lip for a second. It was an ugly thing to watch a man do.

"Why not?" he said. "It will stir up the machines, but they're tearing up the landscape anyway. Let's call her."

He used his private com unit to contact Turov, then handed me the headset.

She didn't answer right off—but I let the channel request continue beeping in her ear. If any other noncom had pulled this stunt, they'd have been up for a court martial by the end of the day. But Turov and I had a connection that I was willing to gamble on.

"What is it, Winslade?" she answered finally. "I have command preparations to make. You can't simply contact me whenever you wish—it's unseemly."

"Uh…yes, Imperator. This is Veteran James McGill, sir. I apologize, sir, but this is quite literally a matter of life and death."

"McGill?" she asked incredulously. "What are you talking about?"

"Have you ever seen the impact point of a barrage from one of these warships, Imperator? Well I have—three times in fact, if you include the bombardment of the squid moon base in this system. In fact, I've aimed and fired them myself more than once. I think I'm the only human in existence who can make that claim."

145

She was silent for a second. I figured she was probably seething.

"That's not officially acceptable information, Veteran," she said. It sounded like her words were coming out between clenched teeth.

The "officially acceptable information" she was referring to was a lie she and I had cooked up back on Tech World. It was generally known I'd been involved in the firing of *Minotaur's* broadsides—but Turov's official story to the brass had left my significant role out. She liked to pretend it was all her idea to fire the big guns.

Actually, our arrangement had been more of a mutually beneficial bargain than a plan. A plan, to my way of thinking, required forethought and…well, planning. We'd made our deal in the heat of desperation.

For all it's flaws, the arrangement had kept me from being permed for misconduct while it gave her the Galactic key. Almost as important, it misled everyone who cared into believing I'd fired *Minotaur's* big guns under her orders.

It was a fiction that had benefited us both for over a year now. If it ever got out that a minor subordinate under her command had changed the course of a battle—and possibly all human history—her career would've been toast. She and I had always pretended my firing of the broadsides at the squid ship was part of her grand scheme—part of her innovative boldness.

"How did you get Winslade's com-set, anyway?" she demanded.

"I borrowed it, sir. Anyway, back to the broadsides—I'm telling the truth, and we both know it. We've seen what these weapons can do. You have to know that the two surviving cohorts down here will die in the blast along with the enemy machines."

"You're correct," she said after a quiet pause. "We'll wait until after midnight when all the machines show up. We'll even send back and forth some radio signals to get them stirred up. I admit that some damage may be sustained due to friendly fire. The machines are so well stacked up, however, we can't afford to miss this opportunity to wipe them all out."

"But you can't use those weapons *here*, sir. They'll destroy everything. I don't think Winslade's cohort would even survive."

"You're wrong. Our techs have done the math. You're sheltering at a considerable depth."

"Sir, we're underground. This land is highly metallic and will carry a seismic disturbance a long way. A cave-in is guaranteed. We'll be crushed."

She was silent again for a second. I had the feeling she was consulting with someone else. "Why are you bringing this to me now?" she demanded. "Is Winslade behind your complaints? Is he hiding in that hole with you?"

I glanced at Winslade. He slowly shook his head.

"This is all me, sir," I told Turov. "Hold your fire. We think we can break out of this mess."

"How?"

"Commit the lifters, sir. We only need three of them. Just think, if the dragons are all wiped out—damn, that's a lot of expensive hardware destroyed. You'll have to explain the loss to Hegemony. After losing *Pegasus*, the bill for this campaign must be pretty high already."

"You want me to risk three lifters to save your sorry ass a death, is that it?"

"It would be the considerate thing to do, sir."

"Do I hear a threat?" she asked suddenly. "You're implying you'll talk about our prior dealings if I don't comply, correct?"

This turn in the conversation startled me. I hadn't been implying anything of the kind. I'd been more hoping to persuade her to see reason than trying to apply pressure.

"No sir, I—"

"That won't work, McGill. All I have to do is withhold your revival indefinitely. After a week, your data could be quietly lost. Regrettable, but it's happened before."

"Told you it wouldn't work," Winslade said quietly.

I glanced at him. He'd either been listening in on my conversation, or he was pretty good at reading my disappointed facial expressions.

I was finally getting mad at Turov. This woman suspected everyone of skullduggery just because she was so good at it herself.

"Listen Imperator," I said, "I'm not threatening you with anything. Our secrets are safe. What I'm suggesting is a way out of this. Don't risk the bombardment. Those broadsides will tear a hole in this planet's crust. You might lose everything. What if the squids show up again after that?"

She was quiet again.

"I get it," she said. "I understand your confidence now. You would not dare to threaten me if you didn't have an ace in the hole, as they say. I haven't forgotten your maneuvering during the elections last year. You must have friends in Varus and aboard my ships. People who will blackmail me to get you revived. I hadn't thought you would—never mind."

I hardly knew what she was talking about. People often attributed near god-like powers to me, but honestly, I only half knew what the heck I was doing most of the time.

But what I did glean from her little monologue was that she was nervous. People who have something to protect can be manipulated by threatening the precious thing they hold so dear. In Turov's case, her downfall was her career. It had been put together on shaky ground, and I knew there were plenty of people who wanted to see her fall. If you were to ask me, I'd say she'd become a bit paranoid about it.

The opportunist in me moved quickly to capitalize on her state of mind. "Well sir, there's an easy way out of all your worries. Just send us the three lifters."

"You want me to risk more invaluable assets?" she demanded. "Fine. But you'll get only one lifter, not three. And I'll only wait four hours for you to complete the evacuation. Tell Winslade that—I can hear him shivering nearby. After four hours, I'm going to fire the big guns and obliterate the region!"

"Thank you, sir!" I said, but she'd already closed the channel.

I gave Winslade a big grin. "She went for it."

"I heard. *One* lifter? That's never going to be enough. We've got a full cohort of exhausted troops and a cohort of heavy cavalry."

Blinking, I nodded. The sneaky bastard *had* been listening in. I had no idea how he'd done it.

"Well sir," I said. "I'll give up my jump seat to a Solstice man if you'll give up yours. Sure, it'll be a squeeze, but if we shove a few units into the top section and stack them up in the officers' quarters, we'll make out."

Winslade looked put out but resigned. "More likely, we'll lose half our men breaking out. That will solve all our weight problems."

I nodded. I'd been thinking that too, but didn't want to say it out loud.

As we prepared for our exodus, I wondered about the bargain I'd made with Turov. From her point of view, I'd blackmailed her. That would probably cost me later on.

Part of my private motivation was to save machine lives as well as human lives. I didn't think they deserved mass extinction, and I still held out hope we could make friends with them at some point.

I hoped these frigging machines would appreciate the effort eventually, but I didn't think they ever would.

-21-

It all went down fast and furious once the lifter gave us the go-code. The lifter pilot hadn't landed yet, mind you, he was letting his clumsy craft drift down toward the LZ, checking out every inch of ground for machines. Watching the operation unfold on the command screens, I could tell the crew wasn't keen on landing in the middle of a pile of giant hungry machines, any one of which was a quarter the size of the lifter itself. That would have been akin to ringing the dinner bell again, and I couldn't blame them for being worried. All that refined metal in one digestible package? They'd be eaten alive—literally.

Winslade began quietly filtering troops out onto the valley floor. For about five minutes, we got away with it. By that time, two full units were out there, one of cavalry and one Solstice unit of infantry. I wasn't sure exactly what the infantry was supposed to do, but I hoped their weaponeers could put some hurt downrange with their belchers if the machines charged us.

For once, I wasn't in the front-line formation. My squad, along with the rest of Graves' unit, was queued up to come out next. We were supposed to sneak out there quietly and hide in a fold of the land, out of sight from the machines—but we never got to that point.

The sneaking ended when somebody transmitted something. We'd all been told to silence our transmissions, of course. We were to run silent, keeping every signal muted. We weren't even supposed to use our suit-to-suit intercoms. But somebody, out of the hundreds, had screwed up. It was bound to happen in a large nervous formation of troops. Hell, some of us couldn't remember to silence our tappers when we went to the movies.

The machines froze. All across the valley, they'd been scooting randomly over the walls between us and the badlands. They all stopped moving for about a second, then reversed themselves. My squad was next in line to come out of our particular hole at that point, and I was provided a front-row seat on the action.

"That's it!" Graves shouted. "Calvary, forward! We'll take up the left flank, right where that big one is bearing down on the infantry. I want each squad to pick a target and take it down. Move!"

We thundered out of the tunnels. Finding themselves underfoot, the Solstice infantry scattered, throwing themselves out of the way of our grinding rush. One down-stroke from my dragon's legs would squash an unarmored trooper as flat as a flapjack.

We couldn't afford to pussy-foot around and make the infantry feel good about themselves this time. They were secondary, and everyone knew it.

My squad followed right behind me. We thundered up a small fold in the land, lining up on top of it. The formation was a strange one as we were operating under the assumption the enemy had no ballistic weaponry of their own. Instead of taking cover and choosing firing positions we knew were safe, we'd opted for maximum viewing range. I felt exposed, and I hoped it wouldn't matter. All Graves' cared about was providing every dragon with a clear line of sight to the approaching enemy.

It was uncanny to watch the machines decide as a single mass to charge our position. The machines didn't spin around—instead they sort of reshaped themselves into metal mounds that leaned in our direction rather than away from us. Like teardrops of mercury, they shunted and shivered their way down the walls of the canyon with new purpose. They came from every direction, and they looked determined.

151

Graves' sudden move placed us in the middle of the action with startling speed. The other cavalry unit that had already been deployed took their time adjusting themselves. They took aim and let loose. They fired first, but they only beat us by about ten seconds.

"Squad, I'm marking our target," I said. "Use your computer-aided targeting. Follow my lead—and don't miss!"

When the target reticle changed from red to green, I squeezed the triggers in my gauntlets. The air cracked, and I could feel the vibration of the big cannon's recoil throughout my machine. Dragons unloaded their spinal cannons on every side of me moments later, and minor secondary shockwaves set my machine swaying. Being on two legs, dragons weren't as stable as wheeled or tracked vehicles, but the gyros whined and motors fought to compensate automatically. My aim would have been spoiled if it wasn't for these computer-guided adjustments.

The opening shells hammered the outer hull of my chosen target machine, punching through that first critical hole. The rest of my squad piled on, nailing the machine I'd painted with plenty more explosive power. The machine was gutted and went into an odd spin for a few seconds before it went down.

More and more were coming, however. We'd waited too long, I realized. It was close to dark, and the lifter should have landed at high noon. The main herd of machines was coming back to feed, and the commotion of battle would surely bring more of them. They didn't seem to have much in the way of fear circuitry. The only time I'd witnessed hesitation in one of them was when we'd met up with the mama machine back near the river. Maybe they behaved differently when protecting young. Other than in that instance, the machines were always eager to feed on fresh metals.

Before the third unit of cavalry was in position to join the fight, our unit had taken out three machines. The other deployed unit had only nailed one. I knew that Graves had told his fellow centurions about focusing all their fire on a single spot on a single machine, but it looked like his peers hadn't taken the suggestion to heart. They were spamming all the machines with fire. Anyone who had a good shot took it. As a result, there were a number of machines approaching us that were damaged and smoking, but they were still in the fight.

I did note a new behavior among the damaged machines, the ones that were still approaching—they were spinning. Going around and around like wheels on a tram. They were becoming flatter, too. That was a puzzle, but there wasn't really any time to worry about it. We had our own problems.

We'd knocked out a number of the enemy, but we weren't doing it fast enough. About ten of them were getting too close.

That's when I heard a whistle and the Solstice infantry around me surged forward. I'd pretty much ignored them up until now. They were helpless in my opinion—but I soon found out I was wrong.

I saw Centurion Belter. She was a dozen meters away, directing her troops on the front line personally. When one of the machines got within a hundred meters, she shouted to Graves.

"We'll take that one!"

Graves' dragon waved a gripper, indicating it was all hers. I noticed that the intended target had started spinning as well— what was that all about? Clearly, they were doing it on purpose. It took a long second, while a dozen light troops surged forward at Centurion Belter's orders, for me to realize *why* they were spinning.

The behavior had to be intended to make it harder to group our shells. I could tell it was working when we targeted our next machine. They were all spinning now, and I found we couldn't punch through the armor as easily. We tried—but failed to stop the machine in a single salvo. The tactic showed an alarming ability to adapt and reason. When they spun, our attacks were nowhere near as effective.

I ordered my squad to extend force-blades. The machine that was bearing down on us wasn't dying peacefully. I felt that it was our duty to stand on our chosen ridge of land and protect the infantry.

Centurion Belter had different ideas. I wanted to shout at her to bring her troops back behind my line—but I didn't. She outranked me, and if she wanted to watch her people die bravely, well, that was her own damned business.

When her troops got to the machine, they threw themselves on their backs, letting it lift its skirt and slide right over them. A bluish glow came from every man thus consumed.

That's when I caught on. They'd been issued grav-plasma grenades. Strange blue-glowing weapons, the grenades didn't work like normal fragmentation explosives. Instead, they gathered up loose surrounding material and then fired it outward with fantastic force. Even water could be turned into a weapon by transforming a puddle into a thousand needles that punched through everything nearby.

The men who went under the machine released their grenades inside the guts of the monster. The effects were dramatic. It stopped spinning, flew off-kilter and sagged. Whatever control mechanism inside kept it moving had died. Mindless, it flopped, shivered, and turned into a smoking wreck.

About half the troops who'd been sent under those skirts managed to crawl back out again. I was impressed by Solstice bravery, having never seen them in action before.

Unfortunately, our efforts hadn't impressed one critical person: the commander of the lifter that was about to land in our midst. We'd done our best to form a circle around the LZ and keep it clear, but there had been breaches. In fact, one of the machines was right there, trying to eat a trio of dragons that it had managed to knock flat.

"Sir!" I shouted to Graves, who was pretty close to my position. "We've got a breach behind us."

"Keep your eyes on your designated targets, McGill. The breach is someone else's problem."

"But sir, the lifter has changed course. I think he's going to land up on the canyon wall."

Graves looked and cursed. "That idiot! McGill, this is a priority directive. All of this fighting is for nothing if the machines take out that lifter. We'll never get out of this valley alive—none of us."

"I got that, Centurion. What do you want me to do?"

"Run your squad up to the lifter. Keep the machines off it until our column can move to support. We can't all run up there now. We'd lose our front line, and the enemy would overwhelm us."

"Roger sir, on my way!"

My squad wheeled and charged uphill after me a moment later. My troops followed me without a single complaint. I figured that was probably because Carlos was already dead. No one had revived him and returned him to my squadron yet—and I couldn't blame them.

We thundered up the steep slope to a plateau where the lifter seemed to be coming down. Sure, the plateau wasn't full of machines at the moment, but once they detected that massive structure of refined metals landing, I was sure they'd flock to the spot. Instead of choosing a safer landing spot, the pilot had ensured that we couldn't protect him.

When we reached the venting lifter and ran around the base of its massive skids, the first of the machines arrived. It wasn't the biggest I'd ever seen, but it was undamaged, and it was spinning.

The fight with this lone machine was brief, but violent. We blasted it all at once at point-blank range. The machine twirled away and crashed down in the valley below.

Making a quick decision I chose a spot near the aft of the lifter to make our stand. I'd no sooner gotten there than I was surprised by a new development. The lifter crew contacted me directly.

"Cavalry squadron, that area is restricted."

The words rang in my helmet. It was a shock since we were supposed to be observing radio silence. Down in the mess of the valley, where a pitched battle was ongoing, I could understand such a breach. But up here, well, we didn't want any new company.

There were no more transmissions for a few seconds as I didn't want to reply and thus create a further breach of my orders. This didn't sit well with the lifter crew.

"This is lifter zero-niner. Are you deaf? Get away from my exhaust ports. If I need to run, I want—"

"Excuse me, sir," I interrupted. "This is a no-transmission zone. You're endangering everyone in the region. Maintain radio silence. Veteran McGill, out."

He shut up after that, and we moved to another spot farther from his jets. I'd just begun to hope that the machines were too busy with the mess in the valley to take notice when the next one showed up, humping over the frosty land like it was late for dinner—which, in a way, I supposed it was.

"Fire on my mark…mark!"

We let loose on the machine and took it down. But it was already too late. A half-dozen more were scooting toward us out of the spikes and boulders.

"Vet," Sargon shouted nearby, "the lifter has put down her ramp. The infantry are boarding."

I took a second to look, and I saw he was right. Graves, Belter and a few other centurions were holding the line in the valley. The rest of the troops, both striding cavalry inside their dragons and the scrambling light troops, were flowing up to our position out of the tunnels. They were moving fast, but not quite in a panic. The lifter ramp had been deployed— the pilot had finally grown a set and committed. I had to give him that much.

Looking back at the approaching machines, I made a grim decision.

"Squad, ADVANCE!" I roared, making my own ears ring in my helmet. I wanted to make sure they heard me over the roar of battle. External speakers allowed me to send my voice booming around me.

Leading the way, I approached the nearest machine, leaving the shadow of the lifter behind. It had just begun to spin when my squad blew it apart.

"Advance!" I shouted again. I have to give my people credit, not one of them disobeyed or asked me if I'd lost my ever-loving mind. They just followed me from one lonely pile of rocks to the next.

The enemy machines were rushing in piecemeal. They were focused on the lifter still, not us. That was not what I wanted, so I opened up my radio. I turned on every channel and broadcast to the entire cohort—hell, I bet they could've heard me up on the big ships above the permanent cloud cover if they were listening.

"Centurion Graves, we're breaking radio-silence to lead the enemy machines away from the lifter. Please don't respond. This is Veteran James McGill, and I'll now serenade you with my best rendition of the *Battle Hymn of the Republic*."

With that, I began to sing. Now, I'll be the first to admit that I'm no songbird. Anyone who'd had the misfortune to attend the same church service I did back on Earth could have told you that. But what I might lack in the area of musical prowess, I more than make up for in sheer volume.

It was an old song, an illegal song in public places on Earth since Hegemony felt it stirred up rebels in certain districts. But I'd always liked it, and I could remember most of the words.

And so I sang—to the legions and to the machines—until the machines were on top of us. We killed two right off, but the next three reached us all at once—about the same time I hit that line about making men holy and letting us die to make men free—when we were knocked down and stomped flat.

Under that last machine, this copy of James McGill made his peace and fired his spinal cannon at suicidally close range.

The concussion killed me, but the machine died as well. My squad, my first command—we were all dead.

-22-

It had been a long time since I'd died and been revived. As such things go, this one was probably the best I'd ever experienced. I returned to life with a gasp and a wheeze, but once I could breathe easily, I found myself to be in an oddly cheerful mood.

"He's a good grow," Bio Specialist Anne Grant announced. She was the chief operator of our cohort's revival equipment. As part of Legion Varus and usually assigned to Graves' command, she'd come along when the rest of us had joined Winslade's cavalry.

I knew Anne's voice instantly. She was an angel to my addled mind. She'd presided over my birth a dozen times more than my own mother had. I considered the woman to be something of a godmother.

My eyes fluttered open. My vision was beyond blurred. Freshly-grown optical nerves were dazzled by light, which they'd never experienced before. My focusing muscles didn't know their jobs either. I struggled to peer up into her face anyway, and I managed it at last. She had severely short dark hair and small features. Her eyes were careworn, but her face was pretty.

Smiling, I coughed, cleared my throat, and then remembered something.

Once, on a different world, a different James McGill had asked this girl for a dinner date. We'd never had that date. Partly, it had been because all hell had broken loose on Tech

World after we'd decided to get together. Unfortunately, there'd also been a number of other females around who'd objected, thus spoiling the mood.

Today, as far as I knew, no woman thought she owned me. Those that had once loved me had long since given up. I'd managed not to get entangled with anyone new on this campaign, probably due to the fact that my promotion and new training had kept me too busy for simple pleasures—or even complicated ones.

But now, eyeing Anne with a clarity of vision that improved every second, I knew what I wanted to do.

"You know what, Anne?" I asked.

"What is it, James?"

"You look harried and rushed, but you're still beautiful to me."

She'd been fussing with IVs and straps, but she paused and stared at me for a second. "Really James? Now? You're going to make a play for the first woman you see—*now?*"

"Uh...the battle's over, right?"

"Yes. You're back aboard *Cyclops*. Legion Varus and what's left of Solstice have all been recalled. But we're redeploying again soon. It's been several days since you died— sorry we didn't get around to your file faster."

"It's okay, I understand. In fact—you know what? I think I've experienced my best death yet. I feel better about things today. I'm alive again, and my last body died well. It was probably the best job of dying I've ever done."

She looked at me oddly and checked my stats again. Maybe she thought I was cracking up, but I didn't care. I really felt great.

Sitting up and stretching, I took a series of deep breaths.

"So, what about it?" I asked her.

"What about what?"

"You owe me a date. Remember?"

Her face clouded, but I kept grinning at her. Finally, she laughed. "You are incorrigible."

"Every man has to reach for the brass ring in his own way. At least, that's what my grandpa used to say."

"Did you really die singing some old war song?"

159

"Yes," I said. "That's probably what made the machines mob us. My singing is pretty bad. By the way, did the evac go smoothly afterward?"

"Well, I wouldn't call it smooth, but about eighty percent of the troops trapped in that valley made it out. The lifter could hardly fly by the time they boarded up."

I laughed. "What about Graves? Did he make it out?"

"No. He fought to the end, the same as you did. Centurion Belter died as well. They've both been revived already."

"What about—" I took a sly look around, seeing no one was listening, I continued, "what about that slippery weasel Winslade?"

"He made it to safety and was air-lifted out," she confirmed, making a face.

"I figured."

I looked down, thinking about the battle again. I'd thought of another person to ask about: Della. But I didn't want to mention that name in front of Anne and freak her out all over again. I'd have to check on Della's status later.

Anne must have seen the serious look on my face, because she touched my hand.

"Don't let that smile you had fade, James. It's so rare to see a man come back happy."

"You know how to fix me," I said.

She sighed. "All right. We've got a date. We'd better hurry, though. We've got a curse hanging over us in that department. Don't forget this time—or start some new war."

"I swear I won't—and hope to die," I said, smiling again.

The rest of the day on the ship went relatively smoothly. Those of us who had lost our dragons had been issued newly refurbished mounts, and best of all we'd been given a full twenty-four hour leave. That was a rare reprieve for a man in the legions in the midst of a campaign. I knew it wasn't because we'd earned it. The officers just hadn't gotten our troop strengths up enough to redeploy us yet. But I appreciated the break, nonetheless.

Anne and I headed to Green Deck to have a picnic. We shared our battle-rations as part of our dinner date. To flavor it up, I found a few packets of food from home that I'd left

160

behind in my locker the last time we'd been ordered to evacuate in a rush. It wasn't much, just a pile of almonds, dried peaches and a few squeeze-bottles of wine. But compared to the insta-hot beige paste the processers were feeding people today, it was pretty good.

"This is so strange," Anne said, sitting on the grass in twilight, "we were down on that nasty, stinking planet for weeks. Now, we're up here enjoying Green Deck."

"Did you die down there?" I asked.

"No. I was never in battle like the rest of you. I stayed back at the base camp with most of the lifters until Turov recalled us all."

"Do you know why they pulled everyone back into space?"

"Well, not exactly, but I think they found another target to attack. Last time, we were just dumping troops on the planet in case the ships were knocked out. Better to get them on the ground than to lose them all. But now there's more of a plan, I gather. The command people have figured out a goal and want to do it right this time."

"That's exactly what I was thinking," I said, reaching out a hand to touch her forearm for a moment. "I mean the part about having a plan and wanting to do things right."

It took a second for Anne to figure out that I was talking about her. She shook her head and smiled.

"Charming," she said. "That's what the ladies all say about you. That you're charming for a date or two then you wander off and forget their names."

"That's a dirty lie!" I complained. "I've never forgotten the name of the girl I'm going out with."

"Okay, okay—but you know what I'm talking about."

"This is just a nice dinner, that's all," I said. "Why do people have to make these things so complicated? Let's talk about something else."

I managed to get her off the topic of my dating habits and our get-together improved. We had a little wine, kissed, and walked around past other couples who were seeking privacy.

Finally, she stopped and looked up at me. "I know what you want, James," she said. "But this doesn't feel right. This place is so artificial. You know that they built it just to let us relieve stress on a campaign?"

"Seems like a damned good idea to me. Just like a nice park in a small town."

"Yes, but…I don't know. It doesn't feel right to me."

"Okay. You want to go back to our quarters?"

"That's not any more romantic!"

I was confused. She'd pretty much said it was over, so I'd figured she wanted to go home.

"Hey," I said, "let me show you something."

I took her down to the little canyon with the waterfall and the lake. There were a few people down there, but not too many. I showed her where I'd fought for my life against the other candidates and veterans of our unit. She seemed honestly impressed.

"You killed *all* of them?"

"Nah, not exactly. Some of them killed each other. I just finished off the last few that were still alive."

"That's so gruesome. To tear each other apart, just to prove who's top dog. As a bio, that's the last thing I'd want to see."

"It's supposed to be a secret contest, so you'll probably never have to see one of these dog-fights in person."

"The officers went along with this barbaric ritual?" she asked, still eyeing the battleground. She might have been looking for old bloodstains, but they'd long since washed away in the artificial rains.

"They sure did. They stood up there on the path and watched."

She squinted in the gloom, eyeing the rocks and the lapping water. The waterfall never let the bubbling surface of the lake smooth over.

"You know," she said thoughtfully. "They turn all this off when we get into battle or engage the warp drive. They drain the water back down into tanks and turn off the pumps. Even the rocks are anchored in case we lose centrifugal gravity or—"

I was laughing, so she stopped.

"You remind me of Natasha," I said. "You're always trying to figure things out. Look up there! Those are *real* stars

162

tonight, not projections like when we're in a warp bubble. Are those good enough for you?"

Anne was miffed, but she got over it. "I'm sorry," she said. "I'm not good on dates. I don't know what to do. I haven't gone out with anyone for years."

Putting a hand on her shoulder, I smiled at her. "You're doing fine," I said. "No worries. I'm having a good time. I've felt great since I came up off that table and saw your pretty face."

"That reminds me. Why did you wake up happy? You never told me."

I shrugged. "I think it was because I *decided* to die this time. I decided to take as many machines down as I could. My aim was to draw them to me and go down fighting. It was all for a good cause, too. The Solstice people had had a pretty rough time of it. I thought I'd let the last thousand or so of them escape. The move saved a lot of equipment as well."

"Okay, you died bravely on purpose. That made you happy?"

"It wasn't just that. Allowing most of the troops to escape saved a lot of the alien machines, too. Turov was planning to bombard the place with the broadsides from space. She'd decided to kill a thousand machines all at once—and us with them. But since we got away, there was no need. Maybe, in a decade or two, those machines will become our allies."

"That seems pretty far-fetched. They're like animals from what I've seen and heard."

"No, they're more intelligent than that." I described my communications with one of their younger members to her and explained my theory that the smaller ones were smarter or at least more reasonable to interact with.

"That's fascinating," she said. "You actually talked to them, and one of them traveled to give you a message? To tell you that they were working with the squids?"

"Yeah," I said, "but keep that part quiet, would you? I think Turov will bomb them for sure if she finds out."

"Why should you care?"

I shrugged. "Graves says that machine life is just one more possible form. We're biological, based on carbon and water.

163

They're different, but this is their planet, and they live here. Who are we to exterminate them without a good reason?"

She nodded thoughtfully. I stroked her hair, but she didn't even seem to notice.

"I didn't think you had thoughts like this, James," she said. "You surprise me, sometimes."

Her words were slightly offensive, but I didn't mind. At least her opinion of me was going in the right direction.

"I think I know what the ladies find attractive about you," she said at last, giving me a frankly appraising look. "There's more to you than meets the eye."

"Uh…does that mean?"

"I don't know. You've been with so many other women, it's disturbing."

My eyes wanted to roll, but I didn't let them. Plenty of guys had been with half the girls in the unit. But I think my affairs tended to be more high-profile, and somehow I'd gotten a rep. Shrugging, I walked off around the shore of the tiny lake.

After a few seconds, she followed me. I led her to the waterfall. There was a small alcove back there where everything was wet with mist. This was the spot where the fireplug lady and the guy with Harris' gun fought to the death—but I was smart enough not to mention that to Anne.

"This is lovely," she said. "I've never been back here."

"You know," I said, "this body of mine has never been with another woman. I'm a fresh grow. You said it yourself."

"That's right," she laughed. "Come to think of it, my body is virgin too."

That did it, I think. She finally relaxed, and we had a good time back there behind the waterfall. Afterward, we enjoyed the temperature-controlled perfection of our simulated environment. It didn't bug me that some engineers had put this place together, planning out our natural activities. Why should it? Every bed in the world had been put together by someone expecting someone else to make love on it. Where was the harm in that?

My reverie was cut short, unfortunately. The first sign of trouble was the waterfall. It stopped falling. The water just turned into a dribble, then vanished altogether.

We sat up, looking in surprise at the lake. It was disappearing, being sucked down into a dark circular drain at the bottom.

"Looks like trouble," I said.

Anne didn't answer. She threw her clothes over herself and let the smart cloth sort out the details. I followed her, both of us half-naked, as we rushed out of there and up the path to the top of the canyon walls.

She worked her tapper, and I couldn't help but notice it was blinking red. So was mine. We'd been summoned to battle stations.

-23-

Somewhere in the officers' command center on Gold Deck, Turov had decided it was time to have a crisis. At first, I was of the opinion that she'd had a hard night without sleep, and she wanted to share the pain. But I was wrong. She wasn't launching this attack—the squids were.

"Listen up, troops," Graves' voice buzzed out of my tapper. I didn't have my helmet with me, but my tapper could carry voice if it had to. "We've got incoming ships," he said. "Their design indicates two of them are enemy vessels. They emerged out of a warp bubble in-system which suggests hostile intent. I want everyone to get to battle stations, fully geared. We might have to repel boarding attempts—or abandon ship."

"Crap," I said aloud. "See you on the other side, Anne!"

She caught my arm before I could run off. She gave me a single lingering kiss then disappeared without a word. She was going to Blue Deck, I knew. As a bio, her place was among her own kind. If there was going to be a battle, she'd have plenty of cleaning up to do.

I was the very last man in my squad to hop into the cockpit of my dragon and run a systems check on it. Something clanged on my spinal cannon, and I rotated the chassis to see who was screwing with me.

Carlos grinned. He'd bashed me with a gripper. I grinned back.

"It's good to see you breathing again, asshole," he said.

"You better not have dented my new dragon."

"It's all good as long as you can still walk and shoot," he said. "How are we going to die today, Vet?"

"It's going to be squids today," I said with certainty. "All squids, all day."

"I just hope I get a few shots in before they blow up the ship. I'd love to see the shock on their faces when they get a load of the twins." Carlos opened his chest panel and exposed two grenade-launchers.

I smiled at that. I hadn't ordered any equipment changes, but his seemed like a good choice right about now.

As heavy cavalry aboard a ship, we were about as useful as tits on a boar—unless the enemy decided to invade *Cyclops*. In that case, we'd come in handy.

My screens lit up, and I fully expected a grim-faced Graves would appear and order me to head to the lifters.

Instead, it was Imperator Turov. She was making a funny expression, something of a cross between a snarl and a smile.

"Get up to Gold Deck, McGill!" she snapped.

I opened my mouth to ask *why*, but she'd already cut the channel. As a mere veteran, faced with a direct order from a high-level officer, I knew what to do.

"Sargon!" I shouted. "You're in charge of the squad until I return. Tell Graves I've been summoned to Gold Deck."

"Was that Turov?" asked Carlos. "I don't frigging believe it. A booty call? Mid-battle, at midnight? That woman has no shame—and precious little sense of timing."

I could have belted him, but I didn't want to take the time, and he wouldn't have felt it anyway in his dragon.

Rushing out into the passageways, I moved to the AI-driven lifts and rode the first one that noticed me up to Gold Deck. That's where the command people hung out.

Clanking into the command chambers, I think I startled a few people. They were all in regular, soft uniforms. I was pretty much the only guy banging around in a dragon.

"McGill!" Turov shouted. "Get over here."

I stomped over to her position. She was tiny, shapely and standing next to a cool-looking three dimensional display system.

She looked me up and down, frowning.

"You're in full kit?"

"I'm cavalry, sir," I said.

"Right. Never mind. Just look at this."

She gestured toward the battle-display system. Three enemy ships were approaching. Two looked like the ones I'd seen before on Dust World. They were definitely squid-made ships. They were big with a dish-like silver structure at each end. These structures rippled with quiet, powerful, amber light. I knew from experience the dish-things propelled the enemy ships.

The third ship was a puzzle, however. It was a trading ship. I'd recognize the design anywhere. It was built by the Galactic Empire, I was certain of that much. Thousands of such vessels traveled between the worlds, ferrying goods from one planet to the next.

A face loomed then, super-imposed on the display depicting the three orbiting ships. The face was that of a squid, and he looked at us as if curious.

"I am Conqueror Engulf," he said. "Where is the one known as the McGill?"

"I'm here," I said.

Turov frowned at me, but I didn't back down. Hell, if she hadn't expected me to speak up, she shouldn't have invited me to this party.

The strangely intelligent alien eyes swept toward me. The being gave me an appraising glance.

"You are dressed for battle."

"I sure am, you damned squid—!"

"I beg your pardon," Turov interrupted. "Can you tell me why the Kingdom has seen fit to come into our star system today?"

The alien eyes moved from me to Turov. "Your system? Does my translator fail me? It must be so. I will have my technicians boiled in caustic ink. They have caused you humans to utter unthinkable insults into my auditory organs."

My mind burned with come-backs, but I restrained myself.

"You heard correctly," Turov said. "This is our territory. We've claimed Gamma Pavonis and all her orbiting bodies."

"You dare such a conceit?" Engulf asked. "Yes, I see now—our moon base has been destroyed. Inexplicable. You should have perished in combat upon first entering this system. I'll have to apologize to the Crown, and I'll demand that the base commander's family be boiled in ink upon my return to the Throne World."

"The internal affairs of your Kingdom don't concern me," Turov said. "But now that our claim to this star system has been made clear, you must state your business before I can allow you to leave."

The squid made a weird, bubbling noise. I wasn't sure if he was laughing or having a gas-attack.

"You say you've claimed this system? For who have you claimed it? The Empire?"

"No. Earth owns these worlds. About your moon base, however, I must apologize. We were attacked by a few insignificant missiles upon arrival and assumed it was a weak effort at local defense by a native species. We didn't realize the Kingdom was involved as no one identified themselves to us."

"There is no need to apologize for our failure. The commander must have been of poor genetic quality if he allowed your ships to prevail."

Turov swallowed. She looked a little sweaty, but I had to give it to her, she wasn't backing down this time. Maybe she'd grown into her job of high-level command over the last year or two. She still looked like a college girl, but the squid didn't know that.

"You requested McGill," Turov said, changing the subject, "and I've brought him."

The squid flicked his strange eyeballs from one of us to the next. "You mean the McGill-creature is not in command?"

"*I* am in command," Turov said firmly.

"Most unusual. The last transmission from our doomed vessel on Tech World indicated McGill was the one who destroyed them. There must have been some misunderstanding."

I knew I should stay quiet. Don't think I didn't know that. But I've always had trouble with the whole quiet-thing, and it's only gotten worse over the years. Deep down, I wondered sometimes if part of Carlos' DNA had been accidentally mixed in with mine during one of my many revives.

"I talked to your Conqueror," I blurted suddenly, "the squid named Glide. He commanded a ship at Tech World. I like to think I had something to do with his destruction, too. Maybe his family made a mistake and should be deep-fried into calamari the next time you meet up with them."

"Such bold talk," Engulf said. "You control a pathetic handful of worlds. Your Empire is crumbling, and it cannot protect you."

"McGill, *please* shut up," Turov said.

"Yes, Imperator."

She gave the squid her full attention again. "How can we help you, Conqueror?"

"You will speak to our ally. He requested that McGill's presence be verified. You will speak to him now."

Engulf's face dissolved, and as for myself, I couldn't have been happier about that. Squids were ugly and downright creepy to look at.

The next face that appeared on the display was even more surprising, however. It was a human face, and I had to admit, I'd never expected to lay eyes on it again.

"Adjunct Claver?" Turov demanded. I could tell from her voice she was as shocked as I was.

Adjunct Claver, better known as "Old Silver," was a Germanica Legionnaire of the worst reputation. He was in fact, a renegade, a traitor, and an enemy combatant turncoat.

"McGill and Turov?" Claver asked, giving us both a secret little grin. "Who else do I see in the crowd? Tribune Drusus, Graves—even that lick-spittle, Winslade. What a bouquet of losers. I should have known they'd send your sorry asses out here to Machine World. Nobody else could be dumb enough or unpopular enough to get such an assignment."

"What do you want, Claver?" Turov demanded. "And how did you get out here in space? I assume you're aboard the Galactic trade ship. Your crimes are innumerable, and I'll have to ask the captain of that ship to arrest you."

"Criminals and heroes are figments of the beholder's imagination, my lady. Now, let's get down to business. I've been working this planet for months. I sold it to the squids and promised them protection from Earth. You're kind of blowing the deal for me—and for our planet."

Turov, for the first time, seemed at a loss. I could have told her Claver was involved in some kind of crazy scheme. From the very first moment I'd seen his face, I'd known this entire situation was a fishy one. He was a liar, a thief, an egomaniac and God knew what else.

"Quit talking big and tell me what you want," Turov said.

"Well ma'am," he said, "it looks to me like we have a few options. We could blast each other, two warships against two, with one innocent trading ship caught in the middle—"

"Don't think you'll be spared," Turov said. "It is very unlikely you'll survive any hostilities that ensue. You probably stole that trade ship in the first place."

"Control your paranoid fantasies, woman," Claver said, making a dismissive motion with his hand. This caused Turov to redden, but she fell quiet. "I'm here to make a deal, that's all. You know me, I'm only interested in mutually beneficial and lucrative exchanges. Let me bring you up to speed: I sold this system to the squids. I can only surmise by your arrival that you're under orders from the Empire to annex the system and make it part of Frontier 921. This brings us into obvious conflict. Now, here's the essence of my proposal—"

"Don't listen to him, Imperator!" I boomed suddenly. "He's a snake-in-the-grass!"

Everyone looked at me except for Turov. She looked disgusted, rather than angry.

"Keep talking, Claver," she said. "McGill, you'll shut up, or I'll have you yanked out of that vehicle and recycled."

Claver produced an ugly laugh. I wondered if he was talking crazy just to set me off and get me into trouble. Why else would he have requested to see my face on Gold Deck with the rest of them? Given our history, the only motive that made any sense was one of revenge. After all, I'd killed the man more than once.

"Here's the score," Claver said, "Earth must declare independence. It's time to cast off the Empire. They aren't helping you anyway. Offer your services to the Cephalopod

Kingdom. They need frontline fighters and allies more than they need another war with a worthless dirt-world like Earth. In turn, I'll make sure that the full output of high-grade metals from Machine World is funneled directly to your planet. You'll have all the resources you need to build a fleet to defend yourselves. What's more, I'll give you wholesale prices. I'm talking the kind of deal I wouldn't offer my own grandmother!"

This time Turov exploded, not me. "Are you crazy, Claver? You offer Earth destruction at the hands of the Empire. We're talking about your home planet, man! How can you have such a lack of loyalty?"

"Loyalty has brought me nothing but pain and death, my fair lady. But it is you who are loyal to the wrong party. You aren't loyal to Earth any more than I am. You're beholden to uncaring monsters from the core of the galaxy. Spurn them! Toss them out! Declare yourselves free!"

Turov didn't shout back. Instead, she looked at him with clenched teeth and half-closed eyes.

I realized then, in my heart of hearts, that she was honestly thinking about it.

This alarmed me. Could I, James McGill, have infected this woman with my particular brand of impulsiveness? The very thought was terrifying. My crazy combined with her ambition? It was a deadly stew I didn't even want to contemplate.

-24-

Five ships stood in orbit over Machine World. It was a big meeting of naval power, by local standards. Oh sure, in the Core Systems where the Galactics wielded supreme power, I'm sure a thousand ships went by on any given Thursday, but out here on the fringe of the Empire, five ships were a big deal.

Two warships floated on each side, with one trader in the middle. No one trusted anyone, and Turov, I think, was probably the most paranoid individual in the system.

Countering her fearful instincts was her driving ambition. I could tell as I watched her that she was thinking about accepting Claver's offer. Maybe the lessons of Tech World had been misconstrued by her scheming mind. She'd gotten away with a lot out there—partly with my innovative help.

"All right Claver," she said after a pause. "I'm going to think about this deal of yours. Let me talk it over with my officers."

"Take all the time you need, little lady," Claver said. "Contact me in an hour. We'll hammer out the details—including your personal incentive package."

I could tell the smug prick was pleased with himself. He'd done the impossible, once again, by appealing to the greed of those in power.

The face superimposed over the ships faded. Imperator Turov rubbed at her fine chin with slow-moving fingers. She was staring at the planet and the five ships in orbit over it. I knew what she was thinking: she'd be rich, famous and something of a hero if she could pull this off.

"Imperator," Tribune Drusus said. "I wish Tribune Francisco was here to back me up on this, but I must protest. We can't trust Claver or his allies. They're clearly the enemy."

She glanced at him, then back at the screen. "Alliances are fluid, Drusus. I value your opinion, but I can't think only of our orders. I have to think of Earth."

Inside my dragon, I wasn't quite sure what to make of that. By alliances, did she mean the Empire? Our affiliation with the Galactics was more than an alliance in my book. They were the legitimate authority in Frontier 921. Sure, the Nairbs and the Mogwa treated us like dirt most of the time, but we'd taken an oath of allegiance to them.

"Imperator," Tribune Drusus said again. "When can we expect Tribune Francisco to be revived?"

I frowned to hear this. Usually, the tribune of a legion was among the first of its members to be brought back to life. As the highest ranking man in Legion Solstice, he should have been right here on the bridge with the rest of us.

Turov's eyes slid to Drusus, then back to the battle display. "There have been technical difficulties. His death certificate has been delayed for some reason."

"I see," Drusus said stiffly.

We all knew what that meant. Turov had set aside his revival for now. But why? I didn't like the implications. She clearly didn't want him around. It seemed to be a god-like power to me, to decide who lived again in whatever order one wished. In Turov's organization, you'd best stay on her good side.

"Let us adjourn to my private office to discuss this," Turov said.

She led the way with Drusus walking behind her. I watched them go, wonderingly. There had been days when she'd invited me into her offices on such occasions. Anything might happen in there once the door was shut.

"Ah, James," Turov said, looking back and noticing my stare. "Come with us. I wish to ask you something as well."

I began to climb out of my dragon. She put up a hand.

174

"No, bring your vehicle. As to the rest of you, don't interrupt unless we're attacked."

"Yes sir," murmured the assembled officers.

Frowning, I did as ordered. I was a little concerned my dragon wouldn't make it through the doorway or fit inside her office, but I needn't have worried. Her personal office was *huge*. We could have had ourselves a good game of half-court basketball in there.

The door shunted closed behind us. Turov eyed us both. "Now, tell me your objections, Drusus."

He did so, in loving detail. He said we had to contemplate the Empire's response carefully. There were entire governmental departments back on Earth dedicated to gaming out such scenarios, and it would be up to them and their bureaucratic masters to decide if we should take such an offer. There was more, but I stopped listening after about two minutes.

During his little talk, the door beeped twice. This annoyed Turov. She answered the door, demanding to know if the ship was under attack. The answer was no in both cases. She slammed the door shut immediately upon receiving this answer and turned back to Drusus.

"Listen," she said, "I appreciate your concerns. But we have a decision to make. Hegemony is not here with their councilors and officials. *We* are here, and we have to make a choice."

"Are you mad?" Drusus demanded. "We can't unilaterally decide to accept an agreement that declares independence from the Empire without—"

Turov put her hand up. "Drusus, don't be so small-minded. We're doing nothing of the kind. If we accept Claver's offer, we can break the agreement at any moment. But in the meantime, we can return to Earth without a new war on our hands. Let the government decide what to do after that. If I fire on them now, aren't I just as guilty of manipulating events as I might be if I decide to accept their offer?"

"No," Drusus said stubbornly. "You're guilty of disobeying orders. We're here to claim this system and defeat all

175

resistance. I'd rather ambush them with our broadsides than let them entrench themselves and—"

"Fine," Turov snapped. "Veteran McGill, I order you to place Tribune Drusus under arrest."

This last statement kind of shocked me. I blinked inside my cockpit and cleared my throat. "Uh, sir? Why would I do that?"

"Because I ordered it, damn you!"

I took in a breath, stepped forward one clanking step and reached out with my grippers. Drusus surrendered his sidearm.

"This is highly irregular, Imperator," he said stiffly. "It will all go in my report."

"No, it won't," she said. "Not after we hack your tapper and erase your latest engrams."

"What?"

She turned to me, and I knew what was coming next. "James, snip his head off."

"Sir? Are you sure about that?"

"You've done far worse. Get on with it."

Drusus looked at me. He was glaring, daring me to do it.

I was seriously conflicted. I liked Drusus, but I was facing direct orders from his superior. I didn't like those orders, and they didn't seem legal to me, but I was new to my rank and wasn't quite sure how to proceed.

Fortunately, I noticed my tapper was blinking. When inside a dragon, a man's tapper was obscured. Someone was trying to send me a private message. Stalling for time, I took the call.

"You disappoint me, James," Turov said. She had her sidearm out, and she was aiming at Drusus. "I'll have to shoot him myself.

The reason why Tribune Francisco had yet to be revived was suddenly clear in my mind. Turov liked complete power, and getting her next-in-command officers out of her hair would allow her a great deal of freedom.

Should I protect Drusus, disobeying Turov? The decision was a hard one, but fortunately, it was made moot by the content of the incoming message.

"Sir!" I boomed, cranking up my external speakers. Both the officers winced. "The enemy is moving! They're landing on the planet!"

The message on my tapper was from Graves. He'd included a screenshot. He might have had some kind of inkling of what was transpiring in Turov's office—or he might have simply wanted to get the message to her.

Turov shot Drusus at that moment. My jaw sagged.

"You disobeyed me," she said. "I will remember that. When I give a subordinate an order to kill, I expect it to happen immediately."

Rotating the chassis on my dragon, I stared down at Drusus.

"How about I do the same thing to you?" I asked her.

She narrowed her eyes and looked at me appraisingly. "Go ahead. I want to hear your explanation to the officers after you walk out of here. Whatever it is, I'm sure it will provide me with a good laugh after I'm revived."

Standing over Drusus like a loyal dog, I glared at her, and she glared back.

"What are you trying to accomplish, sir?" I asked. "Are you in on this deal with Claver?"

"What if I am?"

I nodded thoughtfully. "Of course. Why else bring me up here in a dragon? Why else put the other Tribune on ice then engineer Drusus' death? Worst case, you blame it all on McGill and stiff him with the bill."

Turov bent down and pulled Drusus' arm out of its sleeve. She fished out a shell-like device, the Galactic key. I knew that if she touched her key to his tapper, she could delete his latest mental backup.

We'd done the same thing to a Galactic, sure, but to a legitimate commander? I felt it was an unwarranted violation.

My grippers both extended themselves with sudden decisiveness. Turov gave a little squeal of pain and alarm when I grabbed her wrists and lifted her off her feet. She struggled and kicked my combat machine, but the dragon's armor was such that I didn't even feel it.

"You're under arrest, Imperator. Drusus will be revived with full memories and I'll bear witness to his testimony. Your command is finished."

Saying this, I wheeled around and marched her to the door. The officers were still outside, uncertain about what to do. They might try to kill me, but I figured I'd get a chance to explain before they could get through my dragon's armor. After that, they'd want to know the truth. They wouldn't let Turov erase my mind or Drusus'.

"Stop!" shouted Turov. "James, STOP! I'll do anything!"

Maybe I'm a weak man, but I stopped. Such an offer had possibilities.

Panting, staring at the door and struggling weakly, Turov tried to twist around to see my face. "I'll make you an adjunct—no, a centurion!"

"No, sir," I said. "I don't want that unless I earn it."

"All right. What do you want then, James?"

I thought about it. I felt like a guy on a beach who's been fooling around and rubbed the wrong brass lamp. I knew this genie was a vicious thing, and she would twist my words to her benefit. I had to get something out of her that she couldn't retract later.

"Fire on the squid ships," I said at last. "Blow them away and kick-start this war the right way."

Her eyes widened. I didn't think that's what she'd had in mind. I set her down on her feet, and she rubbed her bruised wrists.

"Are you mad?" she asked. "Don't you understand what I'm trying to accomplish here? Claver and I have worked on this plan for months. We're giving Earth a chance. We're aligning ourselves with the Cephalopod Kingdom. We'll be a much bigger ally to them than we could ever be to the Empire. Have some vision, McGill!"

"I'm a simple man," I said. "I've got simple tastes and more common sense than brains. What my dull mind is telling me right now is that any scheme hatched by the likes of you and Claver is poison."

"You're a bully with the instincts of an animal!" she shouted. "I don't know what I ever saw in you!"

If the situation hadn't been so grim, I would have laughed at that. We'd been lovers once, briefly, but I still wasn't sure who had been more shallow about the relationship.

"I can't let you work this deal without approval from Earth," I said, "even if I am impressed by the sheer balls of the whole thing."

"What if I show you I *do* have approval from Earth?" she asked.

"That would be different."

She reached nonchalantly for her tapper. Instinctively, I grabbed her wrists again. She'd already tapped one button by the time I got a hold of her. The second button, when I looked, was as I figured: security.

"I see," I said. "There's no approval from Earth. You just wanted to call the MPs in here and tell them old McGill went nuts again, am I right? In fact, I'm pretty sure I know now why I'm really here. *Someone* had to be guilty of killing Drusus. Who better than that crazy redneck over there in the metal suit?"

Her face blazed with anger. "Let go of me, James."

"Can't do that. Order the attack on the squids, or I'm frog-marching you out there onto Gold Deck. Everyone will see it. You can't erase all their minds. How would you even manage to kill them all in the first place?"

She bared her teeth, and her eyes darted from side to side. I could tell she was thinking hard. There was no escape, and I could see she wasn't having any luck coming up with another dodge.

The door began to chime again. The officers were probably freaking out, wanting guidance from their top brass.

"You've got ten seconds," I said. "Then I open that door."

"All right, all right! Let go of me. I need to open a line to talk."

Instead of letting go of her, I used her tapper to open the general command chat myself. She looked at the red blinking transmission light. It was active and her words were being recorded. She breathed hard for a few seconds.

I nodded to her, prompting her to say something. I could see in her eyes that she was thinking about yelling for help. But she hadn't erased Drusus' mind yet, and I still had her in my grippers. I might even pull an arm off or something. She had to know that was a possibility. Such things had happened in the past.

"The squids are breaking our truce," she announced at last. "Advance and destroy their ships. Leave the Galactic trade ship alone."

Her tapper beeped as the channel closed. I set her down on the deck as gently as I could. She glared up at me with baleful eyes.

"I'll get you for this, McGill," she said, rubbing her wrists and straightening her uniform.

"Looking forward to it, sir. Uh…what are we going to do about Drusus?"

"Can I erase his memory now, or are you going to man-handle me again?"

I thought about it. "Let's make a deal, Galina. All this will be one more dirty little secret between us. You don't blame me, and I'll back up whatever story you want to tell."

Turov frowned. "I thought you were in love with Drusus or something."

"No sir, you get me all wrong. This isn't about loving anyone. This is about hating Claver and the squids."

Turov nodded thoughtfully. "Maybe you can be useful in this new situation. You've put me in a bad spot. Claver will take this as a double-cross. I'm unsure as to how I'll proceed."

"I'm always good in a war, sir," I said. "Just point me at something you want destroyed. Preferably a squid this time, though."

Turov gave me a half-smile as she erased Drusus' mind. I have to admit, that look of hers creeped me out a bit. She was already working on an entirely new scheme. I knew I was a player in it, and I also knew I wasn't going to like my new role—whatever it was.

The ship lurched then, throwing both of us against the far wall of her office. Drusus' body flopped like a doll. The ship was making maneuvers. I could only imagine what kind of firepower was flying around outside the hull that surrounded us.

My dragon automatically climbed to its feet. I helped Galina up as gently as I could, but she swatted my grippers away. She pointed to Drusus.

"That's our chance," she said. "Snap his neck."

"What about the burn hole in his chest?"

"Let me worry about that."

I looked at Drusus. Sure, he was already dead, but I felt like a ghoul just contemplating breaking a dead man's bones.

"Come on, McGill, don't tell me you're squeamish now!" she growled. She got hold of Drusus, put her knee against his throat and twisted with both hands. The popping sound made me wince.

"There," she said, panting. "We have an accidental death on our hands. A terrible tragedy, a freak incident. We'll avenge his loss upon the squids."

Shaking my head, I followed her next orders. We carried Drusus out onto Gold Deck. People looked at us suspiciously, especially Graves. I think he knew there was funny business afoot, and it made me feel a little self-conscious.

Like some kind of grim reaper, I carried my own tribune down to Blue Deck. There, a familiar face met me. It was none other than the high-ranking bio, Centurion Thompson. She'd always been a sidekick of Turov's. Her attitude told me she wasn't shocked by Drusus' death. She'd been tipped off and probably given orders as to what to do by Turov herself.

Thompson took the body from me with the help of two orderlies. "Cause of death, accidental injury," she said without looking. "Mark him as a shipboard battle casualty."

They walked away from me, hurrying down the passage. The two orderlies looked at one another, frowning. One of them was already fingering the burn-hole.

"But sir, what about this—"

"You have your orders," Thompson said. "Have I been unclear in some manner?"

"No sir. I'm clear."

"Good, now recycle the body immediately. We need to charge our protoplasm tanks with fresh material. He won't be the last to die on this ship today."

181

They disappeared into the bowels of Blue Deck, and I left them to their grim arts.

-25-

The battle with the squid ships was brief but violent. The enemy vessels turned out to be troop transports, not true warships. They fired missiles back at *Minotaur* and *Cyclops* but only scored minor damage.

Each of our ships unloaded a full barrage from their broadsides into the enemy. The enemy ships were torn apart as they hung just above the atmosphere.

Treachery, that's what it was—in more ways than one. The fact that Claver and Turov had hatched this deal outside of government channels against the Empire was the work of two renegades. On the other hand, the squids had been screwed as well. They'd doubtlessly been assured they wouldn't face resistance and hadn't sent serious naval vessels to protect their troopships.

Smiling, I watched the vid over and over again. I could only imagine what Claver must be screaming about Turov on his bridge right now. Unsurprisingly, his trade ship beat a hasty retreat from the system.

I knew Claver fairly well. He was a trader through and through. He wanted to make money, not war. In some ways I could approve of the goal. But he'd always advanced his agenda outside of regular channels, and not for moral reasons. He wanted to cash in, that's all. Greed, pure and simple. He didn't care if a few million citizens lived or died as long as he got his paycheck.

Apparently, his plan had been to set up a trading outpost right here on Machine World, no doubt charging squids and humans alike for his services. The squids were to have military possession of Machine World, while Earth got all the mineral output. That way, both sides could save face and live together peacefully. Come to think of it, the arrangement wouldn't have been a half-bad one if we'd been living with a different political reality.

The trouble was there was this little thing called the Galactic Empire to worry about. They had a million star systems while the squids had an estimated three hundred. Humanity? We were a joke with only two. Millions of star systems translated into millions of warships, and then an extinct species by the end of any conflict that came our way.

As things stood now, it looked like Humanity was going to expand our holdings by a dramatic fifty percent. This third star system would be ours, with all its mineral wealth. All we had to do was evict the squids that had already landed and pacify the ravenous native machines. It should be a piece of cake, really.

"McGill?" my tapper asked me. It was Graves' voice.

I accepted the private connection without hesitation. "What is it, sir?"

"Are you watching this so-called battle? The enemy ships are both down."

"Yes, sir. I can see it. The squids have got to be pissed."

Graves didn't say anything for a few seconds. I thought about closing the connection, but I didn't. It was still open, and he'd made the call. He could decide when the conversation was over.

"McGill?" he asked finally. "What happened on Gold Deck in the Imperator's office tonight?"

"You sure you really want to know about that, sir?"

"No..." he said. "No, I probably don't. I'll just let it go."

"Thank you, Centurion. Anything else?"

"Yes. Were you in on today's events before they began to unfold?"

It took me a few seconds to realize what he was talking about.

"No sir!" I said firmly. "I ended up playing a role in the drama, but I had no idea Claver was going to show up repping the squids, much less that Turov was going to try to play nice with him."

Graves gave me a dirty chuckle. "That's what I thought. Those two should have made sure you were on board before they tried to include you in their schemes. I could have told them that much."

It made me happy to think that my superior had faith in me. I wasn't a schemer. I was an opportunist and a loose cannon, sure, and I didn't always follow orders. But that didn't mean I could be counted on to go along with the random crazy plans of others. I was glad that Graves knew that.

"I guess those two don't really understand me, sir," I said.

"I guess not. Graves out."

The connection closed, and I headed for Blue Deck. My date with Anne had been cut short, and I wanted to see if she was in the mood to continue our get-together.

When I got there, the place was shutting down. Anne had left to go to bed. I couldn't blame her. After all, it was only a few hours until dawn. I went back to my quarters, laid down, and passed out.

* * *

One bad thing about being a squad's veteran was the general expectation that I would wake up before anyone else did. In order to kick people out of bed, a man pretty much had to be dressed and ready to go before the sun touched the sky. I found that part of the job to be difficult—but I did it anyway.

Carlos was my first victim. I kicked him out of his bunk an hour after it was officially dawn in ship-time. In space, maintaining an Earthly clock was artificial. We kept a twenty-four cycle going, but only so that everyone felt at home.

"You've got to be kidding me, McGill," Carlos said from the floor. "Are the squids hitting us again?"

185

"Nope," I said, "but I noticed your dragon hasn't been cleaned in a week. I want to see an oil-change, and I want every ding and dent buffed out."

Carlos heaved himself up and yawned. "This is revenge, isn't it?" he asked.

"I will admit to taking a small amount of pleasure in the situation," I said.

"That's very small of *you*, Vet."

An hour later the squad was showered up, fed and working hard. Harris' crew walked in on us. They shared the same mechanics' bay we did aboard ship. I didn't even look up when he came in. It felt good to get away with that.

Harris ordered his people to work then stared at me for a few long seconds. I knew he was staring, but I didn't even look at him.

Finally, he walked over to me, sighed, and held out his hand to shake. I frowned at it in honest confusion.

"Do I owe you some money, Harris?" I asked.

"No, McGill," he huffed. Then he got a little mad. "Just take it, dammit. Be a man!"

"Why?"

"Because I was *wrong*, that's why!"

This surprised me quite a bit. I could not recall a time I'd heard those words come out of Harris' mouth before. In fact, I doubted they ever had.

I took his hand, and I shook it firmly.

"Why the change of heart, Vet?" I asked him.

"I saw what you did down there in the middle of that shit-storm. You took one for the team, and it worked. I got out of that place alive. Most of my squad did, too. If it hadn't been for you and Graves—well, it wouldn't have happened."

"Okay then...I guess we can call off our little feud."

"Yes, consider it forgotten," he said. "You're a real veteran now. You've earned your rank, and I'm willing to admit it wasn't a mistake. But one thing, James?"

I blinked at the use of my first name. I was pretty sure he'd never done that before, either.

"What's that?" I asked.

"Don't sing anymore, okay? I don't think I could take it."

"I'll try to remember that, Vet. But sometimes, the mood just strikes me, you know?"

We parted ways, grinning. I harangued my squad, and he did the same with his, but we were both in better spirits. It's hard to work alongside a man who you know hates you. Today, I didn't have to live with that.

-26-

We didn't invade Machine World again for three more days. During that time, the revival machines worked night and day, churning out the troops who'd died. Many of them were sad-sacks from Solstice who'd been dead since the first hours of the conflict. They'd died on their ship, *Pegasus*, and had been waiting in line to return to life for over a week.

"It just doesn't seem right," I remarked to Natasha. I'd connected up with her again aboard *Cyclops* as she'd been assigned to working on signal interpretation duties. It was her job to glean whatever intel she could from the scratchy transmissions coming up from Machine World.

"What doesn't seem right?" she asked. She was bent over a device that looked like a microwave oven with the guts of it turned inside out. She wore sensitive headphones as she tested various inputs and outputs. Every time I said something to her, she had to remove the headphones so she could hear me.

"I'm talking about leaving people in the queue so long before revival. They'll be freaked out when they finally regain consciousness—I know how it feels. One time, I was left dead for three days—that's a long time to be dead and gone."

"That's why you keep going down to Blue Deck?" she asked.

"Yes. I'm checking on Drusus."

She looked at me for a moment. "I don't believe you. You're going down there to see Anne, aren't you?" she asked.

"Huh?"

188

"I know you've been going down to Blue Deck every couple of hours asking for her. She's too busy to see you—running the revives night and day. The bio people are pulling double-shifts, and that's putting a kink in your nighttime plans, isn't it?"

I tried not to look embarrassed, because she was partly right. That's the trouble with hanging around smart girls like Natasha.

Now, I liked Natasha, don't get me wrong. We'd had plenty of good times over the years. She'd been my sort-of girlfriend, if it could be said I'd ever officially had one. But she always became possessive after a while, and then we'd break up and things would cool down. On my side of the story, I didn't think I was in the wrong this time.

"Natasha," I said, "you and I aren't sleeping together, right? So why can't I take another girl on a date without you getting bent out of shape?"

"I'm not upset," she said, turning back to her gizmo and fooling with it. She was frowning, but nothing more than that. "I was just putting together the equation, that's all."

"Fine, fine," I said, forcing a smile she didn't return. "If we can drop that now, I'd like to talk to you about our latest dragon load-outs. If we're going up against the squids, possibly allied with the machine-creatures, what do you think we should equip on a front-line dragon?"

Natasha had her headset on again. She lifted the set from one of her ears and glanced at me. I wasn't sure if she'd heard my question at all, or if she was thinking so much she'd decided to ignore it.

"What I object to is your lack of transparency, James," she said in a somewhat stern voice. "You should be more open with women. You should let them know what they're in for before you get involved with them."

"I thought you didn't care."

"I didn't say that. I don't care from a personal standpoint, but I'm looking out for Anne. She's new to the James McGill shell-game."

She put her headphones back on and went back to work.

189

My face twisted up into a grimace, and I sighed. "Sure, you're just thinking about poor Anne. You wanted to rip her hair out last year."

"Did not," she responded.

"You heard that clearly enough."

She pulled her headphones back off. She gave me a sideways glance then went back to her equipment. "Just don't break her heart. Tell her how it's going to be. Tell her you'll get bored around date number four, and by date six or seven you'll be chasing someone else."

"That's not always how it goes."

"Yes—it pretty much is."

"Well…" I said. I felt like I was running out of words. "Look, she's been in the same unit with me for a long time. She knows the score. Besides, when did I ever lie to you about anything?"

She gave me an up-down look. "It's not about lies, it's about critical omissions."

"Like what?"

"Like Della, for instance. When were you going to tell me you'd slept with her again? When were you going to tell me you two had a child together?"

I was floored. First of all, I hadn't thought Natasha knew about these things, and secondly, I didn't think she'd throw them in my face. But these revelations helped explain the generally poor attitude she'd been showing me ever since we'd reached Machine World.

"Natasha, I haven't been chasing you, have I?" I asked.

"No, I guess not," she said, sounding a little hurt.

"Well then, why should I have to tell you every detail of my personal—?"

"Have you told Anne *anything* about Della?"

"Uh…it hasn't come up yet," I admitted.

"You see? That's the problem. Women like to know such details before they get involved. They don't want to be rudely surprised later on. That's the kind of thing that explodes so many of your relationships."

I thought about what she was saying. Maybe she was right, to a degree. When I approached a new relationship with a woman who'd gotten my attention, I generally tried to hide all the bad stuff. Look as good as you can and keep smiling, that was my motto.

"Don't you think starting off with a laundry list of past misdeeds might put a damper on a new romance?" I asked her.

"Well, yes. You have a point there."

We fell quiet for a time. I worked on dragon load-outs on a computer scroll while she kept toying with the listening system, isolating signals and marking interesting ones for focused study later on.

Designing my squad's dragons, I considered shielding, but I didn't select the option in the end. Shields were nice, but they drained your power very quickly, and the projection units were heavy. In my opinion, part of the point of cavalry was being able to move across the battlefield quickly.

After several minutes of quiet, Natasha pulled her headphones off and turned to frown at me.

"What?" I asked.

"Don't you even care about your child? Don't you even care about Della being married? How could you sleep with her in such a situation? I don't get you sometimes, James—then again, maybe I do and I don't like what I—"

"Whoa, whoa!" I said, putting up my hands. "Have you been sitting there stewing all this time?"

She didn't answer, but her expression told me that she had.

"Listen," I said. "Della came on to *me*, and it was after we made love she told me about the kid thing. And the marriage thing. After she dropped those bombs on me, we've stayed apart."

Natasha's mouth was a tiny, straight line. She was pissed under that cool exterior, I could tell. I had to wonder how long she'd been steaming like this and not talking to me about it. Come to think of it, she'd been kind of cold and distant lately—I guess I just hadn't noticed.

"Okay," she said, "you didn't know everything when you chased her. But 'kid-thing'? Really? That's what you call your own child?"

"Maybe it's me," I said, "but I'm beginning to feel a little hostility in the air. Look, here's my kid's picture. She's named Etta. Here's a movie."

I played a short clip on my tapper then another. Natasha eyed these and softened.

"I'm sorry," she said suddenly. "I was an idiot. Forget I said anything. Everyone carries their private sorrows differently, I guess you prefer to bottle yours up inside."

Her statements left me wanting to scratch my head in confusion, but I know it's a good idea to take a breather when your opponent offers one. Sure, I'd looked through the pictures and thought about being a father. I'd been pretty busy fighting and dying to do much of that, but I'd spent a few minutes now and then contemplating these new realities. The truth was, the kid was on another planet and would probably grow up without laying eyes on her real dad. It was more tragic, in my opinion, that her mother had left to fight in the legions as well, because Della had gone off to the stars *knowing* what that meant.

"Look," I said, "you seem more torn up by this than Della herself. The colonists…well, they don't think quite the way we do. They have more of a communal society from what I can see. They raise kids with a group effort. They don't dote on them and take them to theme parks and stuff like that. People on Earth have a much tighter relationship with their children."

Natasha pursed her lips and nodded. "I think you're right. You should be pretty happy about all that. It fits right in with your preferred path through life."

I wasn't certain, but I figured I was probably being insulted again. I stood up and gathered my kit.

"Where are you going?" she asked.

"I'm through here."

She watched me pack my stuff, without talking. Finally, as I was about to leave, she stopped me. She got up, put her hands on my arm, and tugged.

"Don't go away angry," she said. "I'm sorry. I'm jealous. I can't help it. The whole thing with Della—that freaked me out when I heard about it."

"I thought you had a new boyfriend. What about that skinny bio guy?"

She shook her head. "It didn't work out."

Her hands were still on my arm, so I couldn't very well rip away from her. "Uh...are you trying to tell me something?" I asked.

Natasha frowned, not meeting my eyes. "I don't know. Look, you're dropping on the planet again soon, right?"

"We pretty much all are, as I understand the plan."

"Okay. This shouldn't be too hard. We'll wipe out these squid troops in a month and head home. I've got an idea for afterward."

Her rosy scenario concerning the invasion didn't match my own expectations, but I didn't burst her bubble. I'd fought squid troops before, and they were real bastards. Just one of them was worth a squad of men if they got in close.

"What did you want to do when we get home?" I asked.

I don't know what I thought she'd say. Maybe that we should have a drink together in Atlanta and give our old relationship a fresh try. Or that she'd been building one of her illegal bio-nano creatures again, and she wanted to share the secret with me. What she did suggest had never entered my head.

"I was thinking you and I could fly out to Zeta Herculis," she said. "There are regular flights between Earth and Dust World now, you know. They're mostly trade ships, nothing fancy, but it would be at least as comfortable as *Cyclops*. Relatively cheap fare, too."

My mouth must have been hanging open by this time. "Why would we want to do that?"

"To see your daughter, of course!" she said brightly.

The light went on in my skull. "Oh—I guess that *is* possible. I'd honestly never thought of it before. I mean...all our lives we've been stuck on Earth unless we joined the legion and were given a contract in another star system. The idea that we can travel as private citizens—that's all new."

"Yes, yes," she said, smiling. "It *is* new, and I'd like to be one of the first to give it a try."

That was pure Natasha. She'd always been an explorer. If she'd had her way, she'd be flying in a scientific vessel of exploration, not a warship.

193

Then another, even bigger thought struck me—right between the eyes. My smile faded, and so did hers as she watched me.

Della's story about Natasha 2.0 sprung into my mind whole and fully fleshed. It was as if I could see both of them, standing side by side. Twins, but one older and wearing a hard, sun-burnt scowl. The second younger, a little more innocent, standing here and looking at me.

How could I tell her? How could I tell poor Natasha she couldn't ever go back to Dust World? That a crime had been committed, a Galactic violation, and it had been committed by another version of herself? A version of herself who'd been cruelly left for dead in space?

"It's a good idea," I said, coming up with what I felt was a gifted dodge. "But I'll have to ask Della about it. That only seems right, doesn't it? I mean—what if she doesn't want me to interfere? She's got a new husband and all—maybe he wouldn't be too keen on seeing me show up from out of nowhere when he's trying to bond with his stepdaughter."

Natasha's face fell. She nodded thoughtfully. "Okay. You're right. Della would have to know, and she must approve of the idea. It's only right. I'll ask her about it."

She gave me a little kiss and turned away, going back to her work. She didn't see me grimace in concern as I left, shaking my head.

Della wasn't going to like the idea, I knew that much. Who knew what Natasha would read into that?

Damn, why did women always have to make things so complicated?

-27-

The noncoms and officers of the cavalry cohort met together before we dropped. Winslade walked around a central tactical display, skinny arms behind his back, hands clasped. He had the look of a primus, at least, but I still didn't buy the idea that he knew what he was doing. He hadn't earned that from me.

The rest of the troops around me were mostly battle-hardened officers. They looked at Winslade with even more disdain than I did.

I knew the first time we'd dropped under this gentleman's command hadn't won him any points. The entire thing had been a fiasco. He'd stayed hidden under the lifter while we ran around blindly all over an unknown landscape like a bunch of kids in grandma's cellar. Hell, it had taken us *days* just to cross a river. After that, things had gone downhill. We'd ended up taking heavy losses and getting chased off the surface again, accomplishing pretty much nothing at all.

While I'd been down there, these details hadn't been so easy to see. After all, I hadn't been the one in command. I'd followed my orders and marched my squad around to the best of my ability. The strategy hadn't seemed clear to me, but I'd thought at the time that maybe it was because I was new to the role of squad leader.

But after talking to others like Graves and Leeson, who were much quicker to judge than I'd been, I could see now the

195

whole thing had been a gigantic charley-foxtrot from start to finish.

Now Winslade was doing his little walk around the tactical display and making a pompous speech in front of about a thirty sets of unfriendly eyes. He didn't seem to notice that we weren't in love with him. Maybe he was used to that.

"Soldiers," he said, "we've been asked to return to the surface of Gamma Pavonis. This invasion will be different. Last time, we were dropping to evade an enemy attack on our ships. This time, we have a clear goal."

He swept a skinny finger down to point at the three dimensional map. The section he pointed at lit up. A small spike in the landscape was at the center of the region he'd indicated.

"See this startling geographical formation? It's a steep mountain near the equator. Now that we've had time to carefully survey the planet surface after many orbits, we've identified this region as possessing a heavy concentration of titanium ore. Unfortunately, the squids also took the time to analyze the same data. This was their chosen landing spot. The troops they dropped onto the surface ended up here."

His words sparked my interest. I knew that our Imperial ships were built largely with titanium. The metal was light and extremely strong, making it a perfect choice for a ship's hull. With a lead coating to keep out the gamma rays and a few layered electromagnetic shields, you could fly through space in safety and comfort inside a titanium ship.

The trouble with titanium, however, was its rarity. A big mine with a high yield would be extremely valuable to Earth.

"Not only," Winslade continued, "is the ore here plentiful, it's very rich and pure. We'll hardly have to smelt it. Obviously, the squids want this same resource and have moved to take control of it upon landing."

The officers and veterans around me were stirring. I could see their overall attitude shifting. As mercenaries, we were aware of the value of things. We understood fighting for material gain. A big mountain made of pure titanium ore? That had the troops licking their chops all up and down the line.

Winslade surveyed the assembled officers and noncoms for the first time. He allowed himself a sly smile. I could tell he was reading them the way I had. They were no longer thinking about how he'd gotten so many of them killed the last time he'd dropped them on this foggy rock. Now they were thinking of bringing home a treasure to Earth.

"I needn't tell you," he said, lowering his voice, "how much this metal will mean to our home world. Back on Earth right now, Hegemony is buying up interstellar shipments of rare metals, and they're having a tough time of it. Freighters are shying away from Frontier 921. They don't want to venture this far out. The saurian princes of Steel World, our best local suppliers, are still unhappy with Earthlings and refuse to trade with us. Rumors of piracy and outright rebellion all along the fringe of the Empire are rampant as well, making longer distance runs by traders problematic."

That part about piracy was news to me. My eyes widened upon hearing such a thing was possible. How could the Empire allow these violations? I knew the answer, of course, as soon as I'd mentally asked myself the question. The civil war in the Core Systems had changed everything. That was the source of the problem. No one was minding the store out here on the frontier—no one but Earth, that is.

All my life I'd grown up in a very orderly political universe. At the top of the food chain were the Galactics. Races of beings that were so far removed in power and stature from Earthlings that we might as well have been pond scum to them—and pond scum from a rather small pond at that.

But things had changed. The Empire was eating itself from within. The word was that things hadn't gotten any better over recent years in the Core of the galaxy as the conflict spread and progressed. The Mogwa, the particular race of Galactics who "owned" our local province, were nose deep in the war, just like the rest of them. They were slinging ships at other powers, wasting their strength on petty squabbles over who had the right to rule a thousand stars, give or take. They were losing an empire to win an argument.

In the meantime, out here on the frontier, things were becoming more lawless all the time.

Winslade said something else then, something that jarred me out of my reverie.

"There's another angle to this," he said. "A more personal angle. One that involves every one of you in this room."

He had our attention. I couldn't imagine how anything about dropping down again onto a planet Carlos lovingly called "fart-world" was going to personally engage me, but I was willing to listen.

"We need this metal to keep building dragons and other, larger machines we've been planning with those tech wizards out on Dust World. The primary component of their chassis is titanium. A fair amount of it has been mined on Dust World, but nowhere near enough to sustain serious production levels."

Graves lifted a hand. Winslade called on him without hesitation. "Why would the Dust World colonists be our suppliers? And why does this involve us personally, as you claimed earlier?"

"Good questions," Winslade said. "As I understand it, the colonists had originally planned to build their own ship, possibly to use it to escape their desert planet. A grim thought, from our perspective as humans. They might have violated yet another Galactic Law and gotten our species erased. But in any case, they're our modern munitions producers because they haven't been stunted technologically for generations by the Empire. In some ways, they're more advanced than we are."

"And the personal interest part, sir?" Graves asked.

"Do you want to go back to the infantry, Centurion Graves?"

"No, sir. But this hardly seems the moment to make public threats toward my career path."

Winslade fanned away the words with his thin fingers. "I'm sorry. I didn't mean it that way. What I'm trying to say is that the continued existence of this cavalry cohort, and others like it, depends on these metals. We need a surplus just to replace the dragons we've already lost. The fleet wants it all."

We looked at Winslade thoughtfully. Everyone was a little shocked. The words "I'm sorry" had never been in his vocabulary before. I felt an urge to ask a follow-up question. In fact, I almost raised my hand—but I didn't. Maybe it was my recent promotion, or maybe it was an onset of newfound wisdom, but whatever the case, I stayed quiet. Graves was asking the right questions, and it was his prerogative to do so as the senior centurion, second in command of the cohort under Winslade.

"I see my words aren't lost on you," Winslade said, studying our faces. "I know you aren't confident in me as your commander—not yet. But you like your dragons, don't you? All I hear is praise for the hardware. Look how it performed in this last conflict. Without the dragons, an all-infantry force would have been decimated by the native machines."

We couldn't dispute his statements. They were demonstrably true, and they praised us at the same time. Who could argue with that?

"So," Winslade continued, "we're not going to take this ten thousand meter tall rocky spire for Turov. We're not going to take it for Earth! We're going to take it so we can fight in these walking dragons. Unlike our bodies, the dragons must be manufactured and shipped from lightyears away. In order to remain viable, we need a cheap supply of raw materials. Otherwise, this experiment known as a cavalry cohort will be a footnote in the Hegemony textbooks."

Wait a second... Had he just said *a ten thousand meter high spire?*

I looked at the map again, a frown growing on my face. Yes, I could see the scale now. On the map, the central mountain in question looked small, no bigger than a man's nose on an otherwise smooth face. But that was because the display depicted a vast planetary surface.

Ten thousand meters. Holy crap... That was going to be quite a climb.

Winslade went on then with assignments, timetables and launch codes. After about a half hour, he dismissed us. But he called out to Graves before doing so.

"Centurion," he said. "I wish to have a word, if you don't mind."

"Certainly, primus," Graves said, standing stiffly while others filed away. The rest headed down to the dragon bays, planning to pass the briefing summary to their troops.

I hung back, wondering what Winslade was going to say to Graves. I still didn't trust the man. I trusted him nowhere near as far as I could throw his skinny carcass—which I estimated would have been a pretty good distance.

Winslade eyed me sidelong. "I see your chief ape is reluctant to leave. I'm flattered."

It took me about a second to realize I'd been insulted—sort of. The title "chief ape" had its appeal, after all, but I didn't think he meant it that way. Personally, I would have given that title to Harris or Sargon. They weren't as tall as I was, but were about as strong and mean.

Winslade beckoned to me. "Come on over here, ape. If you're going to listen, you might as well do it without straining your huge ears."

I walked back to stand beside Graves. Winslade had a strange look in his eye. He appeared thoughtful. I couldn't recall having seen that expression on this man's face before.

"I owe both of you a great deal," Winslade said. "You both were instrumental in saving my command. Correspondingly, I've recommended you both receive a commendation."

Graves and I blinked at him, stunned.

"Did I hear that right, sir?" I asked. "You're telling Hegemony to give us a medal?"

"Yes. I doubt the request will go through, however. There is a non-neutral party between myself and Hegemony who must approve, and I doubt the motion will get past her desk."

He eyed us. We all knew he was talking about Turov.

"Still," Graves said, "it's the thought that counts, sir."

"Not really, but I'm glad you feel that way. There is another remedy. When Tribune Drusus is eventually revived, I'll ask him to give you Legion Varus' medal of valor. You're still part of Varus as the cavalry cohort is attached to your old legion. I believe he may like you two more than...others do."

"Uh..." I said, "Did I just hear that right? Are you saying Drusus *still* hasn't been revived? It's been days, sir!"

"That's correct. It has been." Winslade didn't say anything else about it. He dismissed us with a wave of his hand.

We left together, and out in the hallway, following the glowing arrows that had appeared on the deck, I turned toward the dragon bays. The arrows weren't displaying emergency colors but were meant to guide troops through the ship to their appropriate destinations. The red arrows were meant for me as I was a combat-arms soldier.

Graves walked with me down the passage.

"That was weird," I said to him.

"Indeed it was. I never would have thought it could come to this."

"Come to what, sir?"

"I'm having second thoughts about Winslade. He barely knows what he's doing, but he's willing to admit that you and I helped him out. That's a serious first step in a commander. What's more, he did a fairly good job of motivating his cohort to fight hard on this new invasion attempt. He tried to provide us with a personal stake in the battle. I don't recall Turov ever doing that."

Still frowning, I nodded in agreement.

"But sir," I said, "what's bothering me most is this business about Drusus. He should be back on the line by now. There's no excuse for leaving him in limbo for three days."

Graves chuckled. "There's always an excuse. Hell, for all we know he's been revived several times and declared a bad grow. I wouldn't be surprised if Turov herself was personally recycling him with a grin on her face."

I winced at that horrible image. The revival machines didn't always reproduce a functional human body. Sometimes people came out wrong and had to be put down and grown again. I'd been declared a bad-grow on a few occasions, but I'd managed to convince people to let me keep breathing until events halted my life yet again.

Who knew, though? Possibly, more than one James McGill had come out with a heart that didn't beat right or a tumor in his lungs. Maybe I'd been put down a few times, struggling feebly while I was being fed into the whirling blades of the recycling chute. I shuddered just thinking about it.

"Don't tell me you've still got the willies about revivals, McGill?" Graves admonished me. "Aren't you getting a little old for that sort of thing?"

"I'm only about twenty-seven—I think."

"Point taken. I'm more than twice that age," he said. "I've been revived more times than you've cut your toenails."

I glanced at him but didn't say anything. Graves was a strange one. No one took a death as easily as he did. Maybe that was the trick. Dying was like anything else; you just had to do it a lot to get over your natural fears.

Graves didn't look like he was sixty or seventy years old, of course. He'd been reset every time he'd died. Physically, his body was maybe thirty-five, tops. Maybe even less than that. My own body was about twenty three by now. I'd lived four years without aging—but it had come at a grim price. Legionnaires might be almost immortal, but only because we got the 'thrill' of dying more than once.

Reaching the dragon bays, I gathered my squad. We outfitted our machines with the battle gear we thought would be most appropriate and made sure every system checked out. When I was finished with that, I had a few hours to kill before the invasion. I let my squad go on break with orders to meet back for the drop an hour before go-time.

-28-

Wandering the halls, I found myself back on Blue Deck. It was with a slightly guilty feeling that I buzzed in, trying to get Anne to answer my call. I had to wonder if Natasha was tailing me with either an electronic trace or an actual spy-buzzer. She'd done both before.

Anne had been ignoring all inquiries sent by tapper since our last date. I figured chiming for her from Blue Deck's security door sent a more powerful message. I wasn't sure why I wanted to talk to her so badly—I guess it was because our one and only date had felt unfinished to me.

At last, the big metal door to Blue Deck opened. The hatchway wasn't like those on the rest of the ship. Blue Deck was closed off to casual traffic, restricted for the lowly likes of me. Combat troops were to stay out, and techs doubly so. The bio-people operated like a priesthood, charged with maintaining their revival machines without interference from the locals.

I'd never fully understood their paranoia—except for the knowledge that their machines were probably the most expensive pieces of alien hardware we had aside from the starships themselves.

When the door opened, I had a little speech all prepared. I'd expected to meet with an orderly, who would be sour and dismissive. Getting past such a person was the first requirement, and I'd done it before.

My bullshit speech died in my throat. Anne herself looked up at me with tired eyes.

"You don't give up, do you?" she asked.

I smiled at her, and she smiled back. Her short hair was pushed back, but strands had still fallen onto her face, glued there by the sheen of perspiration on her cheeks and forehead.

"You're just as pretty as I remember," I said.

She laughed. "Like I said, you never quit."

"Anne, I know you're real busy and all," I said.

"But you want another date. Don't you?"

I did. She was right about that. But I had another more pressing matter to discuss this time around.

"Of course I do," I said. "But that's not why I'm here. I wanted to ask about Drusus."

Her face froze. "I can't talk about that, James."

"Why not? What's the deal?"

She looked over her shoulder then stepped out into the passageway with me. "Turn on that thing Natasha gave you," she whispered.

I knew what she was talking about, and I did as she asked. Some years back, Natasha had perfected a device that would prevent officers and other techs from listening in on her private conversations. It even hid your location from computer monitoring systems, all without tripping security alarms.

At least, that's what I *hoped* it did. Natasha had built it and instructed me on its function. I just used the thing. So far, I hadn't been arrested and executed for using it. As far as I was concerned, the device worked.

"Done," I said. "Now, what about—?"

Anne kissed me. She did so with real feeling. I was surprised, but I went with it. We made out for about ten seconds, and a pair of passing techs snickered behind our backs.

When they'd gone by, Anne removed her lips from mine. Still in my arms, with her head on my chest, she started talking quietly.

"Drusus is on hold. He's not getting a revive—not yet, anyway."

"Turov ordered this?"

"Of course."

My face screwed itself up into a frown. "That's bullshit."

"Don't do anything, James," she cautioned. "Don't do anything crazy."

"The tribune's legion is deploying to the surface today. Solstice is going down, too. Both Tribune Drusus and Tribune Francisco are still on ice, is that right?"

"Yes. We believe she wants to run this invasion directly, without any arguments from tribunes who think it's their job to command their own legions."

I heaved a sigh. "It's a little worse than that. She's got some kind of scheme going. She doesn't want any real brass around to challenge her or to report back to Earth on her activities."

Anne looked at me in concern. "What are you talking about?"

Quietly, whispering in her ear between kisses and caresses, I let her know about what Turov and Claver had been scheming to do. She was alarmed by the end.

"We've got to do something," Anne said. "She can't play god out here on the front lines."

"I have a solution. Why don't you accidentally revive our two tribunes?"

She shook her head. "I can't do that. I'd never get away with it. But I might not have to. Wish me luck."

I didn't know what she was planning, but I knew how to wish her luck. I only let go of her tight little body when she managed to pry herself away. When she went back inside the door to Blue Deck, she gave my hand a squeeze.

"The answer is yes, by the way," she said as she vanished.

"The answer is yes? To what?" I asked the closing door. I stood there for a second, wondering what she had meant. Then I caught on.

There had been, after all, only one question in my mind while I was pawing at her. Apparently the answer to that question was *yes*.

I checked my tapper. It was go-time in forty-two minutes.

I trotted back to the dragon bays, smiling. At least I had something to look forward to when I got back together with Anne again.

The ride down in the lifter was relatively uneventful, until the last few minutes.

"We're getting flak!" my headset buzzed. The voice was that of the transport ship's captain. Her words came as a surprise.

There wasn't supposed to be much in the way of organized resistance on this drop. The enemy had planted troops, sure. But they hadn't taken down much in the way of heavy equipment with them, as far as our techs had determined by studying the records afterward.

Troops. Just a few thousand squid troops. How were they shooting at us in this turbulent, thick atmosphere?

The ship heeled and slew. I heard a thumping sound from below the deck which I knew was the sound of countermeasures being launched. All manner of chaff, beeping decoys and the like were pumped out to obscure the ship from enemy gunners.

About a minute later, while troops barfed and swayed in their dragons, using their grippers to hang on, we took a minor hit.

The lifter didn't depressurize, but smoke filled the hold. After that, the pilot changed tactics. The ship stopped maneuvering and plummeted for the surface instead. I could tell the crew had decided to put us down as fast as possible and to stop trying to be fancy about it.

Carlos was puffing next to me like he was having a baby. "This is not cool, man," he said. "We're going to die before we even get to run off this ship. They should have landed farther from the damned mountain."

"Maybe," I said, "but then we'd just have to march in under fire."

"I'll take my chances on the ground. I hate being meat in a can. Let me out. Let me fight!"

I understood his concerns, and I felt the same way. One of the worst ways to die was being shot from a distance, without any way to defend yourself. When you'd been hit as many

206

times as we had, it was hard to control that panicky feeling. Helpless dread ran through you. Sometimes, I wished I was as cool about dying as Graves was. The man had ice water in his veins.

We made it down about thirty seconds later. This time, the ramp didn't lower itself gently, revealing the world outside. Instead, it dropped with a clang and fell completely out of sight. The crew must have blown the explosive bolts on the hinges. This couldn't be a good sign.

"Abandon ship!" shouted the captain. "Incoming fire! Abandon ship, all hands!"

That was all she had to say. I didn't even get to give anyone an order. The squad was bounding for the opening, taking matters into their own hands.

Dragons were fast and deadly when the rider wanted them to be. Unfortunately, the hundreds of infantry we had with us weren't so fast or nearly as thick-skinned. Light troops were trampled and crushed down as the dragons scrambled to get past them.

I saw Carlos run right over a light trooper, breaking his leg and crushing his snap-rifle with one down-stroke of his machine-driven legs.

I wanted to order them to stop, but I couldn't give that order. The dragon riders were doing the right thing. The bodies of regular light troops were expendable. Hell, they could regrow these people back on *Cyclops* if they had to. All they needed to get back into combat was a new smart cloth uniform and another snap-rifle. The dragons were different. For the duration of this campaign, these combat machines were irreplaceable.

"Get off this ship any way you can!" I ordered my squad, with misgivings. "You're to save your dragons. Allow nothing to get in your way. Blow a hole in the hull if you have to!"

I think Carlos was the first to exit the lifter. I was about the eighth. Behind us dozens more flowed out onto the snowy fields.

In less than a minute, over half the cavalry aboard had evacuated the lifter. Most of those left behind were light troops, Solstice people who'd been too slow or too abused to get away.

The lifter exploded at that point. I saw the enemy missile barrage streaking in at an angle for a split-second. The missiles were quite small, but they packed a punch. They slammed into the lifter with a shattering boom.

The ship broke apart, sending deadly shards and burning chunks of metal in every direction. We were already running, so we kept on running. Everyone in my squad made it out alive except for Sargon. A twirling piece of debris came down out of the roiling mist and knocked him flat. His cockpit depressurized, and with his suit too damaged to reseal itself, he asphyxiated in the deadly non-air of the planet.

It was a tough way to go, with your lungs bubbling and your spine broken. I hoped he hadn't suffered long and that we would meet again soon.

-29-

There was plenty of cover on the mountain, but not much that sheltered us from an attack from above. Unfortunately, that's where the enemy was.

The squids had entrenched themselves high up on the shoulders of the massive spire of metallic rock. They must have had drilling equipment to dig into the ground up there. I didn't really have time to figure it all out. I was too busy gathering my squad and huddling up against a spur of ice and rock at the foot of the mountain.

"All right, sound off!"

They did, and I determined I'd lost only Sargon. I reported this to Leeson.

"That's good," he said, sounding a little out of breath. He was hiding in his own gully a few hundred meters to the west of us. "Harris' group didn't do as well. In fact, half of them are dead—including Harris. I'm going to merge up your squad with his. You'll have Della as your sidekick to replace Sargon."

For some reason, that made me a little uncomfortable. Della and I had been pretty much avoiding each other since she'd been assigned to Harris' squad. Partly, that was because we were both too busy, but partly it was because I was dodging certain realities. Her triple revelations about being married, having had our kid and the whole thing about there being a second Natasha wandering around Dust World—I guess that had just been too much for me. I'd kind of shied away from her since then, not knowing what to say.

A few minutes later when Della trotted her dragon into the shadow of the same boulders where I was hiding, there was nowhere to dodge. We were going to have to live together—and quite possibly die together—one more time.

"Della!" I shouted. "You take the second maniple. I'm leading the first. Split your troops up between the two."

"Hey!" Carlos complained. "She's a specialist, sure, but why don't you give *me* command of Sargon's maniple?"

I thought about it for maybe two seconds then shook my head. "Della's in charge."

Carlos walked his mount away, muttering something about who he had to screw to get command experience. I let it go and ordered my group to prepare to break out.

"We're going to race up to the next point of cover. See that ridge? The enemy missile batteries can't reach that spot easily."

My plans were dashed when Leeson called me again.

"Don't move out yet," he told me. "I need you to protect the infantry. I'm putting a full unit behind your machines. Walk in front of them. Don't leave them out on the open slopes."

I couldn't believe it. "Sir? Are you serious?"

"The squids are mostly using light arms, sniping from way up high. Light arms won't penetrate your dragons."

"Sir, there are small missiles raining down on us. I need all the speed and maneuverability I can get. I can't be saddled with infantry to babysit!"

"You have your orders, McGill, and I have mine. Start babysitting."

Grumbling, I turned back to my expanded squad. There were nineteen of us in all. I explained the plan, and they weren't any happier about it than I was.

"What's the damned point of driving around this metal dinosaur if we can't run at top speed?" Carlos demanded. "Does the adjunct maybe want us to cover up the muzzles of our weapons, too? We don't want to scare the locals, do we?!"

210

Privately I agreed with Carlos, but I couldn't very well say so. A full unit of Solstice light infantry was filtering into our shelter even now. They looked young and scared. I didn't blame them.

"Okay," I said to my squad. "Della, take point with your half of the dragons. We'll moving upslope, but not in a knot. Spread out so we don't all get pasted by a single missile barrage. March as fast as a man can run up this hill. If there are stragglers, well, that's their problem."

About a minute later I found myself trotting my dragon up the hill. In my wake light infantry scrambled to keep up, looking like baby ducks crossing a highway behind a negligent mama. There was incoming fire, but it wasn't very dangerous yet. What surprised me most was the nature of it. Could those be snap-rifle rounds? Yes, the familiar whine and snap along with the telltale orange sparks hitting the rocks around us— they were unmistakable. The enemy must have purchased snap-rifles on the black market somewhere.

"They're shooting at us with our own damned weapons!" Carlos complained.

A round spanged off my chassis, but I soldiered on. Behind me, the infantry hustled to stay close. One went down, and he didn't get back up. He'd taken a round in the throat.

"They must have bought these rifles from Frontier 921 worlds," I said. "I bet the saurians are trading with them. Trade ships are breaking the Empire rules all over the place. Claver might be behind it. Funny, I'm surprised even Claver has the balls it takes to go up against the Empire."

"Funny, but not ha-ha funny," Carlos said. "Maybe the traders know the score better than we do. They get around. Maybe the Empire isn't such a big threat anymore. We're the only ones out here trying to stop anyone from doing whatever they want to."

Carlos' words concerned me. He had a good point. Before I could come up with a response, Della cut in.

"The incoming fire is getting heavy," she reported. She was up ahead of me, leading the first wave. "Permission to employ our shields, Veteran!"

"Hell yeah! Do whatever you need to keep your dragons walking."

I saw the lead machines shimmer, enclosing themselves in artificial fields. Sparks that had been pounding into metal now disintegrated without reaching the hulls of the dragons. I should have suspected that Harris had chosen shields in his load-out. As it had turned out, it was the right choice for this situation. Then again, he'd taken more losses getting off the lifter because his dragons had been slow.

Now that we'd been tasked with marching up a hill, protecting infantry, the shields were an excellent advantage. They burned up energy reserves like there was no tomorrow, but I wished my dragon had them. I'd have switched them on in a heartbeat.

Behind me, light troops tried to keep my churning legs between them and the incoming fire. The squid infantry above and ahead were still showering us with projectiles, but fortunately, they were firing blind. They couldn't see us visually due to the heavy mists. That said, they obviously knew where we were and that we were advancing.

The storm of fire couldn't be stopped entirely by the dragons. Now and then one of the running infantry was hit and sent tumbling back down the slope.

When we finally got to the next major outcropping of cover, Della reported that her power reserves were a quarter down. I ordered her machines to go into standby. They could recharge a little while my group stood guard.

That's when I finally met the Solstice centurion of the unit I was escorting. She was none other than Centurion Belter. Her group had been wiped out the last time we'd fought on this planet, the same as my squad had been.

"What a pleasant surprise," I said to her. "I didn't know you were marching up here with us, sir. Are you in command of this force?"

"Technically, yes," Belter said. "But I don't know anything about these new dragons and their capabilities. I want you to fight your cavalry as you see fit, Veteran. You got us this far."

"Fair enough. Was it an accident that we were thrown in together?"

"Not at all, McGill. I requested the grouping after the confusion I witnessed while abandoning the lifter."

This surprised me. I couldn't recall the last time an officer had requested to throw their lot in with me. Especially not an officer from a rival legion.

I was beginning to like Solstice. They weren't as famous as Victrix or Germanica, which were showboat-outfits in my opinion, more concerned with how they looked in the net news vids back home than anything else. Maybe Solstice people had a little humility and respect for others due to their less storied past. They seemed like hard-bitten fighting troops, accustomed to dying without a thanks or ceremony. Their heavy troops wore armor that was covered in tarnish, dents and burn-marks. The light troops I was grouped with now were equally tough. I hadn't heard a complaint out of one of their mouths yet.

About five minutes after we reached shelter, another two units of infantry and an additional cavalry squad joined us. None of the formations were full-strength by now. We'd lost about twenty percent of our troops already, and we hadn't killed a single squid yet as far as I could tell.

Graves and Leeson were among those who joined us under the overhang.

"This is intolerable," Leeson complained. "What are we—a kilometer or so up from the base? We can't climb another nine thousand meters under this kind of fire. Why didn't Turov just blast the squids from the sky to start with?"

"Because," Graves answered him in command chat, "we're trying to *capture* this frigging mountain full of titanium, not blow it up. The squids were ingenious to land here. They must have known they were safe."

"Either that," I said, "or they've already been mining here and meant to support this mountain as a base. When they landed, they didn't know we were going to fire on their ships. They thought we had a deal."

Graves left the chat channel and contacted me privately.

"Sir?" I asked, opening the connection.

"McGill, you always seem to have nuggets of illicit information. What do you mean the squids weren't expecting to be fired upon?"

213

I realized I'd screwed up. I'd promised Turov I wouldn't mention she was in on the deal with Claver from the start. Graves saved me from confessing, however. He'd already pretty much figured everything out.

"So, the scheme went deeper than I thought. Turov and Claver had this arranged—probably months ago. I can only guess at your involvement. How do you get yourself into these things, McGill?"

"I'm not rightly sure, Centurion," I admitted. "It must be due to my personal charismatic aura."

He laughed.

I took that moment to remind Graves about the native machines who had informed me that they were working for the squids.

"There are trails and familiar swirls all over the surface in this region," I said. "To me, that indicates the local machine population frequents this spot."

"You think the squids have machine allies here?" Graves asked me.

"Yes, I would estimate they do. These patterns in the rock and the ore—they're like identifying teeth marks for the machines."

Graves wasn't happy with my news. If I was right, it meant we weren't just fighting a few thousand squids, we were facing an unknown number of native machines as well.

-30-

We got a break about an hour later. We were ordered to dig in and hunker down. Supporting fire was due to come down within a few hours. The orders were almost impossible to follow as we were on a mountain of titanium ore and methane ice, two substances that were anything but forgiving. We tried to dig foxholes anyway—but failed.

"It'll take an industrial drilling machine to penetrate this!" Kivi complained. Her dragon's claws rasped and scratched pointlessly on the surface.

"It's hard rock," I agreed. "Forget about it. Save your batteries. We'll close ranks and hug up against the overhang. Let's wait it out, everyone."

Belter already had her troops in a fold of protective rock that looked like a crack in the ground. Our dragons wouldn't fit, and I didn't want to have my pilots get out of them, so we stood awkwardly around and waited for whatever was coming our way.

Fortunately, it wasn't the broadsides. Each broadside shell from a big ship was a fusion warhead. They didn't seem to come in designer shapes and sizes, either. They hammered with city-buster force or they didn't fire at all.

What fell on top of the mountain instead was a much lighter attack, but still impressive.

We saw the brilliant blue-white balls falling through the mist. Bright as an arc-welder's torch, they could burn out your retina if you looked at them with the naked eye.

"Visor's down, full shades!" I ordered. My squad hastened to comply.

I hadn't seen this kind of fire from the ships before. It was something new. But the look of grav-plasma balls was unmistakable.

They kept coming down, silent while they were in the atmosphere—but when they hit the ground and the physics effect was triggered, a resounding report rolled down the mountain.

"What are they doing?" Carlos asked me.

"As far as I can tell, they're silencing those missile batteries. Let's hope it works."

Plasma attacks of this kind picked up smaller debris from the region affected and shot it outward in a spray like a fragmentation weapon that didn't have to bring along the fragments. Gravel, shards of ice, anything would do. They were tearing up the squids, I hoped, far up on the mountainside.

Belter contacted me. "We should advance now, while the enemy positions are under bombardment."

I felt unsure. Judging from the immediate vicinity, we weren't getting hit. But if those weapons were walked downslope, and we were exposed—well, we might get taken out by our own artillery. That said, I was a new veteran and Belter was a Centurion.

"All right," I said, without voicing an objection. "Let's move out! Same formation as before, Della, turn on those shields."

We were marching upslope again less than a minute later. Huffing and puffing, the infantry raced after us.

Up ahead, we could see the blue-white flashes as the bombardment crashed down. Now and then, bits of flying debris showered down, hitting machines and men alike. But as far as I could tell, the squids weren't shooting at us. They were trying to hide.

"McGill?" Leeson shouted. "What are you doing? You're out of position!"

"Sorry sir," I said. "Centurion Belter ordered us to advance under the cover of artillery."

"She doesn't have the right! She's not even part of Legion Varus."

"That's an officer-fight, sir," I said, marching my machine a fraction faster. A few snap-rifle rounds were hitting my people now. They seemed to be coming from a nearby position. "I'm just a vet, and this is a joint effort. I follow the orders of the officer who's walking behind me."

One problem with using multi-legion forces came to light when we performed joint missions, which had been a rare event in the past. Historically, our legions were independent rivals. Every legion was like an army from a small country— countries that didn't like each other all that much.

Technically, we were all beholden to Hegemony if push came to shove. But for nearly a century now, the individual legions hadn't had to listen to outside authority while out in the field. On this mission, we'd been told the two legions would be kept separate. Therefore, this kind of thing shouldn't have come up. I'd been briefed on the matter and knew that if it did, the officer on deck was in charge, as I'd told Leeson.

Due to the confusion after our initial landing, we'd been forced to put legions and auxiliary cohorts into one force. The brass simply hadn't foreseen this kind of situation—but in my opinion, they should have.

Cursing, Leeson broke off. I knew he'd go complain to Belter or maybe to Graves or even Winslade. It wasn't my problem. I kept marching my dragon, leading Belter's infantry to the next available pocket of cover.

When we got there, we discovered something shocking. The location was already occupied—by the enemy.

We realized what we were marching into only when we plunged into their midst. They'd been hunkering down, ducking the bombardment that was landing mostly higher upslope. This group must have been one of the lowest posted enemy concentrations on the mountain.

There were about fifty squids, all armed with snap-rifles and wearing that scaled combat-armor I'd seen on Dust World. It was thin, but tougher than it looked.

"Enemy contact!" I shouted, cluing in Leeson, Belter and every dragon rider in my squad. "Use grenade launchers if you've got 'em!"

Fortunately, most of my team did. Della's team didn't have launchers as Harris had put those spinal cannons on them instead. The arrangement turned out to be a good one, however. Her team advanced into claw-range, blasting a few rounds from their big guns as they came. The crack and blast of the shells was deafening, even through my dragon's armored chassis.

Still shielded, Della's front line absorbed most of the enemy snap-rifle fire. The squids seemed surprised and unsure how to handle our marching death-dealers. They poured automatic fire into the shielded dragons, but with little effect.

Throwing themselves prone at the clawed feet of the dragons, Belter's infantry sprayed the squids with snap-rifles of their own.

The squid armor wasn't very effective at stopping this barrage, but squids don't die easily. Many fought on with limbs missing and dark blood pouring out of huge holes in their bodies.

That's when my dragons got into the fight. We were armed with twin grenade launchers, and we tore them apart with the first volley. The enemy was a flopping mass of flesh after we hosed them down with grenades.

I soon called a halt to the firing, and Belter's people charged in to finish the job. There was no mercy on our side. We killed every one of them.

My lips were a tight line. I might have accepted any sign of surrender—but there wasn't any. Squids didn't think like that. They probably didn't find surrender honorable, or maybe they didn't understand the concept at all. They fought to the last, even killing a few troopers by constriction when they got in close. It was a harsh lesson for our dead soldiers who'd never encountered squids before. These aliens possessed a grim vitality.

After it was over, Winslade himself contacted me. I opened the connection without relish.

"Primus, sir?" I asked.

"McGill? Are you in command of that crazy group up high?"

"Uh…not exactly sir." I quickly explained that Belter was leading the infantry, and I was leading the cavalry. "We've done rather well working as a combined-arms force, if I do say so myself."

"Belter, eh? Figures," he said. "She's a grandstander, there's no doubt about it. So are you, for that matter. Could you be bothered to hold your position for the next several hours while more troops get up to you? No one else has advanced so far."

I checked my altimeter, and I had to admit I was surprised. We were about twenty-five hundred meters up.

"We'll gladly wait for the rest of you," I said. "Belter's people are exhausted, and my dragons are about out of juice."

"Understandable. We'll reach you by morning. Winslade out."

Morning? That wasn't encouraging, but night was falling even as I looked around. Since Machine World had an eighteen hour day, the transition from light to dark as night fell was alarmingly fast. The same was true in the dim gray light of every foggy dawn.

Just to be sure I didn't get in the middle of an argument with my officers, I contacted Leeson to inform him of Winslade's orders.

"Good," he said. "We'll be up to your position shortly. This business of command confusion is bullshit."

"I was wondering about that, sir. Who exactly *is* in command when we have so many different groups involved?"

I knew the answer to my question, of course. Barring any special orders, the highest ranking officer present was in charge at any given post. That meant Belter could give me orders whether Leeson liked it or not. If he wanted to change her orders, he would have to find someone higher ranked or convince her she was wrong. In my opinion, he probably wouldn't have much luck in that department.

Leeson knew all this, but that didn't stop him from complaining. "Belter is in charge by default. I hope she doesn't get your dragons smashed seeking glory. Maybe if Turov

219

hadn't been so busy making side-deals with Claver, she'd have set up an appropriate chain of command."

A small hissing sound came out of me when I heard him say this. How could Leeson know about Claver and Turov? There was only one way—Graves or someone else had told him. Eventually, this leak of information would get back to Turov. She'd feel like using her broadsides on the mountain then—focused tightly on my location.

-31-

The hours that followed were long and slow. It was *cold* up here. We were squatting on the side of a spire of rock that seemed to reach right past the limits of this world's envelope of gasses. I'd thought the flat plains down below had been cold, but I was wrong. Up here, there was even less to keep a man warm. It made me think of the fragility of every world. Planets were really oases in a vast frozen desert known as space.

The battle went on hold around us for the time being. The legions moved upslope all night long, and several units filtered into our defensive spot. Others passed on to take higher positions.

The enemy was maneuvering out there too, somewhere, I could feel it. They weren't beaten yet, not by a long shot. They were probably hiding from our plasma artillery.

The officers called a meeting with the noncoms as night fell swiftly over the mountain. Most of our forces were made up of infantry who hadn't done much fighting yet, but they'd done more than their share of the dying.

After the events of the day were analyzed, the commanders had determined the obvious truth: When infantry combined with the cavalry, our formations operated more effectively. Consequently, we were told our dragons would be used to break enemy defensive locations wherever they were encountered during the rest of this campaign. The infantry would be sent in behind us to clean up.

"That's just grand, isn't it?" Carlos asked me afterward.

I mumbled in agreement with him. Being told we were no longer a fast-moving cavalry force, that instead we were destined to become an armored shield for the infantry...well, that wasn't what anyone in Winslade's cohort wanted to hear.

We set up tents that were never warm inside no matter how much hot air we pumped into them. To pass the time, I ate, slept a little and tapped on my tapper. Various people sent me notes wanting to make sure I was still breathing. Mostly, these notes came from Anne and Natasha. They made me smile even as I answered and erased them quickly, so the other girl couldn't find them later. Neither girl would be happy to see I was getting queries about my health from the other.

Kivi showed up and rudely looked over my shoulder. "Still at it, eh, McGill?" she asked.

Startled, I turned to look at her. "Just answering a few notes."

"Yeah," she said. "Here's your goodnight kiss from me."

She kissed her hand and slapped me with it. I caught her wrist and pulled her down into my lap.

Carlos brayed with laughter, and I let her go after receiving a few more slaps. She sauntered off. Her hair was disheveled but she had a smile on her face.

"What's with you and her?" Carlos asked. "It's totally unfair, whatever it is."

"Honestly, I don't know. I have to admit, Kivi and I have a strange relationship."

"Yeah, *real* strange. The end result is you get to screw her and anyone else you can grab. Meanwhile, Carlos is lucky to pick up crumbs."

I shrugged. "Kivi and I do get together every now and then, but she always seems jealous of other women, while I accept her habit of entertaining any number of other men."

"Hey," Carlos said, scooting a little closer and lowering his voice. "I'm hoping to get in on that action soon. You can help me out. Just don't let her have any. Not even if she begs you for it."

"What?"

"You know we're working on a project, right?" he asked. "We're working together to come up with a box to control these stupid machines. That's my in. Chicks love working on a cool project together and being told constantly how smart they are."

Shaking my head, I heaved a sigh. "That's not how you go about it, Carlos."

"Hey, don't be a hater, McGill. Can't you share the wealth a little? That's all I'm asking for. Besides, I'm just imitating you. I watch you play the ladies all day long."

"Whatever."

"Just starve her, okay?" he asked urgently. "If she comes and tries to crawl into that spider-web bag of yours tonight, push her butt right back out again. Preferably, you should aim her in my direction."

Carlos had never been easy to like. There was something about him that was swaggering and desperate all at the same time.

"You got it," I said, which got Carlos to leave me in peace. I saw him pestering Kivi later, and sure enough they started working on some kind of gizmo together.

We called lights out soon after that, and I sank into my sleeping bag of spider-silk happily. It really did keep a man warm even on this ice-ball of a planet. For once, there had been truth in advertising. Maybe the marketing man in charge had screwed up.

I'd barely fallen asleep when someone actually *did* try to slip into my sleeping bag.

This surprised me—I mean *really* surprised me. I'd never have thought Carlos could have been right about something like this.

"Kivi," I hissed. "What are you doing?"

"I'm not Kivi."

It was Della's voice. I felt a pang of embarrassment for the mistaken identity. But really, I shouldn't have. I mean, what the hell was this married woman doing climbing on me in my sleep, anyway?

"Oh," I said. "Uh…what's this about, Della?"

"I've gotten over being angry with you," she whispered back.

This had me frowning bewilderedly in the dark. I hadn't known I'd done anything to make her angry, nor had I noticed that she was in such a state. What should I do now? These were new circumstances to me and presented me with a dilemma. Sure, Della and I had a past, and we were both noncoms. Fraternization should have been a no-brainer. Hell, we'd even had a kid together who was some fifty lights away. But she was supposedly married, and I'd just started things up with Anne, a woman I'd had a thing for that went back years.

"Okay..." I said carefully. "I'm glad you're not angry—whatever it was I did."

She squirmed into my spider-bag, which really wasn't big enough for two, but it stretched accommodatingly. It had been warm before, but now it was getting a little steamy.

"Are you disappointed?" she asked.

"About what?"

"That I'm not Kivi?"

"No, not at all," I said.

She was quiet for a time. I made no moves on her, other than to get comfortable.

"Am I bothering you?" she asked.

"You sure are. I was sleeping—and you're kind of freaking me out."

"Why?"

"Because you're married to someone else!"

"Oh. We colonists don't operate that way. Jealousy is a primitive thing. We've moved past it in our culture."

I chuckled, not believing her for one second. From what I'd seen on Dust World, people were just as jealous as anywhere else. Hell, one little weasel named Stott had killed me over jealousy.

An unexpected full-moon face appeared above us in the gloom of the large tent. It was Carlos, and he was frowning down on us like the face of the Almighty himself.

"Could you two keep it down?" he asked.

The truth was, there was very little privacy at night in a tent full of your entire squad. Often on Machine World, there had been a screeching wind that covered up any noises people made at night. But tonight, it was dead calm outside.

224

"You're just as annoying as people say you are," Della marveled at Carlos.

"Look, McGill," he whispered. "Just screw her and get it over with. We've only got about four hours until dawn."

He went away at last. I hadn't made a single move on Della all this time. I had my arm around her, and I was thinking about doing more—but it just didn't feel right. A marriage was a marriage where I came from.

She grabbed my arm, lifted it up to her face, and activated my tapper.

Curious, I let her do it and looked on. She paged to my photos and vids section. She quickly found the shots of our daughter.

"You've looked at them, at least. Several times, in fact. I can see the date-marks on the files. I'd half-expected to find them all erased."

"Della, why did you come over here and climb into my bag with me?"

She put her head on my shoulder. "I'm not entirely sure. I just do what I feel like in these situations."

I could understand that, so I relaxed and tried to sleep, because that's what *I* felt like doing. I actually managed it for a few minutes before she started talking again and woke me up.

"This bag really is luxuriously warm," she said.

"Yes, it is. Now why don't you pipe down and let me sleep?"

She fell silent for a time, but it didn't last.

"Don't you want to have sex?" she asked finally.

There it was, out in the open.

"Not if you're still married."

She sat up and looked me over curiously in the dim light. "You really are a strange one, James McGill."

"You don't know the half of it, lady," Carlos said. His froggy voice came out of the darkness nearby, alarmingly close.

That kind of killed her mood at last. Della crawled out of my bag, gave me a tiny kiss on the forehead, and left. She went back to her own bed, and I sighed tiredly. I was out like a light after that, but I had troubled dreams for the few hours that remained of the night.

-32-

The gray stillness of dawn was split open by the roar of incoming fire. A bombardment began, one that consisted of green-lit falling objects. They reminded me of the globes they'd dropped on us back on Dust World. Those had been gas attacks. These globes couldn't be gas—we were all enclosed in vac suits so gas was pointless.

I made my way out of my tent into the cold of early morning. I could feel that cold, even through my suit. It cut lines across my body wherever my suit folded up and allowed me to sense what it was really like outside my tiny enclosure.

"What do the squids think they're doing?" Kivi demanded, coming up to stand next to me.

We watched as the green balls popped and liquid splashed the rocky walls of our shelter. They smoked there, melting the methane snow.

"I don't know what that stuff is," I said, "but I doubt it's meant to refresh us. Everyone saddle-up! Get inside your dragons, now!"

This announcement was met with a general chorus of grumbling.

"I haven't even taken a piss yet, Vet," Carlos said.

My people scrambled to obey quickly enough, however, when they saw one of the green globes wobble into our sheltered area and touch our big tent.

The material smoked for a moment, then the tent disintegrated. It sagged like a popped balloon.

227

We climbed into our machines and got them moving. All around us, the infantry were ducking for whatever cover they could find in the cracks and crannies of the gully we were hiding in. I pitied the poor bastards. They didn't have a nice temperature-controlled vehicle to hide inside of. They had to live like cockroaches exposed on the surface.

The genius of the squid attack became obvious when a rivulet of the green stuff ran down under the butts of a half-dozen crouching soldiers. There they were, one minute trying to look in every direction at once, then in the next, their suits were unraveling, exposing them to the brutal elements of Machine World.

People howled and hobbled. Their boots burned away, their legs smoked white. Any exposed skin quickly blistered due to the acidic liquid then froze to a purplish-gray as the frost had its way with them.

Before I could request orders from Centurion Graves, he gave them to me.

"McGill, it's time to advance again. The enemy has zeroed our position and they'll burn us out of here one way or another. I think it's time we took the fight to them."

"Right sir—which way?"

"Check your HUD map. Follow the tactical display. You'll move straight upslope with Belter's unit behind you. The rest of the cavalry will flank."

"Uh…thanks, sir."

I checked on my orders. There was no clear endpoint to our advance. If I was a betting man, I'd say Graves had tapped a likely spot for the enemy position then just ordered me to attack it, hoping there'd be someone to kill when I got there.

"What kind of intel have we got on the enemy positions?" I asked.

"Precious little. Natasha and about a dozen other techs flew buzzers uphill last night, but they were all knocked out before they were a kilometer out. We should have at least that far to go before we encounter serious resistance. It's my opinion that the squids have retreated farther upslope and are bombarding us now to keep us pinned, stalling for time."

"Your *opinion*, sir?"

228

"That's right. Have you got a problem with your orders, McGill?"

"Not at all, sir. I'll let you know when I find the slimy bastards."

I closed the channel and sighed. I decided to relay our waypoint to the squad, but not to pass on the rest of Graves' vague ideas. It was best if the squad believed we knew where the hell we were going.

This march was different. The enemy didn't fire at us with small arms. Maybe they'd realized those attacks hadn't been all that effective yesterday. In fact, they'd only served to pinpoint their locations for the bombardment Turov had launched at the end.

Instead, we marched into the blustery frozen silence of Machine World without facing resistance. It was eerie not knowing what might be a hundred meters ahead. The dragons to either of my flanks were churning uphill, scrabbling on the slippery rock. They were like dark shadows shrouded by mist.

Behind each dragon marched a dozen or more foot-soldiers. Now and then one fell and had to be helped up. I knew some were already injured but terrified to tell their commanders. Under these circumstances, a lame soldier was a liability that would best be put down to start over again at the legion bases at the bottom of this endless mountain.

"Vet?" called Kivi, who was on point. "There's something—come look at this."

I goaded my machine's legs into a faster step. Soon, I was at her position.

What I noticed immediately was the mist. It was thinning out. There were gaps in the white sheets of stuff, like drifting breaks in a thick fog.

Not since I'd landed on this world had I found conditions so clear. I immediately communicated this fact to Graves.

"That's only to be expected," he said gruffly. "You're in a high-altitude zone. You've passed beyond the fog layer, that's all. Now, advance to your assigned coordinates and report in."

Ordering my squad to hold their positions and to be ready for anything, I advanced into the open alone.

It was a strange feeling, walking out of a fog bank that covered most of a planet. For the first time since I'd set foot on Machine World, I saw the sky itself.

The heavens were blue-white. Another cloud-layer, higher than the one that we'd walked up out of, hung overhead. Those clouds looked fluffy and white. I found them strangely normal and inviting. After getting a good look, I retreated back into the mists.

"McGill?" Belter called. "I'm getting reports of the mist breaking up."

"That's right, Centurion. We're getting up out of the fog layer at last."

"That's not good. Not good at all. Hold your position, please."

"I've been ordered to advance to the point on your tactical display, sir. My orders are from Centurion Graves."

"Hold your position, please," she repeated crisply.

I hesitated then did as she asked. I ordered my squad to hunker down in the last shreds of mist.

After about a minute, Centurion Belter got back to me. "Do you know that your centurion is a callous prick?" she asked me.

"You must be talking about Graves," I said. "And yes sir, that's a fair assessment by any measure."

"We're going to do this, but we're going to do this *our* way," she said. "I want you to charge to the designated coordinates. My infantry will follow as fast as they can."

"Uh...why the change of plan, sir?"

"Because I think the enemy is in the clear up there, waiting to ambush us. They'll cut my unit to pieces in the open air."

"Your people did all right when we advanced on forces at the foot of this molehill. You can hide behind our hulls, just like before."

"Listen McGill," she said seriously. "They couldn't see us before. Now, they'll be able to use their scopes. We're walking over bare rock and most of my people are wearing the equivalent of pajamas. They'll shoot right through your legs and take my troops out, shields or no."

230

"In that case why do you think Graves gave us these orders? Doesn't he understand the danger?"

"Of course he does. He thought of this long ago—I think his techs knew about the break in the fog. The sensors from the ships overhead should have given him a warning. He wants us to attack so we'll hold the enemy's attention while the bulk of his force comes around a spur of rock and flanks."

Thinking about it and looking over the maps in my cockpit, I had to admit she was probably right. We were decoys, distractions.

"You're saying as long as we attack," I said thoughtfully, "we're doing our part of this mission for Graves—just not exactly how he's ordered us to do it."

"That's right."

I thought about it, but after about ten seconds of thinking, my com light was blinking again. It was Graves.

"McGill, what the hell are you doing up there? Get off your ass and get moving!"

"Yes, Centurion. Moving out now."

After closing the channel, I opened my squad channel and added Belter to the list.

"Cavalry, it's time to charge," I said. "The enemy might not be exactly where the map indicates they are. When we take fire, we'll veer toward that fire, and we'll destroy the enemy when we meet them."

Della spoke up. "Permission to engage shields, sir."

"Denied. They'll slow you down too much. You're going to be left in the dust as it is with your heavier load-out. If you get in close enough to engage, you can turn the shields on at that time, at your discretion. Sound off, squad! This is it!"

They sounded off. No one seemed happy, but they were grimly determined. That was good enough for me.

We transferred power to the legs of our machines and switched off everything else except for basic sensors and weapons. Charging in a dragon was really a matter of resource management. You had to put as much power into the legs as you could without crippling the machine's effectiveness when you reached the target.

"CHARGE!" I roared, my voice distorting over the com-link.

My dragon's legs began to pump and all around me more than a dozen other vehicles did the same. We thundered about ten sweeping strides upslope before we were out of the fog and in the open.

How we must have looked to the enemy. Lumbering like giant predatory animals of metal, we tore up the slope with abandon. Titanium claws sparked and screeched on stone. Inside my cockpit, my vision bounced and lurched as we crossed uneven ground.

The infantry were racing behind us, but they were lost in the dust almost immediately. My lighter cavalry moved directly upslope at about sixty kilometers an hour over rough ground. This fact gave me a surge of pride. I wasn't aware of any ground force in history that could advance faster under these conditions.

Some small part of me had been holding out hope that the officers were wrong. That the enemy wasn't waiting for us to break out of the fog and become instant targets for everything on the mountain. I dared to think that the green acid-globes hadn't been dropped on us to goad us into attacking. But these faint hopes were shattered almost immediately upon exiting the roiling fog.

"Incoming fire!" shouted one of my squad mates. I didn't have time to look over my displays and identify him.

A storm of small-arms fire swept over my vehicle a second later. At first, it was all snap-rifles, I was pretty sure of that. They splattered us, pitting our armor, but they didn't know enough to concentrate and penetrate—not yet at least.

More green acid-balls arced and fell. They had little effect on my cavalry, but I knew that the infantry in our wake would suffer. We charged on.

Inside my cockpit, it began to feel a little warm. The engine was revving and had gone from a purr to a steady roar.

"Break right, two o'clock!" I ordered. "Up on that snowy ridge—see them?"

We'd all spotted them by now. My HUD outlined them in red and drew little arrows that pointed down to them when they came into direct view. Squid infantry, I was sure of it.

As a group, we veered toward them. Their fire became almost frantic. Still, they weren't focusing enough rifle fire on any single dragon to bring it down.

I began to think this wasn't going to be suicide after all. We were only about three hundred meters from the enemy, and already my comrades were chugging out grenades. Enemy contacts blinked out when we scored a kill.

"Incoming missiles!" Della called. "We've got seven seconds! Six...five...four..."

"Spread out!" I ordered. "But keep advancing. If we get into the ranks of the infantry, they won't be able to pound us with artillery without hitting their own troops."

With a whoosh and boom, the first missile landed behind us, sending up shattered rock in a spray. A half-dozen more landed a second later. They were smart mini-missiles. The later members of the missile swarm learned from the hits or misses of the first ones.

Two dragons were taken out, struck dead and sent rolling down the mountain in a cascade of flame and fragmented metal. I didn't even know who died—I didn't have time to worry about that.

We reached the snowy ridge moments later. The squids, to their credit, rose up to meet us without showing an ounce of fear.

It was an uneven contest. We were encased in titanium with limbs powered by fusion. They were only determined balls of muscular flesh. We man-handled them, tearing off tentacles and throwing the writhing limbs down to steam in the snow. It was a slaughter, but I reminded myself it would have been just as grim if squids had caught and abused our light-troopers.

A dozen of the enemy went down before they got smart. They backed away, spraying concentrated fire at our legs. One machine went down on one knee—it was Carlos. I could see his nameplate. He stopped advancing, but he didn't fall. He balanced painfully on his knees and used his grenade launchers to great effect. The squids tried to close with him to finish him off, but he stopped every attacker that loped in his direction with a well-aimed grenade in the guts.

The rest of them we tore apart. A full company of enemy squids were wiped out.

The troops cheered, and smoke roiled around us. "Centurion Graves," I called, puffing inside my helmet. "We've met and defeated an enemy formation. We lost two dragons, and one more is damaged."

"McGill," he said, "I'm checking on your stats—you're out of position. You left your infantry behind. Worse, you fought the engagement without my flanking troops to help."

"Sir, would you have rather have had me stand on the slopes and wait? We were taking fire from every direction."

"Right—those mini-missiles... Fine, I hereby approve of your tactical decision. In fact, I want you to repeat it."

"Pardon me, sir?"

"Take the next ridge. Look upslope, man."

I craned my dragon's chassis back to gaze uphill. Now that we'd exited the fogbank, the mountain looked more imposing than ever. I could see it in all its pristine glory. The mountain was formed like many others but with the vertical look that all geologically young mountains had. A series of sweeping ridges and stair-stepped plateaus rolled upward seemingly to touch the sky itself.

Centurion Belter's troops straggled in as I looked upward. They were puffing and spent. They'd covered the rough ground as quickly as they could, but I couldn't expect them to keep up if we pressed onward.

"Sir," I said to Graves, "Belter's people can't run any farther. They've reached us, but they need a rest. My dragons have power-levels that are halfway down to the red, too. Besides, I just lost three vehicles, twenty percent of my force."

"Are you complaining, Veteran?"

"I suppose that I am, sir."

Graves fumed for a few seconds. "All right. Wait for the rest of the column. We'll regroup and decide how to proceed. Hide your dragons under an overhang. There are more mini-missiles appearing on the screens now."

These final words goaded me into action. I shouted for everyone to disperse and hug up against a chunk of solid rock.

We rode out the next storm of missiles and then endured three more waves before Graves arrived with his much larger force.

Seeing what we were up against, Graves requested support from above. Turov launched an attack, and the mini-missile battery was silenced.

-33-

When we finally began moving upslope again, we had a lot more troops. There were about seventy dragons, nearly half Winslade's remaining force, and about a thousand infantry.

Strung out in a long, ragged line, my dragons led the ground troops as before, providing them with cover. Graves still wanted to charge again if we ran into enemy resistance, but so far there wasn't any.

Probably the strangest thing about our new formation was the personal presence of Primus Winslade himself. He was riding a dragon around in the rear ranks. This surprised me as I hadn't known he'd been trained to operate one of the vehicles.

Carlos beeped my private channel, and I opened the connection with a sigh.

"What's up, Carlos?"

"You know what's up. I'm screwed."

"Yeah, pretty much," I agreed.

This time, Carlos had a serious reason to complain. His machine had been too damaged to fix in the field. The techs had looked it over and shaken their heads. They left it behind in the snow, and he was transferred into the infantry. This had resulted in an unending fountain of complaints.

"This is what I get?" he demanded. "This is my legion's idea of a hero's thank-you?"

"That's right," I told him. "Only in Varus, it's more of a heroic kick in the pants."

"I must have killed thirty squids in that last battle. All while I was on my knees!"

"Thirty?" I asked as if scandalized. "You wiped out seventy or I'm a liar!"

"You *are* a liar, McGill."

"It's one of my best skills," I admitted.

He was suddenly quiet, but not for long. Carlos was never quiet for long. Even when he died, it seemed like he popped back out of the revival machine with his mouth wide open.

"What's with Winslade?" he asked. "Am I blind, or is he marching at the back of the line in a dragon?"

"You are blind, but you're right, he's driving a dragon like he knows how to do it."

"I bet he got private lessons from Della. Just like you did last night. Hey, I just thought of something! Why doesn't he give *me* that dragon? He's not going to fight if there's another battle. He'll hang back and do nothing. You watch."

"Why don't you ask him about it? I'll patch you right through to his private chat line."

"No thanks…asshole," he said. I thought he might shut up then, but no dice.

"Hey," he piped up a moment later, "that last fight was pretty cool, wasn't it? We charged right up there and smoked those squids. They probably didn't even know what was coming. I think the ones I killed inked themselves at the end."

"That's their blood," I said. "It's darker and thicker than ours. Almost black."

"I say it was ink."

"Fine, it was ink."

He was quiet again for a minute. "You know I'm going to die in this infantry unit, don't you?" he asked. "Belter's crazy, and her Solstice troops are looking at me like they want to pop me right now and get it over with."

I frowned. "Maybe you'll live, maybe not. Centurion Belter has gotten her troops this far. You're exposed, but the cavalry is the top-priority target by now."

"Belter is a real ball-buster. She loves death almost as much as Graves does. I know I'm a dead man. I can feel it."

"So what else is new? Time to shut up, now, okay? I'm trying to listen in on the planning session."

I closed the line with Carlos and tuned into the command chat line. Graves and his officers were discussing our next move. We were advancing now, but not directly upslope. We were spiraling around the mountain, trying to avoid their concentrations while gaining altitude.

The squids, for their part, seemed to be playing a waiting game. We passed camps that showed they'd been here in force but had retreated. They didn't seem eager to face us head-to-head. I couldn't blame them for that. So far, they'd lost every pitched battle. But why were they playing for time by retreating? Did they have a surprise waiting for us? We had no way of knowing.

"I've got Turov looking for enemy concentrations and dumping on them when she finds them," Graves said into my ear. "But there's suddenly a big lack of squids out in the open since we bombarded their mini-missile brigade. Either we got them all or they went underground."

That thought made me frown. I'd seen more than just squid camps on the way upward. I'd seen evidence of native machine life as well. Big divots in the land that left shiny marks of the kind a backhoe might have left in rocky soil at home. We hadn't seen any native machines, though. Only squid infantry. Of course, the big machines might very well be in tunnels in the regions of pure ore higher up.

I wondered if the native machines could digest titanium and what it tasted like if they did. Probably, it was something akin to steak with a fine wine for them.

We trudged upslope for about three solid hours before we reached a good sheltered spot and let the troops rest. The dragons needed to recharge as well.

When we got started again, more than half the daylight had gone by. Nearly half the mountain had been climbed, too.

I have to admit that by the time darkness began to fall, I'd been lulled into thinking this march was pointless. That we'd hurt the squids so badly the last survivors would be hunkering down somewhere, scared and hoping we didn't find them.

Such fantasies were ripped apart just as the sun began to set. The big white ball of heat known as Gamma Pavonis had actually peeked out through the clouds now and then, dazzling our eyes and glaring blindingly on the snow—which was melting in the slight warmth the star provided.

That was when I realized something about this planet. It had big mountains down where we were now, around the equator. There were no real seas, but there were spiky mountains, and where they rose up into the sky enough to pierce the clouds, they revealed their frozen methane to the sun now and then. At that point, the white star melted the frozen methane, transforming it into the thick mists that coated the planet. Everything in the mist froze again, and the cycle was repeated.

All around us, as the frost melted, sheets of hanging white mist rose up. It was like walking in a sauna. At first, I could see every trooper and dragon on the slopes around me. But after half an hour of sunshine, they were vanishing one by one.

When darkness finally came, the enemy attacked.

They came out of nowhere. That's how I remember it. Looking back, I'd have to say they were in tunnels that had been buried by snow. Maybe they'd purposefully buried themselves, I was never sure afterward.

The squids themselves, in close, weren't that much of a problem for our cavalry. The real problem was presented by the native machines that joined their attack.

There had to be at least fifty of the big machines. They rose up from under the ice where they'd lain in wait in our path, like landmines the size of buildings. They heaved up, tossing men and dragons aside, sending them tumbling downhill in an unstoppable avalanche.

One minute we were marching along, minding our own business. The next, we were in the middle of dozens of heaving hills of frosty machines. In between these, we were faced with armed and armored squid troops.

The confusion was overwhelming. Every channel was full of shouting troops and the sounds of panicked, dying men.

I muted the general command channel and switched to squad chat. That way, I'd only be dealing with my own group.

In this kind of mess, there was no front line. There were no formational tactics. We were in a pitched battle at close range. I knew that if Graves really wanted to get a hold of me, he could do so on the unit channel.

"Squad, don't panic. Here's what we're going to do. I want you to pull in tight and put Della's group in the center. Her heavy mounts are the only ones carrying spinal cannons in our squad. Della, link up, focus fire, and take out one machine at a time. Dragons with grenades, keep firing on the squids. You know the drill."

Indeed, Della and the rest did know the drill. She marked her targets and called her shots. The machines began to blow up around us, one at a time.

The process seemed slow and imperfect, but it was working. The machines themselves were undisciplined, as usual. They humped over the ice, gobbling up running heavy troops one at a time and munching on the metal. When they took down a dragon, that took them longer, but they still rasped and churned until the job was done. This gave us the time we needed to take them out.

"McGill?" Graves said in my ear after we blew up our fourth target and were maneuvering to hit the fifth.

"Sir?"

"Are you listening to command chat?"

"No sir, I'm destroying the enemy."

"Normally, I wouldn't complain about that, but Winslade's calling for you. He's in trouble, and wants you to save his ass."

I didn't roll my eyes, but I wanted to. "On my way to his position—sir? I don't see him on my display."

"That's because a machine ate him. He was all alone in his dragon, and apparently he tempted the wrong machine."

"Heading to his last known location, sir. Permission to take Belter with me for support."

"Granted."

I relayed the situation to my cavalry squad and to Belter, who loosed an impressive stream of profanity.

"Not only do we have to march up this icy rock in our underwear, now we have to save Winslade's butt too?"

"That's about right. Let's move out."

"Wait. We'll go in first."

This puzzled me for a second. "What?"

"You heard me, Specialist. Stand your post. My infantry will save the worthless Primus Winslade."

"But sir, how will you deal with the machine?"

"We'll roll under that thing's skirt and light up grav-plasma grenades. You've seen us do it before. If you punch a hole in that machine's upper armor and pound shells inside, you'll only kill Winslade anyway."

"Right, okay. We'll back you up."

I watched Belter's infantry rush the machine, and I had to admit, it was just as impressive a sight as it had been the first time. Carlos tried to connect with me, but I was too busy to listen to his complaints. His light went out about thirty seconds before the machine heaved up and died. I grimaced. He'd bought the farm for sure.

Reflecting afterward, as the enemy broke and fled with us peppering their backsides with our guns, I realized Carlos had been right. Belter *was* a real death-dealer. She liked to get into it, and she was more than willing to lay down the lives of her people, as long as the mission was accomplished.

When we dug Winslade out of the debris, he was still alive. He looked frightened, but he pulled it together when he saw who we were. I ordered my squad to encircle his position while he climbed out of his wrecked dragon and dusted himself off.

"That was excellent work, McGill," he said. "I knew you could pull off this rescue."

"Uh…" I looked around for Centurion Belter, but didn't see her. "The infantry really did it, sir," I said. "They came in under the machine's skirts and took out the guts of it."

"Really? Where is Centurion Belter?"

We both looked around then checked our tappers. She was on the dead list, waiting for revival back at base camp at the bottom of the hill. Carlos' name was just two slots below hers.

"Looks like this unit needs a new commander, sir," I said. "You could appoint Adjunct Leeson."

"What? Leeson? Nonsense. That man is more than unimaginative. He's downright slow. Turov has said it herself."

I looked around, hoping Leeson wasn't hearing this. Fortunately, I didn't see him.

"I'm taking command of this unit personally," Winslade said.

Rotating my chassis, I looked him full in the face.

"You sir? An infantry unit?"

"Yes. I'll have to have a dragon of course. I'd take yours, but you're too damned good at fighting in that thing. Which of your squad members is the least effective?"

Blinking, I couldn't believe what I was hearing. "You want to take another one of our last fighting dragons and use it for a jeep, sir?"

"That's not how I would describe it," Winslade said with his eyes narrowing.

Trying to think fast, I came up with a dodge. "I'll come up with a name, sure. But I'm surprised you're missing out on an opportunity like this."

"What do you mean?"

"Chances to stand out in front of the brass and garner medals for action don't come every day for a new primus. But you know how to handle your career better than I do."

"Yes, I do…but wait a moment—are you suggesting I'd do better on foot?"

"Well, not everyone is a glory hound. Not everyone wants to showcase their versatility in combat, either. No, you're probably better off staying in a dragon, sir. You just got to the rank of primus, anyway. This auxiliary cohort will probably be rebuilt to full strength when we get back home. No need to show anyone you can lead infantry as well. The conclusion will be obvious to anyone back on Earth that you can."

"Hmm," Winslade said, looking around doubtfully. A few of Belter's hard-bitten group were leaning on their rifles, crouching in the snow and staring at us. They didn't say a word, but I had to wonder if a few of them might not end up hating me for this.

"McGill, I've come to a decision," Winslade said. "I'm marching with the infantry until Belter can be revived to relieve me."

"I see sir, very well."

I quickly trotted my dragon away from him before he could change his mind. I organized my cavalry squad and moved closer to Graves, fearing Belter's troops might shoot me in the back.

-34-

The ambush attack turned out to be all the squids had left in them. They didn't come at us again after that. We mopped up a few small concentrations of the enemy and chased off machines that became overly amorous toward our dragons and other equipment.

The mountain of pure titanium ore was ours for the taking—and we took it.

We found large mineshafts in the region where we'd fought the squids to a halt. The enemy had been hiding in these shafts that went deep into the mountain, and the clear evidence was that they'd been here for some time.

"This was their central encampment on the planet's surface," Graves said as he inspected the mining machines and piles of ore.

Small smelters were lined up for hundreds of meters. Perfectly stacked cubes of titanium stood next to every smelter. The squid miners themselves were nowhere to be seen. Perhaps they'd joined the combat ranks of the infantry and died alongside their comrades when we hit them.

"This is excellent," Winslade said, striding around the equipment and refined metals. "We've got a ready-built mine and it's fully operational. The titanium stored in these stacks is enough to form the hull of at least two ships the size of *Minotaur*. What a find!"

Certain things were now clear to me as well. The baby machine I'd conversed with through pictures had told me the squids were already working with his kind. Now, I understood that reference. The tracks inside the mine weren't all squid-tracks. They were the tracks of living machines as well. They'd mined and refined this metal together.

The relationship struck me as both strange and equitable at the same time. The squids had gained an excellent source of raw materials for building their ships. The machines, on the other hand, had been provided a source of gourmet sustenance. For them, this mine was like a winery that produced the finest of vintages. They'd probably been paid in metals, which helped explain how hard and light their bodily structures were. Titanium was a fantastic metal. It was both light and strong and resistant to corrosion.

Winslade contacted Turov with the good news. He insisted on a video connection. He reported in alone, with a huge pile of titanium ingots as a backdrop—but without any of the rest of us in view. He even had us add a few hundred blocks of metal to the top of the stack he strutted in front of, until it swayed and stood unevenly, just to sweeten the image.

Stepping aside, I chuckled while Winslade brayed of his accomplishments to Turov.

"He's a regular chip off the old block," I told Graves.

"He's learned well from Turov, that's for sure," Graves said. "You know what's funny about that? She'll buy it. She'll be behind him one hundred percent, believing his bullshit even though it sounds like an echo of her own."

"Why's that, sir?"

"Well, conmen are like that. A huckster is often a sucker for another huckster. I think they're people who get swept up in the moment. People who can convince themselves their crap is reality are very persuasive. They're also more likely to be swayed by the persuasiveness of another. They're people who get excited about things, and when they meet another of their own kind they like it."

His words didn't make total sense to me, but I couldn't deny what I was watching and hearing. Turov was praising him up and down for capturing the mine, as if he'd killed a couple of thousand squids solo and dug this shaft into the rock with his fingernails.

"Those two are a match made in heaven," I said. "That's for sure."

Graves looked at me sharply. "What are you suggesting?"

"Uh..." I said, wondering what I'd stepped in this time. "Nothing special, sir. They just operate the same way and really seem to get each other."

"You don't know if they have an inappropriate relationship, do you?"

I stared at him for a second, then shook my head. "How would I know about that, sir?"

"You're pretty close to both of them. I thought maybe...never mind."

"Consider it forgotten, Centurion."

But I found I couldn't forget it. Could Winslade be more to Turov than a kiss-up? Even though she looked like she was about twenty now, she was really pushing forty. I knew that she liked younger men—from personal experience. Winslade was barely thirty himself, and that technically made him the younger of the two. He probably wasn't that bad-looking of a guy, in a kind of skinny, slimy way. Of course, I was no judge of male attractiveness. Often in my life, I'd figured a man was an unfortunate troll, only to be told later by various ladies he was positively dreamy.

Turov and Winslade? Could it be? Stranger things had happened—in fact, they'd happened to me. I couldn't discount anything, no matter how distasteful it might seem.

Over the next several hours we settled into the mines, making them our own. The first thing I did was work on my dragon, servicing it. The vehicle had fought well, but it had plenty of damage. There were pits and burns everywhere, and half the joints were squeaking and moving slowly due to heat-warping. Oil, nanite treatments and lots of elbow grease smoothed and resurfaced the fighting machine. I didn't know how soon I'd need the dragon in top operating condition again.

All around me, my squaddies were doing the same as I was—because I'd ordered them to. Our first concern was our dragons. Everything else, even eating, was secondary.

"Hey, McGill—I'm back, and I'm here for revenge!" called a familiar voice behind me.

I turned in surprise. It was Carlos. I shook my head in bewilderment.

"How the hell did you catch a revive so fast?" I asked him.

"Dragon rider," he said, stabbing his chest with his thumb. "I'm marked in the book as a top priority for this push. I don't know who made that choice, but I'm sure glad they did. If they'd known I'd died as infantry, I'd probably be stuck in the slime tanks for another week."

Grinning, I welcomed him back to the squad and shook his hand. More of my people showed up after him, including Harris and Sargon.

"Wait a minute," I asked Sargon. "How'd you guys get up here from base camp so fast?"

"They said the battle was over," Sargon explained, "so they sent a lifter down to move people uphill fast. I'm sure as hell glad I didn't have to walk up the side of this rock. Can you imagine how much that had to suck?"

He grinned at me, and I laughed.

"You're glad you died right off," I assured him.

When we were done shining up our dragons, we found a good place to camp within the mining complex. Except for a few recon patrols, most of us were brought into the mines for shelter. That night, I was completely comfortable for the first time since I'd landed on Machine World. I was even issued a cot to fold out under my sleeping bag. That was heavenly when compared to stretching out on gravel.

Besides the cushy cot, the mines were more livable than the exposed slopes. The interior of the mountain was much warmer than the surface. It had to be about minus ten degrees C in here. That was toasty when compared to what we'd been enduring out in the open.

A storm blew up that night and powdered the land and all the frozen, dead bodies with fresh snow. In the morning, I stood outside on the steep mountainside and admired the view. This world had a strange, crystalline beauty all its own.

Carlos and Kivi found me out there. They had a funny look on their faces.

"What have you two done now?" I asked.

"We found something," Kivi said. She was fidgeting, excited and worried at the same time. "You want to see?"

"All right."

I followed them back into the depths of the mountain. They led me into the offices the squids maintained on the second level above the main entrance. They showed me a big mess of equipment and heated tanks of dark liquid.

"Squid beds?" I asked. "I've seen them before. I'm surprised they're still being heated up."

"The whole thing is on automatic," Carlos said. "We could go swimming, but the water is disgusting. What kind of intelligent creatures float around in their own filth?"

"Well, they filter it and all. It's kind of like a big fish tank." I eyed the cloudy water. I wasn't impressed. "This is why you clowns brought me up here?"

"No, no, we've got a real find," Kivi assured me.

They led me to the squid computers. The cephalopods were nothing if not technologically advanced. Their tech was different than what was standardly available in the Empire, but I was no less impressed by it.

The best thing that Carlos and Kivi found was a computer display system. It looked like a big glass sphere. About two meters in diameter, it played images and sounds from what must have been fully populated squid worlds.

I had to admit after watching the vids in the globe, I was blown away. Say what you want to about the cephalopods, these creatures had an advanced civilization all their own. They had buildings, cities, starships—they were the real deal. Most of the shots were underwater and wavering, but you could still make out what was going on.

"Huh," I said, watching one vid after the next. It was hypnotic, like discovering a new full-fledged version of the internet you'd never seen before. "You realize the Galactics must have planets like these. World after world full of a single proud race of beings. No wonder the squids aren't knuckling under to the empire willingly. They've got too much to be proud of."

"We think we've made a major find, here," Carlos said. "What we want to know from you is how best to play it."

248

"Play it?"

"Yes, James," Kivi said. "To get rank. What did you think this was all about?"

I looked from one friend to the next and shook my head. "That's all you guys think about. Call me old-fashioned, but I really don't work on schemes to gain promotions. I just do the job the best I can. If someone in my chain of command notices and decides to move me up a notch, well, that's good enough. But I'm no expert in digging for such opportunities."

"Oh please," Carlos said. "You're almost as bad as Winslade or Turov, the wizards of rank-climbing."

A frown formed on my face. "Well then, you'd best go ask them how to do it. I've just gotten lucky a few times."

"Hmm," Carlos said, looking at me thoughtfully. "That could be, you know. Kivi, we could be asking a dog how to wag a tail. He does it all the time, but he's clueless about how. Maybe we should talk to Winslade."

"No," she said firmly. "We're not asking anyone else. Winslade would steal the credit for this discovery. We'll take this to the techs directly, with an agreement from them that we're to get the credit when they report it to the brass."

"Sounds like as good a plan as any," I said.

"Thanks for all the help," Kivi said sarcastically. She walked away down the tunnels with Carlos, who put his hand on her butt. She slapped it away playfully.

That got me to thinking. Had Carlos managed to pull off his real goal? I knew he'd been actually digging for rank—but he'd been digging for Kivi, too. I shook my head. Maybe he was getting a little better at achieving his goals in life. He'd failed so many times that I couldn't begrudge him a win now and then.

After they left, I hung around and kept watching squid videos. It took a while, but I found one vid that was different from the rest. It depicted a world of unrelenting splendor. Spires were thrusting up into an orange sky, coming right out of the sea.

I'd figured out by now that squids built cities that were mostly underwater. In fact, they seemed to live on worlds that were largely covered by oceans. This didn't seem strange to me as Earth was mostly covered by water as well.

After watching a few dozen little movies they'd made, I became fascinated by their architecture. The cities were sitting on the bottom of the sea—almost every planet they had seemed to be covered in a lot of water, and only the tallest buildings poked out above the waves into the open air. How did they get those structures to withstand the constant storms and erosion effects?

Reviewing vid after vid, I learned quite a bit. After about an hour, Kivi and Carlos returned. They had Natasha in tow.

"This had better be good," she told them. "I've seen tanks of sludgy wastewater before."

They assured her they'd found a gem, and when they showed her the vid-playing globe, she was impressed.

"James?" she asked. "What are you doing here?"

"I'm playing with this gizmo. Watch this one. I've queued up the best clips for us."

Kivi and Carlos looked alarmed.

"Hold on," Carlos said, stepping between me and the console. "*I'll* show Natasha."

I didn't object. He'd made it plain that they wanted to grab all the glory they could from finding this device. I stepped back and let Carlos do the honors.

Kivi came alive as she narrated Carlos' clips. She sounded just like a tour guide. She explained how they'd found the display system and figured out how to work it. They even knew a few tricks I hadn't figured out yet.

Staying quiet with difficulty, I let them show off the system. They ignored my queue of key videos and concentrated on system operation. They could zoom, pan and even bring out localized audio from any location on any of the three-dimensional vids. I'd never seen the like of it.

They were like two computer salesmen, listing facts and figures and demonstrating the product. But they did this in a rather lackluster way. They were focusing completely on the machine while missing the bigger picture. Finally, I'd had enough of it.

"Hold on," I said. "Let me show Natasha one more thing."

They looked at me with suspicion. A couple of times since we'd gathered around the globe, Carlos had made shooing motions in my direction. I hadn't taken the hint.

"What have you got, James?" Natasha asked.

I showed her the top of the vid collection I'd saved previously. I played the most meaningful one. The movie I'd chosen displayed the world that was different from all the others.

"Look," I said, "see the skyline? There are more buildings up on the landmass, structures that are completely dry."

"So what?" Carlos demanded. "Maybe their oceans dried up. Maybe they've got global warming or something."

"No, I don't think so. I think those buildings aren't built like the rest of them because they're built for different beings. Land-based aliens of some kind."

Natasha was fooling with the controls and rubbing her hands on the clear surface of the globe.

"What are you doing?" Carlos asked.

"The surface of this device is touch-sensitive," she explained, "but the interface doesn't operate in quite the way we're used to. They have tentacles, not fingers. I think the squids—there! I've got something!"

The image blurred and zoomed. We were taken away from the street scene we'd been watching, which showed squids wandering their spires over the waves on ramps between the buildings. We were taken over the ocean at an alarming pace to the landmass nearby. We zoomed in on a cluster of squatty buildings that were entirely dry.

"How'd you do that?" Kivi asked Natasha. She sounded jealous to me. "I've been working with this thing for hours. It never let me select a portion of the image and jump to that focal point."

"You have to think like a cephalopod," Natasha said. "They have tentacles, which are a lot different than hands. I laid my hand down like a single curling appendage, using my forearm, actually, to simulate—"

"What the hell?" Carlos interrupted. "I know that guy! See that freak? He's one of the slavers from Dust World!"

251

Sure enough, we were treated to a shambling giant of a man. He was tall and thin, almost nude, and I knew from experience he smelled *bad*.

"That's one of their slavers all right," I said. "I'd know their kind anywhere. Let's look for a littermate. Humans…just think of it, altered humans are living among the squids on this planet."

We kept working with the system and found evidence not only of the humans they'd specially bred as slaves, but also a dozen other types of beings. They all seemed to live in relative squalor on the land.

"Let's go over what we have so far," Natasha said in her best imitation of a college prof. "This world does seem different. It's more built up than the others we've seen. Far more of the areas are urban and they have enslaved beings from many other planets living there with them. I've noticed many of the enslaved aliens are wearing collars and working at manual tasks."

"Just like the machines here in this mine," Kivi said. "The squids are consistent, at least. They seemed bent on enslaving others."

I nodded thoughtfully, remembering the words I'd heard in conversations with various squids over the last few years. "I remember the guy we met up with on Tech World," I said. "We were calling him an ambassador, but he told us that was wrong. He called himself the Conqueror or something like that. He said he wasn't an ambassador or an emissary. He made it very clear his job was to enslave all aliens he encountered. He seemed to think the idea he was a friendly, talkative representative of his race was amusing and maybe a little insulting."

"A slave culture," Natasha said, nodding. "A kingdom based on slavery and expansion. It's nothing new, but it might help Hegemony understand what we're up against. This is an excellent find, Carlos. And you Kivi, you've shown real progress. I bet when the next exams come around for elevation into the ranks of the techs, you'll be chosen."

Carlos and Kivi both beamed. This made me smile. Natasha was anything but dumb. She had to know that such praise was exactly what they were seeking. I couldn't see any harm in it, all the way around. They were doing exactly what their officers wanted, bettering themselves and making themselves more useful to the legion they served.

Earth's legions didn't handle promotions quite the way militaries of the past had done. In the old days, most armies depended on a steady diet of new recruits. The best of these became experienced and were elevated in rank. The rest were discharged as they got older and were no longer in top physical condition.

In our small independent legions, people didn't age. You could stay a regular in a combat unit more or less forever. Eventually, most people got sick of fighting and dying and left the service. Some did stick with it and eventually rose in rank.

The difference was we didn't use seniority as the primary means for deciding who was promoted. Sure, it was a factor. But the promotional system was largely based on skills and performance. As anyone could stay young and useful to the legions for decades on the front line, an individual had to demonstrate they were special to gain rank. Kivi and Carlos were attempting to do just that, and I had to agree with Natasha, they'd shown promise.

"As your veteran," I said in a formal voice, "I'd be willing to sign any letter of candidacy you might be awarded. Based on what I've seen today, you two have shown you're ready to move up in rank."

"Thanks for your support," Kivi said to me. This time, I could tell she meant it.

Carlos looked like a kid who'd finally gotten the cookie jar out of the kitchen. But he wasn't completely satisfied yet.

"We've still got to get an officer in our chain of command to kick things off in the first place," he said. "I think that'll be the hardest part. Leeson is a prick and Graves only cares about capturing points on maps. But first, we have an arrangement of our own to conclude."

The two left, but they didn't head down to the main chambers. Instead, they went into the dark, unexplored tunnels behind the water tank. There was machinery back there that pumped and heated the water in the tank, making it slosh and gurgle.

I looked after them, smiling. Just before they turned the corner and disappeared, they kissed.

"That's cute," Natasha said, looking after them with me. "Looks like Carlos has learned a few tricks from you."

I glanced over my shoulder at her, eyebrows upraised. She went back to curling her arm into odd positions, trying to get the globe to recognize various touch-commands. Carlos and Kivi were making out in the tunnel for a minute, but then vanished.

"He's bettered himself," I said to Natasha. "He's made himself more useful to the legion. He'll get rank, just as I have."

"That's not what I meant," Natasha said. "Carlos isn't out to become a tech. He's after Kivi. He's hunting tail not stripes, and to me it looks like he's managed to get what he really wanted."

"Oh—that. I don't think he learned that from me. I never had to work so hard to get with a girl. Women just come and go naturally."

Natasha gave me a wry glance. Somehow, I figured my words hadn't made her happy.

She might have said something rude, but right about then a big ruckus began in the room with the squid tank. Carlos was shouting, and Kivi was making a strange, screeching sound.

I ran into the tunnels with Natasha right behind me. In my mind, I figured Carlos had gone too far with Kivi. Maybe he'd grabbed the wrong part of her, and pissed her off so badly she was killing him for it. That's what I honestly thought.

The truth was far stranger. When Natasha and I got to the chamber with the pumps and filters, we found Kivi was in the curled tentacle of a massive squid. The thing must have been hiding somewhere—probably down in that stinking mess at the bottom of their bathing pool, or maybe it had managed to cram itself into the pipes to hide. Either way, the tank of water must have run deeper than we thought.

I didn't care where it had come from at the moment, because a squid the size of a school bus was killing Kivi before my eyes.

Without our dragons, riders like us didn't have much in the way of armor or weapons. We had less equipment than your average light trooper, in fact. But what I did have was the knife I'd always carried at my side. I drew it now, climbed up onto the edge of the tank and slashed at the tentacle that held Kivi aloft.

The whole tank sloshed wildly as the squid shivered in pain. I got the feeling it wasn't used to being cut like that. The giant squid dropped Kivi, who lay limply on the edge of the tank. Natasha and I backed away, dragging Kivi with us. The foot-thick tentacles lashed overhead, but didn't strike us. I figured the massive squid hadn't liked getting a limb amputated.

On a hunch, I raised my knife again, letting it glitter in the monster's eyes. Those eyes showed a malevolent intelligence. But unlike every other squid I'd ever met, this one seemed less interested in self-sacrifice. It didn't want to risk being injured. Normally, squid troops were more than ready to die to kill a man.

"That's right," I said to the squid, even though I doubted it could understand me. "Don't even think about whacking one of us. I'll cut you apart."

Waving my knife to keep it at bay, I dared to glance at Natasha. "Is Kivi still alive?"

"Yes. She might have some broken ribs, but she'll live."

"What do you think this thing is?"

"A fantastic opportunity. Hold it here, James. I'll run down to the main chamber and get a translator. We have the squid language loaded on our bigger computers. We can interrogate it."

"Okay, go," I said, backing away further and standing over Kivi. Unless the squid came out of its tank, it couldn't reach me now.

Natasha ran off, and I looked around quickly. "Where did Carlos go?" I asked Kivi.

255

She groaned in response, trying to stand. I helped her to her feet. She had both arms wrapped around her mid-section, where the squid had squeezed her with its powerful tentacle.

The squid watched us balefully from its tank, one eye lifted up into the air with a hump of brown flesh around it that looked wet and slimy.

Carlos returned to the scene shortly after that. He had a belcher with him—lord only knew where he'd gotten it. Before I could say anything, he charged up to the tank and blasted the squid in the face with the weapon.

The creature popped, sending chunks of flesh, steaming entrails and boiling blood everywhere.

"Boom! I got that fugly mother!" Carlos exclaimed in triumph.

"Was that necessary?" I demanded.

"What? Seriously, McGill? The biggest ugliest squid of them all shows up and you're suddenly in love? Is that it?"

"I didn't think it was dangerous, that's all. It was unarmed. Natasha wanted to talk to it."

"Typical bleeding hearts," he said. "I've got news for you: aliens with tree trunk-thick tentacles don't need weapons. It would have killed you all if I hadn't shown up and blasted it."

And thus ended my one and only chance to converse with a super-squid on Machine World.

-35-

After we'd searched the place carefully and made sure no other squids were hiding anywhere, Natasha and I went back to examining the data-displaying globe. Carlos took Kivi down to the main chambers to get her some medical help.

Whatever I thought of Carlos' actions, Kivi seemed impressed by his efforts to defend her. She was smiling at Carlos, and even gave him a hug as she limped back down the tunnels.

Natasha and I watched them go, and we exchanged smiles. We both figured Carlos might get lucky more than once after all.

The alien globe was a fascinating device, but I sensed I was distracting Natasha somehow. Usually, she'd have been so interested in a new bit of alien tech like this she'd think of nothing else. But she kept bringing up remarks that were strangely off-subject.

"You've been doing pretty well for yourself on this campaign," she said wryly, "as usual."

I didn't bother to say anything because I could see where this was going already. She'd always been the jealous type. She'd never liked the way I wandered from one girl to the next on a whim.

Her next question, however, surprised me.

"Have you ever fallen in love, James?" she asked.

"Uh...yeah. Sure. Lots of times."

She shook her head. "Forget I said that. It was an unfair question."

"Okay," I said, and I really did forget.

There was a brief, uncomfortable silence between the two of us. Finally, I thought of another thing to ask her.

"What are you doing with the globe-thing now, anyway?"

"I'm trying to get a good look at their sun. If we can get a spectroscopic reading and a few other elements of data, we might be able to pinpoint where the star is. That's critical intel, in case this war expands."

"Ah, great thinking," I said, and I meant it. We worked together on the globe for a while, and Natasha got her readings.

"I'm not getting an easy match-up," she said. "Damn the Galactics. If they would only let us use their computers and their nets, we'd have this figured out in seconds."

"You'll get it. I'm confident in your technical abilities."

She rewarded me with a thin smile and a glance. It was the first smile I'd seen on her face lately.

"You want to go back to camp and have dinner?" I asked. "It's getting late, and I'm hungry."

She snorted. "Don't you have a date with Anne going?"

"No, probably not. On this planet I'm always fighting, and when I'm not, she's busy reviving the aftermath of battle."

"Right," she said thoughtfully. "It's like you work on opposite shifts."

"Exactly. So, how about dinner?"

She sighed resignedly. "All right."

We had dinner, and it was better than our usual fare. When a battle was over and we'd won, the legions always brought out the good stuff. The Legion Solstice people had the best food of all. They had shipments of real meat, like whole hams, plus bottles—real glass bottles—of wine and liquor.

One of the best parts of camping in the mines was the increased privacy. We had space and warmth to spare. I'd pitched a private tent in an alcove that once held an alien smelter, and we'd enjoyed the relative seclusion. Natasha used her transmission blocker, and we were on our own all night.

Natasha and I ate, drank and kissed a little, but in the end we didn't make love. Natasha had given me mixed signals on that front, but I'd ignored them. After all, it had only been a few nights since I'd been with Anne. I would have been with Anne tonight if I'd been given the chance, but I'd tried to find her and discovered she was dead tired after reviving hundreds of dead soldiers.

I didn't mind missing out on making love to Natasha. Just being with her was good enough. She was different than the other women in my life. She was passionate, and she felt like home to me.

I woke up the next morning feeling great. Natasha was still there, sleeping off the wine we'd consumed together, and I let her sleep in. I stretched out my toes in my spider-silk bag, sighing in comfort. The morning was a lazy affair. I figured we were done on Machine World.

Slipping out of our shared cocoon hours after my usual waking up time, I dressed and passed through the flaps of the tent into the cool tunnels. I walked a few steps away, looking this way and that. No one was around.

I kept walking down toward the mess tents, where I was hoping to find some breakfast leftovers. No sooner had I done so than my tapper began beeping.

"McGill?" demanded Graves. "Where the hell have you been? We figured you managed to get yourself killed or fell down a shaft of titanium."

"No sir," I said. My mind raced, and I came up with a dodge instinctively. Even first thing in the morning, I was always ready with a glib excuse. "I pitched my tent in a private spot. Maybe I was too close to one of those stacks of titanium bricks, and my tapper was off the grid. Sorry, sir."

The real truth, of course, was we'd used one of Natasha's toys. Techs like to build things, and one of the things they built the most often was a cloaking device that scrambled signals in their immediate vicinity. They knew all too well that officers could check on them twenty-four-seven, and they didn't like it. They knew how to turn off their cameras, their tappers—the works. Whenever Natasha slept with me, she did this as a matter of habit.

"Dammit man, we need you. Our situation has changed. Get to the command module right now."

259

My dreams of breakfast ham vanished. Moving at a fast trot, I reached the command module about five minutes later. Frost and loose gravel crunched under my feet with every stride.

As I ran, the cohort server downloaded all the texts and emails and warnings I'd apparently accumulated while I'd enjoyed myself with Natasha. My arm was vibrating and beeping like there was no tomorrow. I didn't even bother to stop and read them all, I just kept running and saying "shit" to myself every few steps.

"There's McGill," Graves said the second I came in. "Get over here, Veteran."

I trotted to his side. Grim-faced officers were everywhere. I was beginning to worry. What kind of crap was I in the middle of this time?

"It's the Nairbs," Winslade said, staring at me with hooded eyes and crossed arms. To me, he looked like my dad when I came home extremely late on a Friday night. "They're in-system, and they want you on the line before they'll talk."

The Nairbs. Those words struck me with a chill. They were the bureaucrats of our Empire, the proxies of the Mogwa. They were pitiless and precise. If there was a tin credit-piece missing when they finished up their accounting, they'd order everyone in town permed. I'd dealt with them before on several occasions, and I'd have to say that neither the Nairbs nor I had ever enjoyed the experience.

On the tactical display the officers had set up in their command module, I could see the Nairb ship. It was the real deal. I knew those Imperial lines. The ship wasn't equipped for a pitched battle, but I knew they often carried hell-burners— bombs that could extinguish all life on a planet. I'd even seen them in action once, when they'd exterminated a squid colony world.

Feeling little tickles of sweat sprouting all over me, I turned toward Winslade. "Anything you want to brief me on before I talk to them?"

"I don't want you to talk to them at all," Winslade replied. "No sane man would. But Turov has already tried, and failed,

260

to get them to tell us what this is about. They just keep talking about a 'clear violation' and mentioning your name."

Every officer's eye was on me now. I could feel it. The truth was, the Nairbs had a half-dozen good reasons to be pissed off at me personally, and everyone here knew it. Hell, I couldn't even be sure which of my crimes they'd finally figured out and pinned to my name.

"I'm sure it's all a misunderstanding, sirs," I said. "Don't worry."

Winslade snorted and rolled his eyes. Graves sucked in a deep breath and let it out slowly. "McGill, I want you to *think* before you speak. Whatever the Nairbs hit you with, you can't give them an excuse to take drastic action."

"We should perm him," Winslade said suddenly. "Right now."

"Say, what?" I asked, startled.

Winslade didn't even look at me. It was like I wasn't even there.

"We can't take the chance of putting him on line with the Nairbs," he went on. "He'll blab something. We can't risk the erasure of all Earth over one specialist."

"That's already occurred to me, sir," Graves said. "The idea was discussed and rejected before you even got here."

"Rejected? Why?"

By about this point, I had my breath back. Open talk of perming me by my own officers had taken the wind out of my lungs. I wanted to speak up, to object to this line of reasoning, but I managed to contain myself. Maybe Graves had a strong point in my favor. I judged it would be best not to mess that up by opening my big mouth.

"To do so would be a violation," Graves explained. "After reviewing Turov's initial conversation with the Nairbs, one critical element stood out: She admitted to them McGill was present and alive. They asked that question first, before revealing their intent. It's standard prosecutorial procedure designed to entrap the guilty. They know he's alive and with us. If we kill him now, it's tantamount to an admission of guilt."

"We can still do it," Winslade said doggedly. "If he's dead, they can't talk to him. What can they do?"

Graves shook his head. "No offense, sir, but you're out of your league. To the Nairbs, it will smell like a cover-up. They'll widen the investigation. They'll draw up new charges. Frankly, it's the worst thing we could do."

Winslade slid his eyes toward me at last. He looked at me the way I'd looked at my plate of ham last night—only, he didn't seem to like ham.

"I don't know," he said. "He might widen this investigation all by himself."

"Our orders from Turov are to open the channel and present him to the Nairbs as they've requested," Graves insisted.

"I'm in command here, not the Imperator. I think we might have an accident first."

"You're wrong, sir," Graves said firmly. "The Imperator is in-system, and she outranks you."

Winslade's eyes returned to Graves. "So that's how it is? I see. I thought you were starting to care about your career again. Very well, open the channel. Let's hope this doesn't turn into a fiasco that results in our collective funerals."

Once the channel opened, I knew I was in the clear. Winslade couldn't very well off me while I was talking to the Nairbs live. But I was filled with tension anyway.

An ugly green sack of alien flesh known as a Nairb swam into view on the display. I immediately felt I knew how all fugitives felt when the authorities finally caught up to them and made that fateful arrest. There were too many crimes on my rap sheet for me to sit easily in their presence.

As the Nairb began squawking into his interpreting machine, I began to wonder if Winslade had been right. If he'd gotten his way and permed me, things might have turned out better for everyone.

-36-

The Nairb Prefect stared at me without pity or anger. He seemed mildly curious, that was about it. But that didn't mean I was in the clear. Humans were barely interesting to any representative of the Empire.

"This creature is the individual known as James McGill?" the Nairb asked.

I looked around for hints, but Graves, Winslade and the rest of them wore faces of stone. I was on my own.

"Yes sir," I said. "That's me."

"You are an anomaly," the Nairb said. "Our records indicate you were permed more than six years ago. Yet your Galactic Citizenry Identification Number cross-references with several other criminal cases that are still pending. How is this possible?"

"I don't know," I said. "Sometimes on Earth, our computers confuse one person for another. Maybe it's the same with databases in the Core Systems."

Around me, the officers tightened up their faces as if they were in pain. I didn't care. They'd hung me out to dry, and if they didn't like how I answered questions, they shouldn't have put me on the spot with these officials and let me fly solo. They were all too worried about being implicated somehow to openly defend me. Since it was "screw McGill" time, I figured I could say whatever I damn-well wanted.

The Nairb chattered something with another, off-screen compatriot. The second creature answered, and the Nairb then turned his ugly mug back toward me.

"Your suggestion is highly irregular and offensive. Comparing frontier technology to that of the Core Systems is unthinkable. Your comments will be stricken from the official record of this investigation."

I wasn't sure if that was good or bad, so I didn't say anything.

"Let us proceed," the alien continued. "It has come to our attention that this expeditionary force, launched by the level-two civilization known as 'Humanity,' has performed a number of violations in this star system. Your mere presence in this system is unauthorized, and—"

"Hold on a minute," Winslade interrupted in alarm. "I thought you were only interested in this individual, McGill. What are you really investigating?"

The Nairb's green, bulbous face turned to gaze at him. The Nairbs had always looked like seals to me, and I couldn't tell one from the other, so I wasn't sure if I'd dealt with this individual Prefect before or not.

"You will contain further outbursts. They may be construed as attempted interference with an official Imperial inquiry."

Winslade fell silent again. He didn't look happy. People rarely did when they dealt with the Nairbs, and as far as I knew, this was Winslade's first go-around with them.

The Nairb turned back to me. "As I was saying…it has been reported that this expeditionary force fired upon an Imperial trade ship. You were named as a witness to this occurrence. You will render your testimony immediately."

Blinking in confusion, I thought about it for a second. They had to be talking about Claver's freighter.

"We didn't fire on any Imperial trade ships," I said. "We fired on ships from the Cephalopod Kingdom. Ships that aren't supposed to be in this star system, which has been claimed by the Empire."

The Nairb ruffled himself. That indicated he was getting a little bit excited. It was like watching a dog perk up his ears. He thought he was getting somewhere—not a good sign.

264

"You witnessed this attack?"

"Yes, from the command deck of *Cyclops*, one of our warships."

The Nairb checked with his off-screen sidekick again. "We have verification from two sources, then."

My tapper began to buzz on my arm. I glanced over, and saw Graves was tapping away on his tapper, no doubt texting me to shut the hell up. I ignored my tapper and Graves, and I kept on talking.

"No, no you don't have confirmation from me on anything," I said. "Listen, we fired on enemy warships, not the trade ship. The trade ship was undamaged, it retreated intact. Surely you can verify that."

"Immaterial. The neutral warships in question were escorting the trade ship. They had an official charter to do so. By firing on the escorts, you legally attacked an Imperial freighter."

"But the squids are at war with us! We represent the Empire in Frontier 921. If they are fighting us, and we're fighting them, we have to be expected to defend ourselves."

"Your facts are so disorganized they are nearly incoherent. There is no officially recognized state of war between the Cephalopod Kingdom and the Galactic Empire. The jurisdiction of Humans as Enforcers ends at the border of Frontier 921, which you left behind to invade this system. It is your task force that is the aggressor, attacking a neutral entity without authorization to do so."

In extreme cases, even I know when I'm out of my depth. This was clearly one of those occasions. I took a quick look around at the officers who stood in a mute circle. Their faces registered shock and sick fear. None of them looked to me like they knew what the hell to say any more than I did, so I kept on going.

"Claver," I said. "He's behind all this, isn't he? Doesn't the accused have the right to know who his accuser is?"

"Yes. The initial complaint was filed by an individual self-identified as Claver."

"And when was the complaint filed?"

"Fourteen months and six days ago by your accounting of time."

That one stumped me. I opened my mouth, but nothing came out. Claver had ratted on us to the Empire more than a year back? That meant he'd done it after Tech World, where I'd killed him twice.

"Fourteen months ago?" I asked. "How could he complain about an alleged crime that hadn't even happened yet?"

"He did not. He filed a charge of misconduct concerning Human interaction with neutral entities on Tau Ceti. Initially, the charge was dismissed, but an investigation was launched as further complaints came in of misused technology, overreaching of local authority and several other lesser violations. We haven't yet gotten to that part of this investigation. You will be formally charged in due time—the case is quite complex. Be assured, justice will be served and punishment promptly meted out."

I was finally beginning to catch on. Claver had been working with the Nairbs all along since he'd escaped us back on Tech World. He'd been out to screw everyone who'd thwarted his plans then through the byzantine Galactic legal process.

As a general rule, humans avoided Galactic Law. It was just too dangerous. You might want to accuse your nephew of embezzling a few credits from your family-owned company but end up perming most of your relations as a side effect. Normally, no one would want to take that kind of chance.

But Claver—I knew this rodent pretty well. He didn't care who got hurt, as long he reached his goals and got even with anyone who stood in his way. Accordingly, he'd been filing criminal charges with the Nairbs for years. The Nairb ship couldn't have gotten here so quickly if they hadn't been lurking around this region of space. They must have been watching us. They'd waited until they had a serious charge they could nail us with. They'd finally jumped in and slapped us with crimes they already knew we'd committed. It was a setup, a *fait accompli*.

What galled me the most was that they'd used me to confirm the crime and admit our guilt. I felt like the dummy Claver was always claiming I was.

"Let me ask one more question," I said.

"Highly irregular. The accused is wasting the court's time, and the situation is bordering on contempt."

The accused. That's what I was. I was standing trial right here, right now. That's how the Nairbs liked to do things; they knew what was going on, while you were hit with something from out of the blue.

"Nevertheless, I believe I'm within my rights to ask questions that help me understand what I'm accused of."

"Proceed," the Nairb said grudgingly.

"Why isn't there a state of war between the Empire and the Kingdom?"

"Such a state has not been officially declared."

"But this species blew up a ship at Dust World—Zeta Herculis. Check your records on that."

"Immaterial," said the Nairb. "The perpetrators of that crime were annihilated on a neighboring world."

"But the squids have a kingdom," I insisted. "A multi-star civilization. Destroying one of their worlds isn't enough to eliminate the threat."

"The perpetrators are all listed as deceased. The matter is officially closed."

"Then you Nairbs made a mistake."

"Insults will not improve your odds of survival, McGill-creature."

I heaved a sigh. This Nairb was a poster-child for his species. They were unbending, prickly and arrogant.

"All right then, answer me this: How can Claver, a known criminal, just waltz in here and fly a freighter around, negotiating as if he represents the Empire. *We* represent the Empire officially, not him."

"There are no outstanding warrants nor open investigations against Claver. If you wish to file a complaint, the nearest office for doing so is located in Frontier 921—where your jurisdiction ends, I might point out."

Nodding, I thought it over. No one had charged Claver with a galactic-level crime because we'd figured he was dead. He'd as much as told me he had another body going somewhere when he died in our custody back on Tech World, but apparently, no one had been concerned enough to go through all the work it took to involve the Nairbs.

"I've got one more request—" I began, but the Nairb didn't let me finish.

"Request denied. The court has been more than patient with your insolent questions, McGill-creature. Summary judgment has been reached. You will report within an hour to our ship for processing. If you do not, the Human task force will be held in contempt and charged with aiding and abetting a fugitive. Court adjourned."

The channel closed. I was stunned. I stared at the display, which now depicted only Machine World and the ships in orbit above it.

Looking around the group of officers, I was surprised at their expressions. They looked relieved. A few, such as Winslade, even looked happy.

"Well," he said, giving me an appraising up-down glance. "An inexpensive solution has been reached. We'll deliver the guilty party to the Nairbs, and the case will be closed. It could have gone much worse."

"I don't see how," I said, "from my point of view."

Winslade clapped a collection of skinny fingers on my shoulder. "I want to thank you for this sacrifice, McGill," he said. "As your commander, I'll log a note to your parents explaining that although you died as a criminal convicted of Imperial High Crimes, you took your punishment honorably and thereby saved two legions."

Turning slightly, I glared down at him. His fingers retreated hastily, and his smile faded.

"So that's it, huh?" I demanded. "You're just going to let Claver get away with perming me? He's not done with you yet. He'll keep at it. He's the real enemy here—surely you people can see that."

Scanning the faces of the officers, they looked troubled. They studied the displays. Only Graves looked me in the eye—

268

but that man could put a gun in his mother's mouth without showing any emotion if he thought it was the right thing to do.

"McGill," Graves said. "You've got an hour. No one here can do anything to help you. I suggest you spend your final minutes wisely, and then you'll be transported to the Nairb ship for processing."

That was it then. My heart sank. If Graves wasn't going to stand up for me, I was lost. I nodded grimly to Graves.

"All right. I can see I don't have any friends here. Remember me in your dreams, comrades."

I walked out on them but quickly noticed I wasn't alone. A trio of MPs trailed me. They weren't going to let me hide or escape. They'd grab me and drag me to the Nairb ship when the time came.

It was comforting to know that someone finally gave a damn about what happened to me.

-37-

Before I could get to the Nairb ship, I needed to be in space. Accordingly, I took a lifter they had waiting for me up to *Cyclops*. The pilot suggested I just fly directly to the Nairb ship to save time.

"I've got an hour," I said, glowering at him. "And I intend to use it."

There was only one person I could think of who might be able to alter the course of my destiny. I headed over to Turov's office on Gold Deck and tapped on her door.

She took her sweet time opening it. As a man with only forty-odd minutes left to breathe, I felt her delay in my bones.

"McGill?" she asked when she finally answered the door. She appeared to be surprised to see me. "What do you want?"

"May I come in, Imperator?"

She considered for a moment then waved her hand in resignation. "Very well."

She moved behind her desk and fooled with a pile of computer scrolls and her tapper. I stood at attention in front of her, waiting. After a full minute passed, I lost my cool.

"Sir?" I asked. "I've only got a few minutes left to make my case."

"What?" she asked, distracted. "Oh yes, the conviction. Very unfortunate. Now, if you'll excuse me, McGill, I've got a battle report to—"

"No sir," I said. "I can't excuse you. I have to talk to you. There are certain realities between us that must be resolved before I surrender myself to the Nairbs."

"What realities?" she asked, but I could see I had her attention. Her eyes were on me, and they were hooded and distrustful.

"I know about your key—since I found it in the first place. I could tell the Nairbs about it."

"I doubt they would listen."

"Are you willing to take that chance?"

She pinched her pretty mouth into a tight line. "This kind of weaseling is unseemly," she said. "Take your punishment like a man. You deserve it, even you must admit that."

"No less than you do," I said, and I found I had raised my voice a fraction. I was almost yelling—I couldn't help it. "You helped push Xlur's air car off the roof back at Central, same as me. You ordered me to pull the trigger, in fact."

"Slanderous statements. Wild accusations made by a desperate criminal in his final moments."

"That's not—"

"Not true? No, of course it isn't. But that's what the Nairbs will be told. There is no evidence to support your wild charges. Even Xlur himself never made a complaint. You have nothing, McGill."

"Well then…" I said, thinking fast. "Just agree to one thing, and I won't bother to press further. I won't make any accusations at all."

"Name it."

"Revive me when the Nairb ship leaves the system. This doesn't have to be a permanent thing. Put me back on the line in Winslade's cohort. The Nairbs will never notice."

Turov heaved a sigh and for the first time she looked troubled.

"I'm going to lay my cards on the table, James," she said. "If you were anyone else, I'd lie to you. I'd assure you that I was going to revive you. But I can't lie to a man of honor such as yourself. The truth is that I can't allow you to return to life."

"Why not?"

271

"The Nairbs already figured out that something improper happened the last time. If it happens again, that becomes more than a mistake. It becomes a conspiracy. A flagrant disregard for the justice system. They could drag all of Earth into the mess. Can you understand that I can't take that risk?"

What hurt the most was that I *could* see her point of view. It wasn't fair, but if a single man had to be permed to save all of Earth—well hell, I'd do the same thing.

"So I'm screwed," I said, "that's what you're saying?"

"Yes. I'm sorry."

I drew myself up and saluted.

"Goodbye, Galina," I said. She flinched at the use of her first name, but made no complaint. I marched out of her office. Her eyes lingered on my back as I left, I could feel them, but I didn't look back at her.

I took a pinnace to the Nairb ship minutes later. My commanders had it all gassed up and ready to go—very considerate of them.

Moving as quickly as I could through airlocks and security points, I was stripped of weaponry and deposited on the Nairb ship. Checking my chronometer, I had about twenty minutes to go when I arrived.

They didn't even have an escort to greet me. Instead, there were yellow arrows on the floor to guide me to the processing center.

The gravity was light, putting a spring in my step as I followed the arrows like an animal being led to slaughter.

It galled me a little that the Nairbs were so certain of their power and supremacy they hadn't even bothered to put me under guard. It was insulting. I knew from experience that they liked to stay in their offices, but you'd think they could come out to take a personal interest in their prisoners.

I followed the arrows for several minutes. I'd been in Nairb ships before. They were big, empty affairs. Chambers echoed with nothing in them. I'd always wondered what else they might be used for under different circumstances. Maybe the overly spacious ships were built to impress, or maybe they were just examples of wasted tax credits and misallocated funds. Either way, they were lonely places to wander for a convicted man.

When I reached the processing center, I was greeted by a familiar face. Claver was there in one of the witness seats off to the left.

The processing chamber itself consisted of four projectors aimed at a circular scorch-mark on the deck. I could only imagine that I was supposed to stand there and let them burn me down to atoms.

Nairbs fiddled with the controls, and the projectors slewed and tracked upward a bit. I think they were adjusting their execution machine for my considerable height.

"Welcome to the end of the line, McGill," Claver said. "I hope you don't mind if I watch justice as it's being served."

"Not at all. I think I'll join you."

Careful not to enter the central execution area, I circled around the chamber to approach the witness gallery. Claver stood up in alarm and watched me suspiciously.

"What are you doing? Your place is right there. See that burn-mark in the center? The floor there is made of stardust. Material so dense it can't burn. The projectors are powerful and quick. Don't be afraid. You won't feel a thing."

"I'm not afraid," I said truthfully. I gave him a little grin.

We both stood about five seats apart in the gallery. I waved for him to be seated and took a chair myself. The Nairbs ignored both of us while fooling with their equipment and barking at each other in their odd language.

"See?" I said. "Nairbs can count. They know I still have about fifteen minutes to report. They don't care what I do until then."

Eyeing me distrustfully, Claver sat down slowly. Then we had ourselves a good, old-fashioned stare-down. It made me feel happy to see worry in his face. He thought he had the tiger caged—but he wasn't absolutely sure of it.

Claver finally shrugged and tried to relax. We watched the Nairbs go about their work. I reflected that in the old days, prisoners were often treated to the sight of watching their executioners build gallows to hang them with. The difference here was a matter of speed and efficiency. I only had a few minutes left.

What would it feel like to stand there and be blasted into a wisp of white-hot plasma by multiple intersecting beams of energy? Probably, it wouldn't feel like anything at all. One second I'd be standing there, and the next I'd be a puff of expanding steam and dust particles. I tried to tell myself I'd been through worse—because I had—but somehow that wasn't good enough.

"You're going to stand there and let them light you up?" Claver asked.

"That's the plan."

"I can wait for that," he said, crossing his arms.

"So can I," I said, relaxing and leaning back in my chair. It creaked with my weight. It wasn't shaped exactly right for a human, but it worked well enough. I took my boots off and put my feet up on the back of the chair in the row in front of me. I did my best to look like a man who didn't have a care in the world.

-38-

Claver tried to match my performance, working hard to look like he didn't care—but he failed. He looked nervous, and I thought I saw a trickle of sweat run down his cheek. He kept eyeing me, my bare feet, and the execution system.

Finally, he couldn't take it any longer.

"I know you, boy," he said. "You're as dumb as a sack of hammers, but you've always got an angle. What are you trying to pull off? I don't accept for one second you've come here to submit to execution."

In a way, his attitude bugged me. He had no honor, so he automatically assumed others were the same way. In the past this flaw in his character had allowed me to manipulate him. Deciding to have a little fun before I died, I narrowed my eyes and put on a nasty grin. Then I slid my hand into my jacket pocket.

"You want to know if I've got a surprise coming, is that it?" I asked. "You're just the man I'd like to show this to—"

Claver's eyes widened as he stared at my hand in my pocket. "Hold on! Hold on! Easy now, big fella! We've got a misunderstanding here, that's all. I'm on *your* side."

I hesitated. I had nothing in my hand other than a half-eaten chocolate bar I'd kept after yesterday's lunch. For laughs, I twisted my fist around inside my jacket so the rectangular shape bulged oddly under the fabric. Claver watched this display with equally bulging eyes.

"You've always been a man who's willing to die for a cause, I get that," Claver said, talking fast. "But this isn't the time. I can help you out. I know what you want—you want to blast this ship to hell and back, don't you?"

Admittedly, I was taken aback. So that's what he thought? That I was some kind of suicidal, walking bomb? I tried to think of a way to play off his misconception, but I couldn't think of anything good.

For fun, I kept playing the part he'd given me, looking mean and fondling my chocolate bar. Screwing with Claver was the only source of joy I had left.

"You guessed it," I said in my meanest, crazy-redneck voice.

"Okay, I'm with you," he said. "In fact, it's a *good* plan. We can't keep talking here, though. They might get suspicious. I'll just—"

He got up to leave, but I shook my head and stood up with him, my fist big and round in my jacket.

"No Claver," I said. "You're not going anywhere. You're part of this show."

"You should let me help you out—"

"I don't need help, or tricks," I said. "You're going to die, old man. Right here with me. Look me in the eyes. I'm the last sight you'll ever see."

"Hold on! Let me make you an offer."

"What are you talking about?" I demanded.

"I'll revive you after you blow up this ship," he said. "That's the least I can do. Give me your data—I'll do it, I swear. Just let me get off this vessel before you activate your detonator."

I pretended to think about it, enjoying myself.

"Don't worry about my next revive," I told him. "I've got that covered. But you—it sounds like you don't have any way to get out of this."

He looked nervous. "What do you think? That I'm some kind of wizard?"

"Right," I said thoughtfully. "The only revival machines in frontier systems are those brought in on big ships. That means our legion battlewagons and this Nairb Prefect's vessel. Once

276

this ship is gone, that's it, because I'm betting Turov isn't sweet on you right now. At least not enough to bring you back to life on her ship."

He didn't answer, he just grimaced. As I thought about it, I understood his position. He was worried about getting permed himself. That fear had caused him to jump to conclusions about what I was up to. Fear, plus my reputation for reckless behavior in situations like this one, had made my bluff work.

"Maybe we can make a deal, but I doubt it," I said. "You're right, I could let you escape being permed. But what can you do for me? Right now, I'm liking things the way they are. I'm thinking I can solve two problems with a single push of a button. You're gone, the Nairbs are gone, I come back later—everything's perfect."

My thumbnail played with the wrapper and dug into the chocolate a little. He watched and sweated, trying to think of something he could do for me.

"You're going to have trouble getting away with blowing up a Nairb ship," he said. "It's one thing to inconvenience a Galactic by killing him, but a whole Imperial ship—that's worth real credits."

"You only have a few minutes left, Claver."

"You can't have brought and placed a bomb on your own," he said. "Turov has to be behind this. But why?"

The answer to this came to me easily. Glibness in lying is a gift, one I've been blessed with all my life. You can ask anyone from my old elementary school days for confirmation on that point.

"The Nairbs have too much evidence aboard," I said. "Turov figures we can't let them finish their report and send it to the Core Systems on a deep-link."

"Right, right," Claver said, buying it all. "The Prefect will report in the second he has the case closed up, and you've been executed. Nairbs don't like wasting money on services, and deep-link relays are expensive—especially all the way to the Core Systems. One big blip of data is what they'll use, and you're here to stop that transmission."

His ideas surprised me a little. Was I really such a big deal that the Nairbs were going to confirm my removal from the cosmos all the way back to the Mogwa? That seemed bizarre to me. I'd always figured I was small-potatoes to the Galactics.

Claver snapped his fingers and grinned. "I've got it. Your plan is flawed. You can't just blow this ship up with a conventional nuke. There will be an investigation eventually. There's no way around it. They'll trace the radioactives to Earth. What you need is a false trail, a scapegoat."

I was listening but frowning. I didn't know exactly where he was going with this.

"Listen, listen," he said, beginning to raise his voice. "I'll let you finish your mission. Turov will be proud. I'm just going to change the circumstances a little."

"Okay, but hurry the hell up."

He beckoned me to follow him. Figuring I had nothing to lose, I pulled my boots back on and left the chamber.

The Nairbs took some notice of this. They barked after us. I was pretty sure they were pointing out I only had about ten minutes left before my execution. I waved and nodded then disappeared into a passageway, following Claver.

I knew that, in a way, the Nairbs didn't care what I did. They were bureaucrats, not sheriffs. If I didn't report to their execution chamber, they'd grind on, slowly turning their wheels of justice. They'd draw up new charges, maybe expanding them to include the rest of the legionnaires in the system. They'd then order more people to submit to their will.

That was the trouble with Galactic Law, if you didn't give in, they'd just up the ante and come after you again. They were relentless, and I honestly think blindly applying the law to others was the greatest joy in their sorry existences.

Claver and I began to run the second we were out of sight. We took big strides in the light gravity, our boots thumping on the deck as we charged down a long passage. We came at last to the docking area where a strange ship was attached to the Nairb vessel. It had to be Claver's ship.

I grabbed his shoulder when he got to the hatch and started to climb in. "We can't just run from the Nairbs," I said.

"That's not the plan, dummy! Let go of me."

"I'll go in first," I said, yanking him back. I didn't want him zipping away or pulling a gun on me.

Inside the ship, Claver had the oddest collection of crap I'd ever seen crammed into a small vessel. It was a smuggler's ship—that much was obvious. There were loose jewels in buckets, powders in bags, guns packed in crates of oil—he had it all.

"You got a stuffed bear I could buy?" I asked him. "I always wanted one of those."

"I'm fresh out, McGill. Now, why don't you get out of my way so I can show you the weapon?"

"What weapon?"

He rolled his eyes like I was the biggest moron this side of the Moon.

"The squid weapon! What do you think I've been talking about?"

"Why do we need a squid weapon?"

"I can see I'm going to have to spell this out for you. You're not going to use the detonator in your pocket to blow up this ship. You're going to use a squid mini-missile pod instead. They're a little hard to program, but I'll show you how."

"We don't have time."

"Sure we do. The Nairbs will mark you down as a no-show, sure. Then they'll up the charges—but they won't report it in to the Core Systems. Not yet. Not until they've decided on their next step. Nairbs aren't fast. What bureaucrat is?

I had to admit, he had a point there.

"When you don't show up for your execution," he continued, "they'll just grind along down the path they've set. That will buy you the time you need to take the initiative."

He actually had a squid missile pod in his ship. I couldn't believe it. I'd never seen so many stolen devices in a single place—not since Tech World. This made me realize something.

"That pile of junk hidden above the fountain back on Tech World—that was *your* stash, wasn't it?" I asked him.

He flashed me a grin. "Yeah. You were robbing me, not the Tau. Does that make you feel any better?"

I shrugged then smiled. "Actually, it does."

I examined his collection of equipment. Claver called the stuff "trade goods," but I knew a pile of smuggled contraband when I saw it. If the Nairbs had ever seen fit to come aboard his ship and have themselves a private inspection, he'd have been permed right off. I filed that tidbit of information away for the future.

"You'll take this pod, see," he told me, showing me a strange-looking contraption with a mass of missiles loaded into it. The thing looked like a peeled pomegranate, packed with clusters of explosives. "Set it down next to their engine core, activate it manually and direct it to unload its full magazine into the reactor all at once. Boom! You catch a revive, and all our problems are solved."

I stared at him. "Where are you going to be while I'm doing this?"

"Flying out of here."

My eyes narrowed. "Why the hell should I trust you on this?" I asked, lifting my hand inside my jacket. "I've got the bomb business covered."

"Listen, the squids will take the blame this way, I guarantee it. I don't want Earth wiped any more than you do. I need to trade with someone, don't I? These missiles are loaded with radioactives from the squid star systems. Radioactives are made inside the guts of stars. The Galactics can trace them to their source of origin. The signatures will match up to the squids, and they'll take the blame when the investigation comes.

"All right," I said, pretending to be doubtful. "I guess it could work."

Claver looked relieved, but a few seconds later as we unloaded the missile pod and stood in the passageway, he frowned at me. He looked at my jacket again. I'd taken my hand out of there to help with the bulky pod, and it must have looked kind of deflated. Following his gaze, I reached into my pocket again and grasped my chocolate bar like it was a shiv.

"Where *is* your bomb, anyway?" he asked. "On the engine core? When did you plant it?"

The hint of suspicion in his eyes tipped me off. My thin, pathetic dodge was beginning to unravel in his mind. I was surprised it had taken this long. I was only wearing a light infantry uniform, after all. There was no way I could be carrying a bomb on me. A detonator, sure, but not a bomb. And I hadn't had time to plant anything in the Nairb engine room. Anyone who could count should be able to deduce that.

"Of course," I snapped. "I've got the bomb on the core already."

He held out his hand. I glared at his offending fingers, which he used to make grabbing motions.

"What?" I asked, tensing up.

"Give me the key, McGill. That's what you have in your pocket. There's no way you could have reached the core and planted anything down there without the key."

Claver was talking about the Galactic key, of course, the artifact that allowed the Mogwa to break any of the technological locks their subservient races invented. Now I understood the look in his eyes—it wasn't suspicion about the bomb, it was greed for the key.

"Come on," he said, "don't let something so valuable be blown up with the ship. Give it to me."

"All right," I said, pulling my hand out of my jacket at last.

Claver watched, hungrily. His eyes were fixated on my fist.

Instead of receiving an invaluable artifact, he caught my knuckles in his face. At the last second, as my punch slammed home into his nose, he must have realized he was looking at fingers wrapped around a chocolate bar, not a Galactic key, a detonator, or anything else. The baffled look on his face was priceless to me. His greed transformed into confusion and disgust.

But then my big fist nailed him, and he reeled back. He slumped on the deck outside his ship. Behind him was the open hatch full of his piled up, stolen junk.

I picked up the missile pod and heaved it onto my back. There couldn't be much time left to try to pull this off. Fortunately, the gravity on the ship was set for Nairb comfort everywhere aboard, or I couldn't have budged the missile pod. As it was, I was grunting and heaving with it on my back. I must have looked like Atlas holding up the world.

The first obstacle I met up with was a serious one. Heading down the main passage way, I ran into two Nairbs. They were humping along, looking for all the world like a pair a green seals on a beach. They chattered at me in irritation then switched on their translators.

"Beast, you will put that object down and explain yourself."

"Beast, huh?" I asked him. "That's what you really call us, isn't it? Well, it's time to show you I *am* a beast."

I put down the missile pod with a grunt then walked toward the Nairbs. They didn't get it, not until the last moment when I slammed their two heads together.

Now, I'd only planned to crack their skulls together and knock them out. I'd forgotten, unfortunately, that Nairbs come from a low-grav world. They had thin skulls—about the thickness of a sheet of cardboard and not much tougher. Their skulls fractured and gushed on the deck.

Looking down at the mess, I realized I was committed now. Using one of the dead Nairb's flippers, I was able to pass through the hatch to the bridge.

I thought about the engine room, I really did, but I didn't think it would work out. There was no telling how many obstacles might be down there. I didn't know the layout of the ship, and I didn't have a lot of time before the Nairbs got smart and employed defensive systems to put me down. Claver had probably known this, but hadn't cared. He'd just wanted to get the hell away from me and see me dead.

I sealed the hatch to the bridge behind me. I managed to disable the override controls from the inside. Fortunately, Empire design mandated that control systems be universally workable for as many beings as possible, so I had no trouble operating them.

Steering the ship would have been difficult, even so, if I hadn't had such an easy, unmistakable target to aim for. Adjusting the helm and locking in the course, I engaged the engines, full thrust. This caused everything aboard to tip and roll to the back of the chamber it was in. I was pinned to the rear bulkhead for almost a minute before I managed to get crawling again.

I'd almost blown it. If I hadn't been able to move, my whole plan would have been for nothing. But I'm a strong man, and crawling isn't as hard as it sounds, even under three Gs of centrifugal force.

When I reached the missile pod, I engaged it, overriding every safety symbol that popped up, and ordered all the missiles to fire at once.

There was a timer—a short one—that ticked down for a few seconds. What were the Nairbs doing all around the ship during their last moments? Probably, they'd been caught and squished flat by crushing G-forces. I don't know. Hell, they might have all died by now, their hearts unable to pump under this much weight.

I rolled onto my back and looked toward the big display on the forward wall of the bridge. The central star of this system, Gamma Pavonis itself, loomed huge and white-hot. That had been my target, the star itself.

My lips curled back from my teeth, and I tasted metal. That was from radiation poisoning, I knew.

That's all I can remember now, because I died at some point after that, and my memories of those final minutes are lost forever.

It's just as well, I guess. Whether I blew up or burned up, it couldn't have been much fun.

-39-

There was a posse waiting for me when I was reborn. They weren't there to throw me a party, either.

"That's it," the bio specialist said. "He's a good grow—not that it matters."

A collar was clamped onto my neck. That was a new one. An honest-to-God collar, like I was some kind of beagle.

"What the hell…?" I croaked, but that was all I managed to get out before I was roughly hauled off the table.

When you first return to life, your senses don't always work right. For me, the world was a swimming blur, like I was in an underwater universe full of bright lights and barking voices. No one seemed happy with me, I gathered that much.

"I don't see why we bothered to revive this piece of shit again," said someone. I didn't recognize the voice, but it was rough, male, and pissed off.

"He's screwed the lot of us, that's for sure. We're supposed to take him down to detention. The brass wants to know exactly what happened for intel purposes. If he won't talk, we're to use any means necessary to get a full confession."

"Good enough for me."

Naked and collared, I was hauled through some steel security doors and handed over to a pair of hard-eyed guards. They dragged me into another room and threw me into a chair. My wrists were clamped down to the arms of the chair—which turned out to be shiny, cold, stainless steel.

By this time, I had a reasonable level of control over my body, so I kicked the guy who was trying to clamp my ankles to the chair legs. I caught him right in the jimmy, and he grunted unhappily.

I enjoyed the moment, but it was probably a mistake. They punched me for a while until one of them called it quits, pulling back the red-faced guy I'd nailed earlier.

"Give it up, Bill. That's what he wants. If you give him an easy out, he'll avoid talking entirely."

Huffing and snorting with rage, the man named Bill stepped away.

They were both from Legion Solstice. That didn't bode well for my immediate future. Like I've said, Solstice people were a hard-bitten lot, like those from Varus. No legion man really likes a guy from another legion. It was always easier to mistreat someone from a group that you saw as a rival.

I mumbled something through broken lips. They splashed my face with water so I could speak intelligibly again.

"What's that, Varus?" Bill asked.

"I said: you boys are a couple of prime pussies."

This amused them. "Why's that?"

"Strapping down a fresh revive and beating on him for fun? I've always heard that's the kind of thing that gets a Solstice man hard in the morning, but I didn't want to believe it."

For some reason, my words troubled Bill—but not the other guy. The other guy laughed and sneered. "You know what you did? You screwed Earth out of spite. The Empire will never stand for this. Remember what they did to the squids back on Dust World?"

"I sure do, I watched it."

They nodded like they already knew that. "Well, they're going to do the same to Earth once they find out you drove one of their ships right into the local star!"

"But I didn't."

They shook their heads in disgust. Bill leaned over so he could look me in the eye.

"Really?" he asked. "More denials? Simply saying you didn't do something isn't going to wash, McGill. We've heard about you from your own officers. You wrecked the Nairb ship just to screw all of us. Well, now it's payback time. First, we're going to find out exactly what you did, second by second, while you were aboard the Nairb ship. Then, we're going to perm you good."

"What if I don't feel like talking?"

Bill got up and walked away, but then the other guy came close and gave me a grim smile. "This isn't your first time around, McGill. We've already killed you six—no, was it seven times now?"

"Something like that Randy," Bill said. He twisted his lips in thought. "Might be seven. I think it has been seven, in fact."

For the first time, I felt a chill go through me. I couldn't remember any other lives or deaths at the hands of these two, but I knew they might have had the storage backup of my mental engrams turned off.

Could these two goons really have revived me and beaten me to death *seven* times? What was going to make them stop?

"Let me talk to Centurion Belter," I said. "She knows me. I'll tell her my story."

They sighed. "That's not going to wash," Bill said. "Never has, never will. You tell *us* what happened, and then we'll finish you nice and clean. But if you don't give us the truth this time, it'll go badly—all over again."

I was in a quandary now. My heart was racing like it hadn't been since the revival. It was one thing to be dragged around and beaten. I'd experienced plenty of that in my life in the legions. But to hear about my former abused selves—and to know I was about to repeat their fate—I didn't like it and wanted to change the outcome this time.

But how could a man out-think himself? I had to assume all the immediate dodges had already occurred to past McGills, and they'd failed to impress. The only thing I could come up with was something that I knew and my past selves hadn't, that this was my seventh time around. Maybe I could use that.

"Seven was always my mom's lucky number," I said. "You pricks have mammas, don't you?" I looked at the one called Randy, the meaner one, thoughtfully. "Well, maybe not you."

"You're going to insult us?" Randy asked in return, shaking his head. "You've gone down that road. I have to admit, you can come up with some good insults when you want to."

I didn't have an answer. I was breathing hard and testing my bonds. They held me firmly. Steel clamps were good for that.

Randy straightened up and sighed. "Well, we already know where your sensitive areas are so we might as well get started."

He moved around behind me, which freaked me out a little. I couldn't crank my neck around far enough to see what he was up to. The other guy, Bill, put his butt on a table and crossed his arms.

"We know your back isn't that much of an issue for you," Randy said, almost like he was talking about a group project we were all involved in. "Some men don't like a kidney punch, but you suck them right up."

He was right, and that made me feel a bit sick inside because it meant he really did know me.

"Yes, let's speed this up," I said. "Just to check, you already know about Claver, right? That he had a small smuggler's ship docked with the Nairb ship?"

"We know about that," Bill said while Randy fooled around behind my back, rattling metal objects. "At least we've heard that lie before."

"How do you know it's a lie?"

"Because Claver has already communicated with us. If he'd been left unconscious in a docked ship, he would've been dead like everyone else aboard."

"Okay then. I can only assume he escaped."

"Fair enough—the trouble is he hasn't verified one word of your story. He was never on that ship, McGill. He doesn't have mini-missile pods or anything else. He's shown us pictures and cargo rosters. Your lies have already been disproven."

I felt something then, a sharp stabbing pain that went on and on. Someone was driving a needle into my back. I hissed and squirmed, but that didn't make it any better.

"That works pretty good," said Randy from behind me. "You see Bill? This man doesn't mind a punch in the back, but a needle—that's different."

287

"Yeah," said Bill, as if bored and a little uncomfortable.

"Looks like I kicked the wrong guy," I said.

"No, no," said Randy cheerfully. "Bill is just as big of an asshole as I am. Now, next question."

"What's the point?" I demanded between gritted teeth. "You already know my story. There's only one answer for why you're on revive number seven."

"What's that?" Randy asked.

"You're having fun, that's all. This is a kick for you. Bill here, he was honestly pissed. I can understand that. But you Randy—you're the sick fuck, aren't you?"

The needle was driven in again, and it was going for broke. I twisted and writhed.

Finally, Bill's big hand came down on the sadist's wrist. "That's enough. McGill's right. No one dies seven times telling the same story. We're not going to get anything else out of him."

The freak looked disappointed. He sighed. "Yep, I guess it's over. Time to end it. Goodbye McGill. It's been fun, but you're all used up now."

I glared at him while he put a black hood over my face.

"Too chicken-shit to kill a helpless man who looks you in the eye, huh? Just as I thought—a pair of wimps."

They pulled off the hood, and Bill looked at me curiously.

"Why keep lying, McGill?" he asked. "Why keep lying and dying? This is your last go-round. You're permed after this. It's all signed, sealed and delivered."

"I've got my orders," I said. "I can't talk to anyone less than an officer. And besides, I'm not going to be permed." I laughed and let blood dribble on my chest. "If you clowns only knew how many times I've been killed and told I was permed—I'll be back alive in a week."

They looked curious. Maybe I hadn't talked this way before. Maybe past McGills had taken different approaches. Me—I knew I was screwed so I didn't care anymore.

"What do you mean you'll be back?"

I told them real shockers then. I told them about killing a Galactic back on Steel World, being executed for it and coming back. I told them about a few other times, too, where I should

288

never have drawn breath again. They listened, and I could tell they'd never heard these stories before. They seemed a little shocked and upset.

"That's crazy," Bill said. "You can't just go killing Galactics and erasing their tappers."

"We've all got our jobs to do," I said. "Your work is easier than mine, that's all. You get off on it, I understand. Everyone has their dark secrets. But you're not going to perm me. You're just having a bit of fun."

Bill's face darkened at my off-handed assumption he was a sadist. He didn't like to think of himself as a sadist. Randy, on the other hand, never argued with my accusations. I could tell he'd made peace with what he was.

"We've got to report this," Bill said.

"Aw come on, it's total bullshit."

Eventually, Bill called for an officer. It took a while, but they brought in a new face. She was familiar to me, but not really a friend. It was Centurion Belter.

"He keeps telling us that he'll talk to you, sir," Bill said. "He's got some crazy stories—things that might change our status with the Empire. I thought it would be best to bring in an officer as he requested before we perm him."

Belter frowned at them, then at me. She crossed her arms under her small, tight breasts and stared. "What do you have to say, McGill?"

"We aren't screwed. The ship blew up before it hit Gamma Pavonis' corona, didn't it?"

"Yes, but that could be due to—"

"A lot of things, I know. But I know exactly why it happened."

I told her about Claver and his squid mini-missiles. When the region of space and the wreckage that was still orbiting the star was analyzed, the radiation signatures would implicate the squids, not us.

"The Nairbs aren't going to buy it, McGill. Even if you're right. Claver has evidence all lined up to show he wasn't involved."

"Okay," I said. "Then we'll have to blame the squids for an outright attack. We should do that anyway—why not lie? The

Empire should declare war on the squids, not just call them neutrals. This is the second Imperial ship they've destroyed."

"They marked the cephalopods as exterminated back on Dust World and didn't pursue it further."

"Why not?" I demanded. "Because they're weak, that's why not. They don't have a fleet out here, so they don't want a war. We should make them join us. Force them to follow their own policies against the squids."

Centurion Belter nodded tiredly. "You're probably right, but it doesn't really matter. You've been tried and convicted. You're to be permed. I'm sorry about that as I owe you one."

I glanced over at the two fiends. "Take me out of here," I said. "Let me talk to you about something important you don't know. Then you can do what you have to."

She shook her head, and the two guards laughed. "That's not going to happen, McGill," she said.

"All right then, get them out of here, and turn off the recorders."

She thought about it for a minute then ordered the guards to leave. They didn't like it, but she outranked them. She switched off the recorders and faced me.

"What?"

"You've got to know a few things about Imperator Turov."

Her eyes widened a little. "I've heard things—about you and her."

"I'm not talking about personal stuff. I'm talking about geopolitical realities. She ordered me to kill the Nairb ship. Check the logs. She was the last one I talked to before leaving *Cyclops.*"

Belter was frowning now. I had her attention.

"Why the hell would she do that?"

"Because we worked together to kill a Galactic—back on Earth. You remember that 'accident' that happened with an air car on top of Central?"

She nodded slowly. Her frown was bigger than ever.

"Didn't that seem a little odd to you? Well, it was bullshit. Turov and Claver were up to all kinds of shenanigans, and the Galactic found out. She ordered me to kill him, and we faked the wreck together. Then we erased the Galactic's latest mind back-up and pushed him over the side of the building."

She snorted. "That's absurd."

"It happened. I was there. She was there. Check the logs, not the candied up news reports. Here's something interesting—Graves and Leeson needed a revive after that accident, too. Why was that? They weren't in the air car, were they?"

"Shut up for a second," she said. She was working her tapper quickly. She brought up the official reports of that fateful day's events and went over them.

"Okay," she said after a few minutes. "Let's say I believe your crazy story. How the hell did you erase the mental backup of a Mogwa official?"

"Now you're thinking," I said encouragingly. "The answer to that one is in Turov's office. In fact, it's probably in her pocket."

She looked at me curiously. "She wouldn't let us question you and perm you if all this was true. She has too much to hide."

I laughed. "I'm not getting permed. Abused, yes. But not permed. I work for her. I just thought I'd give you a few pointers on how things went around here to help you out. If you stay quiet about all this, now that you know the score, you'll keep your career intact."

I thought I had her pretty bamboozled by now. Most of my story was true, but not my importance, which I was exaggerating. Hell, Turov was probably hoping they'd perm my ass after torturing me for a while.

Belter moved with sudden decision. She unclamped my right arm, then drew her sidearm, pointed it at my chest and stepped back.

"All right," she said. "Free yourself and come with me. We're going to talk with my primus."

"How about your tribune?"

Belter looked troubled. "I don't think he's been revived yet."

I brayed with laughter while I fumbled out of the clamps. "That's old Turov again. She's tricky that way. Doesn't like

291

high-level brass around. They argue too much when she wants to do something off-script."

"She's dramatically off-script on this campaign, I'll grant you that. You'll repeat your story to my primus, and you'll go back to a cell. You won't be permed until you've given a full deposition in front of an officers' court."

I knew now that Belter had taken the bait. She wanted to take on Imperator Turov, and she thought my testimony might be enough. Everyone in Solstice was mad at Turov for a stack of good reasons. I'd been counting on that.

She let me get dressed, signed me out of the detention center and marched me down the passages toward Gold Deck. I didn't move on her until we were in a fairly lonely passageway.

I had a bloody streak down my ribs and was breathing hard before it was over, but she was face down on the deck, unconscious. I dragged her into a data closet and locked it.

Belter had fought well, but she'd made a critical mistake: She'd let me get my hands free.

Leaving Centurion Belter asleep in the data closet with computers humming all around her, I moved on determinedly. I strapped on her sidearm, happy that smart cloth uniforms could stretch to fit anyone, and marched the rest of the way to Gold Deck.

Fortunately, not every man in the task force knew me and my status as a prisoner. As it was a sensitive case, it probably hadn't even gone public yet. No one wanted to create more witnesses than necessary for the Nairbs to question later.

I wasn't challenged until I reached the hatchway that led to the command section, and there I used Turov's name. They contacted her, and I waited and sweated.

Turov allowed me to pass the guards. That was a relief, sort of. I marched up to her office, and the door opened.

We greeted one another with guns in our hands. She was aiming hers at me, and I was aiming mine at her.

We both smiled tightly.

"Who ordered you to be released from detention?" she demanded. "I didn't authorize it."

"I wasn't exactly released."

She nodded, unsurprised. "All right then. What do you want from me McGill, you crazy bastard?"

I looked her straight in the eye. "The Key," I said.

Her eyes widened. She hadn't expected that one. "No," she said quickly.

"I'll bring it back," I said. "I promise."

"No way."

"Then I'll kill you where you stand and take it anyway. Your choice."

She glared at me. There was blood on my face and scabs on my wrists. There was also a determined look in my eye that no one who knew me could completely ignore.

"Why did I let you in here?" she asked.

I wasn't sure if she was asking me or talking to herself.

"I don't know, sir. Maybe you like my smile. But here we are."

She took a deep breath.

"No," she said again. "I can't let you have the key. Not even for old times' sake, James."

"How long has it been since you killed someone with that pistol, Imperator?" I asked her. "This is a duel at two paces. That's harder to win than it seems. And if I win, I promise, I'll perm you."

Her eyes narrowed, and her small fingers tightened on her weapon. "You'd go that far?"

"Yes. I'm on a mission."

"I don't like threats. If I win, I'll do the same."

I shrugged. "I've got nothing to lose. This is all up to you."

She saw something in my eyes or maybe heard it in my voice. She could tell I wasn't bluffing.

"Have you told anyone about the key?" she asked.

"No. Not yet," I lied.

She lowered her gun and walked away into her office. This surprised me, but when I thought it over it made sense. If she went along with my threats, she knew I'd probably let her live. On the other hand, even if I killed her right here on her plush imported carpet, she'd be revived in the end, and I'd be permed for my crimes. The guns didn't even matter in a way, as long as she got me out of her office before I erased her data with the key. For her, dying would be unpleasant but only temporary.

I took her sidearm anyway, just in case she changed her mind, and then I took the Galactic key. She had it in her belt pouch like I figured she would. Something like that was too valuable to leave in a safe or under your pillow. You had to have it handy for emergencies, or it wasn't worth owning.

Getting close to her and searching her body—that did something to me. I could smell her perfume while I dug in her pockets. Her body was warm and firm, and her eyes shone in the office lights as she glared up at me.

Angry, but pretty. I couldn't help but recall a few blissful experiences we'd shared in the past. I wanted to kiss her, but I sensed this wasn't the right time.

"I'll be back in half an hour," I said. "I promise, Galina."

"You'd better be, or I'm going to have you arrested again with fresh charges."

"Wait until I get back, or I'll go public with the key."

After our exchange of threats, she watched me leave. She wore a sour, wistful expression.

As I walked down long passageways back to the aft section of the ship, I reflected on the strange chemistry I had going with this particular woman. It had to be the oddest relationship of my long and storied career with the opposite sex. On any given day, we were as likely to engineer the other's demise as we were to make love. We'd done both, in equal measure, for years now.

She could have had me tracked down and arrested right now, of course—but she didn't. Personally, I think that deep down she didn't want to see the last of me. No matter how much she talked about getting rid of old James McGill, I still turned her on at some primitive level. Maybe we were in a twisted, mutually abusive love affair. One thing was for sure: we were a couple made in Hell.

When I made it back to the detention center, the guards stopped me and moved to arrest me. I was prepared for that. I pulled Turov's face up on my tapper.

"Let him through," she said glumly.

I knew she didn't want me to blab about her key. She just wanted me to get this over with.

The door into the torture chamber opened and slammed shut behind me a few minutes later. My two best friends were there, talking and sipping coffee. Randy—that asshole—he was playing a vid of me on his tapper and laughing about it. On his arm, I was squirming in the chair. It must have been a different version of James McGill, as I couldn't recall having had that many needles shoved into me all at once.

Neither man was armed as they didn't want to risk a prisoner getting his hands on a gun.

Bill stood up and looked at my pistol. He knew the score, and he didn't even say anything. His eyes focused on the bloody stained deck at his feet. That's all.

I shot him in the face, and he sagged down like a sack of meal.

Randy fought. One second, he was smiling and laughing at my video, and the next he snarled like a dog and charged me, getting in close before I could get my pistol lined up properly.

The gun spun away, and we were on the deck, trading vicious blows. He didn't go down easy. I had to pin him. I even ripped out one eye, but he still fought on.

Maybe he knew what his fate would be, too.

When Randy finally lay still on the deck, I used the key on his tapper, and I erased him. Not just his life, but all record that he'd ever existed. Maybe his mamma had a few baby pictures saved somewhere back on Earth, but that was about it.

The only people who would remember him were those who knew him personally and could attest that he'd once drawn breath. As far as all the computers in the galaxy were concerned, he'd never been alive at all.

When I was done, I looked at the key...such power. I'd never permed a man before, and it felt strange.

I tried not to think about it afterward—but of course, I did.

Why'd I do it? Because such a man didn't deserve to live.

What right did I have to perm another human being? I don't know. What right did he have to kill seven versions of me in a row?

Like I said, I tried not to think about it...

But I did.

The detention people were understandably upset when they got to the torture chamber and found both their star tormentors dead on the deck.

They found me sitting on the steel chair, looking down at the bodies thoughtfully.

"Drop the weapon, Veteran."

I did so. Then I held up my hands. On my forearm was a live feed, displaying Turov's face.

"Let Veteran McGill go," she ordered.

"Are you under some kind of duress, sir?"

"No. He has acted under my authority. He is to be escorted to my office immediately. But don't listen to anything else he says."

The guards weren't happy, but they did as she ordered. They muttered and complained all the way back up to Gold Deck.

Centurion Belter made an appearance along the way, and she almost crashed the whole party. She was raving mad, half-naked, and she had a lot of grease and dirt on her. She must have had a hard time getting out of that locked data closet.

"Sorry sir," I said when faced with her shouts and curses.

When the guards explained I was under Turov's protection, she took her sidearm and left me, snarling about traitors and bastards. Since I felt I was neither, I didn't feel the sting of her barbs.

It occurred to me as we reached Gold Deck that Turov might very well have me shot when I got there. But those were the breaks. I'd done what I wanted to do. I'd made my bargain with the devil, and I was going to keep my end of it, no matter how it turned out.

When I got there, she saw I was unarmed and so she waved my escort back outside into the passages. Her office door closed behind me, and we were alone.

I stood at attention as she walked around me, staring up curiously. She stopped when she got around to face me again, and she shook her head.

"You're a wonder, James McGill."

"Thank you, sir."

She held out her hand. "Give it to me."

I put the Galactic key into her small palm. She made it disappear like a magician palming a gold coin. One second it was there and the next it wasn't.

Then she surprised me by putting her pistol on her desk.

"James, I'm sorry," she said.

Of all the things Galina Turov might have said to me, this was probably the last one I was expecting. I glanced down, looking into her face for an instant. Our eyes met, and she honestly looked troubled.

"I reviewed the vid files while you were gone," she said. "I didn't know. I swear it. And I don't want you to blame all of Solstice, either. My orders were to extract the truth. They were overzealous in their efforts."

"You could say that."

She stared at me thoughtfully for a second. "What happened on the Nairb ship? Give me the truth."

I told her. I told her everything. About Claver, the Nairb death chamber, the squid missile pod—even the chocolate bar. She listened, shaking her head from time to time and making sounds of disbelief.

"All right," she said when I finished. "I'm going to trust you on this one. What's done is done, anyway. If the Nairbs don't buy that the cephalopods destroyed their ship, executing you won't have any effect on their condemnation of Earth. Your charges are dismissed."

"Thank you, sir," I said.

"Why did you need the key for simple revenge?" she asked. "You had a pistol—that would have been enough for the McGill I know."

I thought about my answer. She didn't know that I'd erased that guy, Randy. He just wasn't there anymore in the computer systems, and anyone who's ever looked for a ghost can tell you they're not easy to find. You don't even notice when they're not around anymore.

"What would you have had me do," I asked her, "if it had been you in that chair for seven lives?

"Seven...?" she asked, shocked. "I didn't know..."

I took three steps toward her. She backed up one pace and put her hand on the desk near her pistol, but she didn't pick it up.

I touched her shoulder. I don't know why, really. We'd been close once. Maybe that was it. Touching her just felt right.

She didn't even seem to notice. She was looking into my eyes, not at my hands.

298

"Galina," I said, "we've been through it, you and I. Life, death—love and despair. This is one more of those moments, that's all."

"But what did you do?"

"People think I do whatever I want, but it's not true. I did what I had to do."

She finally caught on then. "You *erased* them?" Her eyes were big. "That's why you needed the key. Killing those two wasn't enough?"

"For one man it was—but not for the other."

She nodded as if she understood. Maybe she did understand, I'm not sure.

She looked so young, but she wasn't a kid. She'd seen a lot in her lifetime, just as I had.

"I'll cover it up," she said. "Don't worry about it."

"Thanks," I said, "but I'll never forget this day."

She gave me a little kiss. It was a strangely gentle gesture, coming from her. I took my hand off her after that and left. She didn't try to stop me. She didn't say anything at all. It was hard to know what she was thinking.

I didn't ask because I didn't care. I'd had a long, hard day, and it was finally done.

-41-

Imperator Turov's idea of "covering up" was a little different than mine. She didn't erase records or stage a hearing to clear my name. She just dropped the charges and ordered everyone involved to shut the hell up.

It was effective on a surface level, I had to give her that. The legion officials stopped trying to arrest me, and I was restored to my previous rank and position in Winslade's cavalry cohort. I don't think Winslade was too happy about that part, but he didn't say anything. He had to be wondering what kind of strange power I had over Turov.

No one said much to me at all, in fact. But they did stare, and a few of them sneered. They talked—oh yeah, they talked—but only behind my back.

Carlos was an exception to that rule. He didn't just sneer and whisper, he came right out and bitched about what had happened.

"Another sleazy con job," he said. "Or should I say, blow job?"

"What?" I asked, jolted out of my thoughts. I was running down the pilot's checklist on my dragon. It was all shined up and ready for the parade ground. It'd been a week since our last battle, and that had allowed us to repair and polish our deadly machines.

Carlos and I were standing in the mechanic's bay under the bellies of our respective vehicles. Originally, I'd placed his dragon in a pod at the far end of the bay, but that hadn't worked out. Sure, he'd been less annoying to me, but he'd irritated everyone else. Without me to shut his mouth, his naturally charismatic personality had driven the rest of my squad nuts. Consequently, I'd moved him right up next to me, so I could keep an eye on him.

"You heard me," he said. "Turov still has a thing for you. It's obvious and undeniable. If any of the rest of us had pulled shit like that we'd have been permed instantly. Well, maybe not instantly. They might have tortured us for a while first."

At the mention of torture, I bared my teeth. I could still feel Randy's hot needle in my back. Anne had sprayed several layers of fresh cells over the puncture wounds, but they still ached and stung, especially when I stretched in the morning.

"You don't know what the hell you're talking about," I told him. "And you should stop talking before I stop you myself."

For some reason, he got the message this time. He fell quiet, although he was still muttering to himself about how unfair the universe was. He opened the leg actuators on his vehicle to make some tension adjustments, and I left the bay.

I had a headache, a backache, and I was pissed off. I went to see Anne, who looked me over doubtfully.

"I think you have an internal infection," she said. "How did this happen, James? Did you report these injuries?"

"Sort of."

"What does that mean? Are they from training, or working in the bays or what?"

Hesitating, I thought about my answer before I spoke. Finally, I shook my head. "The injuries were deliberate," I said. "Courtesy of Legion Solstice."

Anne was alarmed and angry about that. "You should report them. This goes beyond hazing and bar-fighting. This is abuse."

She applied salves to my skin and gave me a hefty shot of antibiotics deep in my abdomen. The shot made me a little sick, and the long needle reminded me of Randy again.

She put a hand on my forehead then read the results that lit up her tapper. "Slight fever. Blood toxins are up. Are you sleeping?"

"Sometimes."

She kept prodding me and checking me over. At last, I'd had enough of it, and I gently took her hands in mine.

"Let's go on a date," I said.

She looked into my eyes, still worried. "What happened to you? This could be serious—you didn't have a bad revive again, did you?"

That made me laugh. "I had several of them, in fact. And I don't want to take another trip through the revival machines, if that's what you're suggesting. I just need some cheering up and some time to heal."

"I don't know," she said, looking down at her hands, which were still wrapped up inside mine.

"What? Why not? You promised me another date a while back, remember?"

She nodded, but she still didn't look at me.

"This is the best shot we're going to get," I said. "Things are pretty quiet right now. Everyone's been revived, even the tribunes. If we get into another fight, we'll be separated again. If we fly back home—well, we might not see each other until the next campaign."

Anne pulled her hands out of my grip and sighed. "I know. All right. I'm on break in an hour. Meet me then."

Her words gave me the first smile of my day. I had something to look forward to. Even better, it looked like the general dislike and mistrust I'd been faced with everywhere I went didn't extend all the way to Anne. I was glad about that.

I made some plans and special arrangements, and by the time I met her coming out of Blue Deck's main hatch, I had a picnic basket on my arm.

She looked at it and smiled. "What have you got?"

It was a long list, and there were even a few special items like pickled quail eggs and a bottle of real wine.

"Where did you get all this stuff?" she asked.

"I pulled a few strings."

She gave me an odd look. "With Turov?"

My mouth opened then closed again. I was stumped. Did everyone believe I was some kind of boy-toy for the brass?

"No, with the quartermaster. He owed me one. What kind of rumors have you been listening to?"

We walked together toward Green Deck as we talked. I was annoyed, but I tried to keep my voice light and unconcerned. Even I knew that yelling at your date in the first five minutes wasn't a man's wisest opening move.

We came to the entrance, which was an overgrown arch of leafy vines. It had always looked strange as the vines were in stark contrast to the steel walls of the ship.

We passed inside before she reached out and touched my arm with gentle fingers.

"I'm not being fair to you," she said. "We should cancel this."

"What? These quail eggs aren't going to eat themselves!"

"I know. I appreciate all the effort you've gone to, really I do. But I don't know if I can go through with this today."

"Aw, come on," I said. "Let's talk it out. First off, no, I didn't screw Turov to get out of being permed."

Her eyes were on mine now. She didn't say anything, but I knew I had her full and undivided attention.

"Secondly," I continued, "I didn't kill the Nairb ship and doom us all."

"You didn't?"

"Well—hold on," I said. "Okay, I *did* destroy their ship. But that's been fixed. The Galactics believe it was the squids that did it."

"How did you manage that?" she asked suspiciously.

I gave her the general story, leaving out many of the details. In my version, I was more of a secret agent sent to remove an obstacle than a crazy convict who managed to kill his executioners first.

"So," she said, "that's why you're still breathing? Because Earth won't be blamed?"

"That's right. We're in the clear."

Now, you have to understand that I didn't know any such thing. Not yet. The Nairbs were dead, and as far as anyone could tell, they hadn't reported the details of their fate. The radioactive evidence trail had been effectively planted too, pointing a guilty finger at the squids. But the investigation hadn't come yet, and hadn't made any conclusions.

303

To my way of thinking I wasn't lying, but I *was* embellishing and extrapolating. The results I described weren't certain, but they were likely and preplanned. When I was finished, I watched Anne to see how my words had been received.

She still looked wary, like a cat that just won't come in the door because it suspects you're going to grab it the second it does. She was right, but I kept on smiling and waiting like I didn't have a care in the world.

Finally, she stepped closer and took my hand again. I sighed and we found a spot to eat. Together, we shared a few hours of happiness on Green Deck. No one bothered us, and we thoroughly enjoyed ourselves.

-42-

The only thing I hadn't gotten out of Anne the night before was a promise of more romantic encounters. She'd enjoyed herself, we both had, but she'd stopped short of making a commitment.

In the morning, as I booted people out of their bunks and sent them reeling to the showers and breakfast, I was thinking of her. How was I going to entice her this time? I'd spent a lot of credits and good will getting that picnic together on Green Deck, but a man couldn't pull that stunt every day. For one thing, I'd be broke before the week was out.

Fate had other plans for me in any case. Klaxons wailed, and we were called to battle stations at about nine in the morning. My team was busy doing calisthenics in our module, and we didn't even have our dragons handy to jump into.

"You know what that noise means!" I shouted. "Move your butts, people. Everyone get down to the dragon bay. We're not getting caught with our pants down this time!"

I knew things were bad when red arrows appeared on the deck, leading toward the lifters. I contacted Leeson immediately for directions.

"McGill, the legion infantry is doing a hot-drop. Get your dragons to the lifters, pronto!"

"Will do, sir," I said, waving to my squad who were pounding along behind me at a run. "What are we up against?"

"Unknown ships have entered the system, and they're heading for us. We're deploying Legion Varus on the titanium

305

mountain, with Winslade's cohort to back them up. That's all I know for now. You have your orders, Leeson out."

How many ships? That's what I wanted to know, but he was off the channel before I could ask.

I relayed the information to my squad, and Sargon contacted me privately afterward.

"So Solstice is going to stay in space?" he asked.

"That part didn't get past you, huh?"

"No, Vet. The way I see it, Turov clearly has a plan—and for once it makes a little bit of sense to me. She wants to protect her sole prize on the planet surface and at the same time hold a reserve force in space she can drop anywhere in response to an enemy attack. Our legions are only useful on the ground, so we can take it as something of a compliment that she's chosen Varus to be deployed first."

"That's one way to look at it," I admitted. "We'll find out what we're facing in due course, I'm sure. I'll keep you informed, specialist."

"I know you will. You're not as smooth at this job as Harris was, not yet, but I like your style, Vet."

"Thank you, Sargon."

We disconnected, and I had to smile. Sargon was one of the few men in the unit who hadn't doubted me, not even when I was accused of blowing up an Imperial ship and possibly causing the eventual demise of Earth. He and I understood each other. Sometimes, a man had to do what a man had to do.

We were busy after that, plugging our bodies into our dragons at the same time we were decoupling them from the ship. They came to life as we moved inside them. After having piloted one of these fine machines for months now, it felt like a second skin. When I moved my arm, my dragon's long steel appendage moved. I felt like a giant made of fine metals—and that's pretty much what I was.

Clanking down passages toward the lifters, we made good time. There were arrows to follow on the deck, but we knew the way by now.

The ship was venting and yellow flashers were spiraling around everywhere. It was enough to give a man a headache. The crew was scrambling just as much as the troops were. I

306

knew what that meant, they were getting ready for some fast maneuvering. This might well be a space battle rather than a ground battle. If that turned out to be the case, my cohort might well be the lucky ones. Anyone up here could be caught and destroyed, helpless in their dragons.

When we got to the lifters a line of bios were there, waiting. They had a data system, and they demanded our data disks before we boarded.

At the start of this campaign, each of us had been issued a silver disk about the size and weight of a half-credit piece. There was nothing unusual about that. What was strange was that the bios were asking for them now. I surrendered mine, and the pretty little bio put it into a slot on a data terminal. I wondered if I would get it back—but I didn't.

"Say, Specialist," I said. "What's the deal? Why are we giving up our disks to you shipboard people? Aren't we taking revival machines down to the surface with us?"

"I don't know about what equipment you'll be issued, Vet," she said. "But I know we're supposed to update everyone's data before they get on the lifters."

She proceeded to scan me then, which amounted to plugging into the data ports on my dragon, which connected in turn to my tapper. All down the line they were stopping troops and making these transfers. It took about a minute per man, and I thought it was little strange.

"A full body-scan? Our most up-to-date data? Who ordered this?"

The Specialist pointed upward, at the ceiling. "Gold Deck. The very top."

Turov. It had to be her. But why?

Events moved quickly after that, and I didn't have much more time to think about anything. We were hustled aboard the lifter, with me doing plenty of the hustling for my own squad. I shouted until my voice was hoarse, if only to be heard over the general din of metal clawed feet slamming against the metal deck.

Soon, we were harnessed up and set free. The lifter swooped and shifted under my feet sickeningly. The pilot knew this wasn't a drill, and she was giving it the gas. We were in open space for only thirty seconds before we hit the turbulence of the upper atmosphere.

It's always hard doing a fast-insertion onto a planet. You can't help but wonder if you're riding in the unlucky lifter destined to catch some flak and blow up. But even so, it's better than being locked into a pod and fired at the surface like a cannonball, which is what was happening to the infantry.

Legion Varus had an unusual number of splats that day. Heavy and light troops alike flashed down, looking like white-hot streaks in the sky—but some of their pods never opened after landing. Some punched into the hard ground like bullets, their braking jets malfunctioning. Other men had been crushed when the two halves of their capsules slammed together. Blood that boiled away and burned into a dark stain on the sides of the pods told that story. Still others screwed up, opening their emergency releases too early, too late, or even jamming them and suffocating when their minimal life support systems ran out of oxygen. Such was the lot of the infantry.

Our lifter full of dragons screamed out of the sky like a diving eagle. I was able to watch some exterior events remotely via my tapper. It was when I looked up, craning the viewpoint around to look behind us, that I noticed something unexpected. I contacted Natasha right off. She knew things enlisted people weren't supposed to know, and I valued her opinion.

"Natasha," I said, "I'm getting some strange imagery."

"Relay the feed."

I did so, and she watched with me for several quiet seconds. The engines of *Minotaur* and *Cyclops*, the big ships we'd left behind, were flaring blue. Streaks of white gas and light stretched out behind them for a dozen kilometers.

"Is that what I think it is?" I asked her.

"Undeniably. The ships are pulling out. That's a full burn, and although I can't be sure—I'd guess they're moving to high orbit."

"Where they'll engage their warp bubbles and run?"

"That's a pretty good bet, James. I'm sorry."

"Not your fault. Turov gave the order. I guess you don't have to worry about her being sweet on me anymore. If she is, she's got a strange way of showing it."

"I can't believe she's running out on us."

"How many ships are out there, Natasha?" I asked. "Do you know? What's coming?"

She hesitated. "I can't be one hundred percent sure, because the techs on the bridge who've blabbed sometimes exaggerate."

"Just tell me. How many?"

"Seven ships, Imperial configuration. All of them are headed our way."

I let out a long breath that I hadn't realized I'd been holding. *Seven ships?* That's why Turov was pulling out. She wasn't even going to fight them.

All of a sudden, the fact she'd dropped Legion Varus and Winslade's auxiliary cohort on the titanium mine didn't look like such a compliment. She was bailing out and leaving us behind to defend her prize alone.

It was clear to me now, as well, why the bio people had taken our data just before we dropped. We weren't expected to survive being marooned out here. If we wiped, they wanted a good, clean copy they could use to revive us all at a safe distance.

The lifter touched down, landing with a bounce that made my teeth clack together, and I began unlimbering my dragon. My grippers worked like extended hands, and I felt a certain resolve growing in my heart.

We'd fight, and we'd die on Machine World, just like we were supposed to. But afterward, if by some miracle I wasn't permed, I wouldn't forget we'd been abandoned.

-43-

It turned out in the end that there were seven ships approaching Machine World. They were Imperial capital ships—the same design as *Minotaur* and *Cyclops*. That's why Turov had pulled out. In a way, I couldn't blame her for that part. She had two ships, two sets of sixteen broadsides. Even if she'd wanted to tangle with these interlopers, she would be facing seven to two odds. There was no path to victory for Earth when our ships were outnumbered so badly.

What I wasn't happy about was being dumped on this iceball and left to the slaughter. Turov had chosen to leave a garrison and pull out. Legion Varus was going to have to face the enemy alone.

Fortunately for me, I didn't have time to think about any of these unpleasant details when the lifter opened up and disgorged our dragons onto the steep slopes of Titan—which was what we'd named this mountain over the last week or so.

"All right, listen up," Graves said in my ear as I rushed my people out into the snow. "We'll start this by stealing a page from the squid playbook. We're going to get everyone inside the mines. We'll hide in there to keep the enemy guessing as to our full strength and composition. In the meantime, if they choose to bombard us, we'll be reasonably safe."

"Ha!" Carlos said after Graves dropped out of the channel. "The squid playbook—look how well it worked out for the squids!"

310

I had to admit, he had a point there. But I couldn't openly agree with him on the chat channel, and besides, it was probably the best move we could make.

"Shut up in the ranks," I said. "Dragons, form a wedge. We'll stand guard at the entrance to the mine and cover the infantry as they get out of their drop-pods and try to reach safety."

"What if they start dropping bombs on us?" Carlos demanded.

"Then we'll run over the infantry stragglers to get into the mines. These dragon vehicles are more valuable than our flesh, remember that. *You* are expendable! But your vehicle isn't."

There was grumbling, but it was nothing they hadn't heard before. No one in a real, fighting legion was uncertain about their lack of personal value to the Empire, or to Earth.

We stood outside in the hazy cold, watching troops struggling through the snow from every direction to the mouth of the mines. Thousands of them came in knots and bunches. No one ordered them to form ranks and columns to make an organized march of it—commanders didn't know how long we had, and after the drop, the troops were scattered to hell and back anyway.

In my dragon, I kept one eye on the gray skies. It was pretty pointless to do so, of course. If the big invading ships rolled into orbit overhead, we probably wouldn't see them from the ground in the daylight. If the ships did park on top of us and fire their broadsides, we would only be treated to a few seconds of brilliant falling stars. After that, everything for kilometers around would vanish as the fusion shells landed.

But I still found myself gazing up at the sky, and the rest of my squad mates were doing the same.

A channel request beeped, and I opened it without looking to see who it was.

"McGill here, go ahead."

"You think they're up there?" asked Harris' voice in my helmet. "They say seven Imperial drop-ships, same as ours. What in the *fuck* is that about? Who would have the balls to send troops out here to try to kick us off this planet?"

That was the real question we all had swimming in our heads. Harris had finally voiced it. What the hell was going on? Who was attacking us? This wasn't supposed to happen. Sure, there were the squids and there were the pissed-off Nairbs. But how could either of them have brought in a force in response so quickly?

"I don't know, Vet," I said. "Could the squids have copied our designs?"

"I'd vote no on that theory. I've heard it before—Leeson seems convinced these ships are squid counterfeits, built to freak us out. But that just doesn't seem right."

"Agreed," I said. "I don't think it's the squids. Copying another culture? No, that's not their style. They're too arrogant for that."

"Then we're in agreement. It has to be the Nairbs. They came to have a little show trial, then when that didn't go the way they wanted, they called in back-up."

I frowned inside my helmet and turned toward him. He was standing with his own squad about a hundred meters to the west. We were guarding both sides of this particular entrance to the mines. In between our two squads, a steady stream of infantry trotted over trampled snow, puffing with exertion.

He was looking back at me, but he was too far away for me to read his expression.

"Is that what you think?" I demanded over our radio link. "That my trial with the Nairbs triggered all this?"

"Well? Why shouldn't I think that, McGill? It wouldn't be the first time you screwed up and changed the fate of the human race, now would it?"

I heaved a sigh, and I almost closed the channel. Harris might have finally broken down enough to shake my hand and welcome me into the ranks of the Varus veteran society, but he still had a grudge going. I was the source of all evil in his eyes.

Looking up, I thought I saw something—something I hadn't expected to see. "Harris, I think we're going to have the answer to your question sooner rather than later."

"Why's that, McGill?"

"Because they're dropping troops. Drop pods incoming—thousands of them. By God, they look like stones falling from the sky."

Everyone was looking up, some of the troops paused to squint and point before running faster for the entrance.

I added Leeson to our channel. "I think we should hit them before they get their act together, sir," I said.

"What?" demanded Harris. "Don't hit them, fool! Adjunct Leeson, sir, these capsules must be more troops from Solstice, that's all."

"No Vet," I said, "I have it on good authority our ships have pulled out. They're fleeing the system even now. There's no way Turov would have turned around to come back and drop another legion. Do I have permission, Adjunct?"

Leeson was inside the mines and couldn't see the situation out on the slopes.

"Command your men and fight your dragons, McGill. I'll bring the rest of the platoon out there in a few minutes. Leeson out."

He dropped the channel, and I was left watching the first capsules as they struck ground.

"McGill!" Harris said to me privately. "Don't you go off and do something stupid now, do you hear—?"

I cut him off. "Squad, limber up. We're advancing downslope."

My people had been lounging, but they perked up quickly when I gave the word. My squad was smaller now that I'd lost Della and the rest of Harris' people, but I'd gained Sargon and every one of our dragons was in prime fighting condition.

"Work your battle computers," I said. "Filter out the troops that are already on the ground from those dropping. Mark the new arrivals as hostile until we know the score."

By the time I'd deployed downslope, Leeson came thundering out with another full platoon. Graves and even Winslade himself followed with more dragons.

Our questions concerning the nature of our new arrivals were answered almost immediately. Firefights broke out in a dozen places all around us. Our infantry were caught up in a dozen small gun battles with the invaders. They were definitely not friendly.

"Which squad has anti-air cannons on their backs?" Winslade demanded. A squad from another platoon reported that they did, and Winslade ordered them to shoot down every pod they could get a bead on. Almost immediately, small missiles created plumes of gas and flame. Missiles streaked up to meet the drop pods. A hundred of the pods were converted into fireballs before they reached the mountainside.

The troops who'd been trotting for the mine entrance now became a fleeing mob. Their only orders were to get under cover since they didn't have any weaponry that could shoot down a falling drop-pod.

Our AA cannons missed as many drop pods as they hit, and they kept on coming down. Soon, enemy infantry were climbing out of the pods all around us. Some were kilometers off, others were right in our faces.

The troops—at first, I didn't know what to make of them. They were physically larger than men. About two meters tall and bulky. They stood as dark humanoid hulks outlined against the snow. They had heavy projection weapons, and they wore armor. We faced a heavy cohort—but not a human one.

Then I saw the tails, and I knew.

"Saurians!" I shouted over the unit channel. "Sirs, they're saurian troops! No juggers, just basic raptors."

"We've figured that out, McGill," Graves answered. "The enemy are saurians from Steel World. They're not authorized to breathe on this planet. We're going to correct the error."

"What's that mean?" Sargon asked.

"That means we're supposed to kill all the lizards, you big moron," Carlos said.

I winced when I heard that. Sargon wouldn't do anything now in the midst of battle, but there was sure to be a fresh ass-whooping waiting for Carlos after this was over. Some people never learned.

"Squad, we haven't got any AA," I said. "We're going to use our spinal cannons to blast any group of saurians that gets their act together and forms a cohesive force."

It didn't take long. After about three minutes of total confusion, our troops stopped streaming into the mine. The rest that were still out on the slopes had either been shot or were pinned in defensive positions by the enemy. The steady drumbeat of drop pods from above showed no signs of letting up.

We soon identified organized groups of saurians who had formed up, taken cover and now were laying fire down on our position. My team had gone with heavy armament as our mission this time out was supposed to be a defensive one, not a fast-moving recon effort. Our load-out choices paid dividends today as I ordered my squad to switch on their shields and fire their heavy guns at enemy concentrations.

Troops melted away under fragmentation shells. Rarely, a group of saurians charged in to close with us, but we repelled them with grenade fire at point-blank range.

As we fought, organized Varus infantry came out to help. Centurions led them, and soon, a full unit was supporting every squad of dragons.

The saurians soon figured out they weren't going to take us out with an all-out wave assault. Surprise had helped them initially, and we'd lost a lot of men and dragons out on the slopes. But these gains were easily balanced by the carnage our dragons reaped against their unsupported attacks. It was a slaughter, and my squad only lost three machines while killing several hundred attacking troops.

Finally, the saurians pulled back. The drop pods no longer came down directly on top of us. When new arrivals climbed out of their pods, they ran away, disappearing over the folds of the mountain.

When it grew dark, we retreated as well. We posted guards at the mine entrance, and my squad was relieved. We walked our creaking dragons into the caverns and got out of them, aching and complaining.

"You did well out there, team," I said. "I didn't see a single mistake. Well done, well fought."

My troops beamed and clapped one another on the back.

One clap came down a little too hard on Carlos, however.

315

"What the fu—?" Carlos demanded. His voice was cut off by a pair of huge hands that encircled his windpipe and began squeezing.

Carlos looked at me plaintively. I looked at him and his assailant. Then I nodded to Sargon.

"Proceed, Specialist," I said.

Sargon beat on the smaller man for a full minute. Carlos got in a few good licks—he always did. Sargon looked surprised when his genitals took a hard yanking for example—I could have told him to look out for that one. But in the end, Carlos was down on the ground, heaving, crawling and puking.

I sipped a hot cup of caf and pretended I hadn't seen anything. Sometimes, the life of a Veteran-rank noncom had its little rewards.

-44-

By morning the next day, we were surrounded by around sixty thousand saurian troops. They were crawling all over the mountaintop. Some were above the mines, and some were below us, maneuvering along the ridges and escarpments, hugging stone and ice for cover. A siege had begun, and without support from space, we had no way of knowing what the enemy was up to. Our buzzers had managed to count the enemy troops, but that was all. The tiny spy drones were being caught and destroyed as fast as we could send them out.

After a sleepless night of barricading the mine entrances, the officers were busy filing our unit's after-action reports with Winslade, and I'd been repairing our dragons. We kicked off our platoon's morning briefing at ten a. m. sharp.

"Sixty frigging thousand!" Leeson marveled when we were done with the boring parts. He gave a long, low whistle that made me clench my teeth. Sometimes, when a whistle comes in through sensitive headphones, it's pretty annoying.

"They say they had *seventy* thousand when they first dropped," I pointed out.

"That's right," Leeson said pointing a gauntleted finger at me. "You boys did well. Altogether, our anti-air fire combined with our quick counterattack cost them dearly. Their initial assault was meant to catch us by surprise, but it was an utter failure. They lost the equivalent of a full legion. Just think of it!"

"A lot of those were splats, sir," Sargon pointed out.

317

Leeson shot him an unhappy look. I caught that, and I think Sargon did too. He shut up in a hurry.

"Sure, sure," Leeson said, "half those deaths were due to splats, I'll admit that. The lizards are new to this game. I bet not one of their troops had ever crawled out of a pod into a firefight before. But we gunned down five thousand, we estimate. That's astounding!"

Leeson sounded excited, bloodthirsty even, but I had to feel a small pang for the lizards that'd died yesterday. They'd fought well and fearlessly. The question in my mind—and everyone else's—was why they'd come here to fight us at all?

Leeson thought he had an answer for that. "The best part is these clowns will all be permed for this. They've over-reached this time. They're obviously trying to stop Earth from grabbing a competing source of metals. Hell, their entire sweat-box of a planet might not survive once the Nairbs pass their judgment."

I wasn't so sure about that, but I didn't want to go up against my commander in an argument that was pointless. If this had been a matter of tactics and survival, sure, I'd speak my piece. But not when we were talking about whether something was true or not. Truth had a way of sorting itself out in time, and yapping about it never changed the answer.

"We whooped them," Leeson continued. "That's what it comes down to. And when they come into these tunnels to dig us out, we'll smash them down again. They don't have a chance!"

A few ragged cheers went up from the group. Suddenly, it dawned on me what Adjunct Leeson was doing. He was trying to build up morale. Seen in that light, his rhetoric suddenly made good sense.

These people needed a pep-talk. Anyone with half a brain could see we were all totally screwed, that we were going die in this hole like it was the biggest warren full of rats in history—but it was equally undeniable that troops with hope fought harder.

Accordingly, I stood up and banged my gauntlets together. Harris joined in immediately. Sargon looked startled, but then he stood up with us. He was still walking funny after yesterday's encounter with Carlos, but he was game.

I'd noticed that Sargon was doing everything Harris and I did lately, trying to support us. As a man bucking for rank, that made good sense. In contrast, *my* methods to achieve promotions were unconventional and even accidental.

Graves joined the group, and the applause grew louder. He stared around the team flatly, then nodded when we'd quieted.

"That was well done yesterday," he said. "Our defensive rearguard action helped get as much equipment off those slopes and into the mountain as possible. As far as I'm concerned, we accomplished that mission."

That was vintage Graves. Lives? Deaths? Those meant nothing. Hardware was what he cared about. In his calculus of war, our blood meant about as much as our spit—and probably a lot less. We had more blood in us than we did spit, after all.

He went on to talk about deployments, defensive preparations and supply rationing. After the meeting, we broke up and were assigned specific duties. As my team had taken losses in battle yesterday, so we were spared guard duty. I told everyone to go on break and relax but to keep their dragons ready to roll. We could get called back to the front lines any minute.

"Hey, McGill," said a gravelly voice.

I turned to see Carlos. He was in pretty bad shape. His right eye was swollen shut, and his lips were split and as red as raw meat.

"Ouch," I said. "You fit to fight, soldier?"

"You challenging me again, Vet?"

"No," I chuckled. "What's up? And why haven't you gone to the infirmary to get some skin sprayed over that?"

"It's no big deal. I've been too busy."

"Doing what?"

He smiled, and the blood that outlined his teeth made me squinch up my eyes.

"Kivi, for one thing. She thought it was cool that I stood up for my rights with Sargon."

"Did she hear what you said to him to get your ass whooped?"

"No—and don't tell her about that part, okay? She thinks I was a total victim."

"Don't worry," I assured him. "I think you've paid enough for that mistake already."

"Okay, cool. Let's go."

"Go where?"

"I've got something to show you, Vet. I guarantee you're going to like it."

Figuring I didn't have much to lose, I followed him as he walked painfully down into the guts of the mountain. I was expecting more vids of squids on their home worlds, or possibly another giant squid in a tank. What I got was something entirely different.

The mines themselves were largely unexplored. We'd checked out the upper levels, where there were smelters and transportation systems for ore and titanium bricks, but we hadn't spent much time in the lower tunnels where the actual mining had been done. Carlos led me deep into the uncharted depths.

"Here is the limit," Carlos said, pointing down into dark shaft that led downward at a thirty degree angle. "This is about as far as anyone has ever been in Mount Titan."

"That's because the rest of the mine is empty," I pointed out.

"No, not entirely. Kivi and I found some equipment down there. More stuff that belonged to the squids."

"Why mess with that?"

"What are you? Stu—?" he began, but stopped himself, taking a breath.

That was possibly the first time I'd ever seen him edit himself. Carlos always insulted people who were bigger than he was—hell, that behavior was practically stamped in his DNA.

He shook his finger at me and his split lips parted into a ghastly grin. "No, no way. Not this time. I'm not giving you another excuse. Not so soon."

"Just tell me why you brought me down here."

"Look, the squids had the native machines working for them, right?" he asked.

"Yes, seems like they did."

"And therefore, they had to have a way to tell the machines what to do, didn't they?"

I thought about it. After a few seconds, I nodded. "That stands to reason."

"Exactly. And let me tell you one of the prime rules of tech development: if it's already invented, copy someone else's work. Don't invent your own. It's much easier that way."

I chuckled. "All right then. Did you find a translation device?"

"We did. We found something that appears to be a communication system. Unfortunately, we can't get it to work yet."

Frowning, I turned that statement over in my mind. He led me into a large, dark chamber. There, deep in the guts of the mountain, was a strange workshop. Something was down there—something that moved.

That's when the light went on in my head. "You aren't telling me you've got one of the native machine-creatures down here, are you?"

"Yep. How else could we be testing the translation system?"

That was what I'd been thinking about. "When you said you hadn't got it to work yet, I was wondering how you would know if it was working at all."

"This little guy. He's the answer. Only, he's not talking."

Carlos approached a small native machine-creature. It was one of the young that I'd met up with back along the river and had a drawing contest with. He was a few meters long and about half a meter thick. Like a metal caterpillar, he wormed his way over the stony floor, making scrabbling sounds.

There was a chain welded to his carapace and burn-marks all around the chain.

"We had a hell of a time getting him under control," Carlos said. "We've spent all last night trying to get this moron to talk, but no dice. He might be a dud."

He gave the machine a kick, and it humped and scrambled away to the limits of its chain—which wasn't very far.

"Have you been abusing this thing?" I asked, frowning.

"Abusing it? Sure. Whatever works—but nothing does. We've tried to tell it to eat, to turn around, to play dead. We've worked this translation box sixteen different ways, and this dipshit—"

He moved to give the machine another kick, but I grabbed him and gave him a shaking instead. I wanted to do more, but he was pretty well beat up already.

"Carlos," I said, controlling myself, "I think someone with a gentler hand might do better."

"That's what Kivi said. That's why I brought you down here. But James, please, if you *do* get him to talk, you've got to let us have some of the glory. Don't hog it all, okay? I didn't even tell Kivi I was going to show you. She doesn't trust you at all."

"Don't worry."

To start with, I drew pictures. The machine looked at them, but didn't dare draw its own. It had been traumatized. It shook and squirmed, but wouldn't draw a damned thing in response.

"How much did you beat on him?" I demanded.

"Hardly any," Carlos said. "Okay, maybe a little. But I don't think it was us. I think it was the squids who really did a number on him. See his tail-section and his undercarriage? There are burn-marks and dents everywhere. Maybe he wouldn't work, so they tortured him."

"I'm glad that wasn't all you," I said.

I spent several hours with the little machine that day. I even took out titanium shavings and fed them to him. That got him interested. After a while, I came up with a plan.

"He's not going to communicate out of curiosity," I said. "We've got to get him to cooperate with rewards."

"And punishments?"

"No. Just the withholding of rewards."

Carlos heaved a sigh. "Sounds slow."

"Go get me a bag of titanium shavings. I'm going to run out."

He left, and I tried my best. I drew simple shapes then fed a shaving to the machine when I showed him a circle, for instance. The machine studied it, ate the shaving—but that was about it. I began to think maybe we did have a dud like Carlos had said.

But I kept at it. After drawing the same circle, feeding it a shaving, then erasing the circle and drawing it again about four times, I stopped feeding the machine and began to pretend to feed myself.

Each time I pretended to eat a shaving, I drew a square instead of a circle on the ground. The machine watched raptly as I did this. I slowly drew the square and fed myself another, then another.

The machine watched me move chip after chip up to my faceplate. I secretly dropped them into a fold of my suit, then took another out of the bag.

Finally, the machine lost it. The poor thing was starved. He scuttled forward and erased the square I'd drawn, and scratched out a circle with his feet. As with the first machine I'd managed to contact, his circle was perfectly round. I promptly fed him a shaving. We had made a breakthrough. Circles meant the machine was fed, squares meant I was fed. We had a language of our own.

By the time Carlos returned with a fresh bag of shavings for the machine, we were drawing things back and forth. I would draw a shape then it would draw the same thing—only better than my version. Then I would feed him a shaving.

The machine backed away when Carlos came near, and I pushed Carlos back.

"He doesn't trust you," I said. "Stay over there."

Eventually, Kivi showed up. She was pissed off immediately.

"You brought McGill down here?" she demanded. "We've been working on making a breakthrough ever since we were first posted on the planet, and you're going to let him show it to the brass and take all the credit again, aren't you?"

"I'm just drawing things," I said. "Relax, Kivi."

"No girl can relax around you," she said.

I gave her a glance then shrugged. She was glaring at me. She might have heard about my recent dating activity with Anne. That was typical for Kivi. She'd carry on with other men, but when I dated a new girl she may or may not display a

323

fit of jealousy. If she was in the mood, she'd get mad at everything I did without bringing up what was really bothering her. I guess that came with the territory when you had an on-again, off-again relationship with a girl.

Eventually, I had the machine performing a wide range of tricks. I even managed to have a primitive conversation with it. We'd established that the squids and the machines were interacting, but when this little guy drew the squids, it was with a chain connected to the machines. He didn't seem to be under any illusions. The machines were slaves to the squids, not friends or allies.

"It makes sense," I said. "The squids consider themselves conquerors. They enslave creatures and alter them. Back on Dust World, they did it with humans. Here, they've been doing it with these machines. I wonder if these machines have been altered in design to better meet the squid requirements."

"That would be easier than doing it with selective breeding, you would think," Kivi said.

"Yeah, maybe. But we don't even know how these creatures reproduce yet."

"Why don't you draw two machines screwing?" Carlos asked. "Maybe that will jog this little pervert's mind."

"You're the pervert," Kivi said.

"You should know."

I had to step in before Carlos got himself punched again—by Kivi this time. "Okay, okay, that's enough. Let's stay on task. How does this translation box you stole from the squids work?"

They showed me an odd device. It wasn't entirely made of metal. Parts of it were slimy, like gelatin or thick, pasty oil. When you rubbed it in various ways, the thing produced odd, rasping sounds. The machine took note when we worked the interface, but didn't respond in any sensible way.

"How the hell are we supposed to figure out what this device is saying?" I asked.

"Now you know why we're still working on this," Kivi said.

"Hmm. We should probably bring Natasha in at this point. You guys probably should have as soon as you found this thing. She's better at this stuff than I am."

"No!" Kivi shouted. "You promised, James! Natasha will hog everything."

"Look," I said, "we might be able to get help from the machines if we figure this out. Isn't that more important than a promotion?"

"Not really," Kivi said stubbornly. "You've already got rank, James. This is our best shot."

"But we might all die down here," I said. "The saurians are going to attack, and they outnumber us six to one."

"Leeson said they'll get trashed if they try to come in here," Carlos said.

"And you believed him?"

"No, not really," he admitted. He turned to Kivi, looking disappointed. "He might be right, Kivi. We've failed."

"I know what this is about," Kivi said with sudden anger. "You're just trying to make Natasha happy again. She found out about Della and Anne, didn't she?"

I heaved a sigh and walked out of the tunnel. "I'll be back in about an hour," I said. "If you can make it talk by then, you'll get full credit. Have at it."

I left them behind, cursing my name.

When I returned with Natasha, it was a full ninety minutes later. Kivi was there, but Carlos was gone.

So was the machine.

"What happened?" I asked, shaking my head.

"We tried everything," Kivi said. "We were desperate. Carlos thought this was the last chance we had to get credit for the discovery."

"You guys are crazy," Natasha said. "Kivi, you just have to go through the training and show aptitude. When a slot opens up and your skill level is high, you'll get it. Advancement isn't always about showing off for brass."

"Oh yeah? Is that why McGill, the biggest screw-up in the legion, is two ranks above us? And what about Winslade? Are you telling me he's not a royal kiss-up?"

She had us there, so Natasha stopped arguing. She examined the squid translation box. I'd honestly assumed that when she checked it out, she'd pronounce it to be a squid masturbation aid, or something like that. But she didn't.

"I think this *is* a translation system. It produces sounds like a machine. The interface is strange, but not unlike those that I've seen before. Now, why did you let the machine go, Kivi?"

"Like I said, we were getting desperate. The machine wasn't reacting much other than to draw a few shapes on the ground. We finally realized that it was drawing things that matched the noises the translator was making."

"Ah," I said, catching on. "Did you feed it titanium shavings?"

"Yes, once we figured it out."

Together, Natasha and I examined the drawings. There were dozens of them.

"Did you record this?" Natasha asked. "Do we have data to analyze?"

"Yes," Kivi said. "I'm not an idiot."

"But what happened to Carlos?" I demanded.

Kivi looked down, shamed. "We ran out of room on the floor. It was at the limits of its chain. We decided to cut the chain, to let it have more space. We figured it would stay because we were feeding it titanium."

"Let me guess," I said. "The second you cut the chain, it took off."

"Not exactly. It waited until we ran out of chips."

I rolled my eyes. "So Carlos is chasing after it?"

"I made him go. It was his stupid idea to cut the chain in the first place."

"All right, I'd better go find him," I said.

I left the two women going over the remaining data. Kivi had meticulously recorded the interactions, matching sounds and drawings. She also had many vids of past efforts to communicate, which she grudgingly passed over to Natasha's tapper. I was happy to see them working together. Natasha was wisely heaping Kivi with praise, and Kivi's mistrust seemed to be melting.

The trail left behind by Carlos and the chain-dragging machine wasn't difficult to follow. I found them less than a kilometer farther down in the tunnels.

Unfortunately, the scene wasn't a happy one. Carlos was dead, with his faceplate cracked open. He'd asphyxiated.

The machine was perched on his chest, feasting on the metal bits in his suit.

-45-

The disastrous result of our communication attempts was probably a good lesson for me. I'd come to think of these machines—the small, young ones at least—as harmless. But they weren't. They were like wild animal cubs. It was so easy to forget they were predatory creatures. Just like any lion cub or bear cub, they'd eat you if they could.

I almost killed the machine. It would have been fairly easy to do. Unlike Carlos, I had a heavy beamer on me. I unslung it and aimed it at the head-section of the animal—that's how I thought of these machines now, as semi-intelligent animals—but I didn't fire.

The baby machine didn't flee. Instead, it made a rasping sound. It might have been growling, telling me to get lost. A large number of its cameras studied me, and it kept on chewing while it did so. The machine was feeding, but it wasn't eating Carlos. That would have been too much for me. It was eating his suit. That's all it had wanted, after all.

The poor thing had been starved and abused for who knew how long down here in these tunnels. I could hardly expect civilized discourse after the squids and Carlos had kept it on a chain. Would it be possible to negotiate with these creatures later, when we weren't fighting over who was going to steal their resources? Maybe. One thing was for sure, killing them for eating metal wouldn't help bring peace.

"All right," I said stepping closer and prodding at its hindquarters. "I'm not going to hurt you, but you have to move on. Scram."

The machine was unconvinced. It rasped and whirled on me, threateningly. It was like a feral dog, snarling over a carcass. I gave it a kick, and it tried to bite my foot. I knew as long as I didn't let it get to my faceplate, I was going to be all right. The thing hadn't killed Carlos directly. His faceplate had cracked and the air was poisonous, which was the only reason he'd succumbed.

But I couldn't very well let it chew on Carlos' air tanks forever. That was just going to teach it the wrong thing. So I cranked down the power level on my weapon and gave it a jolt in the butt. Just enough to spot-weld its hind plates together.

It didn't like that at all. It lunged at me, and I zapped it twice more. Finally, the creature got the message and ran off into the dark tunnels.

Grabbing Carlos by the collar, I dragged him back to the chamber where Natasha had been working with Kivi. They looked at Carlos in horror—but they didn't seem all that surprised.

"I've got the data off his tapper," I said. "He'll catch a revive when I report his death to the bio people."

"Did you kill the machine?" Natasha asked.

"No—it wasn't really at fault. The poor thing was only hungry."

Natasha looked worried, as did Kivi.

"What's up?" I asked.

"I don't know if allowing it to escape was a good idea," Natasha said. "I've been examining the vids of the communication attempts made by Carlos and Kivi. At the end of them, the machine clearly understood something they said. That's when it ran off."

"So, something you communicated made it flee?"

"We think so," Kivi admitted.

"Whatever it was," Natasha said, "I'm certain Carlos and Kivi managed to give the machine a coherent message. But I'm not sure what was said."

329

"That's just grand," I said, giving Kivi a scowl. "Let's hope you didn't tell them they could all go to Hell in a hand-basket."

"It could have been anything," Kivi said defensively. "Why are you two assuming the worst?"

"Whatever the message was, it can't be good," Natasha said. "It clearly triggered aggression."

Kivi looked worried, but she shrugged rather than apologizing.

"Do you need to keep working here, Natasha?" I asked.

"No. Without the machine, this particular spot has no special significance. I can take the device with me and review the data anywhere."

"Then let's get back up to the main camp. I need to report Carlos' death, anyway."

We trudged up the tunnels, dragging Carlos' body the whole way. It occurred to me that in times past, a fallen soldier had been treated with great respect and honor. Those days were gone. A body was just a body in my time. We recycled them as fast as possible, sometimes burying them in mass graves or even burning a stack to get rid of them physically. The equipment was what we really needed. The dead were only useful as raw materials for a new body if supplies were short and the corpse was fresh enough.

After delivering Carlos' body to the bio people, who wrinkled their noses and hauled it dutifully away, I returned to my unit's camp. I relayed my findings to Graves, including our previous discoveries of oversized squids and the data-globe. He ordered me to talk to Winslade about everything.

Sighing, I walked up gritty ramps and tunnels to the lofty caverns high up in the mountain's guts. I hadn't wanted to do this. I'd planned to let Kivi and Carlos get their act together and make the report themselves, thus garnering the credit. But in my opinion the situation had changed. We were encircled by enemies and in danger. Secrets withheld from our commanders might get us all permed. I had the duty to report everything we'd found.

In Mount Titan's highest chambers I found Winslade's makeshift office. That's where all the officers held court. Winslade had chosen a pretty spot, complete with a trickling

330

fall of silvery liquid methane and stalagmites that resembled dragon fangs coming up from the floor.

He'd pressurized the entire chamber and warmed it up, so we didn't have to wear helmets in here. That's why the methane was melting. Despite Winslade's efforts, it still smelled too farty for my taste, so I kept my faceplate closed.

"Nice quarters, sir," I commented.

Winslade turned to look at me. He didn't have a smile on his face, he rarely did.

"Veteran, what's this I hear from Graves about you performing unauthorized diplomatic negotiations—again?"

I was taken aback. Winslade was referring to certain activities I'd performed years ago on Dust World, when I'd tried to communicate with the local population of colonists.

"I don't know about any negotiations, sir," I said. "We found one of the machines chained up in a lower tunnel along with a lot of unknown squid equipment. We fooled around with it a bit, but we didn't get very far. The machine ran off."

Winslade narrowed his eyes. He was a cagey one, as slime-balls go. I had to wonder what he was thinking. The question I was hoping he didn't ask was who the "we" in my statement might consist of. I knew Carlos and Kivi were trying hard to get some positive recognition, and I didn't want to take that from them, but I also didn't want to involve them unless things went the right way. At the moment, the whole thing looked like a disaster, so I figured I might as well take the blame myself. People expected this kind of thing from James McGill.

"Up to your usual tricks," Winslade said at last. "This is my first time playing the role of your commander, and I must say I'm sympathizing with all those who've done so before me. You even managed to get one of your troops killed, correct?"

"Not exactly, sir. In any case, we did recover his full kit. He'll pop right out of the revival machine as fit as a fiddle in an hour or so."

Winslade nodded. "I would seek disciplinary action, but your fighting skills are desperately needed at this time. When the saurians first attacked you did well, by every report."

"Thank you, Primus."

Winslade gave me a wry look, indicating he hadn't intended to praise me.

"Dismissed," he said.

I hesitated until he looked up at me with his eyebrows raised. Then I asked another question. "Sir? Is Drusus up and walking around yet?"

"Yes. The Tribune's revival has finally been achieved. Whatever technical difficulty kept him from returning to us has been solved."

I almost laughed at that. Winslade knew full well that Turov had ordered Drusus to be kept on ice until she said otherwise. Now that she'd dumped the legion on this rock and fled the star system, sure, it was time to revive poor old Drusus. Why not let him die again down here like the rest of us?

"You mind if I give my report to him, sir?" I asked.

"I don't see why it would be necessary."

"Uh...you may not be aware that Drusus and I have a standing arrangement when special circumstances like this come up. He wants a full report from the man in the field when matters go beyond the norm and enter the political arena."

Winslade's frown was back. "Is this some kind of threat, Veteran?"

"Not at all, sir. You misunderstand. I'm informing you of a special relationship between myself and the tribune, that's all. It's similar in nature to the relationship you've enjoyed for years with Imperator Turov. Your permission, sir?"

Winslade huffed. "Sounds like you don't need my permission, but I suppose it was courteous to ask. Suddenly, your rapid rise in rank is less surprising to me."

"Thank you sir," I said and left.

I could have said a lot more, and I wanted to. Right off, Winslade had assumed my promotions were illegitimate since his were. I resented that. He'd been flying a desk for the last decade, hassling attractive underlings and kissing Turov's shapely butt. He'd leapt to the conclusion that I was doing the same thing with Drusus as my patron. It wasn't true, but I knew it wouldn't do any good to try to defend myself in the eyes of this man.

Drusus' office was less secluded and more utilitarian. He was just outside the general officers' camp with a standard-issue computer desk and displays encircling the small chamber. He was studying three-dimensional tactical grids that presented the enemy positions around the mountain outside.

"Ah, McGill," he said, glancing at me. "I was wondering when you would come to haunt me again."

"Sorry sir," I said. "It's just my way."

"Understood. What alarming news do you have for me today?"

Drusus had a lot of catching up to do, so I started at the beginning. I told him about my first contact with the native machine life. I also discussed and displayed vids of the dead giant squid, and the data-globe we'd discovered. He expressed mild interest in all these things and promised he'd have teams of techs go over them.

Then I brought him up to speed on each of the incidents of communication with the machine-creatures to the present time. As I explained this, I made an effort to play up the efforts of Kivi and Carlos in the best possible light.

"I'm unsurprised about Kivi's contribution—but Carlos Ortiz?" he asked, as if unfamiliar with the name. He frowned and worked his tapper. "Oh yes, a regular with behavioral problems."

"Same as I used to be, sir," I said. "A few years back."

Drusus laughed. "According to your superiors, little about your aptitude for getting into trouble has changed."

"If you say so, sir. But Carlos does deserve credit for getting the machines to talk using the alien translating equipment. He also discovered and did the initial work with the data-globe."

Drusus made a dismissive wave. "That's not how these things look to me, McGill. Let me explain how an officer of many years sees these reports. The regular known as Kivi accompanied Ortiz on every occasion. When breakthroughs were recently made, you and Natasha—a very capable tech—were both on hand. Even so, disaster occurred, and Carlos managed to get himself killed by an unarmed native youth. As I read this—is this correct? The machine-creature *ate* him?"

"Not exactly, sir," I said, feeling my sympathy for Carlos rising. Sure, I liked to beat on him as much as the next guy, but he was my friend. "The machine wanted the metal in his kit."

"I see, yes... Then you apprehended the creature and destroyed it?"

"No, sir. I let it go."

He eyed me for a moment. "An interesting choice. Most troops would have dispatched an alien after it killed their friend."

"I suppose that's right, sir. But I believed the killing of Carlos to be accidental. Carlos couldn't breathe with his faceplate broken. That's what killed him. And anyway, killing the machine for taking advantage of his death to eat his kit would erase any goodwill we might have developed with our communication attempts. After all, the machine might not understand that breaking a faceplate would result in death. How would it know we couldn't breathe their air?"

He nodded. "A mature response. As to your friends, however...I could see putting Kivi into tech specialist training. Carlos Ortiz...he's a problem. He's definitely senior enough to warrant training. His fighting skills are adequate. But a tech? The idea is absurd."

"Agreed, sir," I said. "He's not a tech. But I think he's ready for a more advanced assignment of some kind. He's been a regular for a lot of years now. He recently reenlisted, in fact."

"A stroke of good fortune for the legion, I'm sure. Let me ask you, McGill, where would you place him? If he's not a tech...then should he perhaps be given a larger, more powerful weapon with greater destructive capacity?"

"Uh...maybe not, sir," I admitted. The idea of Carlos as a weaponeer—it was enough to make a man shudder.

"Then perhaps you see him as a leader of men? An inspiration to his cadre of troops? Perhaps a replacement for Sargon, or yourself in the future?"

The look on my face told the story. Drusus read it and nodded.

"That's what I thought," he said. "A leader must have a clear eye. He must not allow his judgment to be clouded by friendship or sympathy. He must only promote those that deserve it, or the legion will suffer for his mistakes."

"I understand, sir. Maybe Carlos isn't ready."

"I have an idea," Drusus said. "I'll make a note of it. After this campaign is over, assuming we see Earth again, we'll speak further on the matter."

"About that, sir? Have we got a chance to win against sixty thousand saurian troops?"

Drusus turned back to his tactical displays. "Probably not," he admitted. "But that isn't our only purpose for being here. We're to mark a legitimate claim on this world. If Earth is to expand, to become a three-star civilization, we need this planet. It has all the resources that we lack, which is precisely why the saurians are here. They see this world as a threat to their monopoly on heavy metals."

I examined the maps alongside him. The data displayed there was both intriguing and alarming. There were indeed seven Imperial ships parked in orbit and numerous red blocks representing troop formations all over the mountain. In the center was a single large blue block—Legion Varus.

"They'll have to wipe us out soon," I said. "They can't wait around."

"Agreed," Drusus said, "but I'd like to hear your reasoning."

"Well sir, first off there's the matter of those seven Imperial ships parked in orbit. Those don't come cheap. Every day they're out here in the field represents a lot of credits for the saurians."

"Very good. I agree. They have to attack soon. They can't maintain a siege due to the cost, and there's also the threat of reinforcements from a variety of directions. The squids could come back. Earth could deploy more legions—or the Empire itself might send forces."

"The Empire?" I asked, encouraged. "Do you think that could happen?"

"It's unlikely but possible."

"What I don't understand is what the saurians were thinking by coming here at all," I said.

"Are you talking about their motivations?"

"No, sir. Those are clear to me. They're obviously here to maintain their local monopoly on heavy metals, preventing us from gaining a new internal supply. What I don't understand is why they think they can get away with it."

Drusus nodded. "You believe our claim is more legitimate than theirs?"

"Yes. We're the enforcers in Frontier 921. We're fighting a legitimate war against an aggressor species."

Drusus pointed a finger at me. "That's where you're wrong. We're outside the borders of the Empire right now. What happens out here isn't subject to Galactic prohibitions other than directly attacking their assets—such as that Nairb ship you blew up."

I scratched myself through my thin suit and squinted at him. "You heard about that, did you?"

"How could I not have? But that's a topic for another conversation, McGill, should the Nairbs ever figure out that the cephalopods didn't do it."

"So...we reported to the Empire that the squids attacked the Nairb ship?"

"What choice did we have? You engineered the matter masterfully."

"Claver did that, really. I was just caught in the middle."

"As always," Drusus said with more than a hint of sarcasm. "That brings us back to the saurians and their next move—or should I say, Claver's next move?"

I opened my mouth and my jaw just hung there for a time. "Are you saying *Claver* brought the saurian ships here?"

"Of course he did," Drusus said. "Haven't you figured that out yet? Claver's not done with Gamma Pavonis. He won't stop until either he's permed—or we are."

I thought about that as Drusus continued to go over his strategies with me. I'd had the opportunity to perm Claver back onboard the Nairb ship. Maybe I should have permed Claver instead of perming that Solstice legionnaire, Randy, who enjoyed torturing people.

In comparison to Claver, that sadist had been small potatoes.

336

-46-

The saurian assault began three days later. They started off by withdrawing and hunkering down at the foot of the mountain. The alien troops that were posted above our elevation retreated to the snowy heights. Knowing these signs couldn't be good, we took shelter ourselves, keeping well back from the entrance but for a small contingent of troops on lookout duty.

It just so happened that Winslade ordered me and my squad to stand duty at the entrance. To add insult to injury, he ordered us to do it without our dragons.

"But sir," I argued when I received the orders from Leeson, "What good is a cavalry unit without our mounts?"

"You ask yourself that the next time you go off somewhere to play God, McGill!" he shouted back. He was red-faced and pissed-off, and I had trouble blaming him.

"Are you suggesting, sir, that—" I began

"Shut up, McGill. Just shut the hell up. My platoon has been ordered to stand out here in our underwear with beamers in our hands due to your constant meddling. I swear, if I survive this day, I'm going to remember this, Veteran. Graves shouldn't have judged you the winner of that contest back on Green Deck. That's what I know for sure now."

With a sigh, I retreated. Leeson wasn't a bad officer, but he was as emotional as Graves was stern and unflappable. I knew he'd cool off later on—probably.

337

Going over the chain of command, it made sense to me that Winslade had given the grim orders. Turov might have done it—but she had retreated from the system, safe in her two ships. Tribune Drusus was aware of my extracurricular activities, but hadn't seemed overly upset by them. In fact, he'd given me a modicum of faint praise for my part in discovering various squid artifacts in the mines.

No, it had to be Winslade. Of the group, he'd been the one most in favor of perming me the moment the Nairbs had shown up. Maybe this was his way of getting the job done. Better late than never, I guess.

Harris greeted me next with a personal visit, and he wasn't any more pleasant than Leeson had been. Possibly, he was even more hostile.

His big finger jabbed me in the chest. As I wasn't wearing anything thicker than smart-cloth, that finger sunk in and grated on my sternum.

"You asshole," he said. "You just can't hold your shit together, can you? I was a fool. A card carrying fool to think you'd grown up."

"To what do I owe this assault, Harris?"

"You just had to go down into some tunnel and tease some alien until it bit someone. That's what I'm talking about. Winslade explained it to me—at least, he explained enough. Winslade's an ass, but you're worse. If you didn't have rank, I'd make you do push-ups until you puked, then I'd let you lie in it while we all died here in this hole."

In an attempt to change the subject, I pointed downslope toward the enemy positions. "They're pulling back, sir. Not advancing."

"And why the hell would they do that? Because they're going to bombard us, that's why! Maybe they'll use some of that acidic gas that eats your suit. That should make your team extra happy you managed to get our commander to post us out here."

He stalked away, and I let him go without further comment. After all, he was right. Winslade was leaning on my team, and since Harris and Leeson were part of the same team, they were sharing in the pain.

I had to wonder at Harris' mentioning of the discoveries from deep in the mountain. He must have heard about them from somewhere, and that they were the source of Winslade's displeasure. The discoveries themselves were neutral, so Winslade's anger had to be a result of the way I'd handled the situation, rather than the fact I'd done something on my own.

It didn't take long for my slow brain to figure it out. What did Winslade like to do when a discovery was made? Why, he took all the credit personally, that's what. Apparently, he wasn't punishing my people for the Nairb ship disaster, he was unhappy about me stepping over his head and going directly to Drusus, cutting him out of the loop.

As there was nothing I could do about my orders, I stood my post with the rest of them. Everyone was glum and few of them would meet my eye directly.

For about an hour, we watched the skies and the slopes nervously. We moved around in a crouch when we moved at all, wary of snipers and enemy buzzers that were weaponized to kill.

When the attack finally did come, it didn't go down the way I'd expected. There was no storm of missiles or massive bombardment from below. Instead, the attack came from above.

I happened to be looking up—which everyone was doing a lot of—and I saw the gray skies suddenly lighten. A bluish ball fell from the heavens. It was like a ball of lightning, like a falling star of legend.

I'd seen this phenomenon before, but from the standpoint of the man firing the weapon. I'd watched it play out from the tactical control room of *Minotaur* as her broadsides were fired on a planet, causing vast destruction.

The others around me all began to run, but I didn't bother. I didn't crouch or throw myself flat. I stood tall, looming over all those who scrambled past me to get into the mouth of the tunnel at my back.

As that single shell punched through the various layers of the atmosphere, it caused frozen rings of bluish light to encircle it. These expanded on their own, like glowing ripples. It was a thing of beauty in its own deadly way.

I knew there was no time left to run, nowhere to hide. A man might as well face death bravely and make the best of it.

The single fusion shell arced down directly toward my position. One of those seven ships above us had coughed out a single shot, and of every square kilometer on this vast planet, the exact spot I stood upon had been selected for erasure.

I had to wonder if Claver was up there, cackling with glee as the warhead fell. Maybe he'd pinpointed me on a vid report from a saurian tech. Or maybe he'd just gotten lucky.

In any case, one second I stood proud and tall and the next I was just a few atoms of vapor drifting around the mountainside with the rest of them.

* * *

When I awoke, I was surrounded by more than the usual degree of chaos.

"Get him off the table, stat!" shouted a bio.

I was rudely lifted and heaved onto the floor. I squirmed there painfully, my nerve-endings still knitting up and reporting to my brain in a disorganized fashion.

"I'm not sure about the readings, Specialist," said an orderly who was running instruments over my legs. "I'm getting skeletal abnormalities. He might be a bad grow."

This sent a chill through me. Abnormalities? A bad grow? How long was this version of James McGill going to grace Machine World with his presence?

Through sheer effort of will, I struggled to my knees, then my feet. I wanted to cough. I wanted to pitch face-forward onto the slimy floor. But I didn't. I stood swaying, and the half of my mouth that was obeying me twisted upward in a grim parody of a confident smile.

"I'm right as rain, orderly," I said. "Get off me. I've got to get back to my unit."

The bio specialist was one I didn't know. She ran her eyes up and down my person like an auctioneer pricing horseflesh. "He'll do. Give him a uniform and get him out of here," she said to the orderly.

340

Shaking his head, the orderly helped me to a pile of loose clothing and discarded weapons. I took the biggest suit they had on hand, rammed the helmet down over my face, and gripped a beamer in both hands. I noticed as I was doing so I was limping a little.

The orderly kept looking at my bad leg. I took a deep breath and shook my head.

"It's just a charley horse," I said. "I get one every week."

"No," he said quietly, shaking his head. "You've got a torsion in your left femur. Your leg is twisted, and it's going to stay that way. Walking will be difficult, and running will be almost impossible."

I frowned, thinking about that. "I'm cavalry," I said. "I'll get in my dragon and make do."

The orderly shrugged and let go of my elbow. I swayed but remained standing. I walked toward the exit, my left leg moving with my toes pointed inward. I adjusted, and found I could totter along at a reasonable pace—but run? No way.

That was bad. A worse error than I'd ever been born with before. Still, I found I didn't want to give up on my current existence. I briefly considered putting my beamer up against my throat and pulling the trigger, forcing them to recycle me, but I couldn't do it. From the sounds of battle outside the revival center, who knew if I'd ever draw breath again.

It would be one thing to die proudly in battle, getting permed by the enemy because there was no one to bring me back to life. But to kill myself and then sleep forever—I couldn't do that.

In the passageway outside, the chaos intensified. Troops were rushing this way and that. There were injured infantry everywhere, sitting with their backs up against the rough tunnel walls. Bio people knelt beside each in turn and sprayed them with portable flesh-printers to reconstruct what they could. I knew right away things were bad. The bios were patching people up enough so they could stand and get back into the fight. That meant they couldn't afford to recycle and revive. They needed every trooper on the line they could get.

Leeson was along one wall. He was being sprayed along a bare arm that was a bloody mess. The pink of new skin glared against his hairy shoulders, and he glared at me in recognition when I came close.

"McGill? You injured again already?"

He indicated my leg, and I nodded grimly. "It's nothing, sir," I said. "Do I have a dragon waiting for me somewhere?"

"No," he said regretfully. "We lost our mounts in the first counterattack. I didn't see you then. Is this your first time back on the front line?"

Front line? I thought to myself. Since when was the core of the mountain, the inner sanctum where we kept our most holy of tech devices—the revival machines—the front line?

"I'm a little out of touch, sir," I admitted.

"All right. Get me on my feet, and I'll fill you in on the way back to the fight. No, no, dummy! Lift me by the *good* arm!"

I heaved him up with his less injured arm and looked him over. He didn't look like he was in much better shape than I was, but we both had beamers, and we were in the game.

Working our way down long, echoing passages, we passed hundreds of troops gripping their snap-rifles with eyes that rarely blinked. Most of them were Varus light troopers.

"We haven't got dragons," Leeson said. "But I know where there's a stash of heavy armor we can borrow."

I didn't argue with him. I didn't say much at all, in fact. He explained that after the saurians used a single fusion shell to blow open the mouth of the mines, they'd exposed a number of inner chambers and galleries.

"It was like an anthill was cut away to reveal the panicked inhabitants," he said. "The initial blast killed a thousand or so of us. Radiation, cave-ins and follow-up conventional bombardment finished another cohort. But the enemy infantry waited until the next morning to assault on foot—probably to let the radiation levels die down a little."

"Is there any sign of reinforcements, sir?" I asked.

"None. Not from space or anywhere else. But the saurians haven't had an easy time of it, I'll tell you that. We hung back that first day, squatting in the dark until a few thousand of them filtered into the rubble. Then we hit them hard. Booby-traps, dragons charging in close quarters—the enemy was armored, but we pushed them right back out. They don't seem to have any juggers with them, just the smaller raptor troops. They left at least three thousand dead, and in the meantime we've been churning out fresh troops with the revival machines."

That had always been one of our key advantages in battle. A human legion could face a force double or triple its size if it had the time to recycle her troops. If each man died three times, ten thousand legionnaires could do the fighting of thirty thousand.

It rarely turned out that way in practice, however. Once a force reached the breaking point, it was overwhelmed and wiped out. The revival machines themselves could be destroyed as well by deep raids. So far, Varus had held on. But if I had to guess from the look of the people in the tunnels, we were already down to half strength in men, materials and spirit.

"There have been two more assaults since then," Leeson said. "We've tossed them all back out. I don't think the saurians have revival machines, either. Too expensive. They just keep throwing fresh troops at us, and they've got plenty of those."

I scowled. Three assaults? How long had I been in limbo? "How long has it been, sir, since they first smashed open the front entrance?"

"I don't know. About forty hours, I'd guess. They're about to hit us again. Here, these are the heavy suits. Get in one. The exoskeleton will help with that bad leg."

He'd noticed my leg, and I winced at that. When a man came back fresh from a revive with a noticeable physical flaw, he knew he had to hide it. Under normal circumstances, Leeson was well within his rights to order me recycled. He didn't have to put up with a crippled man when he could have fresh grow a few hours later.

But Leeson never even suggested it. A limping McGill was better than nothing. The revival machines had to be used to churn out every soldier they could and get them back on the line. I wondered how many soldiers were hobbling their way to their next fight like I was.

When I found a suit of armor that would fit me, I climbed into it and strapped my beamer to my arm. It felt good to be encased in metal again. I checked the systems and found the suit was fully charged and equipped with shields. I smiled at that.

"As soon as you see the flash of enemy fire, switch on your shielding," Leeson ordered, as if he'd read my mind.

"Can we gather any more of our people, sir?" I asked. "This all seems a little disorganized."

"We'll join our unit at their designated post soon enough. Graves has been charged with holding the entrance to the lower tunnels. It's feared that the enemy will find a second entrance down there and flank us."

I nodded thoughtfully and followed him down spiraling dark passages into the depths of the mountain. Above us, distant explosions rumbled. The walls puffed dust and showered pebbles onto our helmets and shoulder epaulets.

We met up with Graves and my old unit about seven levels down. The sounds of fighting above were distant.

Only about a third of Graves' team was still riding a dragon. The rest had lost their mounts and were dressed in light armor. The only men in heavy armor were Leeson and I. Envious eyes crawled over our equipment.

"Where'd you two steal that?" Graves asked.

"Orders were to make do with whatever we could find, sir," Leeson said.

"Yeah, fine. But turn off your nameplate, Leeson. It says you're Specialist Jane Kinlan."

"Sorry sir," Leeson said, hastily turning off the letters which were emblazoned on his chest.

I'd already removed my insignia, and I couldn't help but smile at Leeson's distress. He was a relatively small man, and whoever Jane was, her armor fit him like a glove.

A few of the troops laughed. Our brief moment of levity was cut short when a warning came down from the upper tunnels. Saurian troops were approaching.

"If they're coming down here," Graves told us, "they must be seeking a way to flank us, a new route through the tunnels. We can't let them come up behind our lines. We'll stop them, right here, or we'll all die trying."

There was a muttered chorus of "yes sirs" but it wasn't enthusiastic.

We hunkered down in the dark, turning down all our suit lights to the barest glimmer and switched on our night vision.

No one talked about the enemy configuration or their numbers. Details like that didn't matter. We were to ambush them and hold our position to the last man.

No one spoke at all as we listened in the dark. The tramp of heavily armored alien feet could be heard echoing down the frosty tunnels toward our position.

I gripped my rifle, and I waited in the dark. The only sounds were the hissing of oxygen from my tanks and the pounding of my heart.

-47-

Right from the beginning, the fight was intense. The two sides met in the darkness, and the ripping sound of gunfire rang from the tunnel walls. We ambushed them, and they used explosives to destroy our strongpoints. Then we fell back to our next defensive line and repeated the process.

Each time, both sides left their dead in the grit. The smoke was so thick, I'd have been choking if I hadn't been wearing an airtight suit.

At one point, they rushed us. They sought to close with an elusive enemy that had been tormenting them.

Leeson was dead. I'd been cut off from the rest of the unit, and we were down to six effectives. As the veteran in the group, all their eyes looked at me for direction.

"Stand your ground!" I ordered my team, remembering how Graves had handled a similar situation underground, facing this same enemy back on Steel World. He hadn't panicked, not even when it was clear we were about to be overwhelmed.

I powered up my shield, and it formed a glimmering shell of force around me. My batteries were low, but saving power wasn't a good idea. It was use-it-or-lose-it time. I was the last trooper in heavy armor present—probably one of the last armored soldiers the legion had. The least I could do was put on my best showing.

My armor was getting pretty dinged up, but once my shield went on, smaller projectiles couldn't penetrate. Taking point, I shed bullets, fragments of explosives and even the gravity-propelled pieces of grit from the tunnel floors like they were so many raindrops.

When they got in close, I dropped my rifle, rose up and extended my force-blades. I'd set them to be thick and short as we were in close-quarters. I didn't want to accidently slash my own troops.

The enemy saurians came in a rush, but they weren't a disorganized mob. They were warriors, intelligent and capable. They fought with greater strength and agility than a man could possess. What they didn't have was shielding or the knowledge they'd live again if they died on this rocky ground.

A raptor engaged me, and all around me, others broke up into small individual melees. We thrust and cut. His twin daggers were high-tech metal, rather than energy, but they could still kill a man. One of his daggers struck home first, but my shielding deflected the blow. My return stroke with a power-blade went in low and took off his right leg.

He went down, but he didn't stop struggling. Inside his helmet, I could see his teeth, his lashing tongue, and his black, jewel-like eyes. We went into a clinch, and my exoskeleton screamed with the force of it. Before the fight, I'd turned down the juice to my arms to a minimum so the power system could support both the force-blades and the shielding. The drain on my cells was still high—I couldn't fight long at this level of power consumption.

A buzzing sensation and a warning light showed the lizard was driving a blade into my belly, intent on gutting me. The weakness of any shielding was a slow, steady attack. The thrust had gotten through to the metal already, and the blade had begun to vibrate. That was the buzzing sound I'd heard.

I finished him with a thrust to the throat, then straightened, sides heaving.

Two more saurians showed up. Behind them, on the ground, lay Gorman. I hadn't even realized he was with my knot of troops. He'd been stationed with another group. He must have lost his position and been driven back to join me at my lonely outpost. He was dead, his guts spilled out all over

347

the tunnel. A steady runnel of blood oozed out of his wrecked body and ran downhill behind me.

The two saurians had a plan, which they'd probably just worked upon Gorman to good effect. Each of them grabbed one of my arms and worked to drive a dagger into my guts. Seconds, that's all I had. The shielding gave way steadily. The armor of my chest plate was thick, but the points of the enemy blades were soon buzzing and penetrating. Had they studied us? Had they brought these knives just to defeat human legionnaires?

The answers to these questions didn't matter, so I drove them from my mind. I was about to die.

I took a chance. Using verbal commands, I ordered my suit to switch off my shielding and transfer all the power to my limbs.

This had two startling effects. Both of the vibrating blades rasped against my armor, slipping due to the sudden lack of resistance. But my arms, at the same moment, became more powerful than any saurian that had ever lived.

I didn't have time for anything fancy. I slammed both the saurian soldiers together like a bully knocking together two boys' heads. This had little effect as they were armored as well, but it did get those blades out of my gut for a moment, and it set the saurians up for my next move.

Slashing horizontally, I swept a force-blade across both their necks. The blade was driven with such force that it beheaded both. They toppled at my feet, and I reengaged my shields.

More came after that. Around me, most of my team died. Hudson, Kivi, Sargon—they all fell. In the end, only Carlos and I stayed on our feet. In the meantime, the attack had been repelled.

"I think…" panted Carlos, "I think they ran out of lizards."

"Maybe," I said. "Let's go find out."

Groaning, he followed my advance. We paused only to touch the tappers of the dead and to lift their power-cells if they had more juice in them than ours did.

We only ran into the lizards one more time, and they didn't want to engage. They were falling back, performing a fighting retreat.

We didn't make it easy for them. We'd linked up with survivors from other squads and units. Graves himself had lived, altogether he led a force of fifteen-odd troopers, all that was left. We dogged the enemy all the way back to the smoke-filled central chambers.

The lizards were falling back, still in good order, but their lines were getting ragged with losses.

"Concentrate fire," Graves ordered. "Aim for the legs to bring a target down then go to the next. Don't pepper them all, they're already retreating. We need to make them pay by taking down every enemy combatant we can."

Coldly, we did as he ordered. It was a slaughter, shooting down fleeing saurians. They threw back fire now and then, but it was only to keep us ducking.

We kept advancing relentlessly. It seemed to take an hour to reach the surface, where we halted for fear they'd hit us with some kind of bombardment. A breathless cheer went up among the survivors as we viewed the aftermath of the battle.

Thousands lay dead, and the enemy was in full retreat.

"That was close, sir," I said to Graves.

He looked at me. "Closer than you think. Most of our lines were broken. Your tunnel held, but it was a rare exception. Good job, McGill."

I frowned. "Sounds like they were winning, sir. Why'd they pull out right before they finished us?"

"I don't know. Maybe even an army of reptiles can have enough death to fill their bellies with fear."

That didn't sound like the saurian troops I'd met. They tended to fight to the death unless ordered to retreat by their masters.

Daring to advance further, I walked out upon the slopes themselves. Graves stayed in the shadowy tunnels behind me.

"You can dream about your death wish if you want to, McGill," he called. "But you'll do it on your own time. I forbid you to run out there into the open and lose a perfectly good suit of armor."

349

"Thanks for your concern, Centurion," I told him. "But you should really come up here and see this for yourself."

Finally, he advanced and hunkered down beside me. Above us, an overhang of cracked rock projected. From the shadows underneath, we could see the mountainside. It ran down about two kilometers to the roiling edge of the thick white mists that covered most of the planet. Just before the edge of the mist, a battle was in progress.

"What the—are those machines?" Graves asked.

"Yes sir, I think they are."

"What're they doing?"

"Eating saurians, sir. By the hundreds—or at least, they're eating their weapons, armor and equipment. They must be hungry."

Graves looked at me, squinting. "Did you expect this?"

"Me sir? How could I know—?"

"The message you sent, using the young machine-creature. Natasha translated it. Didn't she tell you?"

"There hasn't been much time, sir," I said. "I was revived and thrown straight into the fight."

He nodded. "Natasha and Kivi worked on the translation for hours. They figured out it was pretty much a dinner bell, a summons to a feast. They thought it might be the message the squids used to get the machines to come here and chew on the mountain, exposing titanium veins."

I blinked at him. "I had no idea—but it makes sense. Carlos was eaten for a reason after all. He must have accidentally promised that baby machine a dinner, and the machine figured he must have meant to eat his suit."

Graves laughed then. It was a rare sound, an unpleasant chuckle. "Best thing Ortiz ever did. The baby machine took his message off to the nearest herd of native machines and—dinner time!"

Graves laughed some more. I grinned as well. We watched the chaos below for several more minutes before retreating. The saurians had been hit from behind by a hungry mob of machines. The only source of easy metal had been on the saurians themselves, who were new to this odd planet. Flanked

350

by surprise, they'd called a retreat from our tunnels to deal with this new threat.

As far as I was concerned, it couldn't have happened to a nicer bunch of lizards.

-48-

Getting slammed in the flank was too much for the saurian forces—or at least for their commanders. They'd been losing too much strength against us all along, but they'd been buoyed up by the certain knowledge they were driving us back, winning through attrition.

By the time I reached the core of our stronghold, seeking repairs for my equipment and sustenance for my body, Leeson had been revived. He met with me and shook my gauntlet.

"Well done, McGill. You held the line."

"Thank you, Adjunct.

"Even better, they're *still* retreating," Leeson said. "Have you seen the vids coming down from the buzzers?"

"No sir, I haven't had—"

"By damn, I still don't believe it! Those cowardly lizards are tucking their collective scaly tails and running for their lives!"

I echoed his excitement and relief, but I didn't think they were cowardly. Saurians were anything but. I'd once watched one self-execute without a qualm, just because an irritated Nairb had told him to do so.

"I think their commanders are losing heart, not the troops," I said.

"What? Have you fallen in love with another alien race, McGill? How typical. Maybe you should run down this molehill after them and beg them to come back for tea."

"Hardly, sir. I was just pointing out that saurians are very brave as individuals."

"Why the hell are they running, then?"

"To my way of thinking, they've just realized this entire battle is becoming too costly. They've probably spent all their funding on renting ships and arms, not on revival machines. Those choices resulted in a much more powerful force, but a brittle one. They couldn't absorb endless losses. They're probably retreating now because they've lost half their troops. I don't think they planned on that."

"Hmm," Leeson said. "You think their morale didn't break, but the bank did? Interesting. I have to admit, their princes are more money-conscious than they are humanitarians. Well, either way, we're all as good as dead now."

This statement concerned me. Leeson still seemed happy, but I could see a hint of resignation there as well.

"We're dead?" I asked. "Why's that, sir?"

He looked at me in triumph, squinting his small eyes. "Ha! Don't tell me you didn't reason out their next move, Mr. Strategist?"

I frowned at him. Leeson had a naturally abrasive attitude, but he wasn't dumb. I honestly wanted to know what he was thinking, despite his barbs.

"You tell me, Adjunct," I said.

Leeson showed me the unit's tactical display. He ran his finger down the slope toward the massing saurian troops at the base of the mountain. They'd managed to repel the hungry machines, but only after devastating losses. They hadn't been prepared for such an enemy and lacked the heavy weaponry to deal with them. To kill the big machines, groups of soldiers were rushing in close and essentially committing suicide to stop them. I'd seen Centurion Belter employ similar tactics to good effect—but we could revive our losses—they couldn't.

"Think about it," Leeson said. "They're beating the machines but preparing to pull out anyway. Why leave the mountain entirely? They could just siege us from down there. But instead, they're setting up to have transports come down and pick up their battered troops."

353

"Maybe they want to get out of this hell-hole, sir. At least, that's what I think they're doing."

"Nah. They'll pull up stakes, all right, but they won't give up. They'll unleash their big guns again. All of them, this time. Sure, that will destroy most of this mountain and the titanium mine. But the raw ore will survive. A hundred or so fusion shells, that's what I expect will come falling our way once these lizards lift off. You see if they don't."

I was alarmed by his prediction. For one thing, it made sense. For another, there was no way anyone in legion Varus— cavalry or otherwise—could survive such a devastating attack.

"That means we can't let them get back into space," I said. "We've got to stop them."

Leeson shook his head and cracked his faceplate open long enough to spit. "You let me know when you've figured out how to do that, McGill," he laughed bitterly.

Turning away, I began to trot back down the tunnels into the mountain. My pace turned into a thundering run by the time I reached Drusus' office. I'd adjusted my suit to power my legs, so I didn't have to limp.

There were several techs in the tribune's chamber with him. They were rolling up computer scrolls, and they moved with an air of purpose. They weren't panicked yet, but they were sure in a hurry.

"Tribune?" I asked.

He looked up at me, but didn't smile. In fact, his face scrunched up a bit like he smelled something unpleasant.

"What fresh disaster brings you here, Veteran?" he asked me.

"Can I talk to you for a second?"

"No time. We're pulling out. Most of the troops won't make it—I'll have your people go down deep in the mines. To the very bottom, if necessary. Maybe a few will survive."

I watched for a moment as he stuffed a computer scroll into a capsule, then another.

Tribune Drusus spoke to the techs he was working with. I noted with surprise that one of them was Natasha.

"Send out one of these with every flying drone we've got," he ordered. "Send them in every direction."

"Already programmed, sir," Natasha said.

"Good. Fly those birds."

Natasha rushed out with a capsule under her arm and a worried look on her face. Everyone looked like they were about to die—probably because they were.

"Natasha," I said, catching up to her. "What's the plan?"

"Plan?" she asked. "That's a big word for this desperate attempt to survive. We're sending out drones in every direction. They'll fly until they run out of fuel then crash into the snow and wait. If they hear a friendly signal later on, they'll start chirping, hoping to be found."

"Okay…what's in the capsules?"

"Data. Lists of the soon to be dead. Your name, your DNA, and mental backups. Mine too. If someone comes looking and finds them, well, maybe they'll revive us out of the goodness of their hearts."

"I thought Turov took our DNA prints with her when she pulled out."

"Yes—if she made it back to Earth. But there has to be confirmation to get a legal revival. They won't just make a full copy of our legion back on Earth without sending out a mission to confirm our status. These documents will prove we should be revived."

Watching in concern, I frowned at her while she worked. I almost mentioned that she could end up a triplet—but I was smart enough not say that.

"But are you so sure that we'll all die?" I asked. "Drusus said that he was sending the troops deep into the mines."

"It won't matter. Nothing will survive a steady bombardment by the broadsides. We've done the math. They've got seven capital ships up there, James. Grow up. We're all as good as permed, whether we get buried in the tunnels or vaporized out on the surface."

She moved as if to push past me, but I held onto her arm, and she looked up at me, reluctantly.

"Look," I said. "We can't let the lizards fire their cannons."

"How are we going to stop them?"

"You've got to help me," I said. "You've got to get me in touch with Claver."

"Oh no, forget that," she said, shaking her head.

She headed up the tunnels, and I followed. We reached the upper chambers and then the exposed, smoldering galleries. The mess outside was dramatic, and most of it was obscured by fog and smoke.

She set up and released her drone loaded with data scrolls. It looked like a messenger pigeon, but it buzzed rather than flapped. We watched as it darted into the smoke then appeared again. Suddenly, a beam lanced out from downslope and took the drone out. It fell in burning pieces which steamed in the snow.

Natasha made a sound of anguish. "It's hopeless."

"Come on girl, give my plan a shot," I said.

She looked at me for a second then shook her head. "I don't even know what your plan is, and don't want to know. I'm following my orders this time, James. I'm sending out these drones. It's our best hope."

She knelt and began working on another drone. This time, she programmed it to climb up high, hoping to get out of the range of the enemy automated turrets. I didn't think it would work, but she wasn't going to stop trying.

"Look, I'll do that," I said, taking the hand-held terminal from her. "Just get your com equipment out and set it up."

Heaving a sigh, she did as I asked. "You never give up on anything, do you?" she asked.

"No, I guess not."

She got out her tech-specialist computer and put it down in the snow. A small dish extended from the core brick—but then she stopped.

"No," she said. "I'm not going to do this. I'm going to follow my orders, and that's all. Why die violating my tribune's final wishes? You've always gotten me into trouble, James. I see that now. I'll never understand why I listen to you."

This little speech of hers made me angry and desperate at the same time. My mind raced, trying to come up with something I could use to influence her.

I had the answer in less than a second, but I didn't want to use it. Only the fact that the legion was facing a wipe, possibly a permanent one, caused me to say what I said next.

"Natasha," I said. "You haven't always followed the rules, you know. You've come up with some violations all your own. Remember back on Dust World? When you committed a stack of high crimes?"

"What? I did no such thing—not without your urging. It was *you* who shot a neutral air ship and started this war with the squids. That's what I remember."

"Yeah, but before that. You didn't want to die on *Corvus*, remember?"

She looked at me with sudden concern. "You said you wouldn't talk about that."

"I'm just trying to make a point. You reached a situation that made you desperate, and you took your chances. In fact, you and your fellow mutineers took over *Corvus* and escaped into orbit around the local star."

Natasha froze. She turned to face me, her cheeks red. "I didn't do that. I told you I *planned* to do it. That *maybe* there was a twin of me somewhere out—"

"No," I said, my voice becoming gentle. I took her hands in mine and looked her in the eyes. "You didn't try to do it, you did it. Della told me. She knows you very well. That's the real reason she avoids you. She knows your twin, and everyone on Dust World is grateful to her."

I don't think I've ever seen such an odd look on a human face before. It was full of surprise, fear, horror and wonder all at once.

"Della told you this?" she asked in a small voice. "She knows—why didn't you say something?"

"How do you feel right now?"

"Sick."

"That's why I kept quiet," I said. "I'm only telling you now because we're facing that kind of situation. We're here, you and I and thousands of others. I don't want to pretend this body doesn't matter. I don't have a copy out there on Dust World who will carry on in my stead. Even if I'm brought back to life

357

some day, that's not good enough. I want this version of me to live—just like you did back aboard *Corvus*."

"Are you shitting me, James? Because if you are, I'm never going to forgive you."

I shook my head. While she was thinking it over, I programmed and released the drone. It flew off with a buzzing sound and vanished into the smoke and haze. A moment later, it was shot down as well.

"I'm telling you the plain truth, Natasha. I've been carrying this secret with me for weeks now. I didn't want to tell you because I knew it would freak you out. I apologize for telling you now."

"Here," she said, handing me a headset.

I looked at it and then at her. Her eyes were avoiding mine. I gave her a hug and a kiss on the top of the head.

"Just hurry up," she said. "Whatever madness you've got in mind, I want you to do it and get it over with. Now."

Oddly enough, it wasn't that hard to get ahold of Claver. I knew his private channel, and it appeared that no one else was trying to reach him right now.

"Who's this?" he demanded. "Get off the line if this isn't official business."

"It's official, all right," I said. "I want to negotiate a surrender."

"Is this McGill? Ha! No dice, moron. First off, you aren't in charge of jack-squat. Secondly, you're gonna die today. That's what every lizard wants to see, and that's what we're going to give them with these rented ships. I'm going to operate the broadsides myself. I'm their gunner, did you know that? I dropped that first one on your head, and I'm going to enjoy unloading all sixteen the next time."

"Sir," I said, "I'm not going to appeal to your humanity, just to your greed."

Claver paused. "How's that?" he asked finally.

I took a deep breath, closed my eyes, and made my pitch. "I've got access to something you want. Something you would do almost anything to get your hands on."

Claver was quiet for a few seconds.

"The key? Are you telling me Turov left the Galactic key in your country-bumpkin, manure-stained hands, boy? Because if that's your game, I'm not buying it. Turov is six kinds of a bitch, but she's not stupid. She'd never—"

"Sir, what I have is access to Turov, and *she* has the key. If you let us get off this world without operating those big guns for the saurians, I'll procure it and hand it over to you at a later date."

There was another, longer silence. Downslope, I could see the mists swirling. I knew the saurians were still embattled by the machines at the foot of the mountain, out of sight. Occasionally an explosion ripped through the air and flashes erupted in the vapors like lightning bursts inside a cloud.

"Why this? Why now?" he demanded, sounding greedy but suspicious. "Why not just take your lumps and catch a revive back home?"

"Because Turov might not come back. She might scratch this legion from her roster forever. Think of all the baggage she'd relieve herself of if she left us dead and gone."

"Let's say I buy your bullshit. Let's pretend I believe you can get the key, and that you aren't just blowing smoke up my butt in general. Why would you hand it over when you have possession? You might forget about a deal with gullible old Claver at that point."

"I gave the key up before, to Turov. That was a mistake. She hasn't bettered Earth's cause with it. She's used it for personal gain."

"And you think I'm some kind of philanthropist?"

"I'm not under any illusions in that regard, sir. But I think you're trying to build a trading empire while I think Turov is trying to rise to the top of Earth's military. I find you dangerous, but less so than she is."

"Hmmm. You're pulling at my heartstrings, boy. After all, I'm just an old-fashioned softie underneath, and I hate to see a fellow schemer suffer."

I rolled my eyes at his words, but I managed not to laugh.

"Out of the kindness of my inner being," he continued as if he was doing me a tremendous favor, "I'm inclined to accept your terms. I'll do what I can—but I can't offer any promises.

359

These saurians don't want to operate the big guns themselves because they're not licensed to do so, but I'm not under any such proscriptions. Without my help, they may or may not decide to break the rules and do it themselves. My guess is that they won't, but..."

"I'm willing to take the gamble," I said. "For one thing, it's all I've got. For another, I'm betting on saurian respect for the law. They like to follow the rules strictly. They won't work the guns and violate the Galactic statutes. What I don't get is how they had the balls to hire warships and fly out here in the first place."

"Haven't you figured that out yet, dummy? Earth people are Enforcers now, leaving the role of provincial mercenaries open. We lost our monopoly on the mercenary service when we accepted the elevation in status. Now that the job is open in Frontier 921, the lizards are going for it all out. It's not just the metals they were after out here, they want to prove they can defeat an Earth legion on the ground."

"Sucks to be them in that case, sir."

He gave me a long, dirty chuckle that ended in a coughing fit. "You boys pretty much kicked their tails in. I had trouble not enjoying the spectacle. But let's cut the crap. Do we have a deal?"

"Yes," I said. My heart was heavy in my chest.

"When do I take delivery of my prize?"

"You have to give me a year, sir. Shouldn't take any longer than that."

"A year? What the hell kind of—?"

"You could speed that up," I suggested. "If you left us a deep-link by accident, the plan's odds of success would be greatly enhanced. Otherwise, we've got no way to communicate with Earth. We'll have to wait for Hegemony ships to scout the system again before we'd be able to get off this rock."

Claver grumbled and cursed, but at last he agreed that it would speed up the process. Who knew if Turov would ever come back to see what happened on Gamma Pavonis? He couldn't take the risk that he'd let us live but not get home. I couldn't give him the Galactic key if I didn't get back to Turov to take it.

He closed the channel, and I looked up at the skies. Blue-white flares of plasma burned in the upper atmosphere. The saurian lifters were coming down to pick up their troops. Hundreds of lifters for thousands of troops.

I rushed inside the caves to tell Tribune Drusus what I'd done. If he shot down the saurian lifters, even one of them, the deal might fall apart.

-49-

I'll be the first to admit my methods are unorthodox. That I frequently step on the toes of my superior officers—no, that's not right. I *stomp* on them. But when such actions result in miraculous improvements to the well-being of Legion Varus, one might think a little praise was in order.

Instead, when I explained what I'd done, I was met with shocked silence. The silence was unfortunately brief, and was immediately followed by a tirade of swearing.

Tribune Drusus wasn't doing the swearing, however. A certain primus named Winslade was the one creating the stink.

"How *dare* you, McGill?" he asked as if he couldn't quite catch his breath. "How *dare* you?"

"Well sir," I said, "I happen to have a personal relationship with Claver, and I know how he thinks. I only appealed to his better nature and succeeded."

All the officers in the chamber eyed me with a distinct air of mistrust. I found this almost insulting. After all, we were in this together. We were going to die on this rock without help.

"So," Drusus said, stepping forward and putting up a hand to stop Winslade's next outburst. "You're saying *you* talked Claver into leaving without bombing us out of existence?"

"Yes sir, exactly."

"Claver is a trader, not a charity," Drusus said. "What was in it for him?"

"First off, he was their gunner," I said.

"We know that."

"And without him, it's unlikely the saurians will have enough scaly balls to bomb us."

"Fair enough," Drusus said. "But again, what was Claver's source of gain in this deal you arranged? He has to get something out of it."

My attempts to switch the subject had clearly failed. I looked from one of them to the next, blinking and thinking fast. They weren't going to buy any kind of compassion on the part of Adjunct Claver. I couldn't blame them for that. Anyone who'd met the man knew he'd sell his grandma for a bent credit piece and a cup of coffee.

"He wants trading rights," I said quickly. "Not between Machine World and Earth, but between Machine World and the rest of Frontier 921."

There were murmurs and growls at this. They believed it, but they weren't happy about it.

"That's not all," I said. "He wants every ingot in this mine stacked outside for picking up later. Once we've gotten a ship here to pull us out, we're to leave the titanium on the surface and not look back."

There was even more, louder grumbling at that. But eventually, they settled down and accepted the terms.

What choice did they have, really? Who would risk being permed to stop a trade deal? Not these people, and not me, either.

The following hours were tense as we waited for the saurians to withdraw and leave in their ships. They took to the air, vanishing into the sky in their lifters. I was jealous to see it. I'd never watched aliens with such envy.

When they were all hanging up there over our heads, it was hard not to walk in a crouch down here on the surface. Drusus ordered us below, and most followed those orders, but not me. I wandered the rubble-filled tunnels, wondering if I was enjoying the final moments of existence that would ever be allotted to me.

Drusus himself hailed me in the upper galleries. He walked up and stared at me.

"Defiant to the last, McGill?" he asked.

I shrugged. "Sorry sir," I said. "But I figured if a man's going to be blasted to atoms, he might as well walk under an open sky under his own power."

"I can see you're still limping now that you're out of your armor," he said, looking me over. "We can fix that, you know."

"A regrow? What's the point? I'll be dead or alive in a few hours' time, and either way I won't care about my leg."

"Suit yourself," he was quiet for a second, and we both studied the skies. Finally, he had to ask what was on everyone's mind. "Do you think they'll really let us go, James? You talked to Claver, not me. Can we trust him?"

"Not at all, sir. Not for a dime, a dollar or a two-penny candy, as my grandfather used to say. But we can reason through what he wants, and if he wants something we can give, he'll stick to an agreement. He couldn't be successful as a trader otherwise."

"I guess not," he said, and sighed. "It's galling to have to depend on an enemy to—"

Just then, my tapper beeped. I glanced down at it, frowning. No one should have been able to reach me here, standing in the wreckage and blasted craters of the mine's upper chambers. I glanced at Tribune Drusus, who nodded with curiosity.

"Answer it," he said.

"Hello?" I asked. The caller had no ID and no icon. "Who's there?"

"It's me, McGill," said Claver. "I'm sorry to have to make this call, but I'm a man of my word when a deal's been struck. I thought I owed it to you to let you know what happened up here."

My heart sank. "What do you mean, sir?"

"The saurians aren't going for it. Unfortunately, they aren't as dumb as real lizards. They don't want to change their plans just because I've made some kind of under-the-table deal. I'm going to have to drop the hammer on you and your troops."

"Sir," I said quickly, "I've managed to talk the tribune into sweetening the offer."

I explained we would set him up as a dealer and give him the contents of the mines that were already processed and refined.

Claver sounded truly regretful to turn me down. "That *is* tempting, boy," he said. "And I wish I could take it, but I'll be permed myself if I do. The saurians have a gun to my head—literally."

Throughout this exchange, Tribune Drusus watched me, frowning curiously. He could hear both ends of the conversation as I was using the speakers on my tapper and talking out loud. I might have made the call more private if I'd known who was calling—but what was done was done.

I looked up at the gray clouds, expecting falling streaks of light to come down and burn me to cinder at any second.

"Stall them," I said, "stall them as long as you can, Claver."

"What's the point?" he asked.

I told him then about the drones we were flying in every direction.

"The deal could still be on," I said. "Just give us twenty-four hours. Tell them you need to recalibrate or something. Let us spread ourselves out a little, and the odds we'll be permed will be much lower. If we breathe again, even in another place in another time, the deal is still on."

"Hmmm. Okay. But one more thing, I want assurance from Drusus that if I'm permed by these reptiles, I'll catch a revive from your people and be set free afterward."

I looked at Drusus, who appeared troubled but resigned. He leaned closer to my tapper.

"This is Tribune Drusus," he said. "Check my voiceprint. On my word, I'll revive and release you if you require the service after this disastrous campaign."

Claver chuckled. "Well, well, Tribune," he said. "I should have known you were lurking nearby and coaching McGill. He's not smart enough to maneuver old Claver by himself. It's a deal."

The channel closed, and we were left to gaze at the skies in apprehension. Drusus studied me rather than the clouds after a minute or so.

"What did you mean when you told him you'd managed to sweeten the deal by adding trading rights? Isn't that what Claver wanted in the first place?"

365

I straightened my shoulders, but I didn't meet his eye. "Did I say something like that? I'm sorry sir, I must have been nervous and misspoke."

"Right… McGill, you're without a doubt, the most peculiar noncom I've ever met. Just when I think I understand all your twists and turns, you spring another one on me. Sometimes, I worry that I've got a youthful version of Claver in the midst of my own team, hiding in plain sight."

I looked at him and frowned. "I find that suggestion offensive, sir. I've been working hard to save our collective butts. You may not know everything that's in my head, but I'd appreciate it if you'd at least recognize positive results when they're reached."

Drusus shook his head bemusedly. "Lectured sternly by a man who's less than a third my age. I stand rebuffed. But as to recognition and gratitude, remember your rapid rise in rank—despite a thousand infractions."

He walked away, and I regretted having smarted-off to him that way. I gazed up at the skies, wondering as to our fate. It really was hard to think clearly with a mass of fusion shells waiting to rain down upon my head.

Twenty-one long hours passed before the skies spoke to me again. Just in case Claver needed a little more encouragement, I'd spent most of that time pacing around on the surface, watching my tapper.

According to the techs who'd set up dishes to track the saurian ships, all seven had remained parked in orbit. That couldn't be a good sign.

Maybe Claver had come up with a temporary dodge, telling them the broadsides weren't workable for a set period. That would mean he'd followed our agreement to the letter, if not the spirit of it.

If that was the situation, I was as good as dead. At least our drones had managed to spread all over the planet now that the saurians weren't around to shoot them down. If some of them managed to keep from being eaten by the local fauna for the next year or so, we should catch a revive—maybe.

At the crack of the twenty-first hour, something finally happened.

It started off as a streak of blue-white. I'd seen it before, and I'd expected it. The first shell was coming down, falling right toward my position.

I stared at it, unblinking. As a man who's experienced death more times than I can count, I wanted to end it all without cringing. I watched with my spine straight, my mouth clamped closed and my guts still in my belly.

Only at the last second did I realize anything was wrong. The flare of retros—that wasn't right. Shells didn't slow themselves down as they plunged to the ground.

Instead of air-bursting and creating a mushroom cloud, some tiny portion of which contained my fragmented molecules, the falling object blossomed with white flame and landed. When it thudded into the ground not a hundred meters downslope, I ran to it.

My mind was full of possibilities. Could it be Claver himself? Clearly, it was a life-pod. Who else would be crazy enough to come down here now?

I cranked open the hatch, which had bent a little after rolling down the side of the mountain a few meters. Inside, there was nothing living. There was only a polyhedral crate and a note.

Ripping loose the note, I saw scrawled handwriting.

I've been executed. Remember our deal, dummy.

It was signed Claver. I opened the crate and stared at the contents. There was a deep-link unit inside.

For the first time in days, I dared to grin.

-50-

My delight was short-lived. Not ten minutes after I'd dragged the crate containing the deep-link unit out of the life-pod and carried it to the mine entrance, the sky erupted again.

This time, the flash and thunder of explosions were unmistakable. Something else was happening up there. Something big.

I heaved the crate onto my back and trotted into the tunnels, grunting with every step. My breath came in puffs, but I didn't slow down. I lumbered awkwardly into the dark and downward. My left foot dragged behind, but I forced myself to endure the pain. I wished I was still wearing powered armor to help me along, but I'd given that up.

The rest of my legion brothers were down there, deep in mountain, huddling in the lowest tunnels and hoping against hope they'd live to see the morrow. As far as I knew, I was the only crazy son-of-a-bitch wandering around on the surface with the exception of a few drones that tended the sensors and com dishes.

It took me the better part of an hour to reach my comrades. By that time, my muscles were trembling from exertion. The burden on my back, heavier than a full-grown man, had long ago given me an ache I wouldn't soon forget. My limping bad leg had only made matters worse.

Finally, I tottered into the caverns where I was met with the last thing I'd expected: jubilant comrades.

"They did it, McGill!" shouted Carlos, clapping me on the shoulder.

I dropped the deep-link as gently as I could and let myself flop down on my back beside it.

"Did what?" I asked.

"Haven't you been watching the tactical displays? The show has been better than a ballgame."

"I've been carrying this box down from the surface."

Carlos shook his head and loomed over me. He looked down and grinned. "You mean you don't *know?*"

I wanted to kick him, but I was too tired. Instead I closed my eyes and shook my head.

"The squids came back, man!" he said. "We watched it all—live. The saurian ships met them and they fought. There were eleven squid ships, and the saurians still blew them away. It turns out Imperial broadsides *are* good for something besides wrecking innocent planets. They toasted all the enemy ships."

Frowning, I knew something didn't add up. After a moment, I had it.

"But wait," I said. "The saurians didn't have the right license to fire the broadsides."

"Graves mentioned that in the unit announcement," Carlos said. "I guess there is a clause that allows them to fire in self-defense. The Empire owns those ships, and they don't want them destroyed just because no one aboard has a license. They can fire as long as the other side fires first."

I thought about it hazily for a second, still lying on the ground. What a strange, twisted-up set of rules we lived by. Life under the Galactic Empire had always been like that. You often couldn't do what came naturally. You had to check and triple-check countless rules. I could imagine the saurian commanders taking the first few strikes while frantically reading their contracts and consulting with legal experts. In the end, they'd apparently decided they were allowed to use the big guns and had unleashed their power.

Struggling to get up, I groaned. Carlos lifted me to my feet. He frowned at my leg. "You've got to do something about that leg, man."

369

"Later. What about the saurian ships? How many did they lose?"

"Five of them went down! Isn't that great? Only two escaped the system. That'll serve those lizards right. They came out here and got themselves snotted—up, down and sideways. Couldn't have happened to a nicer bunch, huh?"

Another thought occurred to me as I pushed him aside and headed to the command chamber. Maybe I wasn't the hero of the hour. The saurians had been still sitting in orbit, plotting our destruction right up until the squids had attacked. That meant they hadn't given up. Maybe they'd been searching for a way they could legally bombard us, or even calling for a Nairb judgment in their favor. Quite possibly, all Claver and I had been able to do was delay them long enough and tie them up in a legal argument until another enemy arrived.

Tired and sore, I ordered a few lounging recruits to carry the crate for me, which they did without complaint. When I got to the officers' chambers, I was challenged by guards, but they let me through when they figured out who I was. Apparently, they had orders to let me pass.

Tribune Drusus met my eyes the moment I arrived. He looked at me with a mixture of wonder and mistrust.

"Was this battle in space part of your grand scheme as well, Veteran?" he asked.

Everyone was staring at me in silence. I felt those eyes. A dozen officers were present and as many more noncoms. They were curious. They wanted to know how this attack had fallen into place.

I wanted to lie. I wanted to take credit for all of it, but I knew that was a bad path. I couldn't back up any fanciful stories. Whatever I said would fall apart in the end.

"Sometimes," I said vaguely, "a man just gets lucky, sir. I do have one more gift for you, however. A deep-link unit."

That got the attention of everyone, especially the techs. They swarmed me like a pack of hungry coyotes, investigating the crate like it was road kill. Natasha herself was on-hand when the box was opened and did a full diagnostics check on the unit.

370

"The system appears operational," she said a minute later, "except for power. There's no cell. I think we can work around that, though."

The techs then carted it off to their workshop. Natasha stayed behind and gave me a real smile.

"I don't know how you got this," she said, "but you must have dragged it all the way down here from the surface."

"On my back," I admitted. "I'm a little sore."

She kissed me then, and I smiled. Then she was gone, chasing after the deep-link unit with the rest of the techs. You'd have thought it was Christmas.

The excitement of the day turned into exhaustion after that. I found my way to my kit in a lonely chamber. My spider-silk bag was there, and I have to admit, I'd never felt anything quite as good as the moment I eased myself into it.

* * *

I awoke an unknown number of hours later. The chamber was dark except for a few small, glaring lights.

"Have you got the IV in?" asked a female voice. "He's waking up."

"I've got it, I've got it!" Carlos said.

I frowned. *Carlos with an intravenous needle?* The thought was horrific.

Struggling into a sitting position, I caused both of them to squawk and scramble.

"Hey buddy, just relax," Carlos said.

The other voice turned out to be Anne's. I hadn't recognized her at first. I realized then that I'd been drugged.

"What are you two doing?" I demanded.

"Just lie back and relax," Carlos said. "We'll be done in about—"

My big hand lashed out and grasped Carlos' neck. I've got fingers that are longer than normal—it comes with being over two meters tall. I squeezed until his eyes bulged.

"Get that IV out of my arm, you ghoul," I said, slurring my words.

Anne's face came up into my swimming vision. I glared at them both with mistrust.

"James," she said calmly. "This isn't an attack. We're trying to fix your leg."

"I'm not a bad grow," I lied in a growling voice.

"Of course not," Anne said soothingly. "We're not running you through a revival machine. That would have been easier, but we're trying to fix it the old fashioned way."

I looked down at my leg then. It was a bloody mess. She had it open with clamps and artificial veins pumping. They'd bypassed my femoral artery with a smart-shunt, and it was pulsating rhythmically.

"What the hell are you guys doing?"

"We were ordered to kill you and recycle," Anne said. "Graves won't stand for a man with a limp in his unit. Now, could you please let go of my orderly's neck before he passes out?"

I looked at Carlos. He was dressed in surgical greens, and his face was purple. Both his hands were working on my fingers, trying to pull them loose, but he couldn't do it. I was holding onto him and squeezing with the strength of a berserk.

"Sorry," I said, finally letting him go. I lay back down and barely heard his stream of curses and coughs.

"You ungrateful ape," he complained. "My first time in surgery, and the patient tries to kill me. This sucks worse than I expected."

"You'll get used to it," Anne said in a flat voice.

Lying on my back again, my mind calmed. Despite the local anesthetic, I felt them tug and buzz at my leg. They sawed through the femur, twisted it so it would stand straight, then fused it together again using a flesh-printer loaded with bone cells.

"Carlos? Why are you playing orderly?" I asked as they were sealing up my leg.

"I should be asking *you* how I got this job," he said. "Drusus ordered it. Specialist training—the last kind of specialist I've ever wanted to be. No offense, Anne, but being a bio totally blows. It's a disgusting and thankless job."

"None taken," Anne said in that same, flat voice. I got the feeling she wasn't enjoying Carlos' company any more than he was enjoying his new assignment.

I got to thinking of Carlos as a bio. I visualized him working revival machines, caring for the sick and recycling the dead.

A rumble started in my chest somewhere. I don't know exactly where it came from. At first I thought it was a cough, but it turned out to be a laugh.

Still laughing, I passed out and didn't wake up again for a long time.

* * *

Summoned to see the tribune, I hobbled through the tunnels on my weak leg. It was straight now and would heal in time, but it still hurt pretty bad.

Drusus looked me over when I arrived. He shook his head and whistled.

"Still operating on a bad grow, Veteran?" he said. "Graves said you were a chicken when it came to recycling, but I didn't believe it. You're so personally brave in other arenas. Why not embrace death and a quick revive? It solves so much."

Frowning, I shook my head. "Sir, I've been patched up. The leg is straightened and I'll be right as rain in a few days. I didn't want to bother the revival people, they've been churning out troops to replenish our losses for days."

"That's true enough. Well, I guess it doesn't matter. Just try not to limp around Graves, it grates on him."

"Words to live by, sir."

"Now, as to why I've summoned you. We've gotten confirmation from the saurians that the ship Claver was on was destroyed."

He gave me a moment to let that sink in. Once it did, I frowned thoughtfully.

"So Claver is dead, right here in this system. He can't get a revive."

"That's right," Drusus said. "Not unless we give it to him. What do you think we should do?"

I heaved a sigh. "He helped us out in the end," I admitted. "Without him, we'd have probably all been permed."

"That's one way of looking at it. Another way is that without his meddling, we might have never met up with the saurians here. I think he was instrumental in bringing them to this system. What I don't understand is how he knew Earth was coming here at this exact time."

I tossed Drusus a glance then quickly looked away. I couldn't let him read my expression. It was my suspicion that Turov had collaborated with Claver even before we headed out here. It wasn't clear exactly what their plans had been, but I was sure they were self-serving on both sides.

"He gave us the deep-link, and he refused to fire the broadsides on our position in the end. In fact, I think the saurians probably executed him for that before any of their ships were lost against the squids."

"What you say is quite possibly the truth," Drusus said. "That's why I asked you to come here. Among everyone in Legion Varus, your perspective on this situation is unique. In short, we have options, and it's difficult to see how the future might be affected by the choices we make today."

I thought about that. We could leave Claver dead. Maybe the universe would be a better place if we did.

But that was a hard choice for me to make. Claver and I had a deal, and he'd kept his part of the bargain.

"Sir," I said, "Claver was a card-carrying bastard. That man could sell his soul to six different devils and swindle them all. But I made a deal with him. If my vote counts, I'd like to honor that deal."

Drusus nodded slowly. "I felt that would be your choice. Unfortunately, I think I'm going to have to go with my initial instinct and leave the man in his grave. Dismissed, Veteran."

He turned away, and I was left standing there, blinking. My baffled expression transformed into one of annoyance. I shifted from foot to foot then finally spoke up.

"Sir? I'm sorry, sir, but I just can't let this lie."

Drusus frowned at me. He wasn't accustomed to noncoms arguing with him in his office. I could understand that, but I wasn't a man who could let something like that go so easily.

"What are you trying to say, McGill?"

"Tribune, why'd you even ask me to come up here? I mean, if you had your mind made up, why bother?"

"Maybe I wanted to confirm something about you. Maybe I wanted to know how a man guided by principle over logic would judge a case such as this. Now that my curiosity has been satisfied, I'm moving on."

A cold, callous answer. I should have expected nothing less. Tribune Drusus wasn't like Graves. He had a soul in there somewhere, but he also had a great deal of responsibility. He looked at things differently than I did, that's all.

I left his office troubled but resigned. Claver was dead and gone. He was stardust, just like we all once were and would be again someday.

-51-

Earth Central Command was surprised to hear our plea on the deep-link. They grumbled, but three long months after the battle with the squids was over, *Minotaur* came back to Machine World to pick us up.

We rode the lifters away from Machine World with a deep sense of relief. I'm not sure I've ever been happier to leave a planet behind.

From space, the planet looked like a cotton ball. It was all fluffy-white with clouds on top and soft blue-grays underneath. The image belied the turmoil we'd gone through to survive on an intensely hostile world.

Imperator Turov was aboard *Minotaur*, and I could tell right off she wasn't happy about that. Her face was a good ten meters tall, displayed on the ceiling of our unit's module. When she spoke to us, she never cracked a smile. She showed her teeth plenty, sure, but that was only because her lips seemed to curl away from her pearly-whites to punctuate every sentence.

"The heroic actions of Legion Varus have been duly noted," she said, sounding as if she was spitting out nails. "Hegemony has ordered me to provide every member of the legion with the Medal of Honor, bronze rank. Congratulations and welcome aboard, legionnaires."

A mild cheer went up from the assembled troops. It was nice to get a pat on the head from the brass every now and then, even if it came from the hogs back on Earth.

Turov didn't beat around the bush when it came to my role in matters, either. She summoned me to her office on Gold Deck, and this time she had me thoroughly disarmed before I was allowed into her presence. I found this stipulation disquieting, but I walked in as if I didn't have a care in the world.

"Good morning, Imperator," I said.

She eyed me coldly. "James McGill," she said slowly. "The man of the hour, if reports are to be believed."

"Happy to serve, sir. I just do my part the way any other man in the legion would."

She snorted. "Hardly. What other noncom would dare insert his unwanted nose into every official matter that comes up?"

I didn't have an answer for that, so I kept quiet. I was standing at attention, staring at the back wall of her office. There was a picture of Earth there, stylized with an image of Central emblazoned over it. I found the image vaguely disturbing. What was it meant to project? The idea that Hegemony's military ruled Earth? I told myself I was becoming paranoid and tried to listen to Turov instead.

She was reading me a list of complaints by other officers concerning my conduct on Machine World. Even Leeson had a choice comment or two which had gone into my file. That hurt a bit, even if every word of it was true.

"The same old story, McGill," Turov said. "You show initiative—to a fault. You fight well, you lead well. But you constantly disobey even basic orders and place your commanders in compromising positions. Honestly, I'm not sure if you're a genius or an idiot."

"A bit of both, sir, if my mama is to be believed."

She stared at me with hooded eyes. "Let us get to the point. I came to this system with a plan. You're aware of this, yes?"

I took a chance and glanced at her directly. She had that wet-cat look: tail-lashing, pissed off. The cant of her hip as she leaned her shapely butt on her desk told the story, along with the way her arms were crossed and the fact that her eyes were glittering slits.

Glancing back at the picture on the wall, I nodded. "I gathered that you had a plan, yes sir."

"And yet you sought to do whatever you damn-well pleased? Without regard for my requirements?"

"Pardon me, sir," I said. "But am I here to be promoted, demoted, or just chewed out for the fun of it?"

"More insolence. I should never have become personally involved with you. That was a mistake, and it has come back to haunt me in countless ways."

Again, I glanced down at her. I dared to give her a small, private smile. "If it's any consolation, I have no regrets in that regard. I enjoyed myself thoroughly."

"Of course you did," she snapped. "As to your question about your future status, that remains to be seen."

I nodded. I was being judged. My fate was being decided. Calm and unconcerned, I went back to staring at the wall behind her.

"What arrangements did you have with Claver?" she demanded. "Why did he choose death rather than firing the broadsides for the saurians?"

There, she'd put her finger on it. For the first time, I felt a tickle of sweat under my armpits. I couldn't tell her I'd agreed to steal the Galactic key from her. That wouldn't do at all.

"I believe all the details are in the reports, sir," I said, deciding to play dumb.

"I've gone over and over all the reports. They're more than vague in this regard."

My face blank, I gave her the innocent confused look I'd given a hundred teachers, babysitters and friends' moms as a kid. I was proud of that face as it had gotten me out of countless bad spots in the past.

"Honestly, I thought you might be able to shed some light on Claver's actions," I said. "He always was a bit of a mystery to me. I had no idea he was going to come out here and try to set up some kind of titanium trading depot."

She glared at me, and I looked back down at her, straight-on.

"Did *you* know anything about that, sir?" I asked. "I've been meaning to ask you about it. Even more curious was

378

Claver's knowledge that Earth was sending an expedition here in the first place. I mean, what are the *odds* that all these ships would show up in orbit over Machine World at the same time? There are coincidences in the universe, but this one is a doozy."

Turov's mouth got tighter with every word I uttered. By the end of my speech, her mouth was an almost invisible, pink, pinched-looking spot on her face. Finally, as I knew she would, she exploded.

"That's enough with your threats!" she said. "I could crush you—you know that, don't you? Even now, with your friends placed carefully all around the legion, you're not safe from me. Don't think that you are!"

My eyes were dead-ahead again. "I'm sorry sir, but I don't follow you."

She began to pace around me, calming herself down with a force of will.

"All right," she said. "Keep your secrets, McGill. You're not being helpful at all. I'm faced with a difficult decision, and I'd hoped you would shed light on the subject, but you've chosen to be an obstinate ass as usual."

"Uh…what are we talking about now, sir?"

"About Claver, you fool. Should I revive him or not?"

That one took me by honest surprise. That's when I realized this dressing-down wasn't about me at all. She was debating Claver's status. Their scheme—whatever it had been—had fallen apart. But maybe Claver had some hold over her, some promised prize she hadn't gotten out of him yet. If she left him dead, she'd never get it.

That said, she clearly didn't trust the man and wisely so. He was double-dealing everyone, up-down and sideways.

I heaved a sigh. "I made a deal with Claver," I said. "He agreed not to operate the broadsides for the saurians, but he felt the saurians might kill him for refusing."

"And why would he do that?" she demanded.

"To gain the trading rights he planned on in the first place. His first move was to arrive with the squids and a trade ship, cutting a deal. When that failed, he tried a legal approach, backed by the Nairbs. The man is nothing if not persistent.

When I blew up the Nairb ship, he brought in the saurians. Maybe he even knew the squids were coming after that, or he called them, I'm honestly not sure."

"He is beyond slippery," Turov agreed reflectively. "I now doubt my wisdom at ever having had dealings with him—or you."

"He does keep his end of a bargain," I said. "He gave me the deep-link to call Earth. Part of the deal was to revive him afterward if things went badly. In turn, he agreed not to help the saurians fire the broadsides and demolish my legion."

"Hmm," Turov said. "The whole thing almost makes sense. Parts of what you say were written in your superiors' reports, but it was never stated so openly. Fair enough. You made a deal. What do you think now? Should I revive that rat or leave him dead in the gutter where he belongs?"

"I always try to honor a deal, sir," I said. "He kept his part of the bargain, and he paid the ultimate price as far as I can tell. I say revive him."

She stopped pacing and stood directly in front of me, cocking her pretty face and gazing with open curiosity. "You know that he'd betray you in a second, yes?"

"Yes and no, sir. He's a trader. A man can't be successful in such a calling if he doesn't keep his deals most of the time. We might not know all his plans and deals, but I feel confident he will keep to the letter of a given bargain once it is agreed upon."

She nodded thoughtfully. "Yes. Some things are beginning to make sense to me now. He knows you're a man who will keep a deal, just as he himself would. He also knows he can talk you into foolish arrangements. Therefore, his real goal in contacting you must have been to gain an insurance policy. Perhaps he knew he was going to die. Maybe all that about the broadsides was bullshit, and the saurians were going to kill him anyway. Who knows? What we can be sure of is he talked you into agreeing to revive him if he was killed. Now that he is dead, he hopes you will do so, even if you have to do it illicitly."

Turov gazed up at me with sudden suspicion. "You've already done it, haven't you?"

380

"Uh...done what, sir?"

"Revived him. You have friends who are willing to do such things. I know that. I'm a woman who's built up a network of supporters—but you don't need to know about that, it doesn't matter. What I want to know is if you have brought him back yet. Have you, McGill?"

This was the sort of situation I was finding myself in more and more. People thought I was some kind of wizard. Sure, I'd gotten in and out of more than my share of scrapes, but I wasn't Houdini.

"No sir," I said. "Honestly, I haven't revived anyone since Tech World."

"All right. I choose to believe you. And I'll tell you right now, you should not bother. I'm going to do it, quietly."

Surprised, I studied her. The look on her face was calculating, and she wasn't even looking at me. She was working her hands in the air and staring at the deck. I could only imagine what kind of scheming was going on inside that head of hers.

"Why tell me your intentions, sir?" I asked.

She looked back up at me as if she'd forgotten I was standing in front of her. She made a sweeping motion with her hand.

"So you wouldn't try to do it yourself out of some misguided sense of honor! You'd end up making a copy of him. That's all this universe needs—two Clavers. Now, get the hell out of my office. You're dismissed."

Leaving in a hurry, I was left wondering about the conversation all the way back to my quarters. Whatever Claver and Turov were up to, it wasn't over with—not yet.

I had the feeling I wasn't going to like it when I learned the truth.

-52-

Two months later, I was back home on Earth. Weary, and with the haunting light of the stars in our eyes, we marched down the ramps of our lifters, six abreast.

A cheering crowd greeted us bearing tiny flags, waving both Hegemony's blue globe and the Varus Wolfshead pennant. They were mostly relatives, but there were a few others: members of the press, even Solstice people who felt sorry for the troops they'd left behind.

"Is it true that Varus wiped for a fourth time on Machine World?" a reporter demanded, thrusting her audio-wand into my face. A tiny camera drone buzzed over her shoulder, zooming and panning.

"No," I said immediately. "We didn't wipe on Tech World. Not completely. I stayed alive and began the long revival process personally. On Machine World, it wasn't even close. We never lost more than half our—"

The reporter was eating it up, but a pair of hands came out of nowhere and pushed her away. Leeson escorted her and that buzzing drone of hers back into the crowd and hustled me toward the terminal.

"That's enough, McGill," he said, pushing on my back. He propelled me toward the welcoming crowd of relatives. "Noncoms don't talk to the press. Never. Don't you know that?"

"Sorry, sir," I told the Adjunct. "Her questions had implied falsehoods. I wanted to set the record straight."

"That's the job of officers—high level ones. Your job is to keep your damned mouth shut."

"Yes, sir."

My parents were in the crowd. They greeted me with enthusiasm, and my mom cried. She always did that—every time I left and every time I came back.

"I'm good, Mom," I said.

She grabbed me by my jacket lapels and hung on tight, looking into my eyes. "Did you die out there? They said that you *all* died."

"Nah Mom," I said, smiling. "Not this time. Look, I've even got a slight limp. Do you see that? Just an injury, no death. If I'd died, that would have been all fixed up with a new grow. See?"

My little dodge made her happy, and she cried all over again. I hugged them both and headed for the family tram. I was on leave, and I was looking forward to spending a few spring months in my own place on the back of their land.

The best part was my home planet's air. I'd been breathing farts on Machine World, followed by the canned stale air on *Minotaur*, for half a year. In comparison, the fresh breezes of Earth were like heaven.

* * *

That night, I drank a dozen cold beers and passed out happily on my couch. One of the many times I had to get up to pee, I heard a knocking on my door.

It was a timid knock, the kind someone who was unsure of themselves might make. Sighing, I headed to the door and threw it wide.

I had no idea who might be visiting me. It could have been any of a dozen people. By the light of the moon outside, I judged it was the middle of the night, and therefore, couldn't be one of my parents, but that was about the only people I'd ruled out.

My eyes focused in the darkness. Small, female—I thought of Natasha first. She'd come to my door like this on many occasions. But it wasn't her.

Della? I almost said the name out loud, but I caught myself in time. It wasn't her. It *couldn't* be her. She'd headed back to Dust World to visit her own family.

"Anne?" I said, surprised. "How'd you find me way out here?"

She smiled shyly. "I asked around. They said you lived alone—but isn't that your parents' place over there behind the trees?"

"Yeah. But don't worry, they're asleep by now. You want to come in?"

She did so with the mild trepidation all females seemed to exhibit when entering my lair. The interior was dark because I liked it that way. Soft blue lights glowed here and there, illuminating various appliances.

There was only one major place to sit, my couch. She headed there and pushed a few cushions and a thin blanket out of the way.

"You want a beer?" I asked. "Ah—hold on. I'm out. How about a margarita in a can?"

"Sure."

I brought it to her, and she sipped it quietly.

"I'm sorry I didn't call first, or text you," she said, speaking quickly. "I didn't even know I was coming. I was driving around, and I thought I'd just drop by and see where you lived. Once I was here—well, I thought it would be silly not to knock on your door."

Unperturbed, I nodded. The fact that she lived up in Kentucky didn't impinge. It was quite a distance to be wandering late at night. If a man had done the same, they'd call him a stalker. I grinned at the thought, and although I still had a gut full of beer in me, I was smart enough not to say what was on my mind.

Eventually, we got around to the real reason she'd come to my place. We had a great time on the couch, but I didn't remember it very well by morning, so we repeated the process after cleaning up. After that, we went out to breakfast.

There, at a local eatery, we ran into my parents. They were looking at us in embarrassment, not sure if they should say anything or not.

I walked over to them, carrying my plate. Anne followed, mortified.

"James," she hissed. "They'll know I spent the night. They'll have to figure it out."

"They already know," I said. "They aren't stupid. Just make the best of it."

We sat together, talked, and ate. It was nice, and it was something I rarely did. I usually kept my private life and my family apart.

Consequently, my mother was ready to maul poor Anne. I could see she had wedding cakes in her eyes and bells in her ears. It was all I could do not to laugh.

Anne brought up the squids—and I wished she hadn't. They kind of freaked my mother out.

"I've heard about those huge, disgusting creatures," my mom said. "Did you actually see one?"

Anne gave me a wary glance. Obviously, my parents were in the dark concerning my activities while abroad among the stars. I generally edited my stories of warfare. They didn't need to know how bad it really was to be a legionnaire.

I think my dad suspected, of course. When I candied-up my tales of the campaigns, he always smiled with his mouth, but not his eyes. He'd always been able to tell when I was lying better than my mom, back as far as I could remember.

Giving Anne a tiny nod, I took a drink of coffee, and stared into the cup. Anne cleared her throat and started in.

"There was this one cephalopod that was different from the rest," she said. "It was huge, and it turns out it was a female."

This detail surprised even me. Anne and I hadn't talked about the campaign, we'd been too busy enjoying one another's company all night for that.

"Female?" I asked. "How could you tell?"

Anne laughed. "They have sexes, you just have to look. Every squid we've found up until this trip to Gamma Pavonis has been a male. But I've had contact with the team of bios who were tasked with investigating the one you found in that big tank. It was a confirmed female."

"*You* found it?" my mother gasped, staring at me across the table. I had a forkful of pancakes in my hand and I froze. "You never talked about that, James!" she said, raising her voice.

My dad put a hand on her arm. "Hon, you have to know that he doesn't tell us everything."

"You'd think he wouldn't leave out a giant space-squid. Which he found himself, apparently."

"I didn't actually find it first," I said. "Carlos and Kivi did, but I did see it before it died."

My parents eyed me warily. I could tell they wanted to ask exactly *how* the giant space-squid had died, but they didn't.

"Sorry," Anne said. "I shouldn't have brought it up."

"No, no," my mom chimed in, and immediately began trying to make Anne feel better.

They started chatting again about more pleasant things. My mom had switched gears. I could tell she was focused on getting me married off again. Oddly, that was a relief to everyone at the table.

The day went by pleasantly after that, and after staying on for the weekend, Anne headed back to Kentucky. I found myself missing her almost immediately.

About a month later, my door thumped again. It was the middle of the day, not the middle of the night, but for some reason I thought it was Anne, coming back around for another visit.

I pasted my hair down as best I could with the few seconds I dared let pass before opening it.

When I finally did, my grin faded to blank shock. It wasn't Anne at all.

Claver stood there with two centurions. They were in hog uniforms, and Claver was in civvies. My eyes ran from one of them to the next.

"Disappointed?" Claver asked, chuckling. "I have that effect on a lot of people. Come on, McGill. You've been summoned to a meeting."

"What meeting?"

One of the centurions stepped forward with written orders. They were signed by none other than Equestrian Nagata, the man who I'd met with months back. My heart sank. This had to be about Turov and the Galactic we'd killed. That hadn't seemed like an action I'd get away with forever.

"Summoned? To Central?"

"That's right, Vet. You coming peacefully?"

The man was eyeing me, sizing me up. I felt that was a little insulting. Sure, I'd resisted arrest before, but this was different. I was being called by a high level officer to Central. They had written orders and everything.

"The orders seem legit," I said. "I'm not under arrest, am I?"

"Are you refusing the orders?" the centurion asked.

"No sir."

"Then you're not under arrest."

I followed them out to a military air car. It wasn't as nice as the one Winslade had swept me away in months ago, but it was just as fast. We glided over the treetops and soon slipped up into the regulated air-traffic corridors. Applying full thrust, the two centurions whisked me away toward the northeast.

Sitting in the back seat beside Claver, I couldn't help but talk to him.

"Congratulations on breathing again, by the way," I said.

"Thank you," he replied. "I'm equally impressed by the fact you haven't gotten yourself permed yet. I might have misjudged your intellect, McGill. A man can't get lucky so many times by sheer accident."

"Why doesn't anyone like to warn me about these pick-ups?" I complained. "People just come to my house whenever. They could at least send me a note first."

Claver shook his head. "Notes? On tappers? Maybe you *are* a dummy. That would leave an undeniable trace in the computers. If people keep coming to your door unannounced, McGill, it's because they don't want anyone to know they've done it. I, for one, am unsurprised to hear people don't want to make their associations with you public."

I thought about Anne then, and Natasha. Had they come knocking, unannounced, because they feared leaving a trace of their visits? The thought was disturbing. Could I be that toxic to a woman's career?

Claver didn't want to talk business in the back of a military air car with two witnesses, so we discussed pleasantries all the rest of the way up to Central.

At last, after we landed and were walking across the roof, Claver slapped my hand with his.

I looked down at his offending hand and frowned.

"What?"

"Give it to me," he whispered. "And don't tell me you didn't bring it. No one would leave it in a shack unguarded, not even you."

"Give you what?"

He looked at me like I was the dumbest animal on the farm. "The key, you *idiot*. Are you backing out? Because I don't like welshers, McGill."

"I don't have it," I growled back at him. "Not yet. I told you to give me a year."

"Shit," he said. He shoved his hands back into his pockets.

When we were led into Equestrian Nagata's office, the two centurions retreated. The first time I'd met this man he'd been in the Mustering Hall in Newark. But the headquarters building in Central was his home office. As a hog officer, he belonged here.

Claver and I stood there like kids in the principal's office while Nagata fooled around with some computer scrolls on his big, brass-studded desk.

At last, he looked up. "Adjunct Claver," he said, nodding, then turned to me, "and Veteran McGill. Two of the most infamous rogues in Frontier 921."

He riffled through his computer scrolls and selected two of them. He slid one across his desk toward each of us.

I glanced down. Whatever it was, it looked like an official document. Equestrian Nagata's scrawled signature was at the bottom of both.

"What's this, sir?" I asked.

"What do you think it is?" he asked me in return. "An agreement to avoid prosecution—provided you give us the testimony we're asking for."

Frowning, we both picked up our documents and looked them over. Claver read a few words. "Immunity...immediate release....record stricken...good enough. I'm signing."

He touched his thumb to the bottom and an image of his print appeared on the scroll.

I looked mine over with far less enthusiasm. I had no idea what I was facing, and as I paged through the scroll, it wasn't getting any clearer.

"Sir?" I asked. "I don't understand what this is about."

"You're trading your testimony for immunity. You're the small fish, McGill. It's standard practice to allow a few lesser criminals to escape the net in order to capture the big one."

"And who is the big one in this case, sir?"

"Imperator Turov, of course."

"And the charge?"

"In Claver's case, the charge is sedition and racketeering. In your case, it's murder. Namely, the murder of Chief Inspector Xlur. Imperator Turov is guilty of both these crimes."

I'd known the answer to my question before asking it, naturally. I'd just wanted it confirmed. I glowered at the document. It seemed so dirty. Was I going to let Turov hang out to dry? She'd never been a stellar officer, and she was often up to no good, but I felt uncomfortable saddling her with things I'd done at her side.

"Sir...the Galactics aren't behind this prosecution, are they?"

"Fortunately, no. If they ever do bring charges, we'll all be permed. These charges are relatively minor—murder, disobeying orders, endangering the state—the sort of thing you two excel at."

I could tell Nagata didn't like me or Claver. He'd apparently lumped us into the same pot, calling us both troublemakers and criminals. That didn't sit well with me.

"Sir," I said. "Are you aware of the circumstances that led to the unfortunate death of a foreign dignitary on our soil?"

Nagata stared at me. "The Chief Inspector is not a foreign dignitary. He is a Galactic, part of the Empire we all serve."

"You should think that over, sir—"

389

"McGill," Claver said at my side. He'd been quiet up until now, but he'd been growing increasingly alarmed. "Shut that big cracker mouth of yours, for the love of God, and sign!"

I ignored him and stayed focused on Nagata. I pointed at Claver. "This man will tell you whatever you want to hear. He'll sell Turov—or you, for that matter—down the river of your choice without a qualm. But sir, I'm made of different stuff. Honestly, killing Xlur has probably been one of the best things I've ever done. Turov should be commended for her action as well, whatever other faults she might have. Xlur meant to perm *everyone* on Earth. We did what we did because we had to. And now, as a big thank you for saving your collective butts, you've decided to perm us as a reward? I don't get it, sir. Not at all."

"They aren't going to perm you, McGill. Just Turov," said Claver.

I turned on him. "And is that what you want? You want Turov arrested, tried and executed? What do you think will happen during that sequence of events?"

Claver's face froze. He got it. If the hogs caught and tried Turov on the basis of our testimony, he'd never get his key. Turov would either use it to escape her fate, or it would be confiscated.

"I've had a change of heart, sir," he said suddenly. He rubbed his finger side to side over his mark on the computer scroll until it vanished, then tossed the scroll back on the Equestrian's desk, where it rattled with the rest of the documents. "I'm sorry."

Nagata's mouth hung open. He swept his eyes back and forth between the two of us. He was surprised but thinking hard.

"She's got something on you two," he said. "Something so bad, you're willing to risk trial to avoid it. That's got to be quite a lever. I'm impressed by this woman's scheming. Your case isn't unique, you know. I've had my eye on her for years, trying to stop her. Always, my evidence falls apart at the last minute. She has friends in very high places—but she has just as many enemies."

We both gazed at him evenly. I knew now what I was caught up in. A vendetta. A squabble between high-ranking officers. For a mere enlisted man, that wasn't a pleasant place to be, let me tell you.

Nagata stood up suddenly. His body was stiff and angry. "I won't bother to tempt you with bribes. If the threat of prosecution won't sway you from serving your mistress, rank and bank accounts would have even less of an effect. However, my offer stands, and I will seek to come up with a further offer you can't refuse. Know, gentlemen, that I'm a patient man, and that I'll win this contest in the end. You cannot prevail in this political battle in the long run."

"Ah..." Claver said uncertainly. "You said something about an incentive program, sir? Are you sure you don't want to provide more details on that?"

"Get out!"

That was it. We were thrown out of Nagata's office and out of the gigantic headquarters building as well. Claver and I went our separate ways almost immediately. I had to wonder why Nagata didn't have us arrested—but the answer to that puzzle was easy to figure out.

When a fisherman seeks to catch a really big fish, he baits the hook with a small one. Then he lets the line pay out, far, far from the boat...

I went home to Waycross, Georgia, knowing in my heart I was being watched. I was the bait, and that meant I was already on the hook.

I didn't like the sensation. Not at all.

The End

More Books by B. V. Larson:

UNDYING MERCENARIES
Steel World
Dust World
Tech World
Machine World

STAR FORCE SERIES
Swarm
Extinction
Rebellion
Conquest
Battle Station
Empire
Annihilation
Storm Assault
The Dead Sun
Outcast
Exile

OTHER SF BOOKS
Technomancer
The Bone Triangle
Element-X
Velocity

Visit BVLarson.com for more information.

Printed in Poland
by Amazon Fulfillment
Poland Sp. z o.o., Wrocław